MW01005752

The Firebird in Russian folklore is a fiery, illuminated bird; magical, iconic, coveted. Its feathers continue to glow when removed, and a single feather, it is said, can light up a room. Some who claim to have seen the Firebird say it even has glowing eyes. The Firebird is often the object of a quest. In one famous tale, the Firebird needs to be captured to prevent it from stealing the king's golden apples, a fruit bestowing youth and strength on those who partake of the fruit. But in other stories, the Firebird has another mission: it is always flying over the earth providing hope to any who may need it. In modern times and in the West, the Firebird has become part of world culture. In Igor Stravinsky's ballet *The Firebird,* it is a creature half-woman and half-bird, and the ballerina's role is considered by many to be the most demanding in the history of ballet.

The Overlook Press in the U.S. and Gerald Duckworth in the UK, in adopting the Firebird as the logo for its expanding Ardis publishing program, consider that this magical, glowing creature—in legend come to Russia from a faraway land—will play a role in bringing Russia and its literature closer to readers everywhere.

Mahogany and Other Stories

Boris Pilnyak

Translated with Introduction & Notes by

Vera T. Reck and Michael Green

ARDIS PUBLISHERS
NEW YORK, NY

This edition published in the United States and the United Kingdom in 2013 by
Ardis Publishers, an imprint of Peter Mayer Publishers, Inc.

NEW YORK:
The Overlook Press
Peter Mayer Publishers, Inc.
141 Wooster Street
New York, NY 10012
www.overlookpress.com
For bulk and special sales, please contact sales@overlookny.com

LONDON:
Gerald Duckworth Publishers Ltd.
90-93 Cowcross Street
London EC1M 6BF
www.ducknet.co.uk
info@duckworth-publishers.co.uk

Copyright © 1993 by Ardis Publishers / The Overlook Press
Originally published by University of Oklahoma Press, 1988 as *Chinese Story and Other Tales*.
Published by permission of University of Oklahoma Press.

All rights reserved. No part of this publication may be reproduced or transmitted in any form or by any means, electronic or mechanical, including photocopy, recording, or any information storage and retrieval system now known or to be invented without permission in writing from the publisher, except by a reviewer who wishes to quote brief passages in connection with a review written for inclusion in a magazine, newspaper, or broadcast.

Cataloging-in-Publication Data is available from the Library of Congress

Printed in the United States of America
ISBN: 978-1-4683-0153-3

2 4 6 8 10 9 7 5 3 1

Go to **www.ardisbooks.com** to read or download the latest Ardis catalog.

CONTENTS

Introduction 1

Chinese Story 17
Mahogany 109
The Tale of the Unextinguished Moon 165
Mother Earth 211
The Nizhni Novgorod Otkos 273
A Dog's Life 293
A Year of Their Life 307

Selected Works of Boris Pilnyak 319
Index 321

MAHOGANY

and Other Stories

by

BORIS PILNYAK

Introduction

Boris Pilnyak, whose real name was Boris Andreyevich Vogau, was born on October 11 (September 29, O.S.), 1894, in Mozhaisk, a small town in Moscow Province. Both his parents came from the Volga region; his father, a district veterinarian, had married the daughter of an old Saratov merchant family. In an autobiographical sketch published in 1924, Pilnyak says: ". . . within me flows the blood of four peoples: German with a touch of Jewish on my father's side, Slavic and Mongol (Tartar) on my mother's side."[1]

Pilnyak's boyhood passed in the towns of Moscow Province, towns that were clustered about their ancient kremlins. Their poetry entered deep into the boy, and he was later to make them the settings of some of his best stories. The Volga steppe, the homeland of his ancestors, was also part of his boyhood world and would be memorably evoked by the mature writer. Pilnyak records that he began to write at the age of nine and that his very first production described "night and the steppe, the cry of the eagle owl."[2] His career as a writer began in 1915. Some of his early stories are a celebration of the primitive, sensual, unreasoning life—of birds, beasts, and the animal man. "God ikh zhizni" ("A Year

1. Boris Pilnyak, "Boris Andreyevich Pilnyak," *Literaturnaya Rossiya*, Sbornik Sovremennoi Russkoi Prozy, no. 1 (Moscow; "Novye Vekhi" 1924), pp. 257–58.

2. Ibid., p. 258.

of Their Life"), the only work of this period included in the present selection, is an example of his early style.

Other "juvenilia" reveal Pilnyak's debt to Anton Chekhov and Ivan Bunin. By the early 1920s, Pilnyak had become one of the most popular writers in the Soviet Union, his works revolutionary in both style and subject.

"Bliss was it in that dawn to be alive." The brief and heady optimism among the Russian intelligentsia in the immediate wake of the revolution can be sensed in an animal story Pilnyak wrote at this time, which is included in the present collection—"Sobach'ya zhizn'" ("A Dog's Life," 1919), a fantasy of life in a happy animal commune. Pilnyak welcomed the revolution in his own way and for his own reasons. For him it had little to do with Karl Marx and the urban proletariat; it was a "peasant revolt"; it was Slavic Russia erupting and obliterating the alien European civilization so brutally imposed by Peter the Great. Pilnyak's revolution was symbolized by the blizzard and the wolf; it was elemental, anarchic, a creature of the forest. Naïve and romantic as these ideas may seem, they enabled Pilnyak to make sense of what seemed to many a descent into chaos, and even to sound a note of exhilaration in the midst of the cataclysm—to "shout with the storm."

The early 1920s were years of comparative freedom for the "fellow-travelers"—the writers who, like Pilnyak, accepted the revolution but without total commitment. Pilnyak wrote in 1924:

> I am not a Communist, and so I do not acknowledge that I ought to be a Communist and write like a Communist. I do acknowledge that Communist power in Russia was not achieved by the will of the Communists but was brought about by the historic destiny of Russia, and to the extent that I trace (as best as I can, and as my conscience and intelligence dictate to me) this historic destiny of Russia, to that extent I am with the Communists (now, at this time, that means more than ever before, since I cannot be in the philistine camp); I acknowledge that the destiny of

> the Russian Communist party interests me less than the destiny of Russia; that for me the Russian Communist party is only a link in the history of Russia; I know that I must be absolutely objective, that I must not be grist to anyone's mill, not deceive anyone and—I acknowledge that I may be completely mistaken, but I know very well that I am not able to write otherwise than I write now, I do not know how, I will not, even if I wanted to, violate myself; there is a law of literature which prohibits, makes impossible, the violation of a literary gift.[3]

In Pilnyak's prose of this period the influence of Russia's great symbolist master of the word Andrei Bely is unmistakable. This is a prose marked by a loose musical structure, abrupt narrative turns, incantatory digressions, repetition of entire segments and key phrases as a unifying device, obsessive wordplay ("Words to me are like coins to a numismatist"), and experiments with typographical layout. The reader will note Pilnyak's fondness for a line of ellipses that does not, as in contemporary usage, indicate an omitted passage but performs quite another function. This device was not introduced into Russian prose by Pilnyak but has a respectable literary ancestry. Mikhail Lermontov makes use of it in what is in form the most original of Russian novels, *A Hero of Our Time* (1840). In a note to his rendering of this work into English, Vladimir Nabokov, most exacting of translators, informs us: "The line of dots . . . was a stylistic device of the time denoting an interruption or pause, or ineffable things, with nonchalant or romantic connotations."

A more up-to-date trend (no doubt a parallel with the futurist cult of the machine and with constructivism in the visual arts) is a strong predilection for quotations from documents, newspapers, public notices, and popular songs, for new industrial terminology and exotic words. That is the style of *Golyi God (The Naked Year),* a

3. *Pisateli ob Iskusstve i o Sebe (Writers About Art and About Themselves)*, Sbornik Statei no. 1 (Moscow-Leningrad: "Krug," 1924), p. 83.

"revolutionary" novel in every sense, which on its appearance in 1921 immediately established Pilnyak's reputation as a leading writer of the new era. In the mid-1920s he began to move away from this "ragged prose," to which Maksim Gorky objected as the expression of an anarchic vision of life.

The political atmosphere of the middle and late 1920s in the Soviet Union did not favor the bold and outspoken. Politically naïve Pilnyak seemed unaware of the increasing attempts to subordinate literature to the demands of Joseph Stalin's emerging dictatorship.

Two of Pilnyak's works of the period included in the present volume occasioned fierce attacks on the author by representatives of Soviet literary orthodoxy, to say nothing of party activists in the cities and in the provinces, who dutifully called protest meetings and sent resolutions of condemnation to the papers. The newspaper *Vechernyaya Moskva (Evening Moscow)* asserted that Pilnyak's "case" should stand as an object lesson to writers.

In the 1930s the erstwhile nonconformist made a valiant effort to achieve a politically irreproachable stance, but in spite of that he ultimately had to pay for his earlier mistakes. In the era of the Stalinist purges Pilnyak's literary sins and various transgressions attributed to him became crimes meriting the death sentence. According to V. V. Novikov, author of the introduction to a recent Soviet selection of Pilnyak's work: "The literary career of B. Pilnyak came to an abrupt end in 1937. He died on September 9, 1941."[4] It appears that the dating of Pilnyak's death in 1941 is a convenient device to hide the facts. It is generally known that the deaths of many men and women who perished in the purges were later postdated to the early 1940s for the purpose of laying the blame, by implication, on the war and the Germans. Some Soviet sources, for example, *Kratkaya Literaturnaya Entsiklopediya (Concise Literary Encyclopedia),* give the date of Pilnyak's death as 1937, and other evidence confirms that date. In a memoir published in New

4. Boris Pilnyak, *Izbrannye Proizvedeniya* (Moscow: "Khudozhestvennaya Literatura," 1976), p. 5.

York in 1953, R. V. Ivanov-Razumnik, who spent several years in Soviet prisons, records seeing scrawled on the wall of the bathhouse—the prisoners' "post office"—of Butyrka Prison in Moscow in late 1937: "Writer Pilnyak sentenced to be shot."

Pilnyak was all his life an insatiable traveler; he had a reporter's feeling for the arresting detail, and his journalistic writing retains its freshness even today. *Kitaiskaya Povest (Chinese Story)* and *Korni Yaponskogo solntsa (The Roots of the Japanese Sun),* both published in 1927, are sharp-eyed accounts of his travels in the Far East. Several years later *The Roots of the Japanese Sun* became the object of destruction by means of "autopolemics"—creative demolition of a work of literature—an "invention" attributed to Pilnyak. In 1932, six years after his first visit, Pilnyak returned to Japan. The result of that trip was a new book, *Kamni i Korni (Stones and Roots).* It consists of quotations—some of them altered—from *The Roots of the Japanese Sun,* plus "commentary" and some new material. In the new book the writer "destroys" the exotic and colorful Japan of his first visit and presents a new and far less attractive picture of the country. Pilnyak engages in self-criticism, berating himself for his "errors" of observation and judgment on his first trip: "The writer Pilnyak of 1932 informs the readers that his *Roots [of the Japanese Sun]* are worthless," and, "The writer Pilnyak of 1932 asks the readers to discard from their shelves volume seven of the GIZ [State Publishing House] edition of his collected works."[5]

The imaginative writer and the reporter are strangely compounded in Pilnyak: as there are journalistic elements in his fiction, so there are fictional elements in his reportage. *Chinese Story,* which represents Pilnyak's travel pieces in the present collection, is a good example of this duality. It was completed in Moscow soon after Pilnyak's return from his trip to the Far East in 1926. The reader is presented with vivid glimpses of life in Shanghai in the summer of 1926: the unbearable heat and stench, the opium dens and the brothels, the life of the boat

5. Boris Pilnyak, *Kamni i Korni* (Moscow: "Sovetskaya Literatura," 1934), p. 54.

people, the unbelievably primitive conditions within the city, pockets of Western affluence in the midst of Chinese squalor. There are also brief descriptions of Peking—that ancient city, crumbling and filthy, enveloped in the heat and dust of summer, crowded with soldiers, with "thousands—without exaggeration" of beggars on the streets.

The political disarray in China is captured in a number of sharp sketches: feuding warlords, hordes of marauding bandits hardly distinguishable from "regular" armies, attempts by "colonizers" from many lands to gain political power and economic advantage.

Pilnyak chose as his "hero" a young Chinese rebel, the dedicated labor organizer Liu Hua, a real person of whom there is historical record, active in Shanghai in the early 1920s. In typical Pilnyakian fashion, Liu Hua falls in love with Miss Brighton, an American girl of Pilnyak's invention. Of more psychological interest, perhaps, is Krylov, an official of the Soviet embassy—apparently a real person with whom Pilnyak shared quarters. Krylov's marital problems are treated with great insight and form a thread that runs through the entire "diary." This literary potpourri contains a number of interesting ingredients: descriptions of Russian émigrés—former officers of the imperial army whose wives have taken to prostitution—and trips out of town at night in speeding automobiles as a means of "cooling off." Pilnyak's predilection for journalistic quotations as "direct evidence" is illustrated by a number of references to Chinese and English newspapers. Two of the most interesting inclusions are a Chinese tale: resurrection of a bride from her grave brought about by the miraculous power of love and an apparently real occurrence—harsh treatment of an "unobliging" god by the citizens of the town of Kalgan.

The Soviet critic V. V. Novikov, mentioned above, remarks darkly that Pilnyak's novella *Mat' syra Zemlya* (*Mother Earth,* 1924) reveals the influence of "Freudianism." Perhaps that is the reason *Mother Earth,* masterly and politically irreproachable from the Soviet point of view, has yet to be republished in the Soviet Union. The story is beautifully constructed. The wood devil; the forest watchman Kuzya, the teller of tales; the superstitious peasants whose move into a new house is accompanied by a "crawling-in" ceremony complete with a black rooster and a black cat; the forester Nekulyev, whose unfinished letter tells of the "savagery" and "horror" of his Volga outpost, the beautiful tanner Arina, who surrenders to Nekulyev the "heavy wine" of her thirty-year-old virginity—all are given their own levels and tones of voice.

Set at the time of the civil war, in the Volga region where Pilnyak's family had its roots (Volga Germans play a minor role in the story), *Mother Earth* is suffused with a lyricism unique in the author's work. The central character, the forester Nekulyev, is an idealistic and dedicated Bolshevik, but to the peasants he is no less a "master" than was the owner of the land, the prince they had murdered.

On October 31, 1925, Mikhail Vasilyevich Frunze, people's commissar of the army and navy, died after an operation in Moscow, and rumor quickly spread that the surgeons had been ordered to kill the man whom Stalin regarded as a dangerous rival. In May of the following year *Novyi Mir* (*New World*) printed a story by Pilnyak entitled "The Tale of the Unextinguished Moon," in which the circumstances of Frunze's death were set forth in only the thinnest of fictional disguises. Number One—the Unbending Man—the cold and paranoid bureaucrat of the "Tale," has a dangerous resemblance to Stalin, while Commander Gavrilov, the soldier, is closely modeled on Frunze. In Russian, "Unbending Man" describes a man's posture in a negative way—stiff, ramrod straight. Pilnyak's use of this term clearly points to Stalin, who was short and held himself rigidly erect, undoubtedly to compensate for his deficiency in stature. His withered left arm contributed to the general impression of stiffness. Another characteristic of the Unbending Man is his precise, quick, angular movements. Stalin is described by his daughter, Svetlana Allilueva, in her book *Twenty Letters to a Friend* as "impetuous and quick even in his old age."[6] Similarities of this sort between the real and the fictional dictators abound. Pilnyak also introduces some direct contrasts that somehow underscore the

6. Svetlana Allilueva, *Dvadtsat' Pisem k Drugu* (London: Hutchinson and Co., 1967), p. 150.

likeness. For example, the Unbending Man does not smoke and regards smoking as a bad habit; it was generally known that Stalin was seldom without his pipe.

Pilnyak's Commander Gavrilov is a double of the real people's commissar of the army and navy. The writer knew Frunze "slightly" and undoubtedly learned a great deal about him from his friends and from the memorial columns in the papers. The real and the fictional men were very similar in appearance, both being modest and mild-mannered individuals—except in battle, when they became powerful and effective commanders. Their younger years were remarkably similar: revolutionary activity among textile workers, tsarist imprisonment, exile, escape. Gavrilov's disease was ulcer of the stomach; Frunze's, ulcer of the duodenum.

Apparently Pilnyak had an informant in high Kremlin circles who supplied details of Frunze's death and some information about the life and character of the emerging dictator. The informant may well have been Karl Radek, a close friend of Pilnyak's, a member of the Central Committee who was to be among the victims of the Great Purge of 1937. Writer, critic, and editor Aleksandr Voronsky admitted partial responsibility for the "Tale." In July, 1926, writing to Gorky, who was in Sorrento, Voronsky says: ". . . since Pilnyak's story my relations with people in high places have been rather strained. I am accused of having given Pilnyak inspiration. It is true that he did learn a little from me, but of the main thing—I am not guilty."

The issue of *Novi Mir* containing the "Tale" was hurriedly withdrawn, and the editorial board admitted that it had made a "gross and obvious error" in publishing the work. Voronsky, to whom the "Tale" had been dedicated, was quick to reject the honor with indignation, calling the story "a malicious slander on our Party." Two weeks after Pilnyak finished the story, and before its publication, he added an introductory paragraph, possibly at the insistence of the editors, in which he denied any connection between Frunze's death and that of the fictional Commander Gavrilov. The denial has the presumably unintentional effect of focusing the reader's attention on the similarities in the two deaths.

The perceptive portrait of the emerging dictator and the suggestion of his responsibility for Frunze's death led to a fierce official assault on Pilnyak, who was on one of his Far East trips. On his return he "recanted," claiming that "the idea that I was writing a malicious slander never entered my mind at all" and admitting that "I have committed the grossest of errors, of which I was not conscious at the time of writing." It is unlikely that Stalin ever forgot the unflattering picture of himself and the implication of his guilt in the death of Frunze. He avenged himself a decade later.

The "scandal" about "The Tale of the Unextinguished Moon" was revived two and a half years later, when Pilnyak again came under attack, this time for the publication abroad of his novella *Krasnoye derevo (Mahogany)*. The piece was issued by the publishing house "Petropolis" in Berlin. In the 1920s, for reasons of copyright, it was neither uncommon nor "shocking" for Soviet writers to bring out their work abroad before its publication in the Soviet Union, and "Petropolis" was a publishing house "specializing in Soviet writers." Pilnyak did not submit the novella directly to the publishers but sent it through the Leningrad branch of the All-Union Society for Cultural Ties with Foreign Countries (VOKS), which forwarded it to Berlin.

Mahogany had already been accepted for publication, albeit with some cuts, by *Krasnaya Nov' (Red Virgin Soil)*, a leading Soviet literary magazine. Pilnyak was consequently quite unprepared for the savage campaign of vilification launched against him: he was accused of writing an anti-Soviet work and passing it on to a "White Guard" organization for publication abroad.

Official disapproval focused on Pilnyak's caustic treatment of the new Soviet bureaucracy, his dismay at the melting down of church bells—those monuments of ancient Russian craftsmanship—to supply metal for industry, his compassion for the "enemies of the State" (well-to-do peasants who resisted collectivization). Perhaps the gravest of

Pilnyak's "errors" in this piece was his sympathy for a community of political outcasts who lived in a pit near a brick kiln—Leninists and Trotskyites who believed themselves to be "the only real Communists" remaining in the land.

Since very few imported copies of the novella were available in the Soviet Union, critics for the most part had to make do with extracts read before selected groups. This may explain the mutilated quotations to be found in some "reviews." Pilnyak's attempts to defend himself were drowned in shouts of abuse from every corner. The whole of Soviet society, under pressure from the party, seemed bent on destroying the transgressor; very few dared raise their voices in protest, or even in a plea for mercy.

Why should such a virulent campaign have been launched against the author of a book virtually unavailable in the Soviet Union? The answer to this question must be sought in the literary politics of the day. Pilnyak was president of the Moscow branch of the All-Russian Writers' Union, and the purpose of the campaign was to remove him from that position and discredit him at the same time; Pilnyak was not an appropriate person and writer to serve as president of an official body under tightening state control.

Pilnyak was, perhaps, the most prominent though by no means the sole victim of this "campaign" of 1929. Several other writers, including Aleksei Tolstoi, Konstantin Fedin, Vsevolod Ivanov, and Lidia Seifullina, were also accused of publishing "anti-Soviet" work abroad. Foremost among Pilnyak's fellow victims was Evgeni Zamyatin, whose novel *My (We)* appeared abroad in English, Czech, and French; sections of the novel were printed in Russian, "translated from Czech." Although his "crime" was obscure, Zamyatin shared Pilnyak's top position among the accused, at least in the early phases of the campaign, which gave rise to endless newspaper and magazine references to "the case of Pilnyak and Zamyatin." It is clear that the main reason for the attack on Zamyatin was the same as that for the attack on Pilnyak: Zamyatin held a position in the Leningrad branch of the All-Russian Writers' Union analogous to that of Pilnyak in Moscow. The campaign reveals that state control of writers' organizations as well as of writers themselves was the main reason for the attack on Pilnyak and his colleagues.

In the campaign of 1929, *Mahogany* was Pilnyak's principal offense; the case was bolstered, however, by references to other "objectionable" work. "The Tale of the Unextinguished Moon" was recalled and, among more recent stories, "Nizhegorodskii Otkos" ("The Nizhni Novgorod Otkos"). An unabashed approach to sex had characterized much of Pilnyak's earlier writing. In "Otkos" he dealt with incest, a subject verging on the forbidden. Pilnyak's main offense here was not so much his depiction of sexual attraction between mother and son as the parallel he drew between incest and the February revolution of 1917. The act—"foulness, violation of nature, incest"—coincides in time with the February revolution: ". . . the greatest human happiness can sometimes be foulness, as foulness can be happiness." At least one critic concluded on the basis of internal evidence that Pilnyak had in mind the October rather than the February revolution—a far more serious offense.

Another "sex" story, included in the present collection, is "A Year of Their Life," mentioned earlier. In some early publications it is dated December, 1915. Later the date was changed to 1916. The work contains a vivid description of the far north, with its icy winters and long nights lit by the aurora borealis and its brief, rich summers. The focus of the story is the primitive, quaintly romantic life of a trapper and his wife in their first year together. There are scenes of sex and the birth of a child, the kinds of scenes that the Soviet state—which outdoes the Victorians in prudishness—was later to prohibit. The house pet, the bear Makar, is an unusual and most attractive feature of the tale—evidence of Pilnyak's fascination with animals, a fascination later exemplified by the young wolf/fox in *Mother Earth*.

"A Dog's Life," the only story here that might be described as humorous, is a fable that provides another example of Pilnyak's interest in animals, birds, and insects—from bears to termites. The cat and dogs in the piece are endowed with human qualities: they converse politely, are distinguished by good manners, partake of tea and coffee. The world of man that surrounds them is harsh and cruel, and eventually they leave it to settle in the woods as a commune consisting of a cat, several dogs, rats, chickens, and a duck. In the commune all are equal, work hard, and in the evening relax in each other's company, talking about "principles." The happy commune of animals is a wildly idealistic picture of life as it could be in Russia after the revolution.

The literary situation in the Soviet Union today is strange indeed. With the exception of writers who have been described as "the patron saints of Soviet literature"—Maksim Gorky and Vladimir Mayakovsky—complete editions are normally reserved for "safe" nineteenth-century classics. The *Selected Works* of 1976 (reprinted in 1978), certainly the largest selection of Pilnyak's work published in the Soviet Union since his death, does at least include *The Naked Year*, the novel of the revolution, which is still his best-remembered work; but much of his finest writing—much the greater part of the present selection—has yet to be republished, or even, as in the case of *Mahogany*, published, in the Soviet Union.

Fortunately, literature, unlike its creators, cannot be liquidated. There will surely come a day when a selection of Pilnyak's work that represents his genius at its best will be published in his native land. Several stories in this collection (*Mother Earth*, "The Tale of the Unextinguished Moon," *Mahogany*) appeared in a version by the present translators some two decades ago. The two novellas have naturally been polished and perfected this time around, but the changes in "The Tale of the Unextinguished Moon" as presented here are more significant. Our previous translation (as well as another published at about the same time) was made from an incomplete and faulty Russian text published in the West. Since then we have been able to locate a bibliographical rarity: the text of the story as it appeared in the issue of *Novyi Mir* that was confiscated and destroyed because of its presence. It is this version alone that Pilnyak prefaced with a denial that "the death of

M. V. Frunze furnished the occasion and material for it." Who excuses himself accuses himself, as the French proverb has it.

But the main reason for assembling a new collection of stories by Boris Pilnyak is to provide a more representative overview in English of the work of one of the dominant Russian writers of his generation. A peculiarly Pilnyakian genre was the fictionalized travelogue; our author produced three of these—two Japanese and one Chinese—not one of which has previously been translated into English. *Chinese Story*, the product of a Russian in China in the mid-1920s, is at once a prophecy of revolution in a distinctly unorthodox Soviet style and an example of Pilnyak's honesty as a reporter who does not shirk the sordid or ideologically embarrassing detail. This work possesses a historical irony that its creator would surely have savored and is central to this revised and enriched collection.

MAHOGANY

and Other Stories

Chinese Story

One

. . . I am standing on the bank of the Yangtze. All over the world children build towns of sand in the same way; in Russia too. Chinese villages resemble these childish constructions: flat-roofed clay houses, clay-walled enclosures, alleyways of powdery yellow earth—all of it burned out by the yellow sun. They say that some kinds of termites build their termite cities in the same way. Europeans are given to comparing the Chinese with termites and yellow ants because there are a great many Chinese everywhere, and—to a European eye—in the first place, the individuality of each separate Chinese face becomes blurred, and, in the second place, you cannot understand where they are going, where they come from, and what is the purpose of their constant movement. This Chinese village, whose name I will never know, straggles on for a dozen miles. The other bank of the Yangtze is almost lost to sight; this river is about five times as broad as the Volga; it is a river which carries oceangoing merchantmen and battleships; on it run the wooden-sailed sampans—to a European eye—rear end first, the stern being raised while the prow is flat and low. Smoke rises from an English gunboat anchored in the roads.

And here I stand watching. Near to the shore in the yellow water, which looks more like stewed tea than anything else, floats the corpse of a Chinese man. His face is down, his brown back and dark-blue trousers are exposed; the corpse is swollen, and the water carries it along in the most leisurely way, rocking it gently from side to side.

I walk along the shore in the wake of the corpse. A wave has washed it against the shore. An old Chinese man, a fisherman probably—naked but for a dark-blue rag about his loins and wearing an umbrella-like straw hat—pushes the corpse away from the shore with a long bamboo pole. Again the corpse touches ground. And again the old man pushes it away. The corpse moves gently with the current, floating feet first, and is caught in an eddy; it turns around three times, wavers, and floats on, head forward. Silly, but, I must admit, it is less disturbing to see the corpse floating head forward; but there must have been certain physical laws governing the movement of the water and the movement of the corpse, because each time it settled down it would again float feet forward. Yangtze-Kiang—Great Chinese River. . . .

. . . I am living in a settlement, in the international "concession." Beneath the window of the house where I live flows a branch of the Yangtze, the Huang-p'u, alive with steamers, waves, smoke, and sampans because this town is the largest of all the towns along the shores of the Pacific, larger than San Francisco, a huge port receiving daily as many as a hundred oceangoing steamers—a huge wound from which the blood of China flows, pumped out by the Yangtze—a gap in the mighty walls of China through which together with British cannon and dreadnoughts come universities and knowledge, trade unions and dawning revolutions. The house where I am staying is at the confluence of the Huang-p'u and the Nanking Canal. This canal is packed solid with sampans and small boats with roofs. On these boats the Chinese—thousands of human beings—live all their lives within the family circle, tethering their naked children like puppies with leather straps to prevent them from falling into the water. Who can say when the Chinese sleep? At midnight when the tide begins to rise, all at once the Chinese start shouting—it is then, in the midst of all this strangeness, in this dark night—darker than any Russian night—that terror comes. Three large sampans are anchored right by the bridge: it is a temporary graveyard. Rich Chinese must be buried at the place of their birth in the family grave: so the religion of ancestor worship demands. Those who die in this city are brought to these sampans, and their coffins are stacked layer upon layer until the sampan is full. Then the sampans deliver the coffins along the canals of the Heavenly Republic. And in the evenings, when the wind dies down in the sticky murk of that incredible heat, which saps every bit of strength in my body, this sticky smell of the dead men creeps along the bridge, along the canal, wrapping itself about the house. In the evenings prostitutes, all of them European women, stroll along the bridge; the bridge leads to the port, and British and American sailors with their prostitutes are drawn away by the rickshaw men, the only people here who run as fast as a horse. The sailors, all English-speaking, call the prostitutes "chickens." An American dreadnought lies at anchor opposite the house. . . . It would be a terrible thing if Chinese culture turned out to be as overripe as Chinese smells: the entire country is permeated with smells of putrefaction, of rotting things, mold, garbage of every kind, spoiled meat, soybeans, and soybean oils. This rottenness has found its way even into the cuisine: one of the most delectable of all Chinese dishes is chicken eggs that are left to rot in the earth for several years until they turn into a green amber of putrefaction, losing the taste of eggs and smelling of decay; it is then that they are eaten with relish. The Chinese manure the land with human waste, with human dung. There is no drainage system in this city, even in the European quarters: at dawn the Chinese carry away the waste that they gather from beneath the houses to the canals in willow baskets and load it onto sampans; the sampans take the manure to the rice fields—but at dawn the air in the city is unbreathable. . . .

. . . Clippings from a local English newspaper:

Disposal of Corpses

The chief of the Chinese police Colonel Yen Hun-min has issued an order making compulsory the burial of all corpses covered with straw or thin boards which are now to be found in great numbers in the fields around the city.

On account of the terrible heat the corpses decompose, spreading foul smell and infection.

The chief of police proposes that all corpses should be buried within three days. Relatives of the deceased are under obligation to carry out this decree.

In Putung

Reports of the spread of an epidemic of cholera in the Chinese territory, in Putung, where, according to Chinese newspaper reports, cholera is taking a tremendous toll of life among the harbor coolies, are of an extremely alarming nature. The Putung missionary hospital, which daily admits at least a hundred sick, is seriously overcrowded.

Protection Against the Heat

Chinese authorities have at last turned their attention to organizing first aid for persons who suffer sunstrokes or heatstrokes on the streets.

In addition to the fact that at many points on Chinese territory medical corps have been organized, all Chinese policemen have received special training on the administration of first aid to persons overcome by the burning rays of the sun and by heat.

The municipal police have taken the trouble to erect protective structures for policemen on duty at street intersections.

★ ★ ★[1]

China is a country of dragons that symbolize the sun, of pagodas, temples, heaven, ancestors, devillike gods, five hundred Buddhas, tortures, a culture of forty centuries and of the utmost oddity. The dragon is the symbol of China. I am bored in the halls where the gods are assembled because the streets behind the museum, streets which for me are mu-

1. The three stars here and elsewhere was a stylistic device of the time adopted by Pilnyak, denoting an interruption or pause. No text has been omitted.

seum pieces in themselves, have more reality than the gods. I am vexed in the halls filled with books because these are books about China written not by Chinese but by Europeans. I know that for the authors of these books China is the country behind the Great Wall of China. One need not go further into the halls where the wild animals, birds, and reptiles of this country are gathered. But I am being shown through, and I discover a most amazing thing: yes, I am in a strange country, utterly strange; it is no accident that dragons live side by side with the Chinese. In Russia in such museum halls stand the gray wolf, furred beasts, gray birds; there are almost no reptiles apart from the grass snake and the lizard pickled in jars. Here I find an unlimited number of reptiles I have never seen before: in the first place, hairless yellow crabs, tortoises, baby dragons, lizards, crocodiles, fish, seaweed. Here there are hardly any furred animals; most of these beasts are covered with spines or armor; they have lost their fur, and they are all yellow. Birds, on the other hand, are as brightly colored as the robes of Chinese mandarins. A strange world! An incomprehensible world! And a very revealing one, for the animal and reptile world is reflected in day-to-day life, in art and religious beliefs. All these crabs, octopi, fish, and pangolins, which, incidentally, the Chinese eat, are very frightening to my eyes! . . .

I was led to a door and told to look through the glass into the room beyond. There at a white table crowded with retorts, glass jars, alcohol containers, and slides, sitting on a high stool in front of a microscope, was a hunchback. He was dressed like a Chinese houseboy in nothing more than coarse white cotton pants, and was barefoot; his hump was exposed—a hideous lilac-colored thing covered with blue folds of flesh; his face was the very face of China covered with the wrinkles of old age. I was told that this old man was one of the greatest scholars not only in China but in the whole world; he was writing works of very great importance and living in the museum as a watchman, for his keep. . . .

* * *

Every people, every nation has its own particular opiate.

The people of Russia drink vodka, pure, unadulterated alcohol.

The British drink whiskey—barley vodka smoked in the same way as they smoke hams. The people of central Asia smoke hashish. The Chinese smoke opium. How can I convey in words the feeling that opium is no more a chance thing for China, its way of life and philosophy, than vodka is for the Russians, the Russian way of life, and for Russian national philosophy? Opium smoking is not a native Chinese invention: opium was brought to China by the British—the British would take opium anywhere at all—but it caught on and took root only in China, the country where Buddhism teaches the existence of a Chinese-style Nirvana. Chinese opium dens are as filthy as Russian hooch shops. They are forbidden by law: the effect is the same as trying to hold water in a sieve, for Chinese generals and foreigners—consuls included—engage in the opium trade. Chinese side streets smell strongly of opium smoke; there in the mud huts, inevitably in darkness and the most appalling filth, people lie in rows on kangs,[2] smoking, dreaming, and sinking into nothingness.

And it is here, on the thresholds of these dens, in the same way as in the temples and in the streets, that I realize I do not know, do not understand, and never will understand China and the Chinese. I ask questions right and left to find some keys to China, but I do not have these keys, and everything that I look at only adds to my lack of knowledge.

I am told by a sinologist, a professor who has lived in China for thirty years, that the keys to the understanding of China are Chinese gates and walls, for China is separated from the entire outside barbarian world by the Great Wall of China. Peking is surrounded by an outer wall; the central park of Peking is surrounded by an inner wall; every quarter is surrounded by its own wall; every house is surrounded by its wall. In front of the gates are placed two shields of clay in such a way that the yard is completely hidden to protect it not only from evil spirits but also from human eyes. The same shields of blind gates jut out

2. Kang—a raised brick platform occupying one side or end of a room, in winter warmed by a fire beneath and used for sleeping.—Eds.

in the Chinese psyche. Opium is shut off from European understanding by the Great Wall of Chinese ideas. . . .

★ ★ ★

Man-man-ti means in Chinese "Wait a moment," "Don't hurry," "Don't rush," the same as the Russian *seichas*. This *man-man-ti* lies at the heart of Chinese distances, Chinese time, Chinese dealings, Chinese philosophy.

Hankow, June.

. . . I awoke today with the most astonishing sensation of childhood, my childhood in Saratov, in the house of my grandmother Katerina Ivanovna, among the noises of the embankment, the boom of the barge haulers' song. I don't know whether they borrowed this harbor song from us or we from them, but I know that the tune and the rhythm of it here in Hankow, as everywhere else in China, are the same as in Saratov and everywhere on the Volga. I listened hard: the Chinese "Ha-hey-ho!" is exactly the same as at my grandmother's—and the noises are exactly the same—both the roars of the steamers and the shouts of the crowd. And in the morning, freed from the nightmare of sleep under a mosquito net, I went to the embankment to wander through my childhood, for the picture is exactly the same, amazingly so: the same barge haulers wearing a variety of national costumes, the same overseers, men carrying sacks and bales on their backs in the same way (how is it that their spines are not broken?). It is good to remember one's childhood; I feel happy and sad at the same time, and it is certainly not too much to travel thousands of miles to stumble into one's childhood. . . . Strange that what I see here should speak to me of Russia, Grandmother's Russia beyond the Volga.

China is built entirely upon analogies. Already I am a long way beyond Mukden with its tombs and Chang Tso-lin's palace behind thousand-year-old city walls past which the Russian armies fled in 1905, beyond Dairen, the Yellow Sea, the Pei-ho [Pai] River, Tientsin with its dust and palms, beyond the Tientsin-Peking Railway overrun with Chang Tso-lin's soldiers and bringing to mind the year 1918 in Russia—the checking of documents, the pursuit of deserters, the uncertainty of a train's arrival, the storming of railway cars. As might have happened in Russia in 1918, we were about to leave the scorching suffocation of the station platforms after waiting many hours for a train—the porters had already started off with our suitcases—when with no warning whistle a train pulled in; we climbed into the restaurant car through a window. No one could say why the train arrived at this time and not another; no one could say why the train was waiting or why it moved off. I found a place on the car platform; a dozen parties of officials went through checking documents, putting people off, pursuing, making arrests. Europeans in this crush were so many inviolably empty spaces. The heat was scorching; the train was jammed with Chang Tso-lin's soldiers; the stations were jammed with soldiers, army carts and tents, flatcars with cannon, cars with coffins and rice. Cars were taken by storm and by rifle; no one could say why the train waited or moved. On the car platform I made friends with a Chinese soldier, one of Chang Tso-lin's men. He was guarding some sacks; the sun was beating down, and whenever the train began to move, he took off one tunic, then a second, and a third until he was barechested; as we approached a station, he would struggle back into the first, second, and third of his treasures which he had either stolen or won at mah-jongg. . . . Peking—an armed camp—greeted us with the most unbelievable piles of filth, with suffocating heat, walls, gates, and pagodas. We drove through foul streets, knee-deep in dust, through close-packed detachments of troops in the quiet of the Legation Quarter, into the calm of British, American, and Japanese guns.

Peking is a city under arms of Russia's 1918: all the palaces, all the temples are packed with soldiers, cannon stand in the squares, patrols guard intersections—and everywhere are the husks of watermelon seeds!

The Russian year of 1918! . . . But unlike in Russia, foreigners and Europeans are incorporeal, unhindered, inviolable. We take our places in the train that will pass through the field headquarters of Wu P'ei-fu; we have a compartment next door to the restaurant car—that is all that remains of the French "Express Bleu," the most luxuriously fitted in the world. Route: Peking–Hankow. As we leave I am told:

"In the Province of Honan Wu P'ei-fu has collected taxes from the peasants up to the year 1936 inclusive. If you go through Honan, you will see the Red Spears,[3] Fang Chih-min!"

Everyone smiles. The station is lighted by gas lanterns. The night is as black as a Negro. The train moves into the campfires beyond the walls of Peking—and then returns: they are adding a private car for a Chinese general. I am told that General Huang Hsiang-li out of self-respect relieves himself in his private car in the following manner: he stands spread-eagled facing the toilet bowl, supported on either side by two retainers, spitting into the bowl from time to time—then they clean up the tiled floor behind him. Once again the train moves into the campfires, into the blackness of the night. There are two of us; we are elegant; we feel elegant. An army patrol makes its way along the corridor in the most courteous way imaginable. Before us—forty-eight hours of travel according to the timetable, and an unknown number of days and nights according to the demands of reality: we have brought with us enough books for a week. By morning we are lost in an infinity of rice fields, in Chinese destitution, in Chinese toil. What limitless heights might the peasants of China gain if they were really marching forward instead of marking time on the spot as they do, pumping water from the canals to the rice fields and from one rice field to another?! Day after day the Chinese, old men and children, walk the treadmill, turning it, pumping the water, by the weight of their bodies—the children with small sandbags tied to their backs to make them heavier! . . . Toil and centuries of slow working of the land are before us: for who can say how many centuries it took to bring under cultivation, with nothing more than a water-level device, all these plains that

3. A secret society that organized self-defense groups in Chinese villages to protect peasantry from bandits and warlords.—Eds.

stretch so many thousands of miles?! There beyond the train windows, in the abject poverty of villages and fields, dried-up rivers, close by miserable war-shattered hovels are a great many fresh graves and ancient burial mounds. . . . Stations go by with their army bivouacs, their suggestion of the Russian year 1918: freight cars used to transport people, train buffers, soldiers, rifles, machine guns, hours-long delays, dust, watermelon-seed husks, mountains of filth, muddle. . . *man-man-ti!* beggars, peddlers with trays of goods, soldiers in pursuit of the peddlers with their trays, patrols, shouts. Towns are shut off by the gray bulk of walls and the crush of suburbs under the walls. In our international car the conversation moves as the wind blows: words are carried wherever the thought turns; we wander aimlessly back through our lives. On the first day, after we had passed villages buried in loess, underground villages, the Hwang Ho suddenly appeared in the pale blue Chinese sunset. The Hwang Ho, the Yellow River, which every year destroys millions of human lives, which every year changes its course—appeared in the sunset, and the train took leave of it and its loess beds in the deep blue of a moonlit night. In the morning we saw at the station a sheaf of spears similar to those of the Russian Cossacks; tufts of long, red-dyed hair were tied close to the tip of each spear. These spears had been seized from the Red Spears. We were traveling through areas of peasant uprisings: stations are deserted except for soldiers, but in the fields the peasants go on climbing the water wheel as before. Here the most monstrous cruelties are perpetrated: villages are burned to the ground, while detachments of troops and bands of rebels are massacred, women are raped. There is also a band of women—brigands or partisans, as you will—under the command of a woman. They rob merchants and caravans on the road, and the leader takes the most handsome men for herself. This detachment was formed by peasant women driven to desperation by incessant plunder. I remember one particular peasant hut. I saw it in the Peking area not far from the grave of Sun Yat-sen. The hut stood on the slope of a hill by the side of a rice field. On the hillside stood what—to a Russian eye—looked like the kind of shed in which firewood and chickens are kept in

Russian provincial towns: about four paces wide and six paces long, windowless, and with a high door; from the clay stove a pipe led under the kang. The hut was completely empty; an English canned-goods tin served as a cup; on the kang lay a robe of cat fur. At the threshold stood picks and shovels. On the ground in front of the hut sat three females: a mother and her two children. It was impossible to tell how old the mother was: she might have been thirty-two or fifty. She was dressed in the trousers that women wear in China and a blouse which covered her breast; her waist was bare to the sun and as brown as English tobacco, as was her face. The elder girl was dressed only in skimpy pants, and seemed to be about ten years old. The younger girl was about eight and was as bare and brown as her mother's face. The three of them were embroidering women's silk slippers with gold thread, the kinds of slippers that are made for Chinese ladies of noble birth whose feet have been mutilated by binding. Mother and daughters sat in the dust on the flat-trodden earth; silk and gold were spread out on a silk rag. The rice field was next to the hut; there the father worked, up to his loins in water; he stirred up the soil beneath the water with a pick. He was naked, and his queue was tied up in a knot. And this man and his three womenfolk paid me no more attention than if I had been a disembodied spirit. . . .

It was on this trip from Peking to Hankow—the foreigners' express was only two hours late—that we went to what had once been a Russian concesson where to this day on the porch of the Russian church stands an absolutely genuine Russian policeman—complete with epaulets—maintained there by the entrenched remnants of the Russian tea traders. At night I was tortured—by heat and mosquitoes. In the morning I would lose myself in my grandmother's beyond-the-Volga world. A week later the Peking-Hankow railroad, which belongs to the French, was cut by the Red Spears: it was reported in foreign newspapers that the railroad had been partly washed away by the flooding of the Hwang Ho. On the other side of the Yangtze-Kiang opposite Hankow lies the town of Wuch'ang, the cradle of the Chinese revolution of 1911. It is a hill town, gray walled and desperately overcrowded, as Chinese towns are, a place where two men can hardly pass each other in the alleys crammed with guild workshops and small stores. On a hill above the town a signal cannon keeps watch over passing time. From the wall of the fortress on the hill Hankow is gradually lost in the smoke of factory chimneys. An Englishman in cork helmet, dazzling white suit, and white shoes sits in his rickshaw encouraging the rickshaw man with a white hose in the back. The rickshaw man opens up a way through the mass of humanity with hoarse shouts. This is how it is: in Peking, in Wu-ch'ang, as in Hankow, Sikhs—Indians in crimson turbans who are Britain's colonial police—stand at intersections. They hold bamboo sticks with which they paste the thighs of each and every Chinese coolie or rickshaw man that runs past. This is how it is in all British or "international" concessions. Nowhere else are there so many police as there are in China, and nowhere else will you see so much stick swinging and beating as in China! . . . Overhead, stretched across streets, on buildings, in front of buildings hang the gilded, red, and blue hieroglyphs of shop signs, reminiscent of holy banners in Russian churches. These towns are like anthills where the Chinese—there are always thousands of Chinese—are the ants, and everything smells of soybean oil, the national Chinese smell. In Chinese shops you will find the same ground-in dirt, the same slow pace, the same patterns of eight on the floor left by the emptyings of teapots, as you will in the shops of the Tiutins and Sherstobitovs in trans-Volga Russia. . . .

Concessions—this is what they are: the British, French, Portuguese buy a piece of land, build houses in the styles of their native lands, build churches and monasteries; on these pieces of land people live according to the laws of the country to which the concession belongs. The consul is the supreme power; the consular court is the judicial authority; Sikhs maintain order and an atmosphere of European well-being. Park gates carry signs: "Dogs and Chinese Not Allowed"; for killing a Chinese within the concession the consul, sitting in his consular court, imposes on the European killer a fine of the equivalent of twenty-five rubles; Catholic monasteries in the concessions keep up the amber solemnity of church services, hymn singing, and communal monastic life. The parks are shady, and white yachts ride on the canals.

The cork helmets worn by the British are so made that at the slightest movement they give out a humming sound like a stove chimney in a blizzard because of the artificial draft built into them; but from the humming of this cork the head too turns to cork.

★ ★ ★

In China there are many places where you are no more than half an hour, an hour, ten minutes from everything that goes to make up European-American comfort, while three days' voyage from Hankow will bring you to day-to-day Europe with its customs and manner of life. On all passenger steamers throughout the world, the first class occupies the upper decks. A Russian, should he happen to be traveling first class on a steamer and should he find himself sitting on deck pleasantly conscious of being well fed, shaven, and clean, a Russian in such a situation experiences an irresistible urge to go down to the lower deck to those for whom begging and lice are a way of life, to work his way into the tightest crush so as to bring himself to their level. . . . The name of the steamer is the *Chiang-t'ing.* Nobody on board speaks Russian. In the first class there are four passengers: they are Europeans, but their nationalities have been effaced. The ship sailed at 9:15, and at 9:15 the first-class passengers went to bed, while the Chinese crowd in the steerage below kept up a steady hum. Next morning breakfast was served at seven while the ship stood at anchor across from the ruins of a town; I could not find out the name of this town and I shall never know it. I shaved, took a bath, had breakfast, and stretched out in a deck chair feeling well fed, shaven, and clean. The ship began to pull into the shore, and docked. Suddenly there was an avalanche of porcelain, earthenware, and clay Buddhas, dragons, mandarins, vases, copulating pairs of men and women, and tigers. The gods were not admitted to the upper deck, and they dammed up the gangways. I bought myself a god eight inches high—a very cheerful-looking one, made of very good-quality porcelain—for the equivalent of two rubles. On the ship are traveling two European-American old biddies; in the morning one of them, dressed in pajamas, took a stroll along the deck before her morning bath, squinting at the sun like a cat. In this town of porcelain gods and devils we took aboard an Anglo-Saxon.

He to me, energetically, in place of a greeting:

"How do you do?"

I to him:

"Tenk yoo." I speak English badly.

"German?"

"Rashe."

He to me:

"Russian? Whiskey and soda?"

I to him:

"Tenk yoo. Oll rite!"

We were brought whiskey and soda. He turned out to be an American engineer. We began to talk in a mixture of languages; we discuss American industry, Russian culture, Russian art. The American's name is Parker; he is young, lively, likes to joke; undoubtedly he plays tennis very well. Toward lunchtime the ship sailed into the wind. At lunch we sat together. Mr. Parker leaned over to me, smiled brightly English fashion, and said, moving his eyes in the direction of one of the old biddies:

"The lady is observing you very closely!"

I took note of this. We got up from the table. Great Chinese River! It is about five times as broad as our great Russian Volga. The eye loses itself in these watery expanses, and the wind blows like a sea wind. Everywhere sampan sails. Everywhere mountains in the distance. Once these mountains toppled into the water, floated by as rocky steps in the shallows, scattered in stone clusters of islands. Water foamed about the rocks. White clouds floated in the blue sky. The old biddies came out to squint at the sun. Wind. Warmth. Beyond the railing there is the sound of rushing water. Like the wind, trivial thoughts must always be on the move. Mr. Parker shaded his face with his helmet and dozed off. Before falling asleep he said:

"The only great culture is Anglo-American. I don't believe in Chinese culture. Just take a sniff of the place."

I too fell asleep following with my drowsy eyes an island no bigger than a little Japanese house, a deserted rock with a white beacon. Closing my eyes, I thought about *man-man-ti*, about the ocean routes, and about Russia, Kolomna,[4] and the Church of Nicholas-Beyond-the-Walls in Kolomna. There are good things about American culture—the ability not to hurry. . . .

. . . The southern capital—Nanking. Walls as in Peking, scorching heat, palm trees, dust. Soochow or Foochow; a real colonial-style railroad; incredible, impossible, intolerable, dreadful heat; heat that saps the strength, demoralizes, and destroys; heat that cooks a man's brains and dissolves him in sweat. . . .

The Majestic Hotel building is the biggest and most luxurious on the shores of the entire Pacific Ocean; in the Majestic's huge restaurant you could set down the Cathedral of Vasili the Blessed among the palms. Nothing would be easier than to imagine that having passed through the garden town of the French Concession you had suddenly arrived in a real Europe-America. Nanking Road is a reflection of Piccadilly.

⋆ ⋆ ⋆

China! Every town in China has its own government, generals, mandarins protected by their *taels* and *t'ung-tzu-ers*[*] and by their rifles. Though, incidentally, money in China does not belong to the Chinese. Every town has its own bank, and Hankow money is not accepted in Nanking or in Shanghai, in the same way that Shanghai dollars are not valid in Hankow and Nanking. Money! In addition to the fact that each province has its own currency reserves from foreign banks, in China every province has two currencies: one for the Chinese and one

4. A small town 115 kilometers southeast of Moscow, where Pilnyak lived for some time.—Eds.

⋆ Chinese money.—Author.

for foreigners. Foreigners live on Mexican dollars, "big money"; the Chinese, on the other hand, make do with "small money." In theory China has *taels*—theoretical currency units equal to seventy-seven Russian silver rubles; but this money is not to be found even in the vaults of banks, and the Chinese live on *t'ung-tzu-ers* and coppers. One dollar is equal to one hundred cents, and a cent is equivalent to two and one-third *t'ung-tzu-ers*. The rickshaw man, in the first place, avoids being paid in cents and, in the second place, earns fifteen to twenty *t'ung-tzu-ers* a day, and on this he manages to exist. . . . China! Country of wildly divergent contours and also of thousands of kilometers of cultivated land; country ruled by Chang Tso-lin, Wu P'ei-fu, Fêng Yü-hsiang, Fang Chih-min, Sun Ch'uan-fang, by the Cantonese. It is the country of Peking, Shanghai, and that hut which rose up on a hill-side near the grave of Sun Yat-sen. It is the country of K'ou Ying-Chieh's feudalism and the Communist trade-union councils of Canton and Shanghai.

Two

. . . Heat! Heat! *man-man-ti*. . . . Incredible heat, dreadful heat. . . .

There are three of us: Loks, translator Krylov, and I. Our house stands in the placidity of the International Settlement, behind a respectful lineup of lackey boys, in the midst of English rules of conduct, in the cool of refrigerators and the whiteness of Venetian blinds. There are three of us—Russians—in this city of three million souls: we are more lonely than we would have been in a desert because in the evenings in this loneliness we have to don monkey suits. There are three of us: the fourths, the fifths, and the sixths—are my inventions born in the scorching, stifling heat. Krylov and I will soon be on our way.

For me: a Russian ship is to arrive and to take me to Singapore, to Aden by way of the Indian Ocean, to Port Said, to Constantinople, to Moscow. I make inquiries on the whereabouts of my ship: nothing has been heard about it; they tell me that in a few days a ship is going to Siam and try to persuade me to go there in the meantime, although it is possible that my ship might arrive while I am at sea. What dominates my feelings is frightful weariness: my brain is scrambled by the tens of thousands of kilometers left behind; you cannot expose a photographic plate a hundred times in a row—my brain is as worthless as such a photographic plate; I feel like sitting down, saying nothing, seeing nothing, hearing no one—what the hell do I need Siam for!

For Krylov: his wife has left, he must follow her to Russia, to Moscow; he is waiting for the official papers. He has just come in, sat down in an armchair, tossed back his hair; his face is sweaty; he cleaned his glasses and said:

"I know nothing about my wife, how she is traveling—because of her indifference. I know that she is an organized person, and I am wondering if something has happened."

He has a very good wife, a dear and faithful friend. I say that nothing can happen. Our houseboy brings us some soda water.

Every evening we put on monkey suits and go out of town in an automobile—to eat ice cream and to speed for hours on end through palm groves because only during this nightly ritual can we take a breath of air. Every other day I attend banquets.

Man-man-ti! . . . During the past two days I learned what tropical heat is, when your body truly melts. Days pass as ordered. In China—it seems—religion has died: yesterday for the first time I saw a functioning shrine where one could not breathe for incense. . . . Singapore, Hong Kong, Indian Ocean, Bab el Mandeb, Red Sea, Suez. The head on my shoulders—as Esenin[5] put it—is ready to crumble, not in death but in the intoxication of accomplishment, fortitude, and, perhaps, weariness.

June 28th.

It is pouring rain; last night through this rain, stifling as the upper shelf in a steam bath, lightning blinked and thunder rumbled: in daytime you don't hear thunder through the roar of the city. Everything is enveloped in smoke and watery haze. Swarms of mosquitoes fly about the room—we burn antimosquito candles, which make them curl up and could make us curl up too.

It was suggested to me that I take a ship to Siam.

For two days now Krylov had been waiting for a telegram. He came in, smoked for a while, and said:

"It's silly to send telegrams when you don't know where to send them—when, practically speaking, you send them into space."

July 4th.

Scorching heat! . . . No, not exactly; scorching heat is something burning, fiery. This is a steam bath—a shelf in a steam bath; we are living in

5. Sergei Aleksandrovich Esenin (1895–1925), poet.—Eds.

a steam bath. The city lies in the Yangtze Delta; the tropical sky burns above—the Chinese dragon; the air is so thick with warm steam that you cannot cool your organism by quenching your thirst; sweat flows down in streams, neither evaporating nor cooling you off; we are in the wet bouillon of our bodies. Our house-boy makes ice balls in the refrigerator, throws them into icy soda water, and we drink dozens of bottles a day. One cannot take a cold bath or wash with cold water: right after a cold bath comes a heat-stroke, headache, and vomiting; after cold water the body breaks out in boils. The hotter the bath—the greater the relief afterwards. Hands and head droop in the weakening, demoralizing, stifling heat. The sun in the sky is dim in the clouds of steam, and at night the heat does not diminish, but at night—mosquitoes come. All last week I was in a state of collapse: there is a tradition under this sun that in order to adjust oneself to the heat and dampness one must live through a stomach upset. Our clothes are put away in zinc wardrobes to prevent their getting moldy; if you leave out a pair of leather shoes for three days, they get covered with green mold; everything is moldy, damp, runny, and your brain runs too. In Russia, to get an idea of this heat you have to move into a steam bath, to a steam-bath shelf for a week.

No news at all about the *Transocean*. In the office of the steamship company they think that she will arrive only in August. That means I won't be in Moscow until November. That's terrible! . . . Still, I definitely don't want to return by way of Siberia.

Krylov sent five telegrams all at once—to different addresses. He said to me: "My wife always vowed her devotion; of the separation she said that it was boring, unnecessary, lonely and so on. . . .

July 5th.

I have just got back from the office of the steamship company. They told me that the *Transocean* had gone by; she is near Singapore by now. The next ship—the *October*—will arrive in August or September. In Chinese this means ***man-man-ti!*** . . .

July 8th.

Krylov showed me the text of a telegram, ". . . consider silence outrageous, demand explanation." That was in the morning, and in the evening he showed me a letter!

"I cannot understand your silence and our manner of correspondence if this is the word for my unanswered bombardment of you with letters and telegrams. The last note I received from you was dated June 19th. I calculated when my letters and telegrams should have reached you. I checked newspapers to see how long it took them to get here from Peking. To this day I don't know if you're still in Peking or if you're on the way to Kalgan so as to travel on through Mongolia. I cannot accept such casual indifference and carelessness. I am forced to think that there are reasons for your silence. I know you to be a direct and honest person; you are in good health—therefore you must find it difficult to tell me something, or there's something else. But here is what I want to tell you: I wish you all the best, all the best, if this falling-out of ours is catastrophic—I wish you every happiness. I am not going to write to you any more because I don't wish to torment myself and go around an unwanted Tartar. . . ."

I said:

"There is an inexact phrase in the letter; you wrote, 'all the best if this falling-out of ours is catastrophic'; and what if there is no falling-out of any kind—is 'all the best' canceled?"

* * *

. . . if you move your finger over the globe from Port Said east to the shores of the Pacific Ocean, you will run into a town the name of which—for me—is *man-man-ti!* Subtropics. The Settlement.

Night. Up there in the north—in Russia—nobody knows what tropical heat is when matches and tobacco get wet and become covered, like my brain, with mold, when, in addition to everything else, you have to sleep inside a mosquito net and light mosquito candles near you that make breathing impossible. I am now sitting down, having put one of these candles under my chair; the smoke is creeping up into my pajamas. Our house is in the silence of the International Settlement. In the first days after my arrival, at night, we used to drive out of town to out-of-town restaurants—to eat "ice-cream sodas" and the "American Girl"—varieties of ice cream. Now a regimen of a provincial monastery had been established in our house, with bed at eleven. And today, having had a dinner of sukiyaki at a Japanese teahouse—Japanese shashlik at a Japanese restaurant—where people sit and eat on the floor—we went to our rooms at eleven, and I lay down, read, and then extinguished the light.

And now I am up because I can't get to sleep.

Every person must have his household things—and I have mine: in the teahouse this evening I awkwardly shook ashes from my cigarette, and the cigarette holder fell into the ashtray filled with water (English cigarettes, once lit, don't go out); all kinds of people must have thrown cigarette butts into this restaurant ashtray and spat into it, but this little holder, an old one, I had brought with me from Moscow, and good memories make it precious to me. And just now, before sitting down to write, I went into the bathroom and scrubbed the cigarette holder most thoroughly; now it lies before me in a Chinese bowl, soaking in cologne; the cologne has turned brown. . . . On my windowsill—I don't know how it got there several days ago—lies an apparently newborn, tiny, red, hairless dead bat! I did not brush it off and am watching the sun eat it, really eat it before my very eyes; in a few days only the bones will be left.

. . . Damn, it startled me! . . . I was writing, bent over, and I heard a slight noise; I raised my head and saw a big bat; it is now flying under the ceiling—a big one, the kind we don't have in Russia; it is disagreeable; it is unpleasant to be in the same room as this foreign animal. Now it has settled on the curtain. Now it is flying again.

. . . What nonsense!—it flew in and frightened my thoughts away. . . .

Well. Several days from now only bones will be left of the little bat. Then I shall gather them together. That's how the sun eats.

There is more—also my "household things." Before sitting down to write, I went out on our little terrace, and after coming back I looked over my suits—to see if there was any green mold on them. Our house rests in solemn quiet. Our house stands on the shore of a canal—precisely on the corner where the Nanking Canal merges with a branch of the Yangtze. In the canal, on the water, lie, in rows, hundreds of sampans, small Chinese boats, in which Chinese live. I stood on the terrace; from the three large sampans, those loaded with the dead, came the sweet, suffocating smell of dead bodies. One wonders when the Chinese sleep. Just now I interrupted my writing, turned off the light, chased out the bat, and went out on the terrace. It is high tide, and the whole river is howling with Chinese voices, and the whole river is covered with a thousand—thousands of—creeping Chinese colored lanterns. One cannot remain on the terrace for the sweet, suffocating smell of the dead bodies. A mysterious life, which I shall never get to know, has its being on the river! . . .

. . . I know—tomorrow I shall wake up covered with perspiration, crushed by heat, with a sour mouth; the houseboy will bring some soda water with ice and some oranges (they grow right here, next door—anything you may want grows here!) to my bedside; I shall climb into a hot bath, I shall work on my papers until one—until lunchtime—and at two when everything is prickly and sinking hellwards from heat, I shall set out—I shall ride a ricksha (in this heat ricksha men run faster than Moscow horse cabs—incredible!)—to a Chinese movie studio, where I am going to be photographed for a Chinese newsreel—to be more precise, not to a studio, but to some Chinese alleys.

I am thinking of Russia, of my home. When I get back, I shall order a calling card, "B. A. Such-and-Such, once a writer,"[6] and I shall hide myself somewhere far from Moscow; I shall become a member of a cooperative, and instructor, I shall smell of country roads and coarse tobacco: b-u-u-t—I shall not write about the co-operative movement, I shall write about man, death, and love—and make it tougher than life. I am thinking of the death of a Chinese worker, information about

6. Initials for Pilnyak's name and patronymic, Boris Andreyevich.—Eds.

which came into my hands. China! . . . Side by side with dragons there are high-powered plants (today I was at a local sawmill where each machine has its own motor, where everything is moved by electricity brought from hundreds of miles away—a model mill!) Side by side with feudalism, mandarinate, and marshals, there are syndicalist workers' movements, trade unions, strikes, demonstrations, revolution, communism. Side by side with the Chinese living on sampans there is the Majestic Hotel, the equal of which exists only in New York. Every day—every twenty-four hours—into the port come as many as one hundred ships of ocean tonnage—it is the largest port on the shores of the Pacific Ocean. Around the city there are hundreds of mils. The city is submerged in damp, stifling smoke and smell of dead bodies. One wonders when the Chinese sleep. Honky-tonks stretch from the Majestic, where there are tropical thickets and the coolness of fountains in the restaurant hall and where a day's stay costs hundreds of dollars, to Chinese opium dens, where a woman and an opium pipe cost the same—thirty *t'ung-tzu-ers*, or seven and a half kopecks. This nocturnal city is befouled by "whites," white-skinned people, sailors on shore leave, local colonizers and pirates, living in concessions; in this nocturnal city there are multitudes of "white" prostitutes, and they are—wives and daughters of Russian émigrés. In the Settlement, where whites live and where money is made, money is all, and everything is bought and sold—everything and first of all women. . . . Oh, when the Canton revolution smashes through all this—even though three Hindu policemen stand on every corner here—oh, with what chilly joy one looks upon the Chinese who must inevitably be moved—not by marshals, but by revolutions! . . . And now I am thinking about the worker who left the sampans for the streets here and was shot (or strangled—it is not known which). The name of this Chinese worker, librarian, and student was Liu Hua.[7]

. . . Essentially, though, all this is not about me. I don't feel at all

7. A labor leader arrested by the British and executed in 1925 by Sun Ch'uanfang, the warlord governing the area.—Eds.

well. I am very tired. I would like to go home now, to Russia, onto the stove ledge,[8] into thoughts, into books, into quiet—and far, far away from this unbearable heat, horrible and tormenting (I am now sitting here, at three o'clock in the morning, naked—I have taken off my pajamas—I had some soda water, I am sucking a piece of ice, and sweat is running down me in streamlets), from mosquitoes and from the colossal, abrasive loneliness which is now in my heart. I am sitting here like an idiot on a seashore waiting . . . for a ship! I miscalculated—my ship has passed by; when I found out about it, I rushed home to pack my bags and immediately leave for home by way of Siberia—but it turned out that it would take me a month even to get to Vladivostok because the route I had taken here is now cut off either by Chang or Fang or Wu. Tickets to Dairen are sold out to the end of September. More haste, less speed—how very true! . . .

. . . The devil only knows if it's the night that gets me confused! . . . Yes, that's it! Just move a finger from Port Said east to the Pacific Ocean, roughly the distance of one-third of the Earthly Globe—and there lies a city in which it is now night. Outside the window in the blue-gray fog and haze burn the lights of the skyscrapers and the paper lanterns of the canal. And one cannot tell what causes this steam-bath blue-grayness of the night—the heat or the approaching dawn. The bat dominates this night. Too bad our grandmothers are all dead—they knew what bats in the night portended.

* * *

. . . And again it is night, and I cannot sleep.

Yesterday there was a storm, an incredible storm; thunder roared like cannon—never, not anywhere, have I heard such a storm; the streets were flooded so that ricksha men walked knee-deep in water. I was not at home—I was with some Chinese; I came home and saw that the storm had washed my dead bat off the windowsill; so in the morn-

8. Platform over a brick cooking-and-heating stove used as a bed or couch. —Eds.

ing I bought a cricket: the Chinese sell crickets like birds, in cages; the Chinese are connoisseurs of their singing. I bought a cricket, in all likelihood a wild one, because it does not sing when it is light and when I am present. I put some banana in its cage and put the cage under the sofa, and now I am listening to it: when my typewriter clicks, it stops singing, when I stop typing it begins chirping.

How scales and yardsticks change—and—how relative everything is! . . . To the whole world China appears to be fantasy; it appears that way to me when I remember that I am a Russian and that I must "observe," but from the standpoint of everyday life—I am used to everything, I am tired of everything. This has to do with the fact that today was a good day—good in the sense that some Moscow picnic in the Sparrow Hills might be good. This morning my fellow countrymen and I took a motorboat and went to the coast to have a look at the Pacific. The trip there took two hours, the one back—three hours; we had lunch there. We kept passing junks and sampans, and the *Empress of Canada* passed us—it is one of the sixty-thousand-ton ships on which Americans make tours around the world lasting six months; it is a huge thing on which more people live than in Kolomna. I lounged about the deck in the sun and wind (now my hands and face smart with sunburn), and my thoughts blew with the wind. A strange thing: thoughts are like boulders—with each one I can pin myself down—but the breeze was a mere nothing, and still it was in command of my thoughts. And then we had lunch on the seashore: all around us was China with its naked children, with its unbelievable poverty, and in the midst of this poverty, under the palms—an English restaurant immersed in English primness, unhurriedness, whiskey sodas, curry and rice, women like dried fish, and men who understood everything a hundred years in advance. The ocean rolls its waves upon the shore, its breakers thundering, blue as blue; ships are swallowed up in the distance. We came back tired, smelling of the sea; we had dinner, washed; I was busy with the cricket for a while, went to bed, turned off the light—and here I am—writing. . . .

In Russia we don't know anything about China! And it is strange to see, in these days in which we live, how the worlds of national cultures splash over their fences, how a geometrical form—and formula—of the globe moves, equalizing everything over the Earthly Globe. Yesterday, from two o'clock in the afternoon until midnight, I was with some Chinese at a movie studio; incidentally, the same movie studio houses the editorial office of a thick Chinese magazine, the left-front *South Country*. This was in the Chinese City,[9] in a Chinese house—in the garden and inside. Of all the countries I have seen, China is more like Russia than any other country, the beyond-the-Volga Russia of my Russian grandmother—even in its food, although here they eat frogs (the "humanitarian" British try in their own courts any Chinese caught hunting frogs on their, British, "territory") and puppies and swallows' nests and seaweed and rotten eggs. It is no accident that both China and Russia were conquered by the Mongols. For China I have two yardsticks—Russia and Japan (in parentheses: of all foreign cultures, Japanese exerts the greatest influence on contemporary Chinese culture; the best-known literature in China is Japanese; the Chinese intelligentsia goes to Japanese universities to be educated; the most widely spoken foreign language is Japanese; the most widely read foreign magazines are Japanese. . . close parentheses). After Japan, I keep stumbling upon Russia. At the movie studio they had organized—I don't know what to call it—a picnic, I guess: people made themselves comfortable in the house and in the garden, they came on foot, arrived in rickshas and in automobiles, got acquainted, greeted one another, drank, ate, and left. There was only one European there—I. They took motion pictures of me in all kinds of situations. We spoke: Russian (there was not a single person apart from my translator, the Chinese writer Chiang, and me who spoke Russian), English (a great many, nearly all), Japanese (nearly all), German (ten people or so), French (ten people or so). There were: professors, artists, writers, actors, musicians. The number of people present was—oh, about sixty, no less; in any

9. At the time Shanghai consisted of the International Settlement (former British and American Concessions), French Concession, and Chinese City.—Eds.

case, we ate our supper in three rooms (Chinese fashion, using chopsticks). In Japan—to this day a woman is a slave, crawling on all fours, even the wife of a professor specializing in the West; here—things are very much as they were in prerevolutionary Russia: in the corner there sat a covey of girl students who at first gaped at the "celebrities" and reverently collected visiting cards and then, after supper, in a little secluded nook, having purloined a bottle of wine, drank it on the sly and, in antlike voices, sang their songs—exactly like my sister and her friends when they were first-year students. At first all Chinese faces seemed a single face to me—now I can tell them apart as well as I can European faces and am a good judge of Chinese female beauty: I was observing one girl student being "aware" of her own beauty, a charming girl and truly a beauty! . . . Writers' wives, actresses, poets (there were two of them) conduct themselves—exactly—as would our actresses and wives, for example, at my name-day celebrations, had these celebrations been held on a lawn in a garden. As a matter of fact, that was what it was like, except that all were dressed in their national costumes: the great majority of the women were wearing trousers, the men—skirts. We were photographed. We walked about the garden. We were photographed. A drop of wine appeared from somewhere. In a mish-mash of English, French, and German I was talking about the cultures of East and West, about Canton (which those assembled considered the seat of the only healthy Chinese government), about marshals, about the kinship of the Russian and Chinese cultures, about the society I am organizing here—the Sino-Russian Society for Cultural Relations, the "Sino-Russ," as I call this society in my own mind. The actors sang, played musical instruments, recited—if one can use these terms to describe Chinese ways of singing and playing. Others argued. Still others—mainly movie actresses—fox-trotted and charlstoned. There was some drinking. Then came a storm. This was in the evening; I stood on a little terrace, and—I swear to God—I felt like crying at the beauty of the sky rent by lightning and roaring with thunder. . . . And so everybody, men and women, did some drinking—one writer was carried out into the downpour on a deck chair to make him come to, and as I stood on the little terrace, an actress came out (she had learned movie-acting in America); she steadied herself near me, took my hand, said, "My bonny!" and—began kissing my hand, then bit it to bruising. I could have sunk through the floor—signaling my neighbors with my eyes—asking my translator, "What am I to do, Chiang?" Chiang, after a brief conference, said that her husband reckoned it didn't matter, let her kiss—later we'll carry her out into the rain. At this point she wanted to kiss me on the cheek—I ran away; she got angry, said something angrily in Chinese; I understood nothing and turned to the translator. Chiang said that there was no anger there, that compliments were paid in that tone of voice (generally speaking, a European is quite unable to interpret the tone of voice of either a Chinese or a Japanese: it may appear that something rude is being said, and it turns out to be a compliment, or something is said with a sweet smile and it turns out to be an unpleasantness!). Chiang said that the actress intended to pay me a visit—and in the meantime she was presenting me with her photograph. And indeed, she gave me a family portrait: a picture of herself and her husband. In general, the Chinese do not kiss—it is not one of their traditions: the actress did this out of "European politeness," having apparently confused the circumstances—who kisses whose hand; it was for this reason that her husband did not get angry—"So Europe is Europe—one has to observe the etiquette!" Then we drank vodka; the Chinese get drunk in the same way the Russians do: we embraced and said muddled pleasantries in a great mixture of languages. I was led to the car—in the after-rain darkness and puddles—it was as though we were playing "pile-up"—twenty people or so holding onto one another so as to stand up together.

. . . a Russian would understand nothing of what I have just written because a Russian can't imagine Chinese faces, Chinese houses, Chinese politeness, that the Chinese go about with fans (I do too), because their feet, the emotions in their faces, their costumes do not resemble ours in the least, because their music is inconceivable to our ears, and they sing with their faces turned away from the audience toward a wall and recite (after all, in the Chinese theater women are played by men!)

with stony faces—just like masks—in such thin voices that one wonders where they come from.

Yes, I left them. I came home into the quiet of the Settlement. I chatted with Loks. I came home at the hour (and in the darkness) of the high tide, when on the canal the Chinese shout louder than ever. I stood on the terrace, listening, thinking, alone. Far away lightning blazed. Then I went to check my household possessions: I saw that the dead bat had disappeared—my household possessions had become even fewer. . . . And again I am sleepless.

⋆ ⋆ ⋆

. . . The doctor came, and I interrupted my writing. The doctor drives his own automobile, and on his way past our house stops by for a drink of soda water and to exchange whatever news there may be. He is a sexual pathologist or sexual psychologist—I don't know what it is called: his speciality is sexual psychopathology. The doctor told us about a case of a patient he treated today—and the conversation went on about people's sex life. We talked—he and the three of us—about the countless thousands of people who are unhappy precisely because of the ugliness of their sex lives, even in marriage, because of onanism in marriage arising both from differences in sexual temperament and from the present structure of marriage in which the idea of the sex act as an act of procreation has been replaced by the notion of the sex act as pleasure, avoidance of children, with recourse to various unnatural practices which throw everything into disorder—psyche, health, and enjoyment. . . . Krylov said nothing; he did not hear the doctor out; he went to his room and returned only after the doctor had left. Krylov and I went out on the terrace. He said to me: "The doctor talks filth. Just now I was sitting in my room by myself, and I imagined that Katerina and I had a child. I don't know whether it was a boy or a girl, but I was overcome by the sense of happiness, the immense, beautiful happiness of parenthood shared with the woman you love."

"The doctor was talking about that very thing," I said.

. . . The houseboy came to make the bed ready for the night; he picked up a small piece of paper from the floor, unfolded it, looked at it, and threw it away as something unwanted. The houseboy has a remarkable, always inexpressively pleasant face that I examine every time, but when he is not before my eyes, I forget it and worry about not being able to recall it; I go to look at him, I see his blank, impenetrable eyes, his strange smile, his cheekbones and teeth—and I become uneasy; I inquire about his children and ask him to give me some soda water; I leave and again worry about the enigma of his face.

⋆ ⋆ ⋆

Never, never shall I forget our night rides out of town, with the automobile tearing up the expanses of excellent roads, between unfamiliar trees and palms, in those tropical nights when, if it were not for the headlights, it would be impossible to see two steps ahead. And then a strange moon would rise—it would have been beautiful if it were not for the haze of stifling heat and damp; it appears as a cast-off piece of a blue rag in the darkness of a starless, pinched sky. . . . Sometimes the automobile would dash into a swarm of fireflies; they would get crushed against the windshield, slide down and—already lifeless—would still emit their dead phosphorescent glow. . . . Thus the automobile and my brain would spur on the night's kilometers.

⋆ ⋆ ⋆

. . . No, not even in my dreams did I know what heat was! It is now eight o'clock in the morning—and I have already hung to dry two handkerchiefs with which I had wiped sweat so it would not drip on the paper; my shirt could have been wrung out. One cannot see the sun—it is hidden in that bouillon haze which clings to the city and to me with it. It is terrible—terrible—to feel yourself constantly in the bouillon of your own sweat. We Europeans cannot do anything—and we don't do anything, languishing in the heat, sitting under fans—wind makers that resemble airplane propellers—in a state of total emaciation. From the canal drifts the smell of dead bodies. Thoughts are stuck together with sweat, one cannot think.

July 11th.

Krylov showed me a letter:

"My own darling Katerina!

"Allow me to examine my feelings on paper so as to drive away the nightmare of these days. You know the objective conditions of my existence: the troubles with my transfer, weariness, loneliness, uncertainty, heat—all these are trifles compared to what I've been through thinking of you, loving you and suffering over you.

"Yes, I felt, and I still feel, a very great love, a very great pain and—a very great anger.

"I shall begin with the anger, because, no matter what you say, I consider your behavior outrageous, absolutely disgusting in every way. What is the matter? I send telegrams—on June 24 and 27, on July 2, 4, and 6—it is clear that I am uneasy; it is clear that I am sitting here lost in uncertainty. Silence. I have sent letters by registered mail only; it is impossible that you did not get them—I figured out when they arrived. You received my letters of June 17, 20, 22, 24, and 28. You could not find time to write for two and a half weeks—from June 19 to July 5. The hell with it!—if you were bored, you must have had plenty of time and if you were enjoying yourself as a tourist, you could have set some time aside. Particularly because in Peking you found out, before I did, that my transfer would be delayed—which means we won't see each other for a long time; you could have inquired by telegram! . . . So she sends a message after fifteen days—half a month—and doesn't find it necessary to remember to explain the silence, and then, after two more days and through a third party she finds it necessary to inquire about my plans. She writes all sorts of lyrical balderdash about lace, which interests me less than does Chinese snow, which does not exist, and then adds, 'Well, my own darling, I have told you everything my migraine lets me; if I have forgotten something it is for the same reason—my migraine'; and in the telegram you say, 'The tone of your telegram hurts.'. . . And what did the tone of my earlier letters that have vanished without a trace, do to you?' The hell with it! . . . She writes humbug in a positively classical style—like why did we have to part?—and then falls silent for half a month. You filled the six pages of your letter with water, but you did not get around to penning a single line about receiving or not receiving my letters. I hit upon the idea of following you by the newspapers—the dates they were mailed—but, unfortunately, one does not learn a great deal from newspapers! . . .

"What does it all mean? I spend sleepless nights, I wander around in a daze, I worry terribly, I humiliate myself by asking people to give me news of you, I dig around in a pile of guesses, I don't understand anything, I conjecture a thousand conjectures. I come to the conclusion: something has happened that makes it impossible for you to talk to me, that has made you shut yourself away from me; something catastrophic has happened that you want to conceal from me. For how long?! And I am writing you a letter in which, having gathered all my strength, I am taking my leave of you, in order to remove all blame from you, in order to accept the fact that, since it happened, it was meant to happen, because you are an honest, pure, and decent person, and no one has the right to impose his will on another. I was tormented by my anger, and I wrote in that letter that I bless you, wish you happiness and the best of everything. I sat on the terrace all night: this, after all, is like burying someone you love, worse, in fact, because for the first time I understood what jealousy was—it is a loathsome, beastly thing. I sat there all night gathering all my will to banish my anger against you, to keep all the pain to myself and to give you all the joy. It is very difficult and painful. But this is what I lived by all these days.

"Well, and now—point three. Have you read this letter carefully? Really? Then I can do without saying how much I love you. . . . Oh, I love you, love you—and I did not know that I loved you so much, I did not know that you have become a part of my heart, I did not know that I had no strength to tear you out of my heart, my own darling, my dearest, my one and only, my precious. My heart is calm now and I am ready to wait centuries for you, to dream of you—my path to you will be the path of the argonauts in quest of the Golden Fleece of your hands, your eyes, my own darling, my own darling; it turns out that to love in dreams is not a bit worse than to love with caresses."

* * *

Krylov showed me another letter to his wife—the second edition of the above. Krylov was pale, exhausted. I read the letter and said nothing—he went to his room and lay down on the sofa with his face to the back.

Today, July the 14th, is the anniversary of the taking of the Bastille, a national French holiday. Just now Loks has returned from the French consul's in the French Concession. In Russia, in all likelihood, I would not have remembered this day, but here in China the whole city is celebrating it. That is why this old sinner too spent nearly the whole of last night tramping around the French Concession. First we went to the French park, where everything was illuminated, and they sent rockets into the sky with full Chinese splendor, and where with full European decadence, tables groaned under awnings with viands for French sailors and Russian prostitutes. It was boring, and it is not worth talking about the rockets shooting into the sky and roaring like cannon, the bad taste of the illumination of the consulate, its Empire-style mansion lighted with a mixture of Sino-Egyptian curlicues and flowers, and also about the open-air pavilions where hundreds of sailors drank beer and fox-trotted with prostitutes, and the Chinese—by the thousand—stared. But along the Avenue George[10] moved Chinese processions with dragons, fish lighted from the inside, with lanterns on poles, with Chinese music—and that indeed was genuine beauty—fantastic, terrifying and—wonderful. It was in the wake of these processions that I tramped, in their wake that I went into the absolutely fantastic Chinese part of the city. There were many such processions, and everything got mixed up. Dragons, lighted from the inside, with burning eyes, twisted and turned above the crowd, huge fish floated

10. The author probably means Avenue Joffre or Avenue Edouard VII, two of the thoroughfares in the French Concession.—Eds.

above; they were overtaken by dogs, lions, lanterns, people in incredible fancy dress. The air was filled with the sounds of firecrackers, rockets, kettledrums, singing, shouts.

The night was confused. From the French Concession, from the dragons and the noises, we motored to an out-of-town restaurant, first to one and then to another, at first "Del Monte" and then "Dreamland"; we drank white wine with ice and watched people fox-trotting in this heat—in this heat and in white summer monkey suits. . . . Then Loks and I returned home.

. . . I am interrupting myself to tell a story of sailors' love in honor of Comrade Krylov. Krylov and I were in a tavern frequented by sailors. The sailors had been at sea; they had not left their ship for six months in a row; they were American Navy sailors. The women on the dance floor were Russian, Chinese, one Japanese, one Indian, and two Malayan—they could not leave the place until closing time, until four o'clock in the morning. For pennies at the cashier's men bought tickets to dance with the women. The sailors danced with them and had the right to invite them to their tables. I was amused to see how in these huge men—American Navy men—were combined the inevitable idolization of a woman that every man must experience before the sex act, and the dreadful infatuation engendered by the atmosphere of the dive, pitiful and revolting, which flared up constantly either as jealousy, when a dance ticket gave another man the right to dance with the woman, or as overwhelming lust, when, as dancing went on, it seemed that in another moment or so the sailor would crush the woman, tear off her dress, and rape her there and then. . . . But time goes slowly; sitting at an empty table is awkward, and the sailors get drunk without wanting to drink, and fall asleep at their tables waiting for four o'clock. The dive is full of noise and boredom. In their boredom and indifference, out of habit, the women trick the men out of their money—these women who are loved—if only for one night—with such idolatry and passion by the huge, frightening men who at the moment are as irresponsible and silly as children.

We left the dive and Krylov said in despair:

"How ugly, how disgusting—it's dreadful!". . .

After the Chinese dragons and after the honky-tonks of "Dreamland" we went home. It was a black night. Loks and I talked. I went out on the terrace, and I saw: in the darkness of the canal, on one of the boats on the canal, one of a thousand boats, a bonfire was burning; people and shadows of people stood near the bonfire, and firecrackers crackled—a great many of them, very loudly; it was dark, and one could see the leaping sparks of the firecrackers: on the boat someone was dying or a new human life was being born in hard labor, and the relatives crackled the firecrackers to frighten away evil spirits with the noise. . . How to convey the aching anguish aroused in me by those firecrackers on a sampan, heard after a night in the French Concession, by this black night, the bonfire on the sampan, the silhouettes of the people, and the bitter thought that these people were driving away evil spirits with firecrackers—away from someone who was dying or being born, by the fact that there is still so much dark night left in this world! . . .

I went back inside, and Loks and I sat down to drink some soda water, and we talked—long hours—about everything that two fellow countrymen can talk about ten thousand kilometers from home, in a strange land, long after midnight. It could well have been that there was not a tropical night but a polar winter ouside the house. My household possession—my cricket—now sings when I am present. Tomorrow I shall buy myself a turtle; I shall tie it by a leg with a string and lodge it in a pail: let it live and bring me good fortune! . . .

. . . I interrupt my writing. The barber came; he cut my hair, shaved me. Then came lunch. Strange things are happening to me: for many nights now I have slept three or four hours; I am sleepy and I cannot fall asleep.

. . . I continue. The heat is such that my white trousers feel like a Samoyed *malitsa;*[11] they torment with heat. In general, my time is spent

11. Outer clothing made of deer pelts, worn by native tribesmen in the extreme north of the Soviet Union.—Eds.

like this: I wake up at eight or nine in the morning; while I am still in bed, the houseboy brings me some soda water and oranges; then I go into the bathroom, wash, and shave. The houseboy prepares breakfast. Loks and I eat together. At that time Krylov comes out, crushed by the night, but having already looked through the papers. He tells the chargé d'affaires what was in the papers, about the political developments, the civil war, the movements of the armies, the marshals, the mandarins, the universities, the workers. We listen about forty minutes. Then we move into the study and immerse ourselves in the European papers—Russian, English, French. Thus, until lunch. After lunch we go to our rooms. For the second time I get into the bathtub, and then I lie down naked until teatime—or until the time when Loks gets up; he comes to my room (right now—I am pecking at my typewriter, and he is sitting in an armchair, reading); we are silent in the heat, exchanging just a few words. I know that he and I share a very good friendship—we spend many a long night philosophizing—we both need to develop fortitude. At five there is tea. After five I go to see the vice-consul—he has just learned to drive and is a driving enthusiast; we motor out of town, and I find it pleasant sitting in the wind, speeding forward, and thinking. Thus, until eight. At eight—dinner, and then there is always some event; midnight trips out of town—into fireflies and palms—are almost mandatory. . . . And then—night, a book, and insomnia. At night Krylov always drops by; we talk about China, but that is not the most important thing for him; just now he came in and said:

"I got another letter from my wife. You remember I told you that her letters had stopped coming. There is a great cleft within me. I try to plaster over the pain every way I can, but what can you do, if it is there and if it is mixed with anger. The pain and the love are so mixed together that I don't know where one ends and the other begins."

"That's from the heat," I said.

Today we went to a Chinese cinema; nothing special—Chinese costumes, but the principles of acting are American; there is nothing "Chinese" there. One can smoke as in American and English cinemas;

cooling drinks are served in the dark. At night Loks and I drove out of town; we did not stop anywhere, just rested from the heat.

* * *

Nothing is known about my ship.

* * *

July 17th.

Today's entry is devoted to Krylov and his wife. We were in a dive in an out-of-town Luna Park, where for the first time I saw the farce "What Have You Got?" where Russian officers' wives, turned honky-tonk tarts, danced and where Englishmen flashed their monocles. At our table sat the daughter of Admiral Shtark, a local dancer and prostitute. There were four of us. It was quite clear that everything there was exposed to the uttermost, and everything was money and for money. I was lucky, because the other two, who took us around the dives, went not to look, as we did, but to enjoy themselves.

Krylov said to me:

"It pains me to go to such places. The thought keeps creeping into my head that the same thing could have happened to my wife and to my sister. It's dreadful! . . . That prostitute over there"—he motioned with his hand—"finished a Moscow institute of higher education for women. Is it her fault that she followed her husband-officer or her father-general? . . . Look—that violinist is the husband of this prostitute here. People have sunk so low here that husbands do not leave their wives—these prostitutes here—and live on their earnings. . . . This musician and this prostitute have two children. At four o'clock in the morning the husband will go home, and the wife will go to a hotel room with the man who has bought her—or, if the purchaser should so desire, they will go to her own flat. There the husband-musician, a former officer, will quickly change into a servant's livery and will wait on them—in his own house! . . . Dreadful!". . .

And so, in this sort of high spirits we visited three dives—all of them European. Our companions taunted Krylov all evening; they called him a wet rag, said he was afraid of drinking, afraid of getting infected—unlike themselves—and all this with the refrain, "Ah, so you're leaving, you're giving up, we disgust you, well, well!" And so we went to a Chinese brothel, where prostitutes were nine to fourteen years old. This Chinese brothel was spotless, but the doors were open because of the heat, and one could see what was going on in every cubicle. They brought us some—hot—Chinese vodka, and children—girls—began coming in for selection. One of our companions took a nine-year-old girl and went with her to a neighboring cubicle. The other selected a girl of about thirteen but did not manage to go anywhere—he fell asleep, holding the girl in his arms, and she sat there quietly.

Then Krylov had a fit of hysteria. His hands began to shake, his teeth to chatter. I led him outside—he ran down the stairs, eyes lowered. We took rickshas; he looked at the ricksha man's back imploringly, as if urging him to run faster.

"My nerves have absolutely gone to pieces," he said. "I don't know which is more frightful: that these people—without love—and perhaps even without real lust, would copulate for money with a nine-year-old girl or that it could be my daughter, for I am old enough to have a daughter that age, or my wife because my wife comes from the same social stratum as the Shtark woman!". . .

We came home; Loks was still up. Krylov hurriedly got into the bathtub.

. . . Five o'clock in the morning. Yes, yes—and women in dives, when men don't approach them, sit herded together, yawn and talk about which dressmaker is making whose dress: I eavesdropped.

July 18th.

Morning. Today a postal strike began—no newspapers, no letters—that's just fine! . . . There is no sun, above the ground and on the ground—a bouillon consisting of stifling heat and sweat. There are no papers: books, sweat, and thoughts shall be my companions. Tomorrow a ship is leaving for Vladivostok: one has to have great willpower not to take it.

July 19th.

Yesterday I made no notes of any kind because it was a terrible day, the like of which we had not known. All day I lolled in bed, completely demoralized, naked, drenched in sweat, exhausted by this terrible, incredible, impossible heat in which one cannot move, think, eat. Thickening blood throbs in my temples, my body drips sweat, and still there is no salvation—every motion threatens a heatstroke. According to the papers, yesterday there were several-score such heatstrokes. The earth is immersed in steam, there is no sun, all is haze and fog—and in this thick, airy wash mosquitoes swarm. At night, at about eleven o'clock, it started to rain, and Loks and I drove out of town to rest from the heat. We came to a small wood and were engulfed in a swarm of fireflies: this was uncommonly beautiful—these little bugs glowing with the fantasies of Zhukovsky,[12] his romanticism, these little bugs which flew out of the tropical forest. I have written before that I shall never forget these automobile races—no, never!—but you get used to everything and forget everything: it no longer matters to me that out of the tropical night and darkness, away from the speeding road, the automobile will take us into Chinese hamlets, into Chinese alleyways, into this exotica of naked bodies in the automobile's headlights, into the wretchedness of reposing in the dust of the streets, under the sky, in the light of the paper lanterns, into these strange poses of tired bodies sprawled on straw mats.

We returned home. Because there is a postal strike, Krylov had gone to the post office and sorted the letters himself. He was lucky—he

12. Vasili Andreyevich Zhukovsky (1783–1852): poet, one of the founders of Russian romanticism.—Eds.

found a letter from his wife. A disturbed Krylov came to my room; he said:

"If you only knew what my wife has brought me to. She writes, 'Love you, kiss you'—and I am revolted by these words. She does not explain her silence from the 19th to the 5th. Here is this letter, and one can see again that she is not aware of the slap in the face she has given me, which is very hard to patch up and which I no longer have strength to bear. And she does not explain anything! . . . She has no idea how I wait for her letters."

I put an arm around Krylov and led him out for a drink of soda water.

Three

In the morning, Krylov, dazed, translated Chinese newspapers for us. At first my face reflected amusement, then Loks'. Loks chuckled. Krylov asked:

"What's the matter?!"

We burst out laughing: well done, Comrade China!

A translation from the Chinese newspaper *Shih-Shih Hsin-Wen:*

> A report has been received from highly authoritative sources that Marshal Wu P'ei-fu has sent a telegraph order to the *tupan*[13] of the Honan Province Marshal K'ou Yin-chieh to advance immediately against the chief of the partisan detachments Fang Chih-min operating in the Honan Province. Marshal Wu directs Marshal K'ou to abstain from acting in the manner he acted before—occupying a town abandoned by the partisans on their own initiative (as was the case with the occupation of Wentzu) and sending in reports of a bloody battle. Fang Chih-min, as is known, is one of the most powerful partisans in the Honan Province, commanding eight brigades. Marshal Wu directs that Fang be liquidated within a month. At the same time Marshal Wu, having requested help by telegraph from Yen Yueh-chen and Chang Ch'ih-kung, directed brigade commanders Ma, Li, and Yuan to be on the march; in other words, a seventy-thousand-man army was to be organized under the command of K'ou.
>
> Marshal K'ou Yin-chieh replied to Marshal Wu that at present he could not take action because of "domestic circumstances."

13. Military governor.—Eds.

The domestic circumstances, it turns out, are as follows: the famous actress and great beauty Pi Yun-hsia (exact translation—Dew on a Little Jasper Cloud) came to Marshal K'ou as his concubine. It is common knowledge that Pi Yun-hsia plays roles not only in the theater but also in the government of China. For example, in Peking in 1924, in the days of Wu P'ei-fu's Parliament, one of the members of the Parliament, trying to overcome the passive attitude of Dew on a Little Jasper Cloud who refused to become his mistress—and using his "right to parliamentary immunity"—would arrive in his box in the Parliament wearing only an outer robe; he would stick out his bare stomach beyond the railing of the box with the aim of disgracing Jasper Dew's art and thus wrecking Pi Yun-hsia's performances as a guest actress.

> Pi Yun-hsia appeared in Marshal K'ou's house, and in K'aifeng, the capital of the *tupanate*, all activities have come to a halt in confusion and indecision because the mother of Marshal-*tupan* K'ou, an adherent of the old system and old traditions, met Pi Yun-hsia with extreme hostility, constantly analyzing her vices, causing noisy quarrels which sometimes end in blows. All this has such an effect on the *tupan* and his activities as a statesman that he has lost his ability to work, is in a state of indecision, and has sent Marshal Wu a telegraphic reply asking permission to postpone the campaign until the family disorders had ended. The situation in the *tupan*'s household resembles stormy waves at sea.

"What are you laughing about?" Krylov asked.

"Well done, Comrade China!" I said.

... Yesterday I wanted to stay home all day, but some people came and took me to a meeting presided over by the American missionary attached to the army of Fêng Yü-hsiang. Strange, very strange! ... The meeting was in a European-style American theater. Chinese and a very small number of Europeans gathered in the theater. Fêng's army is known as the "Christian Army." And the meeting began with the singing of Protestant hymns in honor of the "Christian General Fêng." The Chinese, standing up, prayed Christian-style for Fêng and his People's Armies; in a chorus they sang the anthem of Fêng's armies. Then they showed misty pictures: Fêng and his soldiers—at a Te Deum, in a bakery, in a metal workshop, in a harness shop, the army on the march, the army at encampments, the infantry, the cavalry, the artillery. . . . Then all those attending the meeting were photographed. Then began a lecture about what a wonderful man, Christian, and leader Marshal Fêng Yü-hsiang, the head of the People's Armies, was; he prayed every morning, worked hard with his own hands, did not ride the rickshas and had forbidden his soldiers to ride them, and together with his men read the Bible and the history of China. . . . The American missionary portrayed Fêng, who is now in Moscow, as a kind of Taborite,[14] an ascetic, a penitent, a Spartacus of his age. . . . The heat in the theater was incredible, worse than on a shelf in a steam bath.

The heat was too much for me, and, exhausted by it, I went home. We had dinner, sat under a fan, and Loks and I stayed there until four o'clock, conversationally tramping around Russia from her past to her present and her future, from north to south, from trifles to great things. We sat in his study, half-undressed, drinking endless soda water and talking: about our beloved Russia for which one should always be prepared to die! . . .

These days I occupy myself with the Sino-Russian Society for Cultural Relations, the "Sino-Russ," and once again I affirm that the foremost word and deed in China is *man-man-ti*—hold it, don't butt in, just a minute! . . . Today news arrived that my ship, the *October*, is on her way to Tientsin, and from there—here; it'll be at sea for three weeks or so. Today wind started blowing from the ocean—at first it swept the dust; now it invigorates. Because the news of the ship at sea has come and because wind is blowing from the ocean and is scattering my thoughts, I feel better, as some kind of action looms ahead. . . .

14. A member of a radical Hussite group who rejected everything for which there was not direct biblical warrant.—Eds.

Man-man-ti! This *man-man-ti* is beginning to seem poisonous to me, the poison of China. . . .

. . . Midnight; the wind is droning outside; my cricket is chirping. Loks is sitting with a book; the door is open. Loks said that before long typhoons would be coming from the ocean. Before me is a long road, a very long road, for only now do I understand how immense kilometers are.

Krylov came in, sat down, said in such a way that Loks would not hear him:

"I found out my wife's address only on the ninth. Right now, it seems, she is in Mongolia, on her way to Moscow. I don't know how she has been living, where she has been, what she has learned, what she has seen, whom she has seen."

Night; no one knows when the Chinese sleep; there is noise outside; the wind has jumbled all the sampans on the canal. Above the sofa before me—the sofa has shelves over it—stands the smiling Chinese god I bought on the Yangtze; the god smiles cunningly, and I am thinking of Krylov and of the poison of *man-man-ti*, of the poison of waiting, of the unknown. The god's smile encompasses this *man-man-ti*, the whole of China, the sea, the ship—that's for me. But for Krylov it is *man-man-ti* that smiles as the god, as China, and as his wife who has disappeared into the kilometers of the unknown.

Four o'clock in the morning. I tried to go to bed but could not fall asleep. I listened to the wind and worked on the policy statement of the "Sino-Russ."

* * *

A Chinese fairy tale—"A fair judgment."

A young man and a girl fell in love and vowed to marry, but the young man was conscripted and fought for thirty years. The girl's parents decided to give her in marriage to another man. She resisted, but the parents prevailed—and the day after the wedding she died. She was buried.

Her betrothed came back from the wars and asked where his bride was. He was told what had happened. He went to the grave. He dug the grave open to take one last look at his beloved. And, when he opened the grave, his love was so strong that the girl arose from the dead. Her betrothed picked her up and carried her to his house.

Then the man to whom she had been given in marriage demanded his wife back through the mandarin.

The mandarin gave his decision:

"A case when true friendship and love could touch the sky and the earth and the laws of nature—to the degree that they returned life to the dead in the name of love—should not be judged by the laws of a mandarin. The girl is to belong to him who led her out of the grave."

This fairy tale was told by Krylov.

* * *

Yesterday at dusk we boarded a ship to see off some fellow countrymen who were going to Vladivostok. We had sailed the Huang-p'u on a motor boat; the water was rough, it was windy, the sun was setting. . . . There is, yes, there is a yearning for strange lands, and it is good to look at ships going to sea, at people carrying their shabby little suitcases (their poverty!), arguing, looking over staterooms, sticking in their little bundles. . . . And it is not good to leave the ship, the one that is about to sail, to get into a boat, the one that is going back, into the port, to the shore! . . . And we returned under the moon, over the waves, in the quiet of the low tide. . . .

. . . It is good to be going somewhere: and so I moved from one room to another; I improvised for myself a bed, a fan, a breeze from the terrace; the houseboy looked in bewilderment on my construction, and Loks and I celebrated my move by drinking a bottle of champagne and a glass of liqueur. To the houseboy I announced in the strictest possible terms that from now on at home I would not be wearing trousers and that for this reason no one was to be admitted unannounced. Because of all these circumstances it seemed to me that I had moved a few degrees to the north: it became easier to breathe, easier to live, to think. Loks is setting up a camera on the terrace: he intends to photograph the canal at night.

* * *

. . . I am making this up now.

. . . on an ocean liner, of the type of the *Empress*, sailing from San Francisco toward the China coast, an American woman or girl is traveling. . . .

Is it really worth joking about the English and Anglo-American manner of living: not walking, but with the aid of the legs carrying one's own dignity, top hat, and dinner jacket; knowing how and when to eat and speak; how to act in the presence of one's father, son, sister, wife, or a foreigner; how to rest, work, be happy, and die? There is solemnity in every minute of their daily lives, a ritual in their day-to-day existence; their life is replete—with time, traditions, and that which fills every minute and has been determined for you, the individual, by the majority, by society, by the nation. This tradition of life exists in all people, beginning with the Russian peasant, for whom this solemnity takes the form of wedding, funeral, and everyday songs, pies on holidays, and the fact that at the table the host is the first to break bread. This solemnity is lacking only in the intelligentsia, the Russian intelligentsia first of all, and that of the countries which culturally—in the western European sense of the word—are below Russia as, for example—in the European view—is China. This is understandable: European "culture" destroys a national mode of life, removing its distinctive qualities, as too inane and stationary, and introduces innovative "individualism" based mostly on illiteracy and the simplest kind of ignorance as it was in Russia at the time of Peter the Great when they cut *feriazi*.[15] In China, this country of Confucian politesse, ceremony,

15. Peter the Great's (1672–1725) numerous reforms aimed at destroying some of Russia's ancient ways-and bringing the country closer to Europe included the abolition or Russian *feriazi*, traditional long, collarless, and beltless outer robes, open in front. In 1701 government officials stationed at city gates fined men wearing beards and old-fashioned clothes, cutting and tearing the latter. On occasion Peter himself cut the beards and *feriazi* of his courtiers.—Eds.

and rules, the intelligentsia, is as faceless as it is in Russia. Thus, gradually, all "pillars" of all national cultures become weakened, but precisely at those spots arises a new, no longer national but world culture; precisely at those junctures come into being such men as Liu Hua for whose sake I am fighting the debility induced in me by the heat. Of course, Russia does not count, for I can see from here that Russia never had a culture of her own. Russia has always been a "distant field" of foreign national cultures: a huge, sparsely populated field with the land not yet finally marked out and consolidated, the juncture of all world cultures. Russia—the land of Udmurtian[16] lack of culture—was under the influence of Byzantium and then Mongolia (it was through Mongolia—after all, the two countries were under the Mongol yoke at the same time—that China strolled through Russia and lodged itself in the Moscow Kitai-gorod,[17] in Kolomna's Zariadye,[18] at my grandmother Katerina's in Saratov; *kitaika*[19] is no accident; neither is *chai*).[20] After the Tartars and Byzantium came Europe, to this day—Europe, Europe with a bit of something Shchedrinian[21]—in other words barbarian—barbarism with a touch of China, the China of deliberations and ceremonies, and the lands beyond the Volga, which I first saw not here in China but at my grandmother's. Russia is a "distant field" of foreign cultures, a pathway "from the Varangians to the Greeks," even in the anthropological sense. This gave Russia the right to be the first to begin the construction of a supernational—world—culture. . . .

16. A native of Udmurt Autonomous Soviet Socialist Republic, small, remote, predominantly Finno-Ugrian.—Eds.

17. A section of ancient central Moscow near the Kremlin, dating from the eleventh century. Although "Kitai-gorod" means "Chinatown," historians believe that the name came from *kita*, a word for a bunch of thin wooden poles used in preparation for laying stone walls.—Eds.

18. Historically, an area adjacent to the marketplace.—Eds.

19. A silk cloth imported from China; later, cotton cloth made in Russia.—

20. Tea.—Eds.

21. Mikhail Evgrafovich Saltykov-Shchedrin (1826–89), satirist.—Eds.

. . . Oh, yes. On a gigantic liner of the type of the *Empress*—far superior to the ship described by Bunin[22] in his story "The Gentleman from San Francisco"—a young American woman was sailing to China—a lady and a member of the Siccawei missionary group;[23] she was traveling with the aim of educating the savage Chinese in the light of Christianity. I am setting aside the conventions of fictional narration where the author must symbolically ram his thoughts into a reader's head: I know that the purpose of this American woman's trip was stupid, that the woman, generally speaking, was stupid, that she needed China as much as she needed Honolulu and was acquainted with it about as well. I know this. But she did not know it.

She woke up early; the sun was shining through the porthole, the breeze was cool, beyond the porthole the ocean rolled its blue waves—everything was as it should have been; tea and fruit were brought to her in bed. Having had her tea, wearing pajamas, she went into the little toilet and then took a bath, as one should in the morning. The toilet and the bathroom were off her stateroom. In the bathroom the Portuguese maid rubbed Miss Brighton's body with a sponge and salt water and massaged it with a shower. Then Miss Brighton dressed, combed her hair, and powdered her face very lightly. The breakfast gong sounded like a siren's wail, and Miss Brighton went to eat her oranges, oatmeal porridge, fish, meat, and kumquat jam and drink coffee. Then she lay on a deck chair on the deck, her hair covered with a scarf, a book in her hands. She was not reading. The ocean breeze enveloped her in calm. She was thinking, with eyes closed against the stabbing brightness of the waves, and dreaming, as a person should in idleness, at sea, with a sunny breeze blowing. The country where she was going was unknown to her: she thought of it in the way all people

22. Ivan Alekseyevich Bunin (1870–1953), writer.—Eds.

23. A Jesuit establishment in Siccawei (Zi-ka-wei, Ziccawei), a village southwest of Shanghai, which included a cathedral, a college, a monastery, a library, an orphanage, a printshop and one of the largest observatories in the Far East.—Eds.

who do not know it think of it—a land of dragons, hieroglyphs, rickshas, mandarin traditions, wedding and funeral processions, temples, pagodas, canals, junks, sampans, palanquins, and other things by the million; she thought of it in terms of her work—the quiet of the missionary cathedral, the monastery, the college with a dormitory where she, not being a nun, would live; she heard the ringing of the monastery bells, saw the sunny luster and desolation of the rows of pews in the cathedral; in her fantasy she walked along a path in the park, above a canal, in the moist vigor of flowers and the morning (. . . later everything was to be just as she had imagined it on the way over, as she had constructed it from the letters of a friend and from photographs—because her life was built on traditions, on the stern tolling of regulations; Americans and Englishmen have no idea of the meaning of the word "abroad," living as Americans even in China and knowing their future three years in advance—to the week—and without mistakes!). That morning on the ship she thought also of liberties, those "liberties" that Americans in China take—for example, a trip to the Western Hills near Peking on the shoulders of men—in a palanquin—just the way it was done in ancient times, the way Cleopatra and other beauties of the world did it, and what woman does not want to dream a little about what it would be like to be Cleopatra?! And, of course, I would not be surprised if in her mind in the tropical Chinese nights she saw the eyes of some Arthur or Stephen—after all, she did not know about the suffocating "charms" of Chinese nights! . . . All in all, this missionary woman on the *Empress* was simply a good American, well brought up, sensible enough, chaste—physically—and almost chaste morally, kind, solemn, knowing her right to life and honor, not bad-looking, thoroughly clean, well fed; she was a good specimen of a female individual of the Saxon race, just a shade on the lean side, just a shade long-legged (and thus deviating from the ideal human exterior). The breeze stirred the salt air of the ocean, air that never causes consumption. Subjectively this woman was right in every way. But objectively. . . .

Ships sail the expanses of the Pacific Ocean carrying cannon, goods, money, people, knowledge. Every twenty-four hours into the port where I am living, into this wound from which China seeps into the world, into this window through which the world is climbing into China, come as many as a hundred ocean ships. . . .

. . . The world is living now in the era when national cultures are cramped behind their fences, when national boundaries are collapsing, when cultures go strolling about the world, not just in the form of ships, cannon, and machinery but also in the form of all kinds of knowledge, all kinds of habits of daily life, when the world is moving toward the leveling of everything there is in the world. And the Great Wall of China is falling. The power of the Shanghai, Canton, and Tientsin mills marches as a commander through China. Around my city mills are smoking. City and suburbs threaten strikes. Thousands of ships come here from all the ends of the earth and leave here for all the ends of the earth, bringing everything that the world produces, leaving everything that the world produces, and in addition—parts of the lives of the people who bring this "everything." Asia and Europe are most horribly mixed together. At night sailors make rounds of dives by way of dark alleys where dog carcasses lie in ditches, where there is no air to breathe. Here too, in these filthy alleys, they play mah-jongg and craps. Here too there is a smell of opium: in the opium dens, on kangs, on the floor, on straw mats, people lie in opium haze, immersed in fantastic visions—erotic and of the kind that alone, perhaps, preserve the "soul" of China. By day, on the wharves, thousands, tens of thousands of people lug and drag bales, bags, barrels, boxes—millions of poods[24] of all sorts of things. Factories and mills are smoking. And here on the wharves, in the mill yards, inevitably coming into being develop capital, strikes, unions, parties, and—revolutions. But beyond the wharves there are alleyways lined with endless stalls: trade and guild smithies, tiny porcelain factories, tea shops, eating houses—all that has existed for thousands of years, that in the course of the millennia has been China's industry, with the guildsmen and shopmen and

24. Pood—a Russian measure of weight, about thirty-six pounds.—Eds.

handicraftsmen making everything that China needed. And there, in those overcrowded alleys, especially in the neighborhood of temples, sit at their tables—sorcerers (as my friend the Chinese poet Chiang translated the word for me), fortune-tellers, prophets, letter writers. . . . The China of the guilds! . . . And beyond the city there are dead bodies lying in the fields and stupendous beggarly labor—the power of China; there over the fields, along the country roads, along the canals and the railroads march Russia's year 1918, death, starvation, victories and escapes. . . .

. . . Krylov was just in and told me that the Fourth People's Army, which had almost deserted the First to join Wu P'ei-fu, betrayed Wu again and returned to Fêng, having exposed the front and pillaged several towns; these civil wars in China exemplify feudalism and imperialism, as well as the country's awakening national pride and might! . . .

. . . No words can describe the filth of the back streets of Chinese existence, the wretchedness and misery—misery in which a *t'ung-tzu-er*—worth half a kopeck—is a big currency unit, itself divided into ten *cash*, misery in which all children walk about naked and adults—half-naked; misery of this stupendous overcrowding when people live not only under roofs but—for months and years—simply under trees; life on sampans is luxury—there live the water "cabbies!" People eat refuse of all kinds, and many practice the profession of gathering dung in the streets and—this is an honorable women's occupation—pushing about the city wheelbarrows full of human excrement (European excrement is valued higher than Chinese, and once there was a riot when foreigners were about to forbid carrying "it" in wheelbarrows, and women rioters poured the contents of the wheelbarrows on the Europeans!). Beyond the Western Gates of my city—newspapers report this every day—they shoot people, chop off their heads, and strangle them. Death by strangulation—a national Chinese invention—is peculiar in the following way: if a person had committed seven crimes, he would be strangled seven times—each time nearly to death and the last time until he was dead. Heads of criminals are kept beyond the Western Gates on poles in cages made of rice straw. Nowhere are police as numerous and beatings in the streets as common as in China.

Europeans live in the Settlement, in the French and British Concessions. Englishmen, Americans, Spaniards, Portuguese, Frenchmen, Italians, Germans, Russians, Portuguese and Arabian Jews—they are all "foreigners" and "Europeans." Within the concessions life is different, non-Chinese, protected by different laws and police. On the gate of Jestfield Park there is a sign "Dogs and Chinese Not Allowed." Right now in the local papers (there are papers here in all languages) a fierce argument is going on—should or should not the courts be placed in the hands of the Chinese, if only in cases involving Chinese; the Europeans are trying to persuade the Chinese that they, the Chinese, would be ill-advised to assume the courts' concerns, expense, and troubles. At a distance from the city stands the missionary Siccawei monastery; there are to be found the quiet of Catholicism and Jesuitism, there are the ringing of the bells, the black—all like one—monks, and the bright park. In their flats the foreigners live a slow, clean, well-fed life, with their motorboats and automobiles driven by themselves, their wives, and their mistresses. One has to take a bath three times a day, change one's pants twice and collar—twice. During the day one has to sit under a fan and drink whiskey sodas. In this barbaric country of constant cholera and plague one has to pay great attention to what can and cannot be eaten. In the evening one must drive to Jestfield Park, out of town, to the Majestic, to an outdoor cinema, where attendants walk along the rows of seats and spray some pleasant-smelling substance under people's feet to prevent mosquito bites. . . . Men must observe how money—theirs and their companies'—is made. So why shouldn't beautiful ladies blossom here, ladies who first study at English, French, and American convent colleges, at home learn to play piano, to draw, and do needlework—and then gain knowledge of the world through overfastidious novels in the cleanliness and clarity of laws and regulations? . . .

* * *

. . . This must be the season for fireflies and cicadas because there are a great many of both of them. . . . All day today I poured forth sweat and the lines above, in heat and stupefaction. And in the evening we drove to Jestfield Park, to a symphony concert. I had no idea how pleasant, attractive, and edifying this park is! . . . It is a thoroughly English park, planned, English-style, over an area of a thousand dessiatines.[25] The trees in the park were decorated with little lanterns; the darkness was blue and, as always, very deep; the moon was shining through the milk of clouds. People, nearly all of them Englishmen, arrived in sedate slowness. In front of the rotunda deck chairs had been arranged in rows. There were very few people present; the Englishmen disappeared behind the backs of the deck chairs, in the quiet of the evening, in the cool of the breeze, among the fireflies. Conversation was quiet and slow. It seemed there were no people there, and the music of the symphony orchestra came through the noise of the cicadas. I don't know and I don't understand music—but tonight I felt very good listening. The music was European. I always argue with Chinese professors that European culture is too realistic; this music could have taken one into "the unreal"; music is a path into the incomprehensible, into that which cannot be measured by a yardstick, into that place where the measurable becomes distorted. I sat there and listened; it felt very good—to leave reality for the incomprehensible. This took me back to my thoughts about Europe and Asia, about how "Europe" created its own surroundings here in Asia, in this colony: fastidious "cleanliness" is well preserved through this music. The lanterns winked soothingly. Then, at the main gate, people got into their automobiles and went home to clean sheets of quiet nights. I was with Loks—we went for a ride out of town. I watched Chinese sleeping on the edges of the road. It is amazing how the English managed to "cut out" with the scissors of their "culture," to cut out of China, this park, this music—this "England"!

25. Dessiatine—a Russian measure of land area equal to 2.7 acres.—Eds.

The music and the beautiful night in Jestfield Park—are not a bit responsible for being beautiful.

* * *

Peking is a military city of the Russian year 1918. All palaces, all temples are jammed with people or are wrecked and stand abandoned and filthy. There are cannon in the squares. There are patrols at the intersections. Everywhere, everywhere there is filth and husks of watermelon seeds. On the gates of the Legation Quarter is a sign: "Beggars Not Allowed." By the gates of the Legation Quarter stand machine guns and British, American, Italian, and Japanese guards. On the parade grounds of the Legation Quarter European soldiers march and exercise, firing volleys and fusillades. At night they let people into the Legation Quarter by password. In the still of the dawn artillery fire is heard, and nobody knows whether it is Chang Tso-lin's artillerymen being trained or a rebellious regiment breaking through. The Imperial Palace and its museums are occupied by soldiers. One can watch soldiers, several men in a row, squatting—eaglelike—on the palace wall above the city and—defecating on the city. In the Temple of Torments, the temple which gave Octave Mirbeau the occasion to write his novel *The Garden of Tortures*, there are dust, desolation, and a fat, half-blind monk who does not talk, bemused with opium, but immediately demands a dollar; in the dust of the temple stand gods representing graphically all kinds of tortures, horrible tortures, which are now covered by a layer of dust about two fingers thick and have been forgotten in general, and in particular because all these kinds of tortures have gone out into the streets of the civil war and spread all over China. Heat and dust in Peking are incredible. In the commercial part of the city thousands—without exaggeration—of beggars roam. At an intersection stands the leader of the beggars—he is a leper; he is completely naked, and his ribs are exposed—the skin, shriveled into green scabs, has slipped off them; he stands firmly. The beggars move about in crowds. The beggars are organized into a union; formerly one of the younger sons of the emperor was ex officio chairman of the union; now there are no emperors, and beggars' chairmen are millionaires, although it is impossible to give anything to beggars because if you do give something to even one, a whole thousand of them will storm you, they will howl, grab your clothes, push you, rave, dance in front of you, spit. . . .

. . . and so our heroine, Miss Brighton, she who had sailed aboard the steamer *Empress*, arrived in Peking. Europeans are inviolable in Peking. She really was carried in a palanquin, as once Cleopatra was, to the Western Hills and the Summer Palace of the emperor—reclining on cushions, she was carried by four Chinese. But this isn't the main thing. Near Peking, behind the commercial section of the city, is the Temple of Heaven, a most majestic, grandiose edifice, disposed not upon a thousand dessiatines like Jest-field Park but on many thousand dessiatines of quiet, beauty, majesty, centuries. In the middle of a multitude of squares, pagodas, passages, groves, avenues, walls, beneath the sky there is a marble altar, consisting—mystically—of eighty-one slabs, for this entire temple is built on the mystical number nine. The altar is round; it is sculptured of yellow marble, warm as the sun. The slabs of the altar are so arranged that every slab has its echo, every step on them reverberates around with a resounding echo, and the closer to the center the more unusual the echo. Above this altar is the blue sky, completely unobscured. Around the altar stand marble urns, where (I don't think it's true) was gathered the blood of those sacrificed to Heaven. It is true, though, that under imperial power in China, once a year, the emperor, the Son of Heaven, would journey to this temple to pay his respects to his father—Heaven. Having passed through the resoundingly echoing slabs of the altar, which he alone could ascend, the emperor would lie down on his back on the central stone and gaze at the sky. The surrounding crowd of thousands would freeze in silence. The echo of the emperor's steps would fade. In the majestic silence of the scorching heat the emperor would gaze at the sky, contemplating his father—Heaven. There are no emperors now. The temple is neglected, dusty, befouled with human excrement; all structures have been turned into barracks; all open spaces are blocked by artillery batteries. The central courtyard, the one where the marbles of the altar lie beneath the sky, is deserted, overgrown with tall weeds; to one side, having constructed a hut from boards, live two watchmen, who have most likely installed themselves on their own initiative; during the day they sell sweet drinks and sleep—while at night. . . .

Miss Brighton got to know a group of Americans in Peking, ladies and gentlemen. The gentlemen had a most exotic suggestion. In the evening, wines, sweetmeats, and fruit would be taken to the Temple of Heaven, to those two ragamuffins who guarded the altar of the temple; the lackeys of the American gentlemen would be left with the wines, sweetmeats, and fruit. And toward nightfall, when the heat abated and endless patrols walked the streets, the ladies and gentlemen would ride to the Temple of Heaven, would make their way through the patrols to the altar, whispering excitedly. Every slab of the altar had its own echo. The ladies and gentlemen fox-trotted and charlestoned on the slabs of the altar, each one of which had its own echo. They danced to a portable gramophone, which had been brought together with the sweetmeats; the music of the gramophone and the rustle of their shoes on the floor were repeated by the sacred echo. Having danced, they would rest, drink wine, eat sweetmeats—and dance again. The ragamuffins who guard the altar arranged pitch torches at the altar rails. On one occasion, during an intermission, with pears in their hands, Miss Brighton and her gentleman went down the marble path away from the altar into the darkness of the trees to take a look from there at the torches.

"Look," said the gentleman, "into these very urns was poured the blood of sacred animals and of those people who were sacrificed to Heaven."

She made no reply.

"What beauty, what majesty!" said the gentleman, and came to a standstill.

She made no reply; she also came to a standstill. She leaned on his arm. He took her hand. It was the first time in her life: the gentleman raised her hand to his lips and softly kissed it—it was the first time in her life that a man had kissed her hand when they were alone. But she had no strength to resist; her head was going round in the midst of this incredible exotica. She laid her head on his shoulder. But this was a moment of weakness. She straightened herself and said drily,

"Yes, very beautiful, let's go and dance," and she led the way.

Again the gramophone began creaking; again the majestic echo came from the slabs as people jerked in the charleston. Toward morning they, the ladies and gentlemen, excited, tired, stunned by the colonial exotica which breaks the rules, a little bit like schoolchildren, rode in automobiles into the coolness of their homes to take a bath and go to bed.

* * *

. . . It is said, "Chinese marshals go to war only because they have armies which have to be put to work, and because feudalism is the marhsals' mode of life." I know that Marshal Such-and-Such was with Chang Tso-lin today; Chang insulted him, and since Chang didn't manage to cut off the general's ears and nose, break his bones, and throw him on a dung heap—this general left Chang, either for Wu P'ei-fu, or for the bandits; after spending six months or so with the bandits, he will write to Marshal Sun Ch'uan-fang and send his respects and chests of tea, and he and all his soldiers will become regulars in the marshal's regiments. Europeans draw up schemes: Chang Tso-lin is the protégé of the Japanese, the three northern provinces are in essence a Japanese colony, Marshal Wu P'ei-fu looks to the British and the Americans; Fêng Yühsiang—to the USSR; the Cantonese—also to the USSR. But about two years ago a treaty of friendship with the USSR was almost signed by Marshal Wu. Schematically, it is understandable that the British and Japanese, to a lesser degree the French and Portuguese, those countries which own land and buildings in China, want to see China such as it now is and hold as tightly as they can to the treaties of the last century. The Americans entered the world market and the Far East later; they have no property in China, but they do have goods, and they wish to see China a powerful national-bourgeois state which would have a single currency, would be able to buy and would sell raw materials; the Americans have established in

China thirty thousand primary schools and more than ten universities and take Chinese children to their States by the thousand. The USSR intends to see the entire Earthly Globe free, endowed with equal rights, working and educated. I don't understand Chinese affairs at all—but it is clear that the Republic of China, what is known as the Republic of China, is the most strained knot of world politics. I said "what is known as the Republic of China," because in reality this republic does not exist: Chang Tso-lin is not in the least subordinate to Wu P'ei-fu; Canton is not in the least inclined to be subordinate to Chang, or Wu, or Sun. Governments and governing cabinets are created in Peking one after another, but no one subordinates himself to them; they exist fictitiously, mainly so that foreign states should have someone to talk to. Marshal Chang, an illiterate man, at one time the leader of a *hung-hu-tzu*, which is to say bandit, detachment (in 1904, at the time of the Russo-Japanese War, he plundered Russian supply trains), Marshal Chang, when his closest generals are guilty of misdemeanors, cuts off their noses and ears. Marshal Wu, who received a mandarin education, considers a day lost if in the course of that day he has not written a poem, a lyric one, according to the Chinese rules. Marshal Feng says prayers to the Christian God—every morning. *Tupans*, provincial governors, generals, and colonels constantly desert one general for another, betraying now one, now another, depending on who will pay a higher salary and give a better province to plunder. This year, 1926, Marshal Wu in the Honan Province has collected all taxes up to 1936 from the peasants, and he has done this not only to plunder but also—Chinese wisdom!—to strengthen the allegiance of this province; another general, says he will start collecting taxes all over again. . . . Impossible to understand anything!—but you can understand that going on fourteen years now cannon thunder over China; towns, fields, and villages are plundered; people are reduced to beggary; more and more burial mounds arise in the fields—in this immense Chinese crush of four hundred and fifty million people. On the thresholds of the diplomatic quarters and the foreign concessions stand machine guns. In the roadsteads of the ports gray hulks of dreadnoughts and cruisers, American, British, French, Japanese, lie restless. . . .

★ ★ ★

. . . I'm writing all this—in this dreadful heat—to tell the story of a Chinese man, the delightful and unhappy Liu Hua. Perhaps he was born on a sampan near our bridge, on our canal: he was just the same sort of scamp as those naked kids I see from my terrace, who are tied up with ropes to stop them falling into the water. . . . At this point in writing I deliberately went out on the terrace to have a look at them: a windy day, waves, rising tide, a convoy of junks hauling muskmelons and watermelons; bales are being unloaded; the unloaders are groaning out their Chinese heave-ho; the sky is tattered with clouds; the canal is buzzing with shouts, groans, the hooting of launches and steamships, the honking of automobiles and trams rolling over the bridge; in the distance smokes a gray American dreadnought. These sampans, on which people live, are covered with straw mats against the sun, are silent, and—in the noise of the canal and the city, beyond these noises—I hear coming from these boats the crying of several unseen children, children hidden from the sun by straw mats. . . . This boy I'm talking about found within himself the capacity to climb out of these boats onto the earth, onto the wharf, onto the streets. He mounted an extremely complex social ladder, by the age of eighteen finding himself in the typesetting room of a Chinese printshop. He must have had a talent amounting to genius—Lomonosov-like[26]—apart from the social ladder, he also went the difficult way of knowledge and meditation, for by his twenty-fifth year he was a librarian at the local Chinese university, set up with American money and in the English style—he, the hero of my tale, learned several languages and while acting as a librarian sat in on courses at the university. The quiet of the library in

26. Mikhail Vasilyevich Lomonosov (1711–65), the leading Russian poet and scientist of his day, was the son of a fisherman on the White Sea coast.—Eds.

the university park did not prevent him from emerging from the university as a man who had grasped very well what books had to tell him, had completely (in the same way as that goodly tribe, our own students) rid himself of the daily routines and conventions, understanding that revolutions were under way in the world, could not but be under way, that his homeland was a great and rich country with a mighty future, that the mandarins of his homeland and the feudalism of the marshals were an ancient muzzle, that his duty was to go and to do. Very rarely are born people with very clear brains—almost always people have "muzzles" and "masks," when they either are incapable of seeing and thinking simply or obscure their vision with traditions, ceremonies, customs: but this one did not have any traditions, apart from the traditions of his brain and his knowledge; he knew how to see and did not wear any kind of mask; he tried everything on the tooth of knowledge.

. . . From there, from those embankments, from bales, barrels, poods, tons, shillings, dollars, *t'ung-tzu-ers*, "big" and "small" money, from poverty and from wealth—others as well as he went to other embankments, into the suburbs: to the embankments—American skyscrapers of commercial firms, general stores, banks; to the suburbs went mill and factory villages, mill and factory yards, clouds of smoke, hooting; from the embankment marched the national Chinese—comprador—bourgeoisie to be established at the tops of the social ladders, in the best suites of skyscrapers, in country villas, while the ragged throng of Chinese workers marched at lower levels to the suburbs, and there talk of the proletariat of the world originated. Those from the suburbs did not lose their umbilical connection with the port embankments. This man, the hero of my tale, chose the fate of being spokesman of those from the suburbs: he arose against the foreigner-Englishmen and the native compradors. This man was killed, we don't know how—hanged, shot, or strangled—but we do know by whom: the British and the compradors together. This man had a year like a cinema thriller, when in this city of millions he—deputy chairman of the council of trade unions—addressed meetings, organized strikes, escaped all kinds of police with heavy bags of *t'ung-tzu-ers* and *cash*, the union members' money, without a home, without a roof over his head, without rice, never resting at night.

He was arrested by the British on Chinese territory. He perished because of two poods of *t'ung-tzu-ers*. He escaped by way of the roof when the police arrived. But he did not manage to carry off all the money. And he stole back into the building occupied by police to recover it. He rescued two poods of copper. But he himself was killed. At the moment arguments are going on in the local press about the court, about who is to be the judge. The British have lost the right to try and condemn to death those Chinese who have been caught committing a crime not on "their" territory. This man was captured on "Chinese" territory. . . .

In China everything is in confusion, from the feudal lords, from the colonizers to the bourgeoisie (Chinese nationalist, comprador, European-educated, militant, young, piratical), to the proletarians (among the students, professors, in ports and factories). This area is governed by Sun Ch'uan-fang, a military governor, marshal, feudal lord, mandarin-educated man. Sun lives permanently in the "Southern Capital," in Nanking, his residence. Sun came to our town. The brokers arranged a banquet in his honor, in the Chinese fashion, when hundreds of dishes consisting of sugared meat, swallows' nests, super-rotten eggs, shark fins, and bamboo roots and shoots are eaten, and after the dinner everyone goes to a brothel to smoke opium and copulate. The British gave a banquet for the marshal in European style, where the ladies were in evening dress and the gentlemen in monkey suits, with flowers on the tables, with speeches and all kinds of roast beefs, wines, fruits, witticisms, and foxtrot. And later, when Sun was leaving, right at the railway station (it should be remembered that according to Chinese tradition one should always talk about business "by the way," should "make excuses" for talking business), a representative of the brokers and a representative of the consulates in an ultimate gesture of politeness and brilliance of wit requested they be presented with the head of the criminal. Sun "presented" it. The Chinese have invented many ways of doing away with a human being: strangling, hanging by the feet, cutting up with a saw, beheading, skinning alive, shooting: today it was announced in a newssheet that tomorrow they would be shooting people outside the Western Gates. The manner of Liu Hua's death is unknown—whether he was strangled, skinned alive, hanged, shot, where, when, and how nobody knows, but Chinese poets are already writing poems about him, and one such poem is in my possession. One can imagine that night, a cell of the Chinese torture chamber in the city wall, there where the prison is, the night—the executioners, the death rattle of a man being strangled, the calm of the executioners; a Chinese revolutionary told me how his friend was shot in his presence; there were several witnesses, everyone was calm, and the man about to be shot was picking his nose before his execution—the Chinese are not afraid of death. . . .

. . . All right then, about the girl who arrived at the beginning of my yesterday's writing, on a steamship of the *Empress* type and who is subjectively right. This girl borrowed books from Liu Hua when he was a librarian, she was at the banquet arranged by the British in honor of Marshal Sun (more accurately—in honor of Liu Hua), and at the time Liu Hua was being strangled she married the secretary of the British consulate, the very man who represented Britain in that "Mixed Court" for the "freedom" of which the British are so keen to fight and which naturally applied its hand to the case of Liu Hua.

. . . This hero of mine, Liu Hua, together with his comrades, set himself against a great deal—the foreign colonizers, the barbarity of the mandarin system, the dragon marshals and the merchants, the factory owners, the compradors, those for whose freedom America fights—against everything, against everyone—for "what is reasonable is real," but not "what is real is reasonable." He took off the Chinese robe of daily habit and dragons and discarded all kinds of muzzles. He perished trying to rescue two poods of copper. But it was not by chance that I began yesterday with such a clean, well-fed, honest, and chaste girl, she who got married at the time of his death.

He, my hero, was a *man*, but love is free: a great deal of space was devoted to her in the diaries kept by this Chinese, for he loved this woman in such a way as one can love wind; he loved the woman, this love being his only "muzzle," one leading to unreality, in the same way the music at the symphony concert yesterday led me. This woman never knew that she was loved by a half-naked librarian who could not follow her into Jestfield Park, since "Dogs and Chinese Not Allowed.". . .

* * *

. . . I just went out on the terrace. The moon is shining, reflected in the oily water; there is a smell of something rotten, of dead human flesh; women on the sampans are quarreling; launch lights race along the river. Sometimes I'm overcome by such—I can't find words for it: there's no sense in leading a monkish existence, but there's nothing I want, and there's nothing to do in this heat; there's nothing to read, and I'm tired of reading; there's no one to talk to, and I don't feel like talking; there's no sense in sitting like this without doing anything, but I don't feel like doing anything; I ought to be thinking, but I don't feel like thinking—I don't feel like anything, but it's impossible to sit here like this, and it's almost impossible to sleep. Heat! Heat! . . . I undressed and lay in the bath for a whole hour, to the point of stupefaction, because I didn't feel like getting out of the bath either! . . . The girl who was sailing on the *Empress* could have not got married, could not only have eaten her fill and kept herself thoroughly clean and been honest in the subjective definition of her own traditions; she could have been a remarkable human being, as out-of-the-ordinary as he, my hero, the strangled Liu Hua; let us suppose that she had a touch of the qualities of Liza Kalitina,[27] the lucid beauty of purity, faith, and chastity—and of the faith that the main thing in the world is love, which is a thing unto itself, as knowledge is and heroism—but in any case Liu Hua's romance

27. The self-sacrificing heroine of Ivan S. Turgenev's novel *A Nest of Gentlefolk* (1859).—Eds.

would have run its course and had to run its course in the way I have described it.

Dogs have been howling on the canal the entire evening, in a variety of pitches, dolefully. I saw in the distance: a whole sampan of dogs had come floating up. I asked the houseboy what the matter was. It seems that these dogs have been brought by way of the canal from the province and that they are to be slaughtered for food. We—Loks, Krylov, and I—are living here because the Russian Revolution has sent us, because we, the Russians, are now against the entire world. Loks is sitting in the dining room at a table piled with a mountain of orange peel, reading an English book about China; once Loks spent a year in solitary in a fortress—he says that there he got into the habit of talking to himself; I am typing, and I can hear him commenting aloud by himself in Russian while reading the Englishman. . . . Again I went out on the terrace; the Bund disappears in the gloom, the Huang-p'u and the canal are covered with lantern lights, wind is blowing, dogs are barking, the clouded moon passes over the earth, absolutely green, as back home in wintertime—perhaps this isn't really summer and China at all, but deep Siberian exile?! My cricket has died—of thirst, I suppose.

. . . At this point I broke off writing; Loks and I decided to play a game of sixty-six—a convict game. . . . I searched the entire house and couldn't find any cards. We made a firm decision—to buy some cards and mah-jongg tomorrow. Nothing is known about my ship.

* * *

A clipping from a local newspaper. . .

Again About the Parks

The British colony finds it hard to reconcile itself with the fact that, not wishing to aggravate relations that are already strained, the Settlement authorities without issuing any new regulations have decided to pay no attention to Chinese who gain entrance to those parks to which they were not admitted only a short time ago, and also settle on the lawns of the Bund, also until the current summer inaccessible to them.

Yesterday there again appeared in the pages of the *North China Daily News* an indignant letter from a foreigner, in which he asks whether the municipality had reconsidered the regulations relating to the use of the parks, and if it had reconsidered them, why no word had appeared in the newspapers.

And further the indignant foreigner tells how he and his wife tried for four hours one evening to find room for themselves on the benches on the Bund lawns, but all the benches were crowded with Chinese coolies. The behavior of the coolies lying on the grass shocked the letter writer's wife. . . .

* * *

About Peking.

Peking is a city of mandarins, temples, pagodas, gates, walls, squares, a city of Confucian politesse and quiet, a lotus city of lakes, canals, temples of Heaven, the Sun, Silence, Tortures, the Five Hundred Buddhas, the capital of Chinese culture, together with the Egyptian the most ancient in the world, where the palaces, temples, and remembrance of the past are as solid as the pyramids. Peking. . . .

Peking. . . .

In the story about Liu Hua the American Miss Brighton danced the charleston on the altar of the Temple of Heaven. . . .

At the embassy of the USSR in Peking one of the embassy secretaries gave me a copy book of verses given to him in turn by their author, my fellow countryman, kept under guard in the Peking State Prison for murder. The author gave the verses to the secretary when embassy employees were inspecting the prison.

China—Peking—the Chinese prison of Peking. . . .

Here are the verses of my fellow countryman and fellow creative artist. . . .

The Steamboat!

The steamboat is a river ship
Always under steam,
Pulling barges, carrying freight,
It puffs upon the stream.

Firewood keeps the furnace hot,
Though coal is quite all right,
Without repair our steamboat sails
For years, both day and night.

Some steamboats carry passengers,
Are crowded fore and aft,
The lovely ladies and the men
Gaze through the porthole glass.

A jealous bunch they are somehow,
Not slow to quench love's thirst,
Not hoity-toity in the least,
Though you expect the worst.

When the occasion comes her way
You'll be her cabin guest,
And in that cabin she grows wild,
Demanding to be kissed.

The matter ended with a smile,
We laugh both she and I,
So smart she is, so out to please,
We make a compromise.

Our trip was going merrily,
But when three days had passed

I felt a sudden biting pain—
Could she have been the cause?

The sickness long did trouble me,
Doc gave me something strong.
A steamboat now I'll never board,
I'll hate them all life long!

. . . The Temple of Heaven, the Temple of the Sun—China—Peking—centuries, the silence of the centuries and lakes overgrown with lotus. . . .

What human vulgarity! The embassy secretary who gave me this copybook packed with such verses told me the story of this poet, my fellow countryman and fellow creative artist. The poet is a murderer and a thief. He was sentenced to ten years by the Chinese. He's been in jail about four years already. He's pleased with his lot. The prison where he is kept is a model one from his point of view: for a bribe women are allowed to visit the men once a week. The poet's sister lives in Peking and earns her living by prostitution. Once a week she visits the poet in prison—not as a sister but as a mistress—and the poet beats her mercilessly when she doesn't bring what he had ordered—silk socks, vodka, opium.

I've mentioned this story about the poet for the sake of Krylov, a nice man who is so mixed up that he becomes enraged when his wife sends him kisses in her letters, which he finds offensive, although his wife is also a nice, good person who is not guilty of anything. This story is for Miss Brighton too.

FOUR

July 23d, morning.

In Moscow they'd say: It's a fine day today, sunny, cloudless, quiet—days like this at this point of July are particularly fine, when the first barely discernible gossamer appears, haze among the trees, distances have become translucent, and the first leaf, the first fallen leaflet, suddenly rustles underfoot; there is silence in the trees, and the air is so blue, so transparent that concepts of perspective change and things could only be painted in watercolor—y-yes. . . .

. . . And today in the local newspapers:

"Air! . . . Air!

"Today it is 117 degrees. As for the moisture that suffocates, that doesn't let you breathe, who can tell that the limit has not been reached beyond which begin prostration, distraction, madness. In these three July weeks the city is not so much melted down as boiled soft, stewed, steeped, drained, exhausted. Air! Air! . . . Oh, for a breath of fresh, pure, invigorating air! . . .

"77 deaths in a day.

"In the Settlement 23 persons died yesterday, 17 fell ill. In the Chinese territory 42 persons fell ill and died. In the French Concession 6 persons died, 19 fell ill. In all. . . ."

. . . Impossible, astounding! Words fail me! . . .

News has arrived from the sea. My ship will be here between August 10th and 20th; from here we'll go to various Chinese ports to pick up tea, then to Singapore, then to Ceylon. *Man-man-ti*—for me—is metaphysics!

Another clipping from a newspaper, an official announcement:

> All foreigners are duly warned that trips to Su-chou, likewise to Hang-chow, can only be undertaken at the present time, in

view of the unsettled condition of these provinces, at their own responsibility and risk; the Chinese authorities are not issuing passes to these areas. This serves as additional evidence that neighboring areas are once more becoming unsettled! . . .

Civil war! Revolution! . . . We live in the name of revolution, but we live in the utmost calm. The houseboy brought in mah-jongg.

. . . How great is the Earthly Globe! Listening to today's news from the sea, I keep myself in mind, and again I feel a longing to be on the move, to look, to see, to travel—to the limits, to the brink. Before setting off for here, I inscribed a book for Dmitri Furmanov:[28] "If I die, do not think ill of me. I'm prepared to die any way at all, only not in bed"—I'm alive, Furmanov is dead—news has arrived. And really, it isn't so bad, not to have anything, to renounce all, for the sake of the roads, for the sake of the winds. I think such thoughts, and I feel good and at peace with myself; I stop thinking about Moscow, and all I want is to be on the move—how great is the Earthly Globe! . . .

July 24th, twilight.

Yesterday the heat was 117 degrees: today it must be even higher. Incredible! All day I lolled beneath a fan (and reasoned that a fan, that electric device constructed in the form of a propeller, could well be an illustration of the theory of atomic energy: if this propeller were revolved a few thousand times faster, it would turn into a solid mass of material, no longer copper of which the blades are made; it would be very light, wouldn't even drive the air; it would be possible to hold it in your hands. I suppose even an airplane propeller has a limit to speed of revolution, after which its effectiveness would begin to—must—diminish; it would also be possible to hold it in your hands like a piece of very light metal—and: how much energy there is in this world, to

28. Dmitri Andreyevich Furmanov, (1891–1926); writer. His *Chapayev* (1923) was praised by Soviet critics as the best novel of the civil war.—Eds.

reason in reverse, when this unknown piece of metal formed by colossal speed of rotation—what energy in this colossal speed—again turns into blades of copper abandoned by electricity! . . .)—all day I lolled beneath a fan, delirious and tormented with the heat. I talked to Krylov and made the following conjecture: it would seem that, even without achievements, love can be very great, very strong; a beautiful love can be diverted into such channels of the heart when—in the name of that love itself, in the name of its pride and splendor—it is necessary to reject its object, for love can be sublimated, separated from the body, possessions, and time of its object, in such a way that the tender words of this object begin to seem insulting to love, in such a way that the body must be freed of the object, so there remains solely a pure chalice of love, chaste, transparent and undefiled; it would seem that love is able to bury the very thing that is considered a manifestation of love—tenderness, caresses, possession—bury it in its own name and in the name of its purity. . . . And I also thought, in this universal bouillon of suffocation in which it lives, this whole country surrounding me, how wise the world is, how everything conforms, nothing is incidental, and everything is joined by an endless series of laws, of beautiful truths, which, alas, cannot take man into account as an end in himself and in which man is made equal with—with a pawn in a game of chess, and with every variety of those mosquitoes, thousands of kinds of which come flying into my room every evening. All I read about these days is China. It is very entertaining to observe yourself, to observe how two lives can go on at the same time in a man: one—my own, not connected with any place, anything dependent on place and time, my own, mental—and the other, the Chinese life, the everyday life of a writer, when I walk, look, see, listen. . . . "Everything in life is only a means," and I often think, I often feel inclined to put into shape in my writing, to analyze this world of man, where man passes into unconsciousness as music does into unreality—not by instinct, not by feelings, not emotionally, but: by means of his brain, consciousness, objects, science—by means of knowledge.

Loks has changed clothes before going to dinner. We are leaving.

Someone has just come; we'll have to stay a minute. The houseboy has brought some mosquito candles. Sky, river, the Bund—everything fades into evening, and in this evening dampness everything is silvery. The moon has already risen—I love the moon; it always speaks to me of a beautiful romanticism and of love's great mystery of romance, such a mystery as I have never experienced or never noticed and which apparently does not exist in the life of reality but only in the life of images—the moon has risen, it is utterly blue, the kind it never is at home. The lighthouse beacon and the lanterns are already reflected in the water, but smoke from ships and from factories beyond the Huang-p'u can still be seen rising in the sky, escaping from the bouillon of suffocation—toward that heavenly blue which is now replaced by this silvery-greenish vomitlike mist. . . . Another thing: I just haven't been able to find anything by Pushkin here, and I don't know him by heart—and Pushkin is almost a physical need in this mistiness and vagueness—to cool this hot mist by means of the "purple dawn" of his transparent clarity: dawns are always cold and fresh! I just went out on the terrace; and suddenly the moon was reflected in the blue water in transparent clarity. During the day the water of the canal and of the Huang-p'u is as yellow as the skin of a bass drum. . . .

Night of the 24th–25th.

When you look for a very long time at an object, it begins to reel, melt away; there are circles before your eyes, and everything disappears. That's how it was with me today in Jestfield Park—the rotunda dissolved before my very eyes, everything sank into invisibility, and only music remained. Music is a real communion with all that is beautiful; I didn't know that before. Apparently the art of music has found another champion in me—I hadn't even suspected before the loftiness and beauty that music engenders in a man. We were at a dinner party and then went on to a symphony concert—and then we were supposed to go to a countryside restaurant. But after listening to music I didn't feel like "slumming," so I went back home.

China! . . . If a ricksha man or a fisherman has no luck for an entire day, the ricksha man knows that an evil spirit is in pursuit of him—and then he has to run across the road in front of a motorcar, while the boatman has to sail under the very bow of a ship so that the evil spirit should be left on one side and he on the other—to escape the evil spirit. This is speaking in general. It's also true in general that the Chinese don't respond to automobile horns and—you can blow your horn as much as you like—won't yield the right of way. To take a particular instance: we were riding along today, an urchin came running toward us; by pure luck we didn't run him over; the entire automobile screeched as the brakes were applied; the Chinese driver got out of the automobile, grabbed the boy, and gave him such a boxing on the ears that I went to his rescue—the driver smiles; the urchin smiles; we drive on. . . . Nowhere have I seen so many street fights as here: a ricksha man is running along; a Hindu policeman beats him with a bamboo cane; two men are in disagreement; they don't quarrel; they are silent—they just beat each other up; in a class by themselves are the police—there are a hell of a lot of them of all nationalities and odd types; all this is in general. And in particular—I very much regretted today that I don't know how to fight. We were coming out of the park after the concert, a crowd of foreigners. And unfortunately two Chinese were locked in combat near the park gates. For reasons incomprehensible to me, no doubt on a "humanitarian impulse" and for the sake of order, a certain American went to separate them. Two other whites went to his aid. They dragged the fighters apart and went back to get into their automobiles. But the Chinese again began fighting. Then the American got angry: he struck one of the Chinese in the face; the Chinese swayed; the American kicked him in the back; the Chinese fell down and picked himself up, intending to say something to the American, something not in the least malicious, but the American struck the Chinese—in the chest—the Chinese fell down like one dead. It seemed to me that the American had killed the Chinese. Apparently the American was also in doubt, because he bent over and touched the naked body of the Chinese with his white shoe. But the Chinese got up, and then the American once more—with a sigh of relief—kicked him in the back. The Chinese ran away from the American like a beaten dog. About two hundred spectators stood about. . . .

25th, morning.

At this time people will be gathering to embark on the motorboat for the seaside. In daytime, at night, in the evening, in the morning—over this land there is always a smell of corpses and human excrement. The main religion in China is the veneration of ancestors, of those whose corpses give off such a smell. And if Chinese culture in its entirety smells as do those corpses, then this might be said—sadly enough—to be the national odor! . . . I feel nauseated today with this heat and the odors—my head feels as if I had just got up after a long illness.

. . . I watched Krylov unobserved. He was sitting on his bed, with his right knee up against his chin, against his lips (when you sit in that position a dimple forms on the knee)—and he was kissing the dimple on his knee. His face was sad and serious. I have invented a prescription: when a man is very lonely, when he has nowhere to turn, then let him kiss his own knee, for then he will feel a certain incomprehensible tenderness toward himself, and pity, and a man is relieved, as though the knee becomes, can become, his friend and share his loneliness! . . .

Now Krylov has already got up, is reading Chinese newspapers. The base of Wu P'ei-fu, Liao-yang, has been flooded, the dikes have been ruptured, water has overflowed the canals, the city has sunk a fathom under water; around the city walls is a boundless sea: so far, five thousand people have perished. The snows of the Pamirs are melting.

26th, morning.

Yesterday I understood what the Chinese dragon is, and why it is a dragon. We went to the seaside. Having had lunch there in the English restaurant beneath the palms and with ice, we set off (the devil made us!) for the forts, right for the shore, the women in wheelbarrows,[29] the men on foot. We managed to get there under that scorching sun. And from there. . . the sun was burning as if our bodies were touched with pieces of red-hot iron, everything was soaked with sweat, just as if a man had jumped in the water, and the first thing you felt was not the pain in the head but an ache in the limbs as from rheumatism, as from cold, a strange, tormentingly pleasant ache. After that suddenly came a dreadful pain in the head, at the back, from the neck to beneath the skull, thence to the temples, a terrible pain, a terrible weakness, a fearful indifference, when everything sinks out of sight. And during the return journey—four hours—I lay on the deck, in the shade of the tarpaulin, seeing nothing, ready to die in terrible pain. There were eight of us, four men, one boy, three women: the women endured the sun, of the men only Loks escaped heatstroke. At home in the evening, Loks, a former convict, sat by my bed, solicitously reading me poetry—but I didn't care, if only I could rid myself of this dull, nagging pain. Today—in spite of the fact that yesterday I was wearing a cork helmet—I can't touch my chin or my neck: they're burning, inflamed. And my arms and legs ache all the time; Russian peasants get rid of the ache in a bath-house on a shelf—here it's the other way around. Devil take this dragon!—a deep blue dragon—in a whitish, empty, bleached sky.

Krylov:

"In Shantung bandits raid entire villages and small towns, take everything, massacre people or tie them up and lay them on roads. The bandits buy weapons from local military units of General Chang Tsung-chang."

2 o'clock in the afternoon.

In Moscow it's now seven in the morning. In my room in Moscow the blinds are still down. How one can distract oneself with nonsense for

29. In China a not uncommon way of traveling for women, children, and old men—Ed.

hours on end—such as my spending hours reconstructing unimportant things, trivia, a room's semidarkness, a lamp on a table! . . .

4 o'clock.

Impossible to breathe! . . . Dreadful! . . . But in Moscow there is the coolness of nine o'clock in the morning.

6 o'clock.

In Moscow it's eleven o'clock in the morning. Is the sun shining outside the window, or has there been a thunderstorm? Outside my window the day is dying, the city hums, the river groans. Somewhere a European military band is playing: a colony, devil take it! . . . Another day passes. Loks has lain down with a book, dozed off. This evening my companions and I decided to play preference. I don't feel like anything; my mind is blank. I wrote a letter to Russia, to a childhood friend, in whose company in Bogorodsk I used to collect Tartar earrings[30]—I asked him if he would gather some Tartar earrings and take them to my house in Moscow; the fellow will think I'm not all there—a letter from China, he'll say, and all about Tartar earrings! . . . And where I am now there's a smell of corpses from the canal all the time.

8 o'clock in the evening.

Extinguished the light, went out on the terrace; the night is dark as dark can be, stars—a great many stars—completely unknown to me, strange, not our stars, not at all those I'm familiar with from childhood, from the days of Mozhaisk.

30. A popular name for a spindle tree, a small tree or shrub that produces colorful, pendulous fruit.—Ed.

2 o'clock in the morning, 26th–27th.

Here it is night—in Moscow seven in the evening. All this time I've been playing preference. We went out on the terrace just now; windy—and an enormous, beautiful moon hangs over the water; the water has a phosphorescent gleam beneath the moon; people make noise on the canal. And suddenly everything is mixed—this wind—this moon—these waters—these noises: in Russia it's fall now, but here all of a sudden came a breath of spring; a customs launch broke the silence with its wailing siren, and the echo did not die away for a long time, as only in the springtime at home. That's because at home only in spring during floods is the air so saturated. But we don't ever have a moon like that; at home it's poorer, weaker. . . .

. . . The consul joined me on the terrace. Night. We are silent. The wind—how good it feels! Naked, I was standing in the wind—here it is, my body. It feels good to be in the wind: you don't need anything, everything passes with the wind—and it's a good thing that it passes. The Chinese saying, "The guitar strings are broken," signifies a falling out between lovers. I don't have a lover. Long live comrade wind! . . .

. . . I greet, I greet everything!

. . . . a ginseng sprout from the bowels of the earth assembles love's languors for an aged man and for a mortal doubles the life span granted by heaven. And in this hazy hour of the bull, obedient to the galaxies, with the prayer of your forefathers take a deer horn, and dig the mysterious root shaped like a man!—

—This is a translation from the Chinese about ginseng, about real events and legends connected with this root, like mandragora—about this "mysterious root shaped like a man." What's all this about?—yes, both I and everything else are as mysterious as music, as these muscles of mine hardening and bulging beneath the skin, the ones I have just exposed to the wind, which in this wind have started to swell with strong blood, telling me that they live in their own way, and in their own way can dictate me their own laws of being. . . .

Loks has a habit of talking to himself. Just now, before going to bed, I took a bath and suddenly caught myself saying, "Well, let's crawl into the bath and soak ourselves!"—and noticed that I too talk to myself aloud, amiably, benevolently, as to our old friend—that's me chatting with my feet, my hands, my chest, the soap. Silent interlocutors!

27th, morning.

Yesterday, going to bed, I glanced at my watch: three o'clock. I woke up just now, glanced at my watch: three o'clock. The proverb that happy people, etc., is out of date. Loks is asleep; houseboys are not here. I read the papers: all about the same things, about the heat, cholera, wars, strikes. The houseboy brought the mail—and I was thunderstruck by the joyful news that my ship will apparently be going back to Vladivostok, that is to say that my trip is going to be postponed for another month. To hell with it! *Manman-ti*—truly a poisonous thing! . . .

At breakfast Krylov was reading Chinese newspapers. Together with K'ou Ying-chieh—that makes it even better!—Fang Chihmin, a partisan from Honan Province, threw out the slogan "Honan for the People of Honan!". . . And then K'ou Ying-chieh, a Honan *tupan*, sent a letter to the mandarin of one of the most remote districts of Honan, in which mention was made that K'ou was born in that district, that K'ou's father died when K'ou was two years old, that K'ou and his mother left his birthplace when he was five years old, but he remembers that a brother remained there—and K'ou asks the mandarin to find his older brother, whose name he, K'ou, has forgotten because of the remoteness of the time. The mandarin, overjoyed, replied that indeed there lived in his district a Chinese with the family name K'ou, an illiterate ferryman on a raft—and that this ferryman did in fact remember that in very early childhood he had a brother who later disappeared. K'ou Yingchieh, a *tupan*, a general, went to meet his older brother, and a solemn encounter took place between *tupan* and indigent and illiterate ferryman. They acknowledged each other as brothers with full Chinese ceremony. The beggar received the rank of colonel and traveled to K'ai-feng together with the *tupan*. Everything was splendid, but. . . in K'ai-feng lived the *tupan*'s mother, who turned out to be exactly two years older than her newfound older son! . . . Newspapers were full of amused comment, but the new brother still receives high posts. K'ou needed all this to prove himself a native of Honan. This serves as an illustration of the feudal Chinese way of life, of the nature of Chinese mandarin politics and how the *tupans* fight against the slogans of the partisans.

I glanced at my watch: its hands still registered three o'clock—I had forgotten to wind it—I wound it.

* * *

. . . In Russia the days are now transparent, clear. In the countryside distances have expanded, the reaped fields lie vacant, rooks gather in flocks, and a "party" of crows flies over a coppice. The crescent moon comes out early, hangs pointlessly for a long time, and then is frosted over by the night—or is warmed by it—and then a wolf comes out of the forest, makes its way silently along the forest edge, without stirring a fallen leaf. The shadows from the moon in the forest are deep blue, almost black. In the forest grow Tartar earrings—they cannot be seen in the night; I just know that they are there. The empty twilight lasted a long time. The wolf lay long in a hollow. No hares were to be heard—they had gone into the fields. Human loves bloom in various ways. It is good if love has bloomed in the spring (even if it's October), borne fruit in summer—then such a love will have its spring every year, and then every fall it's so good to rummage in your desk that smells of the past winter, to sort through papers and letters, and to gather them together, the ones from last winter, to tie them in bundles and thrust them into the bottom of the lowest drawer—perhaps to see them in the last—human—winter, and sometimes not to remember them—even in this last human winter. Such is the course of simple human life. . . . But the wolf came out to the edge of the forest at night in an autumn as transparent as Pushkin, when there is hunting along paths still free of snow, and hunting horns celebrate autumn, the wolf caught sight of the glassy moon with his glassy eyes. But—this is autumn too—there is rustling, droning, moaning, rustling, howling, weeping—one cannot tell who or what it is—perhaps the wind, perhaps wolves, perhaps the forest itself. And a fine rain is falling, falling, a cold rain, the sort that makes it frightening for a man, if he is walking through the forest, to move, frightening to think that only yesterday, this morning, he was calmly whistling something from *The Merry Widow*. It is frightening to imagine that suddenly the wind might take over and begin whistling over the forest the same tune from *The Merry Widow*. At such a time a man has to stop, to lean against a tree, to pull his cap down over his forehead and—to begin whistling a tune from *The Merry*. . . "

The Moscow mail has arrived, I'll read the newspapers.

8 o'clock in the evening.

I just washed my hands: out of the tap from which cold water usually comes came hot water—that's how the sun had heated it in the pipes.

After lunch I slept. I woke up because Loks arrived and sat down close by, in silence. I drank some soda water, ate an orange, smoked a cigarette to get my eyes unglued—I looked at Loks; he looked at me in silence. I understood everything, and I said:

"Should we have a game of sixty-six?"

"Exactly," answered Loks.

Heat. The fan whistles like a snowstorm and does not bring any rest. Here's the advantage of a typewriter: it is impossible to write by hand because the paper would be swollen with sweat.

Today we had a visit from Chiang Kuang-tz'u and T'ien Han, Chinese men of letters, poets and dramatists, my friends. We talked about the "Sino-Russ." In the metaphysical system of *man-man-ti*, the society flowing in subterranean springs is now emerging onto the earth's surface. The society will have its own journal, *Nankuo* (*Southern Land*). We rode with them to have dinner at a Chinese restaurant, to eat swallows' nests, pigs' fetuses, beetles, sugared meat.

5 o'clock, morning of the 30th.

Yesterday I had a muddled day, rare in our solitude: Chinese in the afternoon, in the evening, at night. . . .

Now it's five o'clock in the morning: in Moscow it's eleven in the evening; the day after tomorrow it's August; a blue evening, stocks in bloom. . . . Dawn—it's an empty time when the earth is not sown with light. Just now I stood on the terrace: everything's enveloped in fog, but in such a fog as does not exist in Russia, through which one cannot see only what is happening on land—in the heavens red craters are forming a dawn, along the river under full sail in the fog move sampans and junks: a thousand-year-old landscape! . . . Russia—dawns purify everything.

Since midnight I have been in the company of my fellow countrymen, local artists of local music halls, musicians and dancers. These people have gathered in my honor—and that is a tribute such as I have never experienced before! One man played Khlestakov;[31] another simply suffered from hysteria. Organizer: "Do you like her? Take a bottle and go upstairs; there's a dark room there." Hysterical man: "Do you want to know what we are? Give her twenty-five rubles then. . . ."

All these people were Russians. I was ashamed that I too was a "man of the arts." . . Russia—dawns purify everything. A colony, China—incomprehensible, terrible! . . . In a few days' time these actors will carry "Russian art" to Java, to Batavia, to Manila. . . .

One night outside a window near our building I heard someone swear in Russian. A woman was getting into a ricksha; an American sailor was waiting for her in another ricksha. A Russian wearing a tattered officer's uniform was demanding money from the woman. The woman rode off. Then the man began to yell after her that he was her husband, he might not want her to spend the night with the sailor, and might not allow her to—he demanded two dollars. The woman rode

31. The central character in Nikolai V. Gogol's comedy *The Inspector General.*—Eds.

off. To me—to my way of thinking—it seemed that he would immediately begin cursing us, the Russians, the USSR, the Bolsheviks, threatening our—Bolshevik—home, but, no, he cursed only his wife. . . .

. . . Very unpleasant to see such "actors": Russians, my comrades in art, must be entreated not to travel, not to go on "tours" of the East, of the colonies, for here females are inevitably transformed into kept women, and men into pimps, here where everything is for money. . . .

6:30 in the evening, 30th.

I didn't sleep all last night. During the day I worked for the "Sino-Russ" people. After lunch I contrived to have a little sleep, although I sank onto the sheet as into a Sahara of heat. Hurrah! Hurrah!—My ship will be here on the 8th! . . . Sweat flows in streams, drips onto my glasses, gets in the way of seeing and writing.

I woke up lively and happy. Still in half sleep between sleeping and waking, a certain half-conscious something remains from sleep, something which simply makes you feel good, and then the brain fills its hollows of consciousness, memory, affairs, and then—"Oh yes, so the ship will be coming on the 8th!"—and that's it. And that "it" is very sufficient, for the dead point is beginning to move, is liquidating this piece of my life, essentially the most fantastic and—the most difficult in terms of fantasy, fantastic in terms of difficulty, but such a one at any rate where are intertwined the warped shapes of *man-man-ti*, time, nights, corpses on the canal, incomprehension, suffocation, revolution. . . . This paragraph is badly written; I can't improve on it. "All is for the best in this best of all possible worlds!" shouted Doctor Pangloss when they were dragging him to the scaffold.

Hurrah! Hurrah! My ship is arriving on the 8th! . . .

Morning of the 31st.

I was reading the papers. Of course, it's a completely different world. There—somewhere—is Europe, and here—Panama, Batavia, Manila, these equatorial oversteamed bouillons of heat, Singapore, gales at the equator, Sun Ch'uan-fang, Fang Chih-min, Chinese, Hindus, Malayans, their life, their interests—Portuguese, Arabian Jews, Spaniards, Frenchmen, Englishmen—colonies and mother countries—colonies. And here am I, suffocating in the smell of dead human flesh drifting from the sampans, living the everyday life of the diplomatic corps in the diplomatic quarter, in a way I have never lived before, in leisure and comfort; today the senior houseboy on his own initiative emptied my suitcases, sorted through the contents, and hung it in various wardrobes, having beforehand taken everything made of wool to the dry cleaners, the way it is done for all gentlemen; the houseboy decided that things ought not to be in suitcases if the gentleman was not going anywhere. It's very important that I have got out of the habit of sleeping, because nights give new dimensions to everything. When I quit this heat, when my thoughts, all that I have seen, my will, and nerves get back into order—it will be a journey out of the fantastic. I look at my body in the mirror: I think strange thoughts about my body having become completely sexless—this is a big chapter from the fantastic tale which is being written for me by life itself.

. . . If you were to take off from this Earthly Globe and in some stupendous flight look at it from above, then you would see that it is not in the least concerned with man, but hostile to man by its very dimensions, by north and south—the poles—being hidden from man by cold, by ice, by snowstorms, by the south now being immersed in eternal night, the north in eternal day, by mists of clouds, storm clouds, fumes, molds drifting about the equatorial lands in deadly suffocation, by winds, calms, scorching heats, rains, thunderstorms, snowfalls, glooms, bursts of light that pass over this Globe flying in the void. Yes, that's how it is. And—yes, great is the human brain, which, Kant notwithstanding, can see "things in themselves."

9:30 in the evening.

This morning bought a deck of cards for solitaire. All day I lay out solitaire. The Paris mail arrived; Loks is buried in French magazines. I don't go anywhere; no one comes to see us.

10:30 in the evening.

Have been laying out solitaire to the point of stupefaction, and it still refuses to come out.

11:30 in the evening.

Yet again embarked on combinations of cards, reasoning that there must be a vast system of laws governing cards, this solitaire which refuses to come out.

Midnight.

It's come out! Twice in a row! . . .

And I went out on the terrace, looked at the stars: a great pity that the dead bat has been washed away by the storm—and an absolute pity that mankind has not yet mastered the ability to put people in a condition of anabiosis: I would very willingly put myself into the state of anabiosis until my ship's arrival.

August 1st, 3 o'clock in the morning.

Well, July is now past—hello, August!—and on the canal August was met with a cannonade of firecrackers, fireworks, met with the death of some Chinese, about whom I shall never be able to find out anything, however much effort and thought I expended. A wind came up in the evening; it's blowing from the ocean, rocking the lamp, strong and fresh—and it's easier to think. In an automobile, in this wind, in the darkness, we went racing out of town, in silence, everyone keeping to himself, gloomily. No fireflies any more.

8 o'clock in the morning.

All night a fierce wind was howling, tearing, hurling, and now it's roaring in such a way that our house is like a ship at sea. The sky is vacant, like the sea. The newspapers write about typhoons in the ocean. The Indian Ocean will greet me in September, and, oh, will it give me a rocking so that I would know the meaning of travel around the world! . . .

1 o'clock in the afternoon.

Wind! Wind! Loks came in and said that the wind makes him ten years younger and that last night he slept without nightmares for the first time this summer. A golden, golden, golden day, the kind about which, according to Mayne Reid,[32] it is said, "A fine tropical day has arrived. . . ."

11 o'clock in the evening.

Now it isn't just a wind but a hurricane that is whistling, howling; the windows have been closed; everything is shaking; now is the time to "say a prayer" for those at sea! . . . Ooo-eee-yooyooyoo!—it roars, howls, sobs. The night is black, the canal is still, empty, the trees toss beneath the terrace. I love the elements! . . . A typhoon! . . .

Why—China and not Norway? This feeling of loneliness and vigor I now have were given to me by Hamsun. Loks arrived with a pack of cards; we played sixty-six; he won. Every man should have his household things: I am absolutely convinced that this howling wind here is an item of my household and of my material existence, side by side

32. Anglo-Irish Writer (1818–83) known for his novels of adventure.—Ed.

with games of solitaire. The night is black as black, the stars bright, and this roaring wind, blowing blackness upon the earth, shares the darkness with the stars.

9 o'clock in the morning, the 2d.

The wind has dropped.

Krylov came in and showed me the text of a telegram he sent his wife this morning: "All that is mine I place in your hands, if they are clean." This Russian hysteria written in Latin letters will be driven by the force of electricity as far as Moscow, over one-third of the Earthly Globe.

★ ★ ★

. . . China! . . .

I was told to put on a friendly face. We were walking through the workers' quarter; there wasn't a single European there. I saw how an entire worker's family, with an old granny and a dozen kids, lives in a tent, the kind of thing used by tradesmen at village fairs back home, the kind where the walls are made of rags and are lifted during the day; the granny and the mother were clothed only in rags about their loins; the children were completely naked. So by way of the workers' quarter we reached the temple. The temple belongs to this district. The temple is a beggarly one. Actually it is a little town of temples, where you can find anything—from oratories according to the class and rank of the worshipers and dying, to workshops, to the cubicles (near to the gods) of the sacred prostitutes (I've seen them, these sacred prostitutes—they sit in a little herd, young and old, given by their fathers to the god; they embroider, drink tea—peaceful creatures). The temple has a name—Temple of the Queen of Heaven. In my presence two Chinese women brought two hens as sacrifice to the goddess. It's half-dark there, very quiet, sleepy, smelling of sandalwood incense. It was there that my head began to go around, to get bleary and to ache from the heat—and we made for home. According to Chinese rules a person may not be taken to prison from a temple. I visited this temple because it was from here that Liu Hua was taken by the police. In the temple there are semidark stalls behind grilles, with clean-swept floors: people in ecstatic prayer may lie there for hours; many who have nowhere to lie down and sleep come there, lie down "ecstatically," and sleep. The smell in Chinese temples is stupefying. I've heard the Chinese yawning: they yawn very differently from us—they sing as they yawn, in the same way, no offense meant, as dogs howl. Liu Hua went into hiding in this temple and concealed the members' money here. The police took him from the temple.

* * *

. . . Heat—heat—heat! Krylov arrived: yet another front has come into existence; General Chu Pei-teh has invaded western Kiangsi. Today there's some sort of solar typhoon; I really don't know what it is, because there's no wind at all, not a breath, and the air is wet and hot, as—as when you break a loaf of bread just taken out of the oven. Krylov recounted how the people of Kalgan had quarrelled with their God of the City Wall. Listening, I lay in bed, sick from the heat, on a sheet wet with sweat.

The summer of 1924 was very dry. The people of Kalgan prayed to their chief god—the God of the Wall—prayed to him all together, begging him to help them: he didn't help. Then the people of Kalgan carried the god out from his shrine into the sun, so that he himself—the god—should feel the heat. They carried him out—and the following day rain fell in such torrents that there was a flood, the town was inundated, people sailed about town in junks, many people were drowned. Then the people of Kalgan dragged the god into the rain, set him in a puddle, and gave him a whipping. And then, when the flood was over, they put the god back in his shrine and—forgot about him until the New Year celebrations of 1925. Just before the New Year the soothsayers established that, while the god's image remained in the shrine, the god himself was not there, for he had gone to the heavens to complain about the people of Kalgan to the chief (I forgot his name) god of heaven. And without this God of the Wall the New Year had never been welcomed and was impossible to welcome. The New Year had to be canceled. They canceled it. But all the same at midnight before the New Year the whole town went to the Western Gates to beg the god's forgiveness. They approached the gates with lanterns, opened the gates and fell on their faces before them, begging the god to make peace and return to the town. At half-past three in the morning it became known through the bonzes that the god was at the gates, was in a swaggering mood, and would assume his place in the shrine only if the people would lure him back by crawling. And that's what they had to do: they crawled on all fours from the gates into the town, face to the gates, backside to town, they crawled back-to-front right to the shrine: this is the way they lured the god back. They crawled to the shrine, settled in fan shape around it, heads facing inward. The god passed through the crowd into the shrine and settled into his image. People closed the fan. And then—oh, then!—they flung themselves on the god in the shrine, gave him a fierce beating, and locked him up so that he couldn't run away any more—and: on the occasion of the New Year they went to play mah-jongg, devoting three days in a row to the game! . . .

Krylov swears this is not invention but fact, an illustration of the old China alive to this day. I went out on the terrace, smoked, threw my head back. No, we don't get skies like that: here they are much darker and deeper, more remote—and such bright, unfamiliar stars. I can now write a good story about the meaning of exile.

* * *

. . . This morning at eight o'clock my friend, the poet Chiang Kuang-tz'u, came bursting in. I was asleep. He said that an automobile was waiting, that we had to go and take part in making a film for our "Sino-Russ." I hurriedly shaved and washed, and we left for the studio. There—the end of the world, everything is upside down, lanterns are being hung up, pictures are being hung high on the walls, tables are being set up: they're making an artistic café. I'm the one who will walk into the café, the artistic café, which in fact isn't there, with a Russian woman artist (they invited a Russian artist friend of mine), with a Chinese sculptor (a genuine, renowned Chinese sculptor, who studied in France for six years), a professor (a real one, a teacher of literature from the local university, a popular man), and a poet, my friend and translator Chiang Kuang-tz'u. We'll sit at a table, we'll converse, we'll be served by two girls—I, as a democrat and as the son of a revolutionary people, will suggest that they have a drink with us, sit down with us—they will join us, and Sofia Grigorievna (the Russian artist) will draw one of them. The café is crowded. The students recognize me and ask to be introduced. We exchange visiting cards. We talk. They, the students, say that they welcome me, a Russian revolutionary writer. We all get up to drink a toast together—the students and the maids and we, science and art. And I put the hands of the students in the hands of the maids—European fashion—as a symbol of the alliance of science and democracy, the alliance of labor and learning! . . . So it was contrived by T'ien Han.

That's not quite how it was played out. The confusion was super-Babylonian! . . . They were working on the café until noon. The roasting heat was incredible. In the bustle everybody spoke only Chinese. At twelve o'clock, at a command that meant nothing to me, the entire gathering, some thirty people, without fuss, worker-fashion, moved to a neighboring Chinese eating house to have lunch. Half-dozen soups, frogs, lotus, morsels of dog were served. Sofia Grigorievna almost threw up, not that she ate anything. I ate, drank, and sat pouring sweat. We went back. Still more people had assembled. Babel. And this is where my sufferings began.

They started filming. I was seated in the center; all the floodlights were directed on me, and in addition to the floodlights they set up some shields that reflected real sunlight on me. These shields were my downfall: in the first place, they scorched with tripled heat, and, in the second place, they blinded me! . . . People took their seats. Although the film was silent, a musician played the violin, and a man sang; but Chinese music and singing—to a European ear—seem the ultimate degeneration of hearing; my teeth began to ache from the singing and the violin just as they ache when cork is rubbed against glass. Everyone spoke at once, and there was an incredible din I could make nothing of. Chiang Kuangts'u was supposed to be acting as well as translating what was said to me: people shouted at him at the top of their voices; he would turn away from the camera and yell at me. This is how it began. We came out, sat down, removed our hats, ordered wine, which the girls brought: everything was in order. But at this point the students arrived and sat down in such a way that the shield (damn it!) was opposite my eyes. I got up to greet the students and give them my visiting card, and—went blind, literally; I realize that I can't see anything, make an effort to open my eyes—again a shaft of that incredible sunlight; again I close my eyes and try to cover my face with my hands. The operator is cranking the camera—I understand this isn't the proper way to get acquainted. The director yells at Chiang. Chiang yells at me. Everyone yells. Can't understand anything. And I stand there weeping, tears flow from the light and the pain in my eyes. Music howls. They've started filming this part over again. I understand the circumstances: they have invited important people, respected and well known, and I don't want to look a fool either; I agreed to this entire operation—although I do understand that it's a bit silly—only for the sake of "Sino-Russ" friendship and for the sake of the decent people who also agreed to participate in this stunt, one that seemed to say: here you are—China as it really is, ornamented with well-known names! . . . But I noticed that all the Chinese had long since given up "acting" and—are struggling only with the sun and with these accursed sun shields that blind and roast a man; and so everything comes out all right—it is an illustration of how people suffer from the sun and do not dare to look at the dragon. Music plays, the singer sings, the sun incinerates, sweat pours, everyone yells in Chinese; there's no understanding anything. The director yells at Chiang. Chiang yells at me. I am blind and deaf.

Thus till four o'clock. Then—again precisely as on command—everyone gets up to drink tea. I asked to be allowed to go home—

begged off!—and on arrival, without wasting a moment, got into the tub. . . . Once, when I was called in by the military for enlistment and my myopia was being checked, they dropped some atropine in my eyes: I was half-blinded, and my pupils lost their ability to expand and contract; now my eyes, after these cinematic operations, are as incapable of seeing as after atropine. And, all the time in my throat and in my head—those lights, those howls, that music.

FINAL CHAPTER

* * *

2 o'clock in the morning.

A very strange condition arises when you lay out hands of solitaire for hours on end: everything merges before your eyes; you can't tear yourself away from the cards, but you can't concentrate on them either—the cards merge; the cards grow to enormous size; the cards sink away, shrinking to pinheads. And it seems that the table, the typewriter, the cards on the table—everything is moving, crawling, living. And then your thoughts disappear somewhere. Loks talks to himself. And dreams become confused in your waking hours: a nightmare of floodlights that blind you, steamships, Chinese music and hubbub, shrines, alleys. I walked through the rooms of our house. On the table in the dining room—soda water and liqueur, oranges and a deck of cards for solitaire, litter of ashes and orange peel. In the drawing room—magazines rummaged through a hundred times. The air in the study is unbreathable from the leather of the armchairs. There, beyond the walls of our house, people work, wage wars, die, betray, win victories, trade, die from heat, drought, from floods, from starvation, from cholera, conspire, rebel—the Chinese—there, beyond our—this!—city, over the vast thousands of kilometers, where lives the most populous nation in the world, the one that invented the printing press, gunpowder, the compass, that is to say, the things that made Europe powerful, the one that lives in terrible poverty and barbarity, in dirt, in the suffocating stench of corpses, from which I in particular shall soon begin to lose my mind. . . . I spread my brains in bewilderment, as philosophers spread their hands: I am very tired, worn out—and over cards my thoughts have learned how to double, to treble, and in general to be only "fractions," having lost the ability to coordinate problems with "many unknown quantities." Loks talks to himself: Loks lives in this world because the Communist revolution must pass over the entire Earthly Globe. Here in our house—winter and exile.

⋆ ⋆ ⋆

. . . It's August now in Russia. Night. A fine rain is falling, falling, a cold rain, the sort which makes it frightening for a man, if he is walking through a forest, to move, frightening to think that only this morning he was whistling something from *The Merry Widow*. But the rain has stopped, and the crescent moon hangs pointlessly in the sky, frosted by the night—and then the wolf comes out of the forest, without stirring a fallen leaf. . . . Ah, Russia, my Russia—my distant field! . . . With glassy eyes the wolf looks at the glassy moon.

Moscow
Povarskaya Street
February 7, 1927

Mahogany

One

Paupers, soothsayers, beggars, mendicant chanters, lazars, wanderers from holy place to holy place, male and female, cripples, bogus saints, blind Psalm singers, prophets, idiots of both sexes, fools in Christ—these names, so close in meaning, of the double-ring sugar cakes of the everyday life of Holy Russia, paupers on the face of Holy Russia, wandering Psalm singers, Christ's cripples, fools in Christ of Holy Russia—these sugar cakes have adorned everyday life from Russia's very beginnings, from the time of the first Tsar Ivans, the everyday life of Russia's thousand years. All Russian historians, ethnographers, and writers have dipped their quills to write about these holy fools. These madmen or frauds—beggars, bogus saints, prophets—were held to be the Church's brightest jewel, Christ's own, intercessors for the world, as they have been called in classical Russian history and literature.

A noted Muscovite fool in Christ—Ivan Yakovlevich,[1] a onetime seminarian—who lived in Moscow in the middle of the nineteenth century, died in the Preobrazhenskaya Hospital. His funeral was described by reporters, poets, and historians. A poet wrote in the *Vedomosti:*[2]

1. Ivan Yakovlevich Koreisha (ca. 1780–1861), for many years an inmate of a Moscow institution for the insane; his followers regarded him as a saint and a seer.—Eds.

2. *Moskovskiye Vedomosti* (*Moscow Gazette*), a conservative Moscow daily.—Eds.

What feast is in the Yellow House[3] afoot,
And wherefore are the multitudes there thronging,
In landaus and in cabs, nay e'en on foot,
And ev'ry heart is seized with fearful longing?
And in their midst is heard a voice of woe
In direst pain and grief ofttimes bewailing:
"Alas, Ivan Yakovlevich is laid low,
The mighty prophet's lamp too soon is failing."

Skavronsky, a chronicler of the times, relates in his *Moscow Sketches* that during the five days that the body lay unburied more than two hundred masses for the repose of the dead were sung over it. Many people spent the night outside the church. An eyewitness of the funeral, N. Barkov, the author of a monograph entitled *Twenty-six Muscovite Sham Prophets, Sham Fools in Christ, Idiots, Male and Female*, relates that Ivan Yakovlevich was to have been buried on Sunday,

> as had been announced in the *Police Gazette*, and that day at dawn his admirers began flocking in, but the funeral did not take place because of the quarrels which broke out over where exactly he was to be buried. It did not quite come to a free-for-all, but words were exchanged, and strong ones they were. Some wanted to take him to Smolensk, his birthplace; others worked busily to have him buried in the Pokrovsky Monastery, where a grave had even been dug for him in the church; others begged tearfully that his remains be given to the Alekseyevsky Nunnery; still others, hanging on to the coffin, tried to carry it off to the village of Cherkizovo. It was feared that the body of Ivan Yakovlevich might be stolen.

The historian writes: "All this time it was raining, and the mud was terrible, but nevertheless, as the body was carried from the lodgings to

3. Institution for the insane.—Eds.

the chapel, from the chapel to the church, from the church to the cemetery, women, girls, ladies in crinolines prostrated themselves and crawled under the coffin." Ivan Yakovlevich—when he was alive—was in the habit of relieving himself on the spot:

> He made puddles [writes the historian], and his attendants had orders to sprinkle the floor with sand. And this sand, watered by Ivan Yakovlevich, his admirers would gather and carry home, and it was discovered that the sand had healing properties. A baby gets a tummy ache, his mother gives him half a spoonful of the sand in his gruel, and the baby gets well. The cotton with which the deceased's nose and ears had been plugged was divided into tiny pieces after the funeral service for distribution among the faithful. Many came with vials and collected in them the moisture which seeped from the coffin, the deceased having died of dropsy. The shirt in which Ivan Yakovlevich had died was torn to shreds. When the time came for the coffin to be carried out of the church, freaks, fools in Christ, pious hypocrites, wanderers from holy place to holy place, male and female were gathered outside. They had not gone into the church, which was packed, but stood in the streets. And right there in broad daylight, among the assembled, sermons were preached to the people, visions called up and seen, prophecies and denunciations uttered, money collected, and ominous roarings given forth.

During the last years of his life Ivan Yakovlevich used to order his admirers to drink the water in which he had washed: they drank it. Ivan Yakovlevich made not only spoken but also written prophecies that have been preserved for historical research. People wrote to him; they would ask, "Will so-and-so get married?" He would reply, "No work—no supper. . . ."

Kitai-gorod in Moscow was the cheese in which the fools in Christ—its maggots—lived. Some wrote verse; others crowed like roosters, screamed like peacocks, or whistled like bullfinches; others heaped foulness on all and sundry in the name of the Lord; still others knew only a simple phrase which was held to be prophetic and gave the prophet his name; for example, "Man's life's a dream, the coffin—coach and team, the ride—as smooth as cream!" Also to be found were devotees of dog barking who with their barking prophesied God's will. To this estate belonged paupers, beggars, soothsayers, mendicant chanters, lazars, bogus saints—the cripples of all of Holy Russia; to it belonged peasants and townfolk and gentry and merchants—children, old men, great, hulking louts, brood mares of women. They were all drunk. They were all sheltered by the onion-domed, sky-blue calm of the Asiatic Russian tsardom; they were bitter as cheese and onions, for the onion domes atop the churches are, of course, the symbol of oniony Russian life.

* * *

. . . And there are in Moscow, Petersburg, and other large Russian towns other kinds of queer fish. Their family tree is rooted in the Russia of the emperors rather than the Russia of the tsars. The art of Russian furniture, established by Peter, came into its own under Elizabeth. This serf art has no recorded history, and the names of its practitioners have been obliterated by time. It was an art of solitary men, of cellars in towns, of cramped back rooms in servants' huts on country estates. It was an art that had its being in bitter vodka and cruelty. Jacob and Boulle were the teachers. Serf boys were sent to Moscow and Saint Petersburg, to Paris, to Vienna—there they were taught their craft. Then they returned—from Paris to the cellars of Saint Petersburg, from Saint Petersburg to servants' cramped back rooms—and created. For decades a craftsman would work on a great sofa or dressing table, or on a small bureau or a book cabinet—would work, drink, and die, leaving his art to a nephew, for a craftsman was not supposed to have children, and the nephew would either copy his uncle's art or develop it further. A craftsman would die, but the things he had made would live on a century or more on the landowners' estates and in their town houses; people made love in their presence and died on the great sofas, hid secret correspondence in the concealed drawers of secretaires; brides looked closely at their youth in the little mirrors of the dressing tables, and old women—at their old age. Elizabeth—Catherine—rococo, baroque—bronze, scrolls, palisander, rosewood, ebony, curly birch, Persian walnut. Paul is severe, Paul is a Knight of Malta; Paul has soldierly lines, Paul has a severe repose, dark-polished mahogany, green leather, black lions, and griffins. Alexander—Empire, classic lines, Hellas. Nicholas—Paul again, crushed by the majesty of his brother Alexander. Thus have epochs given their shape to mahogany. In 1861 serfdom came to an end. The serf craftsmen were replaced by furniture factories—Levinson, Thonet, Viennese furniture. But the craftsmen's nephews survived, thanks to vodka. These craftsmen no longer make anything; they restore the past, but they have kept all the skills and traditions of their uncles. They are solitary men, and silent. They take pride in their work, like philosophers, and they love it, like poets. They live in cellars as before. You can't put such a craftsman in a furniture factory; you can't get him to restore a piece made later than Nicholas I. He is an antiquarian; he is a restorer. In the attic of some Moscow house or in a barn on some country estate that has escaped burning, he will find a table, a three-leaved mirror, a sofa—dating back to Catherine, Paul, or Alexander—and for months on end he will worry away at it in his cellar, smoking, thinking, measuring with his eyes to bring back life to dead things. He will love these things. And—who knows?—he may find a yellowed bundle of letters in the secret drawer of a small bureau. He is a restorer; he looks back to the prime of these things. He is sure to be a queer fish, and in his queer-fish way he will sell the restored piece to a collector, as queer a fish as himself, with whom, to seal the bargain, he will drink brandy—poured from a bottle into a square glass measure of Catherine's time—out of a wineglass that had once been part of the imperial diamond set.

Two

The year is 1928.

The town is a Russian Bruges and a Muscovite Kamakura. Three hundred years ago the last tsarevich of the House of Ryurik was murdered in this town; on the day of the murder the children of the boyar Tuchkov played with the tsarevich—and to this day Tuchkovs survive in the town, as do the monasteries and many other families of less illustrious ancestry. . . . Relics of ancient Russia, the Russian provinces, the broad upper reaches of the Volga, forests, swamps, villages, monasteries, country estates, a chain of towns—Tver [Kalinin], Uglich, Yaroslavl, Rostov-Veliki. The town is a monastic Bruges of feudal Russia, a town of narrow streets overgrown with camomile, of stone witnesses to murders and centuries. Two hundred versts from Moscow, and the railroad is fifty versts away.

Here ruins of country estates and mahogany are still around. The head of the local historical museum walks around in a top hat, a cape, checkered trousers, and has let his side whiskers grow, like Pushkin's; in the pockets of his cape are kept the keys to the museum and the monasteries; he drinks tea in the tavern and vodka in solitude—in his storeroom; his house is piled with Bibles, icons, archimandrital cowls and miters, surplices, stoles, cuffs, cassocks, chasubles, chalice cloths, palls, altar vestments—of the thirteenth, fifteenth, seventeenth centuries; the furniture in his study is mahogany and once belonged to the Karazins; on the writing desk is an ashtray in the form of a nobleman's cap with a red band and a white crown.

Barin[4] Karazin—Vyacheslav Pavlovich—served at one time in the Horse Guards and resigned some five and twenty years before the

4. A member of the gentry; also, a form of address and reference roughly equivalent to "squire" or "master." The word remained in use among peasants for some time after the revolution.—Eds.

Revolution, because he was an honest man; one of his colleagues had been caught stealing; he was sent to investigate, reported the truth to his superiors; his superiors covered up for the thief—this was more than Barin Karazin could stand, and he submitted a second report—his resignation—and settled down on his estate, going into his district town once a week to make purchases; he rode in a huge, old-fashioned carriage, accompanied by two footmen; with a white glove he would give a sign to the shop clerk to wrap up for him half a pound of the best caviar, three-quarters pound of *balyk*,[5] and a small sturgeon; one footman would pay the bill; the other would receive the purchases; on one occasion the shopkeeper made as if to shake hands with the Barin, but the latter withheld his hand, explaining this refusal with a curt "No need for that!" Barin Karazin wore a nobleman's cap and a greatcoat in the style of Nicholas I; the Revolution had forced him from his estate and into town but had left him his greatcoat and cap; Barin Karazin stood in queues wearing his nobleman's cap, preceded by his wife instead of footmen.

Barin Karazin existed by selling off old family possessions; it was to this end that he used to call on the museum curator; at the curator's he would see things that had been taken from his estate by the will of the Revolution and look at them disdainfully; but one day he noticed on the curator's desk the ashtray in the form of a nobleman's cap.

"Take it away," he said curtly.

"Why?" asked the curator.

"The cap of a Russian nobleman cannot serve as a spittoon," replied Barin Karazin.

The two connoisseurs of antiquities quarreled. Barin Karazin went away in anger. Never again did he cross the curator's threshold. In the town lived a saddler who remembered with gratitude how Barin Karazin—when the saddler was a youngster and an errand boy in the Barin's service—how the Barin with one blow of his left hand had knocked out seven of his teeth for not jumping to it.

5. Dried and salted filet of sturgeon.—Eds.

In the town impenetrable silence was congealing, howling with boredom twice a day in steamers' whistles, and ringing the ancient denizens of church belfries—until 1928, that is, for in 1928 the bells were taken down from many churches for the State Ore and Metal Trust. High up in towers, with the aid of pulleys, beams, and hemp ropes, bells were dragged from their belfries; they hung over the earth; then they were cast down. As the bells crept along the ropes, they sang an ancient lament—and this lament hung over the town's closed-packed, ancient stones. The bells fell with a roar and a great sigh and sank a good two arshins into the ground.

In the days of the events described in this story, the town was groaning with the groans of these ancient bells.

The most useful thing in town was a trade-union card; in the shops there were two queues—those with cards and those without; to take a boat out on the Volga cost cardholders ten kopecks, and the rest forty kopecks, an hour; cinema tickets—to the rest twenty-five, forty, and sixty kopecks, to cardholders five, ten, and fifteen. A trade-union card, if there was one in the house, occupied the place of honor next to the bread card; as for bread cards—and that meant bread, too: four hundred grams per person per day—they were issued only to those who had the vote; to those who had no vote and to their children no bread was given. The cinema was in the trade-union park, in a heated barn; it had not been thought necessary to provide the cinema with a signal bell, but a signal was sounded from the power station to the whole town at once: first signal—time to finish your tea; second signal—put on your coat and be on your way. The power station operated until one, but when there were name days, *oktyabriny*,[6] and other unofficial festivities in the house of the Executive Committee chairman, or the Industrial Combine chairman, or of other higher-ups—electric lights were late going out, sometimes all night, and the rest of the population contrived to have their own festivities on these nights. And it was in

6. Secular ceremony of the naming of a child, taking the place of baptism. Its name derives from October, the month of the Bolshevik Revolution.—Eds.

the cinema one day that a representative of the People's Commissariat of Domestic Trade by the name of Satz, or maybe Katz, while in a state of perfect sobriety, bumped accidentally, simply through clumsiness, against the wife of the Executive Committee chairman; she, overflowing with disdain, uttered the words, "I am Kuvarzina"; representative Satz, being unaware of the power of this name, apologized with raised eyebrows—and for those raised eyebrows was subsequently forced to leave the district. The higher-ups in the town lived in a tight little group, keeping a watchful eye, out of inborn suspiciousness, on the rest of the population; they substituted squabbles for constructive activity and every year reelected themselves to one important district post after another, depending on the alignment of squabblers, on the principle of robbing Peter to pay Paul. The economy was juggled on the same principle. The combine ran everything (the combine came into existence the same year that Ivan Ozhogov—the hero of this story—became an *okhlomon*).[7] The board of the combine consisted of Executive Committee Chairman Kuvarzin (his wife's husband) and Workers' and Peasants' Inspection Representative Presnukhin; Nedosugov acted as chairman. Their way of running things was by the slow dissipation of prerevolutionary resources and stupid bungling, to which they brought loving care. The oil mill operated at a loss; the sawmill—also at a loss; the tannery—not at a loss, but not at a profit either, and without a depreciation fund. The previous winter a new boiler had been hauled over the snow to the tannery by forty-five horses and half the population of the district; they got it there and left it—because it was the wrong kind—entering its cost in the profit-and-loss account; they bought a bark crusher and abandoned it, too, as useless, entering it in the profit-and-loss account; then, for the purpose of crushing bark,

7. Word, probably derived from Greek *ochlos*, "mob," and *monos*, "alone," meaning "apart from the mob" and, therefore, "outcast." An early translater of Pilnyak, who must have consulted the author about the meaning of the word, says, "The author affirms that it means just what its use in the novel implies." —Eds.

they bought a chaffcutter—but abandoned it, since bark is not straw; that too was written off. They set out to improve the living conditions of the workers with a housing project: they bought a two-story wooden house, moved it to the tannery—and sawed it up for firewood—five cubic *sazhens*[8] they got out of it—because the house turned out to be rotten: there were only thirteen sound beams in it; to these thirteen beams they added nine thousand robles—and built a house just as the tannery shut down because, although unlike the other enterprises it made no losses, it made no profits either; the new house remained empty. The combine covered its losses by selling off equipment from enterprises idle since before the Revolution and also by such deals as the following: Chairman of the Executive Committee Kuvarzin sold lumber to Member of the Board Kuvarzin at the fixed prices with a 50 percent discount—for twenty-five thousand rubles; Member of the Board Kuvarzin sold the same lumber to the population at large, and to Chairman of the Executive Committee Kuvarzin in particular, at the fixed prices without discount—for something over fifty thousand rubles. In 1927 the board expressed a desire to rest on its laurels; Kuvarzin was presented with a briefcase; the money for the briefcase was taken out of public funds, and then a subscription list was rushed around among the natives in order to return the money to the cashbox. In view of the narrowness of their interests and their lives, passed in secret from the rest of the population, the higher-ups are of no interest whatsoever to this story. Alcohol in town was sold in two forms only—vodka and sacramental wine; there was nothing else; vodka was consumed in quantity, and sacramental wine, too, although it was somewhat less in demand—for Christ's blood and *teplota*.[9] Cigarettes on sale in town were "Cannon," eleven kopecks a pack, and "Boxing," fourteen kopecks a pack; there were no others. There were two queues for both vodka and cigarettes—trade-union and nontrade-union.

8. One *sazhen* is equal to 1.89 yards.—Eds.

9. In the Russian Orthodox church, wine diluted with warm water, given to communicants during Communion.—Eds.

Steamers called twice a day, and in the ship's restaurant one could buy "Sappho" cigarettes, port, and rowanberry brandy—and "Sappho" smokers were obviously embezzlers, since there was no private business in town, and official budgets made no provisions for "Sappho." The townsfolk were looking forward to the day when the town would no longer be an administrative center, and they would live on their vegetable patches, supplying one another's needs.

Near Skudrin Bridge stood the Skudrin house, and in the house lived the peasants' agent, Yakov Karpovich Skudrin, a man of eighty-five; besides Yakov Karpovich Skudrin there lived in the town—but not under the same roof as Yakov Karpovich—his two much younger sisters, Kapitolina and Rimma, and his brother, the *okhlomon* Ivan, who had changed his name to Ozhogov; more about them later.

For the last forty years or so, Yakov Karpovich had suffered from a hernia, and when walking he supported this hernia of his with his right hand through the fly of his trousers; his hands were puffy and greenish; he salted his bread thickly with salt from the common salt dish, crunching it between his fingers, frugally sprinkling what was left back into the salt dish. Over the last thirty years Yakov Karpovich had lost the habit of sleeping normally; he would wake at night and keep vigil over the Bible until daybreak and then sleep until noon; at noon he always went out to the public reading room to read the papers: there were no papers on sale in town and no money to take out subscriptions—papers were read in reading rooms. Yakov Karpovich was fat, white-haired, and bald; his eyes watered, and as he got ready to speak he would go into protracted wheezings and snufflings. The Skudrin house had once belonged to the landowner Vereisky, who went bankrupt as an elected justice of the peace after the abolition of serfdom; Yakov Karpovich, having served his time in the prereform army, worked for Vereisky as a clerk, became adept in courtroom chicanery, and, when Vereisky went bankrupt, bought him out of house and position. The house had stood untouched since Catherine's time; in the century and a half of its existence it had darkened like the mahogany inside it, and its window-panes had taken on a greenish tinge. Yakov Karpovich remembered the days of serfdom. The old man remembered everything, as far back as the *barin* of his serf village, as far back as the recruiting for Sevastopol; he remembered all the names, patronymics, and surnames of all the Russian ministers of state and people's commissars, all the ambassadors to the Russian Imperial Court and to the Soviet Central Executive Committee, all the foreign ministers of the great powers, all the prime ministers, kings, emperors, and popes. The old man had lost count of years and used to say:

"I've outlived Nikolai Pavlovich, Aleksandr Nikolayevich, Aleksandr Aleksandrovich, Nikolai Aleksandrovich, Vladimir Ilyich—and I'll outlive Aleksei Ivanovich too!"[10]

The old man had a nasty little smile, at once obsequious and malicious; his whitish eyes watered when he smiled. The old man was hard, and his sons took after him. The oldest, Aleksandr—this happened long before 1905—having been sent to the landing stage with an urgent letter and having missed the steamer, received from his father a slap in the face accompanied by the words, "Get out, you good-for-nothing!" That slap was the last drop of honey; the boy was fourteen; the boy turned, walked out of the house—and returned home only six years later, a student of the Academy of Fine Arts. Sometime during those years the father had sent his son a letter in which he ordered his son to return and swore to withdraw his parental blessing, laying on him an eternal curse; on this very letter—just below his father's signature—the son had written, "To hell with your blessing," and sent it back. When, six years after his departure, Aleksandr walked into the parlor one sunny spring day, the father went toward him with a gleeful smile and hand raised to strike his son; with a cheerful grin, the son took hold of his father's wrists, smiled again—a smile that sparkled with strength; his father's hands were held in a vise; the son forced his father to sit down in an armchair near the table by applying the slightest of pressure to his wrists, and said:

10. Nicholas I, Alexander II, Alexander III, Nicholas II, Lenin, and Rykov (the last chairman of the Council of People's Commissars, 1924–30, executed in Stalin's purges in 1938).

"Good day to you, Daddikins—don't put yourself out, Daddikins—take a seat, Daddikins!"

The father began wheezing, tittering, snuffling; malevolent kindliness passed over his face; the old man called out to his wife:

"Maryushka, yes, hee-hee, a drop of vodka, my dear, bring us a drop of vodka, cold from the cellar, and a bit of something cold to go with it—he's grown up, our boy, grown up—he's come back, our boy, to blight our old age, the s-son of a bitch!"

His sons went their ways: painter, priest, ballet dancer, doctor, engineer. Two of the younger brothers took after the oldest—the painter—and after the father; the two youngest left the house, like the oldest, and the younger of the two, the engineer Akim Yakovlevich, became a Communist; he never returned to his father's house, and on his visits to the town of his birth stayed with his aunts Kapitolina and Rimma. By 1928, Yakov Karpovich's eldest grandsons were married, but his youngest child, a daughter, was only twenty. She was his only daughter, and, amid the thunders of the Revolution, she was given no education of any kind.

In the house lived the old man; his wife, Maria Klimovna; and their daughter, Katerina. Half the house and the attic were not heated in winter. The house lived as people lived long before Catherine, even before Peter, although it was mahogany of Catherine's time that inhabited its silence. The old people lived off their vegetable garden. Industry supplied the house with matches, kerosene, and salt—nothing else; matches, kerosene, and salt were doled out by the father. From spring to fall Maria Klimovna, Katerina, and the old man toiled over cabbages, beets, turnips, cucumbers, carrots, and licorice, which took the place of sugar. On summer dawns the old man could be met in his nightclothes, barefoot, his right hand thrust through his fly, a long switch in his left hand—grazing cows outside the town in dew and fog. In winter the old man would allow the lamp to be lit only when he was up—at other times mother and daughter sat in darkness. Every day at noon the old man went to the reading room to read the papers, soaking up names and news of the Communist Revolution. At those times

Katerina would sit at the harpsichord practicing Kastalsky's[11] spiritual songs; she sang in the church choir. The old man came home at dusk, ate, and went to bed. The house sank into women's whisperings, into darkness. Then Katerina would go to the cathedral for choir practice. Her father would awake at midnight, light the lamp, eat, and bury himself in the Bible, reading it aloud from memory. About six o'clock he would fall asleep again. The old man had lost all sense of time, having ceased to fear death, having forgotten how to fear life. Mother and daughter kept silent in the old man's presence. The mother cooked porridge and cabbage soup, baked pies, baked[12] and curded milk, prepared pigs'-feet jelly (saving the knucklebones for her grandsons)—in other words she lived as the people of Russia lived in the fifteenth and in the seventeenth centuries; the food she prepared was also of the fifteenth and the seventeenth centuries. Maria Klimovna was a dried-up old woman; she was a wonderful woman, the kind still preserved in Russia in the villages, together with ancient icons of the Virgin. The cruel will of her husband, who, fifty years earlier, the day after their wedding, when she put on a raspberry-colored velvet bodice, asked her, "What's that for?"—she did not understand the question—"What's that for?" asked her husband again—"Take it off! I know you as you are without the finery, and there's no cause for others to stare!"—and with this, licking his thumb, the husband painfully showed his wife how she should pull her hair back from the temples—the cruel will of her husband, which forced the wife to put away her velvet bodice in a chest forever, which banished her to the kitchen—was the wife's will broken by it, or was it tempered by subjugation? The wife became forever submissive, dignified, silent, sad—and was never false, not even in her heart. Her world did not reach beyond the gate—and there was only one path that led outside the gate: to the church, which was like a grave. With her daughter she sang Kastalsky's psalms; she was

11. Aleksandr Dmitriyevich Kastalsky (1856–1926), historian of Russian choral music, composer, and choirmaster.—Eds.

12. A method of preparing milk by slow cooking in an oven.—Eds.

sixty-nine years old. Pre-Petrine Russia was stiffening in the house. At night the old man read the Bible from memory, having ceased to fear life. Very rarely, once every few months, in the silent hours of the night, the old man would approach his wife's bed; he would whisper:

"Maryushka, yes—kheh, hmm! . . . yes, kheh, Maryushka, this is life, Maryushka!"

He would be holding a candle; his eyes would be watering and laughing, his hands trembling.

"Maryushka, kheh, here I am, yes—this is life, Maryushka, kheh!"

Maria Klimovna would cross herself.

"Shame on you, Yakov Karpovich! . . ."

Yakov Karpovich would put out the light.

Their daughter, Katerina, had little yellow eyes that seemed unable to move from endless sleep. Around her swollen lids freckles bred all year round. Her arms and legs were like beams; her bosom was huge, like the udder of a Swiss cow.

. . . The town is a Russian Bruges and a Russian Kamakura.

Three

. . . Moscow rumbled with truckloads of actions, beginnings, achievements. Automobiles and buildings hurtled into distances and into space. Poster shouted Gorky's State Publishing House, cinemas, and congresses. Noises of streetcars, buses, and taxis affirmed the capital from one end to the other.

The train was leaving Moscow to enter a night black as soot. The feverish glows and thunders of Moscow were abating, and very quickly vanished. Fields stretched out in black silence, and silence settled down in the car. In a double compartment of a first-class car sat two men—the brothers Bezdetov, Pavel Fyodorovich and Stepan Fyodorovich, mahogany men, restorers. There was something puzzling about their appearance: they were dressed as merchants dressed in Ostrovsky's time, in frock coats and Russian-style overcoats, and their faces, although shaven, had the true Slavic cast of Yaroslavl folk; the eyes of both were empty and intelligent. The train was dragging time off into the black expanses of fields. The car smelled of tanned hide and hemp. Pavel Fyodorovich took from a suitcase a large bottle of brandy and a small silver tumbler—poured, drank—poured and silently handed the tumbler to his brother. His brother drank and returned the tumbler. Pavel Fyodorovich put the bottle and the tumbler back into the suitcase.

"Are we taking beadwork?" asked Stepan.

"Certainly," replied Pavel.

Half an hour passed in silence. The train was dragging time along, bringing it to a halt at stations. Pavel took out the bottle and tumbler, drank, poured his brother a drink, put things away.

"Do we treat the girls? Are we taking porcelain?" asked Stepan Fyodorovich.

"Certainly," replied Pavel Fyodorovich.

And after another half hour of silence the brothers each drank another tumbler.

"Are we taking so-called Russian Gobelins?" asked Stepan.

"Certainly," answered Pavel.

At midnight the train reached the Volga, and a village famed throughout Russia for its handicraft boot industry. The smell of hide grew stronger and stronger. Pavel poured a final tumbler for each of them.

"We're not taking anything after Alexander?" asked Stepan.

"Out of the question," replied Pavel Fyodorovich.

At the station were heaped mountains of Muscovite boots—not a philosophical observation but a concrete confirmation of the nature of Russian roads. The goods smelled of pitch. The darkness was as thick as the pitch it smelled of. Bootmakers ran about the station. Beyond the station everything was sinking into mud. Wasting no words, Pavel Fyodorovich hired a cart to the landing stage for forty kopecks. In the darkness coachmen were swearing like bootmakers.[13] The damp rolled in from the vast dark of the Volga. The far bank glowed with the electric lights of bootmaking. In the ship's restaurant a party of Jewish buyers was getting drunk; a young woman wearing a monkey-fur wrap kept things lively, poured the vodka; the party left after the third whistle. The steamer dimmed lights. The wind began to grope the Volga's vastnesses; dampness crept into the cabins. The waitress, an enormous woman, while serving the Bezdetovs was making up beds on the tables in the restaurant and talking about her lover, who had stolen a hundred and twenty-two rubles from her. The steamer was carrying off inside it the smells of boot leather. Deck passengers were singing bandit songs to keep out the cold. In the gray dregs of morning landscapes loomed—not from the fourteenth but from some prehistoric century—banks untouched by man, pines, firs, birches, boulders,

13. "to swear like a bootmaker" and "to swear like a coachman" are Russian proverbial expressions.—Eds.

clay, water; the fourteenth century according to European chronology was present in rafts, ferries, villages. By noon the steamer had entered the seventeenth–eighteenth century of the Russian Bruges: the town came down to the Volga with its churches, its kremlin, and the ruins left by the fire of 1920. (In that year a good half of the town—the central part—burned down. The fire broke out in the District Food Committee headquarters—the townsfolk should have been fighting the fire, but instead they began hunting *burzhuis*[14] and putting them in jail as hostages; they hunted the *burzhuis* for three days—exactly as long as the town burned—and stopped hunting them when the fire had burned itself out without any interference from firemen's hoses or population.) At the hour that the antique dealers disembarked, crazed flocks of jackdaws were flying over the town, and the town was moaning the strange moan of bells dragged down from church towers. Rain was getting ready to drip awhile over the town.

Pavel Fyodorovich—without wasting words—hired a tarantass to Skudrin Bridge, to the house of Yakov Karpovich Skudrin. The cab rattled off over ancient cobblestones overgrown with camomile; the driver told them the town's bell news, explaining that many people in the town had developed nervous disorders from the strain of waiting for the bells to fall and for the thunder of their fall, like inexperienced riflemen who screw up their eyes in anticipation of the shot. The Bezdetovs met Yakov Karpovich in the yard; the old man was chopping kindling for the stove. Maria Klimovna was pitchforking manure out of the cowshed. Yakov Karpovich did not immediately recognize the Bezdetovs, but when he did, he was pleased to see them; he broke into smiles, began groaning and snuffling; he said:

"Aah, the buyers! . . . I've thought up a theory of the proletariat for you!"

Maria Klimovna bowed to the guests from the waist, tucking her hands under her apron, and sang out hospitably:

"Dear guests, long-awaited guests—welcome!"

14. From *bourgeois*, often in the sense of "profiteer," "exploiter," etc.—Eds.

Katerina, dirt-smeared, her skirt hitched up to her thighs, dashed into the house—to change. Above the rooftops a falling bell roared, sending flocks of crows reeling; Maria Klimovna crossed herself; the bell boomed louder than a cannon; the glass in the windows facing the yard rang; it certainly was bad for the nerves.

They all entered the house. Maria Klimovna went through to her pots and pans; the samovar began to hum at her feet. Katerina came out to the guests, a young lady now, and curtsied. The old man took off his felt boots and circled his guests barefoot, cooing like a pigeon. The antique dealers washed off the grime of their travels and sat down at the table, side by side, in silence. The eyes of the guests were empty, like those of dead men. Maria Klimovna inquired after their health and set out on the table a variety of seventeenth-century food. The guests stood a bottle of brandy on the table. During the meal only Yakov Karpovich spoke; he tittered, hmm-ed, talked about places to look for antiques that he had noted for the benefit of the brothers Bezdetov.

Pavel Fyodorovich asked:

"So you mean to hold out? Not sell?"

The old man fidgeted and tittered, answered in a whine:

"That's right, that's right. I can't, no, I can't. What's mine is mine; I can still use it myself—time will tell, yes, kheh. . . . Better let me tell you my theory. . . . I'll outlive you all yet!"

After dinner the guests went to take a nap—they pulled the sqeaking doors to, lay down on the feather beds, and silently drank brandy out of antique silver. By evening the guests were thoroughly drunk. All afternoon Katerina sang psalms. Yakov Karpovich hung about the doors to the guests' room, waiting for them to come out or to speak, so that he would have an excuse to go in and talk with them. The day was carried off by the crows; all though sunset the crows were agitated, stealing the day piecemeal. Dusk was carried from door to door in water carriers' barrels. The eyes of the guests, when they came out to tea, were utterly dead, dazedly unblinking. The guests sat down at the table, silently and side by side. Yakov Karpovich squeezed himself in behind them to make sure of having their ear. The guests drank tea from saucers, lacing brandy with tea, unbuttoning their frock coats. A torchère of Catherine's time was smoking near the table. The dinner table was round, of mahogany.

Yakov Karpovich was choking on this words as he hastened to have his say:

"I've got an idea ready for you, kheh, an idea. . . . Marx's theory of the proletariat will soon have to be set aside, because the proletariat itself will have to disappear—that's my idea! . . . And that means the Revolution was all for nothing, a mistake, kheh, of history. By virtue of the fact that, yes, two or three more generations and the proletariat will disappear: first of all in the United States, in England, in Germany. Marx wrote his theory in an epoch when muscular labor was supreme. Nowadays machines are replacing muscles. That's my idea. Soon there'll be only engineers tending the machines, and the proletariat will disappear; the proletariat will all turn into engineers. That, kheh, is my idea. And an engineer is not a proletarian, because the more cultured a man is, the less need he has to show off, and he's more content to have the same standard of living as everyone else, to spread material well-being evenly, so as to liberate thought, yes—take the English, both rich and poor sleep in the same way, in jackets, and live in the same kind of houses, the three-story kind; but the way it used to be with us—compare a merchant and a peasant: the merchant decked himself out like a priest and lived in a palace. But I can go around barefoot and be none the worse for it. You'll say, kheh, yes, there'll still be exploitation. But how can there be? The peasant, who can be exploited because he's like a beast—you won't let him near a machine: he'd wreck it, and it costs millions. A machine is too costly to try to save a few kopecks on the man who operates it; the man must know the machine; the machine needs a man with knowledge—and there'll be one man where there were a hundred before. Such a man will be pampered. That'll be the end of the proletariat! . . ."

The guests drank their tea and listened with unblinking eyes. Yakov Karpovich grunted, hawked, and hurried on—but he did not have time to develop his idea to the full: Ivan Karpovich, his brother, arrived—

the *okhlomon*, who had changed his name from Skudrin to Ozhogov. Neatly dressed in hopeless tatters, his hair neatly cut, galoshes on his bare feet, he bowed respectfully to all and sat down apart from the rest, in silence. Nobody responded to his bow. His face was the face of a madman. Yakov Karpovich fidgeted and showed signs of unease.

Maria Klimovna said sorrowfully:

"Why did you have to come, brother dear?"

The *okhlomon* replied:

"To have a look at the different forms of the Counterrevolution, sister dear."

"What Counterrevolution could there be here, brother dear?"

"As far as you're concerned, sister dear, you are the everyday Counterrevolution," *okhlomon* Ozhogov began in a soft, mad voice. "But I have made you weep—that means that you have the seeds of communism in you. But Brother Yakov hasn't wept once, and I very much regret that I didn't put him up against the wall and shoot him when things were going my way."

Maria Klimovna sighed, shook her head, said:

"And how's your boy?"

"My boy," answered the *okhlomon* proudly, "my son is finishing university, and he doesn't forget me, he visits my domain on vacations, warms himself by the stove; I make up revolutionary verses for him."

"And your wife?"

"I don't see her. She manages the Women's Division. Do you know how many managers we have for every two production workers?"

"No."

"Seven. Too many cooks spoil the broth. As for your guests, they are the historical Counterrevolution."

The guests drank their tea, pewter-eyed. Yakov Karpovich was flooding with violet rage; he began to look like a beetroot. He advanced on his brother, tittered with politeness, began to grope about with his hands, rubbed them together energetically as if he were out in a frost.

"You know what, brother dear," began Yakov Karpovich in a

hoarse whisper, very politely, "get to the Devil's mother out of here. I ask you in all earnestness! . . ."

"Beg pardon, Brother Yakov, I didn't come to see you, I came to take a look at the historical Counterrevolution, and to have a few words with it," Ivan replied.

"And I'm asking you—go to the Devil's mother!"

"I'm not going to the Devil's mother!"

Pavel Fyodorovich Bezdetov slowly turned the pewter of his left eye to the brother and said:

"We can't be talking to fools; if you don't leave, I'll have Stepan throw you out on your neck."

Stepan returned his brother's glance and shifted in his chair. Maria Klimovna pressed her palms to her cheeks and sighed. The *okhlomon* sat in silence. Stepan Fyodorovich got up slowly from the table and moved toward the *okhlomon*. The *okhlomon* timorously rose, crouching, and started backing toward the door. Maria Klimovna sighed again. Yakov Karpovich tittered. Stepan stopped in the middle of the room—the *okhlomon* stopped by the door, grimacing. Stepan took a step toward the *okhlomon*—the *okhlomon* disappeared behind the door. From behind the door he entreated:

"In that case, give me a ruble twenty-five kopecks for vodka."

Stepan glanced at Pavel; Pavel said:

"Let him have enough for half a bottle."

The *okhlomon* went away. Maria Klimovna saw him to the gate, pushed a piece of pie into his hand. The night beyond the gate was black and motionless. The *okhlomon* Ozhogov was walking toward the Volga through dark alleys, past monasteries, across vacant lots, following paths known to him alone. The night was very black; Ivan was talking to himself, mumbling unintelligibly. He went down to the combine brickyard, where he squeezed through a hole in the fence and started across the clay pits. A kiln was burning among the pits. Ivan crawled down into the kiln pit—there it was very warm and very stuffy; through the cracks of the kiln door came a red glow. Here on the ground several derelicts lay about, overgrown with matted hair—

Ivan Ozhogov's Communists, men who had a tacit agreement with the combine: they kept the brickyard kiln going for nothing—the kiln whose fire baked the bricks—and they lived by the kiln for nothing, these people who had brought time to a standstill in the era of war communism, when they elected Ivan Ozhogov their chairman. On some straw by a board that served as a table lay three derelicts, taking a rest. Ozhogov squatted down by them, shivered for a while warming up, as people shiver in fever, put down the money and the piece of pie on the table.

"They didn't weep?" asked one of the derelicts.

"No, they didn't weep," replied Ozhogov.

For a while no one spoke.

"It's your turn to go, Comrade Ognyov,"[15] said Ozhogov.

Two more men in beggars' rags, with matted beards and whiskers, crawled into the clay of the underground cave, lay down beside the others, put money and bread on the board. A man of about forty, an old man already, who had been lying in the darkest warmth—Ognyov—crawled over to the board, counted the money, and started to climb out of the cave. The rest remained sitting or lying in silence—except that one of the newcomers announced that in the morning they would have to start loading a barge with firewood. Ognyov soon came back with bottles of vodka. Then the *okhlomons* moved closer to the board, brought out their mugs, and sat down in a circle. Comrade Ognyov poured a round of vodka; they clinked mugs, emptied them in silence.

"Now I shall speak," said Ozhogov. "Once there were some brothers whose name was Wright; they made up their minds to fly up into the sky, and they perished when they crashed to earth, having fallen out of the sky. They perished, but people have not abandoned their work; they haven't let go of the sky—and people are flying, comrades, they are flying over the earth like birds, like eagles! Comrade Lenin perished like the brothers Wright—I was the first chairman of the

15. The names of all the outcast Communists derive from words related to fire.—Eds.

Executive Committee in our town. In nineteen twenty-one everything came to an end. We are the only real Communists in the whole town—and look what things have come to: the only place left for us is this cave. I was the first Communist here, and I'll remain a Communist as long as I live. Our ideas will not perish. And what ideas they were! Now nobody remembers that except us, comrades. We are like the brothers Wright! . . ."

Comrade Ognyov poured a second round of vodka. And Ognyov interrupted Ozhogov:

"Now I'll have my say, Comrade Chairman! What deeds were done! How people fought! I was in command of a partisan detachment. We were pushing through the forest: a day, a night, and then another day, and another night. And suddenly at daybreak we hear—machine guns. . . ."

Ognyov was interrupted by Pozharov; he asked Ognyov:

"And how do you slash? How do you hold your thumb when you're slashing, bent or straight? Show us!"

"On the blade. Straight," answered Ognyov.

"Everybody holds it on the blade. You show us. Here's a knife, show us!"

Ognyov took the cobbler's knife that the *okhlomons* used to cut bread and demonstrated how he placed his thumb on the blade.

"You do it all wrong!" shouted Pozharov. "That's not the way I hold the saber when I'm slashing—I slice with it like with a razor. Give it here; I'll show you! You do it all wrong!"

"Comrades!" Ozhogov said quietly, and his face was contorted by raging pain. "Today we must talk about ideas, great ideas, not about slashing!"

Ozhogov was interrupted by a fourth man, who shouted:

"Comrade Ognyov, you were in the Third Division, and I was in the Second; do you remember how your outfit let them get across the river near the village of Shinki? . . ."

"We let them get across? No, it was you that let them get across, not us! . . ."

"Comrades!" again Ozhogov spoke in a soft, mad voice. "It's ideas we must talk about! . . ."

At midnight the men in the cave were asleep by the kiln—these derelicts who had stumbled upon the right to live in the kiln pit of a brickyard. They slept in a heap, one resting his head on another's knees, their rags pulled over them. The last to go to sleep was their chairman, Ivan Ozhogov: for a long time he lay near the mouth of the kiln, a sheet of paper before him. He lay on his belly with the paper spread on the ground. He wet the lead of his pencil with his tongue; he wanted to write a poem. "We have raised a worldwide. . . ," he wrote and crossed out, "We have set ablaze a worldwide. . . ," he wrote and crossed out. "You who warm your thieving hands. . . ," he wrote and crossed out. "You who are lackeys, or idiots perchance. . . ," he wrote and crossed out. Words would not come to him. He fell asleep with his head on the scratched-up sheet of paper. Here slept Communists who had been called to duty by war communism and discharged by the year nineteen hundred and twenty-one, men of arrested ideas, madmen and drunkards, men who, living together in a cave and working together unloading barges, sawing firewood, had created a strict fraternity, a strict communism, having nothing of their own, neither money nor possessions nor wives: their wives had left them, had left their dreams, their madness, their alcohol. In the cave it was very close, very warm, very bare.

Midnight was passing over the town, inert and black as the history of these parts.

At midnight Stepan Fyodorovich, the younger of the restorers, stopped Katerina on the stairs to the attic, touched her shoulders, solid as a horse's, felt them with a drunken hand, and said quietly:

"Pass the word on to your. . . sisters. . . . We'll do it again. Find a place, tell them. . . ."

Katerina stood submissively and submissively whispered:

"All right, I'll tell them."

Below at that very moment Yakov Karpovich was expounding his theories of civilization for the benefit of Pavel Fyodorovich. On a round table in the parlor stood a frigate of bronze and glass intended to hold alcohol, which, poured from the little tap into tumblers and from tumblers down men's throats, would enable them to sail in this frigate, over alcohol, from fancy to fancy. The frigate was an eighteenth-century piece. The frigate was filled with brandy. Pavel Fyodorovich sat in silence. Yakov Karpovich fussed around Pavel Fyodorovich, hopping up and down like a lovesick pigeon, supporting his hernia through his fly.

"Yes, kheh," he said. "What do you think, then, keeps the world moving, what moves civilization, science, steamships? Well, what?"

"Well, what?" Pavel Fyodorovich repeated the question.

"What do you think it is? Labor? Knowledge? Hunger? Love? No! Civilization is moved—by memory! Just picture to yourself—tomorrow morning everybody loses his memory—instinct, reason remain, but memory is gone. I wake up in bed—and I fall out of bed, because it's through memory that I know about space, and once memory's gone, I don't know about it. My pants are lying on the chair; I'm cold, but I don't know what to do with the pants. I don't know how to walk—on my hands or on all fours, I don't remember yesterday, and so that means I'm not afraid of death, for I know nothing about it. The engineer forgets all his higher mathematics, all streetcars and locomotives have come to a standstill. Priests can't find their way to church, and what's more, they don't remember anything about Jesus Christ. Yes, kheh! . . . I still have my instincts—though you might say they're a kind of memory too; but let's suppose I have them: I don't know what I should eat, the chair or the bread left on it from the night before, and when I see a woman, I might take my daughter for my wife."

The northeaster that filled the sails of the alcohol frigate on the table clarified Yakov Karpovich's thoughts: in company with the frigate the eighteenth century had left behind among the parlor's mahogany a Russian Voltaire. Beyond the windows of the eighteenth century moved a Soviet provincial night.

Another hour and the Skudrin house was asleep. And then in the sour silence of the bedroom Yakov Karpovich's slippers flip-flapped toward Maria Klimovna's bed. Maria Klimovna, an ancient lady, was sleeping. The candle trembled in Yakov Karpovich's hand. Yakov

Karpovich tittered. Yakov Karpovich touched Maria Klimovna's parchment shoulder; his eyes watered with pleasure. He whispered:

"Maryushka, Maryushka, this is life, this is life, Maryushka."

The eighteenth century sank into Voltairean darkness.

In the morning bells were dying over the city, howling as they shattered. The brothers Bezdetov woke up early, but Maria Klimovna had gotten up even earlier, and with morning tea there were hot mushroom and onion piroshki. Yakov Karpovich slept. Katerina was half-asleep. Tea was drunk in silence. Day came gray and slow. After tea the brothers Bezdetov went about their business. On a piece of paper Pavel Fyodorovich had drawn up a list of houses and families they were to visit. The streets lay in the silence of provincial cobblestones, stone walls, tall weeds under the walls, elders among ruins left by the fire, churches, bell towers—they sank even deeper into silence when the bells began to whine and screamed with silence when the bells bellowed in their fall.

The Bezdetovs would enter a house silently, side by side, and look around them with vacant eyes.

1. On Staraya Rostovskaya Street stood a lopsided house. In this house the widow Myshkina was ending her days; the widow was an old woman of seventy. The house stood with one corner to the street, because it had been built before the street came into existence. The house had been built not of sawed but of hewed wood, because it was put up before Russian carpenters used saws and when the ax was their only tool—before Peter's time, that is. In those days the house might have been a boyar's. The house preserved a tiled stove and stove ledge dating back to that time; the tiles were decorated with sheep and boyars and were ochered and glazed.

The Bezdetovs walked in through the gate without knocking. The old woman Myshkina was sitting on the *zavalinka*[16] in front of a pig

16. An earthen ledge—part of the foundation—surrounding the small Russian house. In village life it has the function of the front stoop.—Eds.

trough; a pig was eating scaled nettles. The Bezdetovs bowed to the old woman and sat down beside her without a word. The old woman responded to the greeting, flustered, pleased, frightened. She was wearing torn felt boots, a cotton skirt, and a bright Persian shawl.

"Well, are you selling?" asked Pavel Bezdetov.

The old woman hid her hands under the shawl, lowered her eyes to the pig. Pavel Fyodorovich and Stepan Fyodorovich exchanged a look, and Stepan winked—she'll sell. With her bony hand, lilac-nailed, the old woman wiped the corners of her mouth, and her hand trembled.

"I just don't know what's to be done," said the old woman, and glanced guiltily at the brothers. "Our grandfathers lived here and left it to us, and their fathers before them, and further back than anyone can remember. . . . And when my lodger died—God rest his soul—things just got too much for me; he did pay me three rubles a month for the room, and bought kerosene besides—I didn't lack for anything. . . . And you know, my father and mother both died on that stove ledge. . . . What's to be done? . . . God rest his soul, the lodger was a quiet one; he paid three rubles and died in my arms. . . . I've thought and thought, how many nights I haven't slept—you've upset my peace of mind."

Pavel Fyodorovich spoke:

"There are a hundred and twenty tiles on the stove and on the stove ledge. Twenty-five kopecks a tile, as we said before. And that makes thirty rubles for you all at once. That'll last you the rest of your life. We'll send the stove setter; he'll take them out and put bricks in their place and give them a coat of whitewash. And all at our expense."

"I'm not saying anything about the price," said the old woman. "It's a rich price you're offering. Nobody around here would offer such a price. . . . And who needs them but me anyway? If only it wasn't for my parents. . . . I'm all alone. . . ."

The old woman was lost in her thoughts. She thought for a long time—or was she thinking at all? Her eyes became unseeing, sank deep into their sockets. The pig had finished its nettles and was poking its snout at one of the old woman's felt boots. The brothers Bezdetov were looking at the old woman, businesslike and stern. Again the old woman wiped the corners of her lips with a trembling hand. Then she smiled guiltily, glanced guiltily around her—at the leaning fences of the yard and the vegetable garden—lowered her eyes guiltily before the Bezdetovs.

"So be it then, and God's blessing on you!" said the old woman, and held out her hand to Pavel Fyodorovich—awkwardly and shyly, but as time-honored trading custom required—passing the tiles from hand to hand.

2. In the cathedral square in the semibasement of what had been their own house lived a family of landed gentry—the Tuchkovs. Their former estate had been turned into a dairy. In this basement lived two adults and six children; the adults were two women—old Tuchkova and her daughter-in-law, whose husband, a former officer, had shot himself in 1925 as death from tuberculosis drew near. The old colonel had been killed in 1915 in the Carpathians. Four of the children were Olga Pavlovna's, as the daughter-in-law was called; the other two were the children of the younger Tuchkov, who had been shot for counter-revolutionary activities. Olga Pavlovna was the breadwinner; in the evenings she played the piano in the cinema. At thirty she looked like an old woman.

The basement was unlocked, as are all poverty-stricken dwellings, when the brothers Bezdetov arrived. They were met by Olga Pavlovna. She nodded several times, inviting them to come in; she ran ahead of them into what was known as the dining room to cover the bed so that the strangers would not see that there was no bed linen under the blanket. Olga Pavlovna glanced at herself in the triple mirror on a mahogany dressing table in the Empire style of Alexander's time. The brothers were businesslike and brisk. Stepan turned chairs upside down, pushed the sofa away from the wall, lifted the mattress from the bed, pulled out the drawers of the commode—examining mahogany. Pavel went through the miniatures, beadwork, and porcelain. The young old woman, Olga Pavlovna, still had a girl's lightness of movement and the ability to be embarrassed. The restorers wreaked silent havoc on the rooms, dragging dirt and poverty out of every corner. The six children clung to the mother's skirts, curious about these strange goings on; the two eldest were ready to help with the work of devastation. The mother was embarrassed for the children; the younger ones were sniveling as they held on to her skirt, distracting their mother from embarrassment. Stepan set aside three chairs and an armchair, and he said:

"These are odd pieces, not a set."

"What did you say?" Olga Pavlovna asked, and turning to the children, cried helplessly, "Children, please leave the room! This is no place for you, I beg you to. . . "

"These are odd pieces, not a set," said Stepan Fyodorovich. "There are three chairs, but only one armchair. The pieces are good, I don't deny it, but they'll need a lot of repairing. You see yourself—you live in a damp place. You'll have to get a complete set together."

The children quieted down as soon as the restorer began to speak.

"Yes," said Olga Pavlovna, and blushed, "we did have it all—but I doubt if it could be got together now. Some of it remained on the estate when we left, some was carried off by peasants, some was broken by the children, and, then again, there's the damp—I carried to the barn. . . ."

"I suppose they gave you twenty-four hours to get out?" asked Stepan Fyodorovich.

"Yes, we left at night, without waiting for an order. We foresaw. . . ."

Pavel Fyodorovich joined in the conversation; he asked Olga Pavlovna:

"You understand French and English?"

"Oh, yes," answered Olga Pavlovna, "I speak. . . ."

"These miniatures wouldn't be—Boucher and Cosway?"

"Oh, yes! Those miniatures. . . ."

Pavel Fyodorovich said, glancing at his brother:

"We can give you twenty-five for each."

Stepan Fyodorovich interrupted his brother sternly:

"If you get together even half a set, I'll buy everything. If, as you say, the peasants have some of it, you could go to them."

"Oh, yes!" replied Olga Pavlovna. "If half a set. . . It's thirteen versts to our village—not much more than an easy walk. . . . Half a set can be got together. I'll go to the village today and give you an answer tomorrow. But if some of the pieces are broken. . . ."

"That doesn't matter, we'll reduce the price. And don't bother with just an answer, bring the things direct, so that we can receive everything from you tomorrow and have it packed. Sofas—fifteen rubles; armchairs—seven and a half; chairs—five each. We'll take care of the packing."

"Oh, yes, I'll go today; it's only thirteen versts[17] to our village—not much more than an easy walk. . . . I'll go right away."

The oldest boy said:

"Then you'll buy me shoes, Maman?"

Beyond the windows was a gray day; beyond the town lay the country roads of Russia.

3. Barin Vyacheslav Pavlovich Karazin was lying on the sofa in the dining room, with a squirrel-skin jacket, worn almost bald, thrown over him. His dining room, like the study-bedroom that he shared with his wife, had the appearance of a museum squeezed into the lodgings of a mail-coach driver. The brothers Bezdetov halted at the threshold and bowed. Barin Karazin subjected them to a lengthy scrutiny, barked:

"Out, s-swindlers! Out of here!"

The brothers did not move.

Blood rushed to Barin Karazin's face, and he barked again:

"Out of my sight, you scoundrels!"

The shouts brought his wife into the room. The brothers Bezdetov bowed to Karazina and retreated behind the door.

17. One verst equals about 0.7 mile.—Eds.

"Nadine, I can't stand the sight of those villains," said Barin Karazin to his wife.

"Very well, Vyacheslav, you go to the study; I'll talk to them. Oh, Vyacheslav, you know how things are!" replied Barynya[18] Karazina.

"They have disturbed my rest. Very well, I'll go to the study. Only please, no familiarities with those serfs."

Barin Karazin left the room, trailing his jacket behind him; the brothers Bezdetov entered the room in his wake and again bowed respectfully.

"Show us your Russian Gobelins, and also tell us the price of the small bureau," said Pavel Fyodorovich.

"Won't you sit down, gentlemen," said Barynya Karazina.

The door of the study flew open; the Barin's head thrust itself out. Barin Karazin shouted, looking to one side, at the windows, lest his eyes should accidentally fall on the brothers Bezdetov:

"Nadine, don't allow them to sit down! What can they understand of the beauty of art! Don't allow them to choose! Sell them those things which we find necessary to sell. Sell them the porcelain, the porcelain clock, and the bronze! . . ."

"We can go, if you want," said Pavel Fyodorovich.

"Oh, just a moment, gentlemen; let Vyacheslav Pavlovich calm down; he's very sick," said Barynya Karazina, and sat down helplessly at the table. "We do have to sell a few things. Oh, gentlemen! . . . Vyacheslav Pavlovich, I beg of you, shut the door; don't listen to us—go for a walk. . . ."

* * *

Toward evening, after the jackdaws had torn the day to pieces and the bells had ceased howling, the brothers Bezdetov returned home and had their dinner. After dinner Yakov Karpovich Skudrin got ready to sally forth. In his pockets were money and a list provided by the Bezdetovs. The old man put on a wide-brimmed felt hat and a short sheep-

18. Feminine equivalent of Barin.—Eds.

skin coat; on his feet were the remains of a pair of boots. He was on his way to the carpenter's, to the drayman's for ropes and matting—to make arrangements to have the purchases packed and taken to the wharf for shipment to Moscow. The old man was in his element; as he left he said:

"What we should do is leave the carrying and packing to the *okhlomons*; they're as honest as they come, even if they are idiots. But it can't be done. Dear Brother Ivan, their number-one revolutionary, wouldn't allow it—he wouldn't let them work for the Counterrevolution, hee-hee! . . ."

The brothers Bezdetov settled down in the parlor to rest. And the earth settled down for the night. All evening people kept knocking stealthily at Maria Klimovna's window; Katerina went out to them, and people, fawning like beggars, offered—"They say you have guests staying with you who buy all sorts of old things"—ancient rubles and kopecks, broken lamps, old samovars, books, candlesticks; these people did not understand the art of the old days—they were poverty-stricken in every respect. Katerina did not let them into the guests' presence with their copper lamps, suggesting that they leave the things until the morning, when the guests, having rested, would take a look. The evening was dark. At sunset a wind rose, bringing clouds; a fine rain, immutably autumnal, began to fall; through the forest, through the mud of country roads (the same mud in which Akim Skudrin was soon to get stuck), walked Olga Pavlovna, a woman with an old woman's face and movements as light as a young girl's. The forest moaned in the wind, and was terrifying. This woman, with a young girl's terror of the forest, was walking to her village to buy from the peasants armchairs for which peasants could have no use.

About eight o'clock in the evening Katerina got her mother's leave to go first to choir practice and then to a friend's; she put on her best clothes and left. Half an hour later Stepan and Pavel, the two Fyodoroviches, went out into the rain. Katerina was waiting for them on the other side of the bridge. Stepan Fyodorovich took Katerina's arm. In pitch darkness they set off along a path that followed the edge of a ravine, toward the outskirts of the town. That was where the old Skudrin aunts lived. Katerina and the Bezdetovs sneaked like thieves into the yard and from there, like thieves, into the garden. At the far end of the garden stood a dark bathhouse.

Katerina knocked, and the door half opened. There was a light inside the bathhouse; three girls were waiting for the guests. The girls had blanketed the windows and moved a table to the steps leading to the steam shelf. The girls were wearing their Sunday best; they greeted the guests solemnly.

The brothers Bezdetov took out from their pockets bottles of brandy and port that they had brought from Moscow.

The girls set out on the table—on paper—boiled sausage, sprats, candy, tomatoes, and apples. The oldest of the girls—Klavdia—brought out a bottle of vodka from behind the stove. They all talked in whispers. The brothers Bezdetov sat down side by side on the steps to the steam shelf. On the shelf a tin lamp burned.

In an hour the girls were drunk—but still they talked in whispers. The faces of drunken people, and women in particular—when they are very drunk—become set in expressions that are the creation of alcohol. Klavdia was sitting at the table, propping her head with a fist, like a man, her teeth bared, her lips frozen in an expression of contempt; from time to time her head would slip off her hand, and then she would pull at her cropped hair, without feeling any pain; she was smoking one cigarette after another and drinking brandy; her face glowed pink, and she was hideously beautiful. She was saying with disgust:

"Drunk, am I? Yes, I am. So what? Tomorrow I'll go to school again and teach—and what do I know? What is it I teach? And at six I'll go to a parents' meeting I called. Here's my notebook, everything's written down here. . . . I'm drinking—oh, what the hell!—and here I am drunk. And what are you? What have you to do with me? You buy mahogany? Antiques? You want to buy us, too, with your wine? You think I don't know what life is? You're wrong, I do—I'm going to have a baby soon, but who the father is I don't know. . . . So what—so what?"

Klavdia's teeth were bared and her eyes staring. Pavel was after

Zina, the youngest, a short-legged, giggly girl with a head of blond curls; she was sitting on a block of wood, a little apart from the rest, legs spread wide, hands on hips. Pavel Fyodorovich was saying:

"I bet you won't take your blouse off, Zina, I bet you won't undo your brassiere, you wouldn't dare!"

Zina clapped her hand over her mouth so as not to burst out laughing, burst out laughing, and said:

"Oh, yes, I will!"

"No, you won't! You wouldn't dare!"

Klavdia said contemptuously:

"She will. Zinka, show them your breasts! Let them look. Want to see mine? You think I'm a drunk? No, the last time I was drunk was when you were here before. And I came today to get blind drunk—blind drunk, you understand? Blind drunk! . . . What the hell! . . . Zinka, show them your breasts! Don't you show them to your Kolya? . . . Want to see mine?"

Klavdia yanked at the collar of her blouse. The girls rushed up to her. Katerina said sensibly:

"You mustn't tear your clothes, Klava, or they'll know at home."

Zina was barely able to stand; she embraced Klavdia, grasping her hands. Klavdia kissed Zina.

"I mustn't?" she asked. "Well, all right, I won't. . . . But you show them. . . . Let them look; we're not ashamed, we don't hold to old-fashioned ideas! . . . You buy mahogany?"

"All right, I'll show them," Zina said meekly, and set about unbuttoning her blouse.

The fourth girl went outside; she felt sick. Of course the Bezdetovs felt themselves to be buyers; buying was all they knew.

Outside the bathhouse it was raining; the trees rustled in the wind. At that hour Olga Pavlovna had already reached her village and, happy and grateful to Grandpa Nazar for selling her some chairs and an armchair, was falling asleep on a bed of straw on the floor of Nazar's hut. At that hour Barin Karazin was writhing in a fit of senile hysteria. At that hour the *okhlomons* in their kiln pit were affirming with the eyes and voices of madmen the year nineteen hundred and nineteen, when everything was shared equally—both bread and labor—when nothing lay behind them and ideas lay before them and there was no money, because it was not needed. And in another hour the bathhouse was empty. The drunken women and the brothers Bezdetov had all gone home; at home the drunken girls were creeping quietly to their beds. A notebook had been left lying on the floor in the bathhouse. In the notebook was written, "Call parents' meeting at six o'clock on the seventh." "At meeting of Local Committee suggest everyone subscribe to government industrialization loan to amount of month's salary." "Suggest Aleksandr Alekseyevich reread *ABC of Communism.*"

In the moring the bells were whining again, and in the morning cartloads of mahogany—Catherines, Pauls, Alexanders—were being dragged toward the wharf under Yakov Karpovich's supervision. The brothers Bezdetov slept until noon. By that hour a crowd waiting to know the fate of their old rubles, lamps, and candlesticks had collected in the kitchen.

The town is a Russian Bruges.

Four

. . . And it was about this time, two days after the brothers Bezdetov, that the engineer Akim Skudrin, the youngest son of Yakov Karpovich, arrived in the town. The son did not go to his father's house, staying with his aunts Kapitolina and Rimma. The engineer Akim was not in town on business; he had a week free.

. . . Kapitolina Karpovna goes to the window. The provinces. A crumbling red brick wall abuts on one corner an ochered house with a belvedere, on the other a church; beyond—the square, the town scales, another church. It is raining. A pig is sniffing at a puddle. A water cart comes around the corner. Klavdia goes out the gate; she is wearing greased boots, a black coat reaching to the tops of the boots, a blue kerchief on her head; she lowers her head, crosses the street, walks along the crumbling wall, turns the corner into the square. Kapitolina Karpovna's eyes are bright; she watches Klavdia for a long time. On the other side of the partition Rimma Karpovna is feeding her grandchild, the daughter of her older girl, Varvara. The room is very bare, very clean, very neat—nothing has changed for decades—as the room of an old maid, an elderly virgin, should be: a narrow bed, a small worktable, a sewing machine, a dressmaker's dummy, curtains. Kapitolina Karpovna goes to the dining room.

"Let me feed the baby, Rimmochka. I saw Klavdia leave. Did Varya leave too?"

These two old women, the two Karpovnas, Kapitolina and Rimma, were seamstresses and dressmakers, hereditary, honored members of the lower middle class of ancient standing. Their lives were as simple as the lifelines on the palms of their left hands. The sisters were born within a year of each other; Kapitolina was the elder. And Kapitolina's life was filled with the dignity of middleclass morality. Her whole life had been laid open before the town's eyes and lived in full compliance with the town's rules. She was a respected member of the middle class.

And not only the whole town but she herself knew that all her Saturday evenings were spent in church, that all her days were bent over the hemstitching and openwork of blouses and shifts—thousands of shifts—that not once had any man outside the family kissed her; and only she knew the thoughts, the pain of life's soured wine, that wither the heart; and yet her life had had its budding, its bloom, its Indian summer; and not once in her life had she been loved, had she known secret sins. She remained a model of obedience to the town's code, a virgin, an old woman who had soured her life with chastity, God, tradition. But the life of Rimma Karpovna, also a seamstress, had taken a different course. It had happened twenty-eight years before; it had gone on for three years—three years of shame, shame which was to remain with her throughout her life. It had happened at a time when Rimma's years were sinking beyond thirty—years which had taken away her youth and sown hopelessness. In the town lived a treasury official, an amateur actor, handsome, and a swine. He was married; he had children; he was a drunkard. Rimma fell in love with him, and Rimma could not resist her love. Everything about it was shameful. In this love there was everything that shames a woman in the eyes of small-town morality, and everything went wrong. All around were woods where the secret could have been kept—she gave herself to this man one night in one of the town's little parks; she was ashamed to take home her torn, blood-stained (sacred blood, in truth) drawers—she stuck them in the bushes, and the next morning they were pulled out by some boys for all to see; and not once in all the three years of her shame did she meet her lover under a roof, meeting him in the woods and in the streets, in the ruins of houses, in deserted barges, even in fall and winter. Her brother, Yakov Karpovich, disowned her and drove her out of the house—even Kapitolina turned against her sister. In the streets people pointed fingers at her and snubbed her. The treasury actor's lawful wife went to give Rimma a beating and egged on the local roughs to beat her as well; and the town and its code were on the side of the lawful wife. Rimma gave birth to a daughter, Varvara, a proof of her shame and an embodiment of it. Rimma gave birth to a second girl, Klavdia, and Klavdia was another proof of her shame. The treasury amateur left town. Rimma remained alone with two children, in desperate poverty and shame, a woman then well past thirty. And since that time almost thirty more years have passed. Varvara, the elder daughter, is married, happily married, and already has two children. Rimma Karpovna has two grandchildren. Varvara's husband is in government service. So is Varvara. Rimma Karpovna runs a large household; she is the founder of a family. And Rimma Karpovna—a kindly old woman—is happy in her life. Old age has made her shorter, happiness has made her plump. How kind and how full of life are the eyes of this plump little old woman. And only one thing concerns Kapitolina Karpovna now: the lives of Rimma, Varvara, Klavdia, the grandchildren; her chastity, her town-wide reputation for uprightness, have turned out to be for nothing. Kapitolina Karpovna has no life of her own.

Kapitolina Karpovna is saying:

"Let me feed the baby, Rimmochka. I saw Klava leave. Did Varya leave too?"

Outside—the provinces, fall, rain. And then in the hall the door pulley squeaks, a man's boots stamp the floor to shake off wet and mud—and into the room walks a man, looking around helplessly in the way that all nearsighted people do when they take off their glasses. It is Akim Yakovlevich Skudrin, the engineer, the image of his father fifty years before. He has come—no one knows why.

"My respects to you, dear aunts!" says Akim, and kisses Aunt Rimma first.

The provinces, rain, fall, the traditional samovar.

Engineer Akim was not in town on business. His aunts welcomed him with the samovar, hurriedly prepared flat cakes and that warm hospitality found in the Russian provinces. Akim did not go to see his father or his superiors. Dying bells whined over the town; the streets were sound under their covering of camomile. Akim stayed a day and a night and left, having established that he had no use for his birthplace; the town did not accept him. The day passed with his aunts, in the roamings of memory through time, in the futility of memory, in the desperate poverty of his aunts, of their concerns, their thoughts, their longings. Things in the house were as they had been twenty, twenty-five years before, and the dressmaker's dummy, which had been terrifying in his childhood, no longer frightened. At dusk Klavdia came home from school. They sat down together on the sofa, cousins, ten years between them.

"How's life?" asked Akim.

They talked about this and that, and then Klavdia spoke of what was most important to her; she spoke very simply. She was very beautiful and very calm. Dusk lingered and deepened.

"I want to ask your advice," said Klavdia. "I'm going to have a baby. I don't know what I ought to do; I don't know who the father is."

"What do you mean, you don't know who the father is?"

"I'm twenty-four," said Klavdia. "Last spring I decided it was time I became a woman, and so I became one."

"But you have someone you love?"

"No, I don't. There were several. I was curious. I did it out of curiosity, and after all—it was time; I'm twenty-four."

Akim was at a loss what else to ask.

"I was concerned not with love for someone else but with myself and my own emotions. I chose men, different kinds of men, so as to experience everything. I didn't want to get pregnant; sex is joy, and I didn't think about a baby. But I did get pregnant, and I've decided not to have an abortion."

"And you don't know who the man is?"

"I can't say for sure. But it's of no importance to me. I'm the mother. I'll manage, and the state will help me; as for morality,. . . I don't know what morality is, I've been taught not to know. Or perhaps I have my own morality. I answer only for myself and of myself. Why is it immoral to give myself to a man? I do what I want to do, and I'm under no obligation to anyone. The man? I don't want to tie him in any way; men are fine, but only when I need them and when they're not burdened with responsibility. I don't need a man in bedroom slippers, and

I don't need a man to give birth. People will help me—I believe in people. People like you, if you have pride and aren't a burden to them. And the state will help. I slept with men I liked, because I wanted to. I'll have a son or a daughter. I'm not sleeping with anyone now; I don't need it. Yesterday I got drunk, for the last time. I'm telling you this as it comes into my head. I'm disgusted with myself for getting drunk yesterday. But perhaps the child will need a father. You left your father, and I was born without a father and never heard anything except filth about him; when I was a child, this hurt me, and I used to get angry with my mother. Still, I've decided not to have an abortion; the child fills my being. It's an even greater joy than. . . I'm young and strong."

Akim was unable to collect his thoughts. On the floor in front of him lay rag runners, the pathways of poverty and meanness of spirit. Klavdia was calm, beautiful, strong—very healthy and very beautiful. It was drizzling outside the windows. The Communist Akim wanted to hear that a new way of life was coming; the old way of life was rooted in the ages. But Klavdia's morality was both new and strange to him; but could it be right, if Klavdia saw it that way?

Akim said:

"Have the child."

Klavdia cuddled up to him, laid her head on his shoulder, tucked her feet under her, became soft and helpless.

"I'm very physical," she said. "I like to eat, I like to wash, I like to do exercises, I like it when Sharik, our dog, licks my hands and feet. I enjoy scratching my knees until the blood comes. . . . But life—it's big, it's all around me, I can't make any sense of it, I can't make any sense of the Revolution—but I believe in them, in life, in the sun, in the Revolution, and I'm at peace with myself. I understand only what touches me. As for the rest, I'm not even interested."

A tomcat walked along the runner to the sofa and made his customary leap onto Klavdia's lap. Outside the windows it had grown dark. On the other side of the partition a lamp was lit and the sewing machine began to stitch. Peace had entered the darkness.

In the evening Akim went to see his Uncle Ivan, who had changed his name from Skudrin to Ozhogov. The *okhlomon* Ozhogov came out of the kiln to greet his nephew. The earth around brickyards is dug up and the roofs of brick sheds are long and low—and because of this brickyards always look like places of ruin and mystery. The *okhlomon* was drunk. It was impossible to talk with him, but he was very pleased, very happy, that his nephew had come to see him. The *okhlomon* could hardly stand up, and trembled like a dog.

The *okhlomon* led his nephew into the brick shed.

"You've come, you've come," he whispered, pressing his trembling hands to his trembling chest.

He turned a wheelbarrow upside down and made his nephew sit on it.

"Have they thrown you out?" he asked eagerly.

"Out of where?" asked Akim.

"Out of the Party," said Ivan Karpovich.

"No."

"No? They haven't thrown you out?" Ivan asked again, and sadness came into his voice—but he finished cheerfully, "Well, if they don't throw you out now, they will later; they'll throw out all the Leninists and Trotskyites!"

Here Ivan Karpovich fell into delirium; in his delirium he talked about his commune, how he had been the first chairman of the Executive Committee—what years they had been and how they were lost, those stormy years; how he had been driven out of the Revolution, and now went among the people to make them weep, and remember, and love—and again he talked about his commune, about the equality and brotherhood there; he insisted that communism was, above all, love, the intense concern of man for man, friendship, brotherhood, shared labor; communism was the renunciation of material things, and what mattered most in true communism was love, respect for human beings, and—people. The neat little old man trembled in the wind, running his bony fingers, which were also trembling, over the lapels of his jacket. The brickyard spoke of ruin. Akim Skudrin, the engineer, was flesh of Ivan Ozhogov's flesh. . . . Paupers, beggars, soothsayers, mendicant chanters, lazars, wanderers from holy place to holy place, cripples, blind psalm singers, prophets, fools in Christ—all these are the double-ring sugar cakes of the everyday life of Holy Russia, now sunk into eternity—paupers on the face of Holy Russia, fools of Holy Russia for Christ's sake. These sugar cakes were the adornment of everyday life, Christ's own, intercessors for the world. Before the engineer Akim stood a pauper and beggar, a lazar and fool in Christ—a fool of Soviet Russia for Justice's sake, an intercessor for the world and for communism. Uncle Ivan must have been a schizophrenic; he had his own particular obsession: he walked the town, he went to the houses of acquaintances and strangers, and he implored them to weep; he delivered fiery and insane speeches about communism, and in the street markets his speeches made many people cry; he made the rounds of government offices, and it was rumored in town that at such times certain important personages rubbed their eyes with onion to gain, through the *okhlomons*, some much-needed popularity. Ivan was afraid of churches, and he cursed the priests, unafraid of them. Ivan's slogans were the most leftist in the town. In the town Ivan was revered as the people of Russia have learned over the centuries to revere fools in Christ, through the mouths of whom Truth makes itself known to men, and who for Truth's sake are willing to go to their deaths. Ivan drank, destroying himself with alcohol. He gathered around him men like himself, cast out by the Revolution that had created them. They found a place for themselves in the underground cave; they lived in true communism, brotherhood, equality, friendship—and each one of them had his own madness: the obsession of one was to correspond with the proletarians on Mars; a second proposed that all fully grown fish in the Volga be caught and that iron bridges be built over the Volga, paid for by the sale of the fish; a third dreamed of laying streetcar lines in the town.

"Weep!" said Ivan.

Akim, tearing himself from his thoughts, did not understand Ivan at first.

"What did you say?" he asked.

"Weep, Akim, weep, this very minute, for communism lost!" shouted Ivan, and pressed his hands to his chest, bowing his head as people do in prayer.

"Yes, yes, I am weeping, Uncle Ivan," Akim replied.

Akim was strong, tall, massive. He stood up next to Ivan. Akim kissed his uncle.

The rain beat down. The darkness of the brickyard spoke of ruin.

⋆ ⋆ ⋆

Akim was making his way back through town from his *okhlomon* uncle's by way of the marketplace. In a solitary window a light was burning. This was the house of the town eccentric, the museum curator. Akim went up to the window—in times past he and the curator had together rummaged around in the kremlin cellars. He was about to knock, but he saw something strange and did not knock. The room was piled with surplices, stoles, chasubles, cassocks. In the middle of the room sat two men: the curator poured a glass of vodka from a huge bottle and lifted it to the lips of a naked man; the man did not move a muscle. On the head of the naked man was a crown of thorns. And then Akim realized that the curator was drinking vodka in solitude with a wooden statue of a seated Christ. The Christ was carved of wood and was life-size. Akim remembered—as a boy he had seen this Christ in the Divny Monastery; the Christ was seventeenth-century work. The curator was drinking vodka with Christ, lifting glass after glass to the lips of the wooden Christ. The curator had unbuttoned his Pushkin-style frock coat; his side-whiskers were tousled. The naked Christ with his crown of thorns seemed alive to Akim.

Late that night Akim's mother, Maria Klimovna, came to see him. The aunts left the room. His mother had come in a plain housedress; she had thrown a shawl over her shoulders and come running. She wore a pair of spectacles—held together with thread—to have a better look at her son. And the mother was solemn, as at Communion. The mother embraced her son, pressing her withered breast to her son's chest; the mother ran her bony fingers through her son's hair; the mother pressed her head to her son's neck. The mother did not even weep. She was very grave. Not trusting her eyes, she felt her son with her fingers. And she blessed him.

"You won't come, you won't come to see us, son?" the mother asked.

Her son did not reply.

"And me—what have I lived my life for then?"

The son knew that his father would give his mother a beating if he found out that she had been to see her son. The son knew that his mother sat long hours in the dark, while his father slept, and thought of him, her son. The son knew that his mother would keep nothing from him and would tell him nothing new—nothing—and the old was accursed, but she was his mother—his mother!—all that is most rare, most wonderful, most beautiful, his mother, a saint, a martyr, a part of him by everything she had lived through. And the son did not reply to his mother, said nothing to his mother.

* * *

Next morning the engineer Akim left. The steamer did not leave until evening; he decided to go fifty versts by carriage to catch the night train. A tarantass and a pair of bays were brought up. The day was changeable—rain one minute, sun and blue sky the next. They took the Moscow road. Mud came up to the wheelboxes and the horses' hocks. They rode through thick forests; the forests stood gloomy, wet, silent. The driver, old and taciturn, was perched on the box. The horses went at a walk. Halfway, when Akim was already beginning to worry that he might miss the train, they stopped to feed the horses. In the co-operative tearoom they were told that vodka was not sold there, but they managed to get some from the stiller across the street, the secretary of the village soviet. The driver had a bit too much to drink and began to talk. Tediously he told the story of his life—how he had worked for thirty years, as he put it—in meat, but gave it up when the Revolution came, being no longer needed. When the driver was thoroughly drunk, he began to wonder at the ways of authority. "Well, there you are, that's how things go, God help us—I was in meat for thirty years and this commissar came and did it all in three weeks, and three weeks later he got rid of my brother, who was in flour, and my brother had been in the business thirty years, like me!" And there was no telling whether the driver spoke in bewilderment or in derision. They fed the horses, set off, again were silent.

The engineer Akim was a Trotskyite; his faction had been crushed. His birthplace, his town—it was clear to him now—was no longer of any use to him; he had set aside this week for thought. He should have been thinking about the fate of the Revolution and of his party, of his own fate as a revolutionary—but these thoughts would not come. He looked at the forests—and thought of forests, wilderness, marshes. He looked at the sky—and thought of sky, clouds, space. The horses' ribs had long been covered with foam; the horses' bellies heaved in labored breathing. The road was deep in mud; lakes had formed in the road—for the simple reason that the road was there. Dusk was already falling. The forest was mute. Thoughts of forests, of country roads, stretching for thousands of versts, led Akim to thoughts of his aunts Kapitolina and Rimma—and for the thousandth time Akim justified the Revolution. Aunt Kapitolina had led what was known as an upright life—not a single sin in the eyes of the town, not a single transgression against town morality; and her life had turned out to be empty and of no use to anyone. In Aunt Rimma's passport there would always be written, as would have been written in the passport of the Virgin Mary had she lived in Russia before the Revolution, "Spinster—has two children"; Rimma's children had been her shame and her grief. But her grief had become her happiness, her dignity; her life was full, fulfilled; she, Aunt Rimma, was happy, and Aunt Kapitolina lived on her sister's happiness, having no life of her own. One must be afraid of nothing; one must be doing; every deed, even a bitter one, can be a happiness, but nothing—remains nothing. And Klavdia—wasn't she happier than her mother because she didn't know who the father of her child was?; her mother knew she had loved a scoundrel. Akim's father came to his mind: it would have been better never to have known him! And Akim suddenly became aware that his thoughts about his father, Klavdia, his aunts were really thoughts not about them but about the Revolution. For him the Revolution was the beginning of life, and life itself—and the end of life.

The forests and roads darkened. They came out into open country. The west had long been dying, the red sunset its mortal wound. They drove through fields—fields the same as they had been five hundred years before—entered a village, dragged through the mud of its seventeenth century. Beyond the village the road dipped into a ravine; they crossed a bridge; on the other side of the bridge was a pool that proved to be impassable. They drove into the pool. The horses lurched and came to a halt. The driver struck the horses with his whip—the horses pulled but did not budge. All around was deep mud; the tarantass was sinking deeper and deeper in the middle of the pool—above the linchpin of the left front wheel. The driver braced himself on the box and booted the shaft horse in the rump—the horse jerked and fell on top of the shaft, then sank up to its collar into the mire. The driver lashed the horses until he realized that the shaft horse could not get up; then he waded into the mud to unharness the horse. He took a step and sank knee-deep into the mud; he took another—and he was stuck; he could not pull his feet up, his feet came out of his boots, his boots were left in the mud. The old man lost his balance and sat down in the pool. And the old man burst into tears—bitter, hysterical, helpless tears of rage and despair—this man, this specialist in the slaughter of cows and bulls.

The Trotskyite Akim missed the train, as he had missed the train of time.

Five

The art of mahogany was an anonymous art, an art of things. Master craftsmen drank themselves to death, but the things they had made were left behind and lived; in their presence people loved and died; to them they entrusted secrets of griefs, loves, business affairs, joys. Elizabeth, Catherine—rococo, baroque. Paul is a Knight of Malta, Paul is severe—severe repose, dark-polished mahogany, green leather, black lions, griffins. Alexander—Empire, classic lines, Hellas. People die, but things live on; ancient things give forth "effluences" of bygone days, of epochs dead and gone. In 1928—in Moscow, in Leningrad, in provincial capitals—antique shops appeared, where bygone days were bought and sold by pawnbrokers, by the State Export and Import Office, by the State Museum Fund,[19] by museums; in 1928 there were many people who collected "effluences." People who bought ancient things after the thunders of the Revolution, indulging their passion for bygone days in the privacy of their own houses, breathed in the living essense of dead things. And Paul, the Knight of Malta—straight and severe, without bronze and scrolls—was held in high esteem.

The brothers Bezdetov lived in Moscow on Vladimiro-Dolgorukovskaya Street, on the Zhivodyorka,[20] as Vladimiro-Dolgorukovskaya Street used to be called in the old days. They were antiquarians, restorers—and of course they were queer fish. Such people are always solitary, and silent. They take pride in their work, like philosophers. The brothers Bezdetov lived in a cellar; they were queer fish. They restored Pauls, Catherines, Alexanders, Nicholases—and they were visited by queer-fish collectors, who came to look at bygone days, at workmanship, to talk about bygone days and craftsmanship, to breathe

19. Not a fund but an organization established in 1918 for the purpose of confiscating and disposing of privately owned objets d'art.—Eds.

20. Literally, Flayer's Street.—Eds.

in bygone days, to set their heart on something, and to buy it. If the queer-fish collectors bought anything, then the purchase would be christened with brandy poured into a square glass measure of Catherine's time and drunk out of glasses that had once been part of the imperial diamond set.

. . . And back at Skudrin Bridge—nothing is happening.

The town is a Russian Bruges and a Muscovite Kamakura.

Yakov Karpovich would awake about midnight, light a lamp, eat, and read the Bible aloud, from memory, as always, as he had done for forty years. Every morning the old man would be visited by his friends and by petitioners—peasants—for Yakov Karpovich was a peasants' agent. In those years the peasants were bewildered by the following—incomprehensible to them—problematical dilemma, as Yakov Karpovich put it. The problem's incomprehensibility lay in the fact that the peasants were divided about fifty-fifty. Fifty percent of them got up at three o'clock in the morning and went to bed at eleven, and in their families everyone, young and old, worked day in and day out; if they were buying a heifer, they went over everything ten times before buying; they carried home any brushwood they found on the road; their huts were kept in good repair, as were their carts; their cattle were well fed and well cared for, as they themselves were well fed and up to their ears in work; taxes in kind and other state dues they paid promptly; they feared the authorities; and they were considered enemies of the Revolution, no more, and no less. The other 50 percent of the peasants each had a hut open to the winds, a scraggy cow and a mangy sheep—and that was all they had; in spring they went to town to collect a state seed loan; half the seed loan they ate, for they had no grain of their own left; the other half they scattered—shouting distance from seed to seed—and so there was no harvest in the fall; they explained the poor crop to the authorities by the lack of manure from the scraggy cows and the mangy sheep; the state relieved them of tax in kind and repayment of the seed loan; and they were considered friends of the Revolution. Peasants among the "enemies" maintained that, as far as the "friends" were concerned, 35 percent of them were drunkards (and here, of course, it is hard to determine whether poverty came from drunkenness or drunkenness came from poverty), 5 percent or so had bad luck (chance isn't always on your side!), and 60 percent were idlers, gabbers, philosophers, loafers, bunglers. In all the villages the "enemies" were harassed with the aim of turning them into "friends" and thus ensuring that they would have no means of paying their taxes in kind, while their huts became the property of the winds. Yakov Karpovich wrote affecting and fruitless petitions. Among Yakov Karpovich's visitors was one Vasili Vasilyevich, an enemy of the Fatherland, a man who had gone out of his mind. Before the Revolution, Vasili Vasilyevich had been a clerk of the council—the District Council; he became interested in agriculture and read every book about it he could lay his hands on. In 1920 he went to the land; he was given one dessiatine; he came to his dessiatine, a man of forty, with nothing but bare hands and boundless enthusiasm. In 1923 at the All-Russian Agricultural Exhibition, he was awarded a gold medal on paper and certificates of merit by the People's Commissariat of Agriculture for his cow and milk and for his work as chairman of the dairy collective; in the spring of '24 he was offered forty dessiatines to build a model farm—he accepted twenty, and by '26 he had seventeen cows; he hired a farmhand and—that was the end of him: he had become a kulak; by '27 he had five dessiatines and three cows left—the rest had gone in taxes, dues, and government bonds; in the fall of '28 he gave up everything, having decided to return to town and to clerking, in spite of the fact that in the fall of '28—on rafts crossing the Volga, on country roads, in pothouses, and in marketplaces—the peasants were talking figures: they gave you a ruble and eighty kopecks for a pood of rye at the cooperative, but if you bought a pood of rye at the same cooperative—on a coupon—it was three rubles and sixty kopecks, and if you sold a pood in the market—you got six rubles. Vasili Vasilyevich returned to town and—went out of his mind, not having the strength to break away from the kulak way of life. In these parts you don't come across too many villages and hamlets—mainly forests and swamps.

Yakov Karpovich had lost his sense of time and had lost his fear of life. Besides petitions of no use to anyone, he wrote proclamations and philosophical tracts. Vile—heartachingly, nauseatingly vile—was Yakov Karpovich Skudrin.

The town is a Russian Bruges and a Muscovite Kamakura. In this town in the sixteenth century Tsarevich Dmitri was murdered. It was then that Boris Godunov ordered the great bell of the Church of Our Savior in the Kremlin to be taken down—the very bell that the priest Oguryets had struck to cry the murder; Boris Godunov punished the bell, tore out its ear and tongue, scourged it in the town square together with other tongueless and earless citizens, and exiled it to Tobolsk, in Siberia. Today the bells are dying over the town.

Yakov Karpovich Skudrin is alive—his life is uneventful.

* * *

In 1744 the leader of an expedition to China, Gerasim Kirillovich Lobradovsky, upon arriving at the outpost of Kyakhta, took into his party one Andrei Kursin, a silversmith and a native of the town of Yaransk. Kursin, on orders from Lobradovsky, journeyed to Peking to obtain from the Chinese there the secret of making china, *portselen*, as china was called in those days. In Peking, through the agency of Russian "apprentices of the rank of ensign," Kursin suborned a master craftsman from the Imperial China Works with a bribe of a thousand *lan*, two thousand rubles of the time. This Chinaman demonstrated to Kursin how to make *portselen* in abandoned Buddhist shrines thirty-five li from Peking. When Gerasim Kirillovich Lobradovsky returned to Saint Petersburg, he brought Kursin with him and wrote a report to the empress about the secret of *portselen* making, which he had carried with him out of China. There followed an imperial ukase, conveyed to Baron Cherkassov by County Razumovsky, that the new arrivals from China be sent to Tsarskoye Selo. Kursin was showered with honors, but his thievery did him no good, for, as it turned out, the Chinaman had deceived Andrei Kursin, had "acted perfidiously," as was reported at the time in a secret court circular. Kursin returned to his native Yaransk, fearing a flogging. In the same year, on the first of February, 1744, in Christiana,[21] Baron Korf concluded a secret agreement with Christopher Conrad Hunger, a master china maker, who had learned his craft, he claimed, at the Meissen Works in Saxony. Hunger, striking a bargain with Baron Korf, came secretly to Russia, to Saint Petersburg, on a Russian frigate. Hunger began building a china works which subsequently became the Imperial China Works—and began to conduct experiments, which he combined with drunken brawls and cudgel fights in company with his Russian assistant Vinogradov; he was thus fruitlessly engaged until 1748, when he was expelled from Russia for charlatanry and incompetence. Hunger's place was taken by the Russian mining engineer Dmitri Ivanovich Vinogradov—one of Peter's protégés, a hopeless drunkard and a man of great natural gifts—and it was he who founded the craft of Russian *portselen* in such a way that it owes nothing to anybody, being the invention of Vinogradov; nevertheless, Andrei Kursin, the man from Yaransk, who was roundly duped by the Chinese, and Christopher Hunger, the German, who duped everyone around, dangling Europe before their eyes, must be considered the fathers of Russian *portselen*. And Russian china had its golden age. Master craftsmen—of the Imperial Works, of old Gardner, of the "*vieux*" Popov, Batenin, Miklashevsky, Yussupov, Kornilov, Safronov, Sabanin—flourished under serfdom in a golden age. And continuing the tradition of Dmitri Vinogradov, those who gathered around china making were connoisseurs and queer fish, drunkards and skinflints: the factories were run by the princely Yussupovs, the Vsevolozhskys of ancient lineage, by the queer-fish Bogorodsk merchant Nikita Khrapunov, flogged on the order of Alexander I for making a statuette of a monk bent under the weight of a wheat sheaf wherein was hidden a young peasant maid; all the masters stole secrets from each other, Yussupov from the Imperial Works, Kisselyov from Popov; Safronov would spy on a secret process through a hole in an attic late at

21. The name of Oslo until 1925.—Eds.

night, like a thief. These master craftsmen and queer fish created beautiful things. Russian china is the most marvelous art adorning the Earthly Globe.

Yamskoye Pole
Volkov's house
January 15, 1929

THE TALE OF THE UNEXTINGUISHED MOON

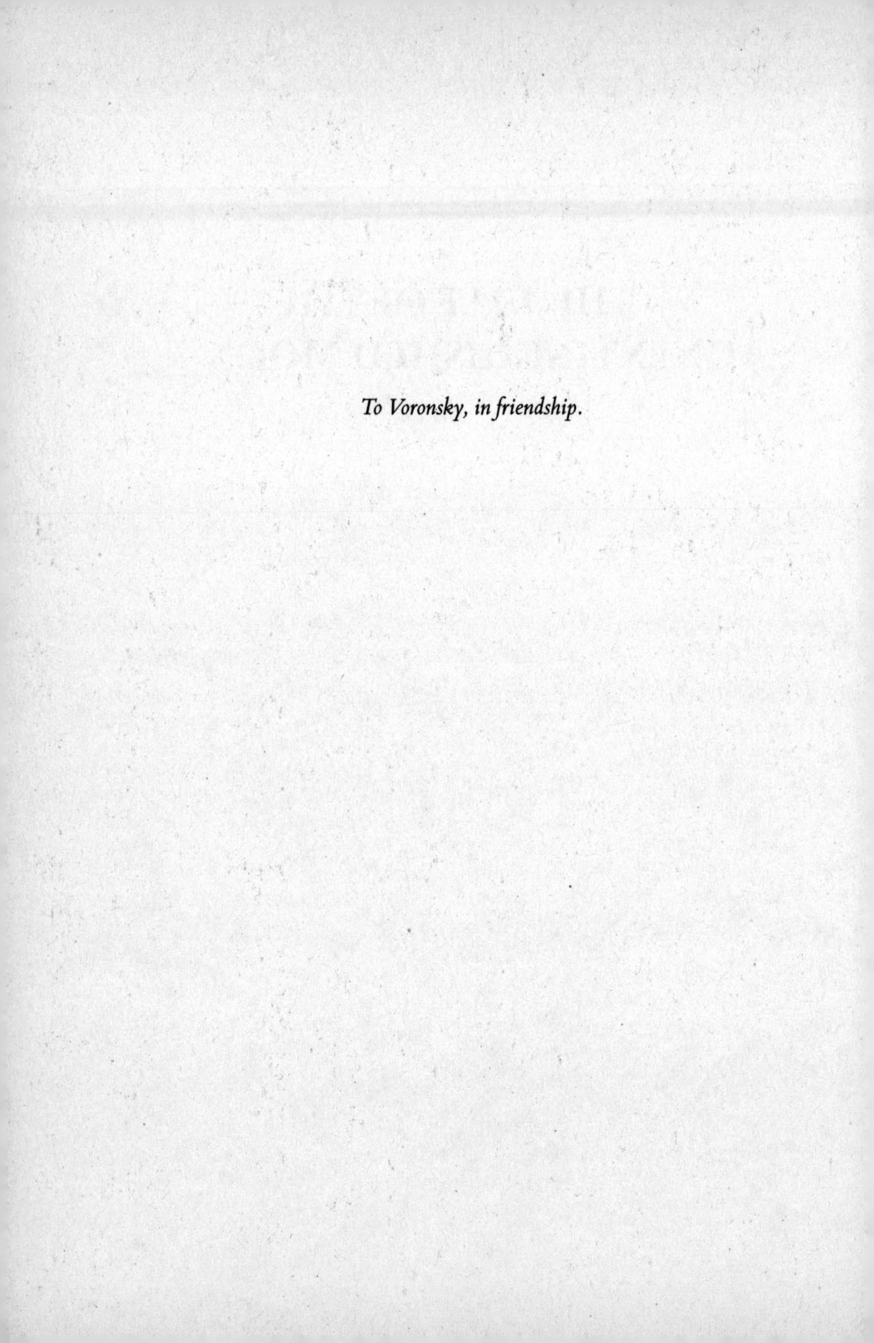

To Voronsky, in friendship.

The Tale of the Unextinguished Moon

Introduction

The plot of this story suggests that the death of M. V. Frunze furnished the occasion and material for it. Personally I knew Frunze very slightly, was barely acquainted with him, having met him, perhaps, twice. I do not know the actual details of his death—and to me they are not essential because the purpose of my story is anything but a report on the death of the People's Commissar for Military Affairs. I find it necessary to inform the reader about all this, lest he should look for facts and real people in the story.

Moscow **Boris Pilnyak**

January 28, 1926

One

At dawn factory whistles sounded over the city. A gray murk of night, fog, and sleet trailed in alleyways, dissolving in a dawn that seemed likely to be cheerless, frosty, and gray. Factory whistles wailed a long time, slowly—one, two, three, many of them—merging into a gray howl over the city. In this hushed hour before dawn factories wailed, but from the outskirts came shrill, irritating whistles of railway engines arriving and departing. And it was quite clear that these wailings came from the city, the soul of the city now befouled with gray murk. At that hour in newspaper printing plants rotary presses were bringing out the final copies of the papers, and soon from the dispatch yards boys were hurrying through the streets with bundles of papers; one or two of them stood at deserted street corners shouting as if in rehearsal for the day's shouting ahead:

"Revolution in China! Army Commander Gávrilov arrives! Army Commander sick!"

It was at that hour that a train drew in at the station where trains from the south arrive. It was a special train. At the end of it was a blue lounge car—quiet, with sentries on the footboards and heavy curtains drawn behind plate-glass windows; its sides gleamed grayish where light struck them. The train had come out of the black night, from fields that had squandered the summer on luxuries and now had only winter left—fields that had been plundered in summer and abandoned to a hoary old age. Slowly and with little noise the train crept beneath the roof of the station and was switched to a siding. The platform was deserted. It was no doubt by chance that extra militia with green stripes on their uniforms stood at the gates. Three officers with rhomboids on their sleeves went through to the lounge car. There they returned salutes and stood for a while by the steps as the sentry whispered to someone inside the car; then the three went up the steps and disappeared behind door hangings. Electric light flashed on in the car. Two army electricians began bustling about, stringing telephone wires to the car under the station roof. A man wearing a threadbare spring coat and an unseasonable fur cap with earflaps approached the car. This man saluted no one, and no one saluted him. He said:

"Tell Nikolai Ivanovich that Popov is here."

The Red Army man looked slowly at Popov, examined him, noted his worn, unpolished shoes, and replied slowly:

"The Comrade Army Commander isn't up yet."

Popov gave the Red Army man a friendly smile and for some reason began to speak in a familiar manner. He said amicably:

"That doesn't matter, sonny; just you go and tell him that Popov is here."

The Red Army man went in and came back again. Then Popov climbed up into the car. Night was still trapped there—the curtains were drawn, and the electric light was burning. The south was trapped in the lounge, since the train had come from the south: there was a smell of pomegranates, oranges, pears, good wine, good tobacco—there was a smell of the benedictions of southern climes. On the table next to the lamp lay an open book, and near to it was a plate with some half-eaten gruel; behind the plate lay an unbuttoned Colt holster, its leather strap twisted like a snake. At the other end of the table stood several opened bottles. The three officers with rhomboids on their sleeves sat in leather armchairs to one side of the table along the wall, sat very respectfully at attention, holding their briefcases in silence. Popov squeezed behind the table, took off his coat and cap, laid them beside him, picked up the open book, and glanced at it. An attendant, indifferent to everything in the world, came and cleared the table; the bottles he put somewhere in a corner; he brushed pomegranate rinds onto a small tray and, having spread a tablecloth, placed on it a solitary glass in a holder, a plate of stale bread, an eggcup; he brought in two eggs on a plate, salt, several small medicine bottles; he lifted a corner of a curtain, took a look at the morning, then drew the curtains back from the windows—the cords made a forlorn hissing sound—and switched off the light; into the lounge crept a gray, frosty autumn morning. Everything became very ordinary; in the corner one could discern a crate of wine bottles and a rolled-up carpet. The attendant stood in the doorway, like a statue, motionless, with a napkin in his hands. Every face was yellow in the gloom of the morning—the thin, watery light was like a yellowish discharge from an infected wound. An orderly appeared in the doorway and stood next to the attendant; the field office was already in operation; the ringing of the telephone broke the silence.

Then the army commander came out of the sleeping compartment into the lounge. He was a rather short, broad-shouldered man, fair, with long hair combed back. His tunic of green army cloth with four rhomboids on the sleeve was ill-fitting and wrinkled. Although his spurred boots had been polished with the utmost care, their worn-down heels bore witness to long service. This was a man whose name stood for the heroism of the Civil War, for the thousands, tens of thousands, hundreds of thousands of men who had stood behind him—for thousands, tens of thousands, hundreds of thousands of deaths, agonies, mutilations—for the cold, hunger, the ice-covered ground, and the scorching heat of long marches—for the thunder of cannon, the whistle of bullets and night winds—for bonfires in the night; for marches, victories, and routs; and—again—for death. This was a man who had had command over armies, over thousands of men; who had had command over men, victories, death—over gunpowder, smoke, broken bones, torn flesh; over those victories which vast crowds with hundreds of red banners had acclaimed in the rear and of which the news had flown by radio around the world—those victories after which deep holes had been dug in the sandy soil of Russia for the corpses, holes into which thousands of human bodies were flung in heaps. This was a man whose name was overgrown with legends of wars, feats of leadership, boundless valor, boldness, stubborn determination. This was a man who had the right and the will to send men to kill other men and to die. Into the lounge walked a rather short, broad-shouldered man with the good-natured, slightly weary face of a seminarian. He walked quickly, and his gait revealed both a cavalryman and a man who was very much a civilian, not at all a soldier. The three staff officers sprang to attention: for them he was the man—the man at the wheel of that enormous machine known as the army—who commanded their lives, mainly their lives, successes, careers, failures—their lives, but not their deaths. The Commander halted in front of them, did not offer his hand, made the sign that allowed them to stand at ease. And in this way, standing in front of them, the Commander heard their reports: each of the three stepped forward, came to attention, and reported, ". . . as commander of. . . ," ". . . in the service of the Revolution. . . ." The Commander shook hands with each man in turn as he finished his report, probably without having listened to the reports. He then sat down in front of the solitary glass, and the attendant suddenly appeared to pour tea from a gleaming teapot. The Commander picked up an egg.

"How are things going?" the Commander asked simply, brushing aside formalities.

One of the three began speaking, told him the news, and then asked in his turn:

"How is your health, Comrade Gavrilov?"

For a brief moment the Commander's face took on a distant expression; he said with some annoyance:

"Well, I've been in the Caucasus for treatment. I'm all right now." He paused. "I'm well now." He paused. "See to it that there are no official welcomes, no guards of honor; in general. . . ." He paused. "You may go, comrades."

The three staff officers rose to go. The Commander shook hands with each of them without getting up. They left the lounge silently. When the Commander came into the lounge, Popov had not greeted him; he had picked up the book and turned away from the Commander as he leafed through it. The Commander had given Popov a sidelong glance and had not greeted him either, pretending not to have noticed the man. When the staff officers had left, the Commander asked Popov, still without a word of greeting, as if they had seen each other the evening before:

"Would you like some tea or wine, Alyoshka?"

Popov had not time to reply, because an orderly stepped forward and began to make his report to the "Comrade Commander": the automobile had been unloaded from the flatcar, some official letters had been delivered to the office—one of the letters was from House Number One, it was marked "secret," had been brought by his secretary—an apartment had been made ready for him at staff headquarters; a pile of telegrams and letters of welcome had arrived. The Commander dismissed the orderly, saying that he would continue to live in the car. The Commander had not come to rejoin his army but to visit an alien city: his own city, where his army was, lay several thousand versts away; it was there in that city, in that area, that he had left his concerns, cares, the routine of his life, his wife. The attendant, without waiting for Popov's answer, placed two glasses on the table, one for tea and the other for wine. Popov got out of his corner and sat down by the Commander.

"How's your health, Nikolasha?" Popov asked with concern, as a brother might.

"My health is as it should be; I'm back to normal, I'm well—but, who knows, perhaps you'll have to stand in a guard of honor by my coffin," Gavrilov replied, perhaps joking, perhaps in earnest; if it was a joke, it was a grim one.

These two, Popov and Gavrilov, were bound by ties of longstanding friendship, by the underground work which they had carried on side by side, by their work together at a factory long ago in their young days when they had started life as weavers in Orekhovo-Zuyevo; there in their youth was lost the River Klyazma, the woods beyond the Klyazma along the road to the town of Pokrov, to the Pokrov hideaway where the committeemen met; there was their ragged weavers' youth with underground pamphlets, with editions of *Donskaya Rech*[1]—with *Iskra*[2] like the Bible—with workers' barracks, meetings, secret

1. A liberal social-political and literary newspaper published from 1887 to 1905.—Eds.

2. First "all-Russian" Marxist newspaper, established by V. I. Lenin in Leipzig in 1900.—Eds.

addresses—with the wide square in front of the railway station where in 1905 Cossacks' bullets and lashes whistled over crowds of workers; later they were prisoners together at Bogorodsk, and still later they shared the life of professional revolutionaries: exile, escape, underground work, Taganskaya Transit Prison, exile, escape, emigration—Paris, Vienna, Chicago—and then the thunderclouds of 1914—Brindisi, Salonika, Rumania, Kiev, Moscow, Saint Petersburg—and then the storm of 1917, the Smolny,[3] October, the roar of cannon over the Moscow Kremlin, and finally—one of them is Chief of Staff of the Red Guards in Rostov-on-the-Don, and the other the elected representative of the proletarian nobility, as Rykov wittily remarked, in Tula; for one in those days—wars, victories, command over cannon, men, and death; for the other—provincial committees, executive committees, the Supreme Economic Council, conferences, meetings, projects, and reports. For both of them, everything—life, thoughts—devoted to the greatest revolution in the world, the greatest justice and truth in the world. But to each other they had always remained Nikolasha and Aleksei, Alyoshka, always the close friends of their textile-mill days, without rank or formality.

"Tell me, Nikolasha, how is your health?" Popov asked.

"Well, it's like this: I had a stomach ulcer—perhaps I still have it. You know—pains, vomiting blood, terrible heartburn—nasty business." The Commander spoke quietly, leaning toward Aleksei. "They sent me to the Caucasus for treatment—the pains subsided; I returned to work, carried on for six months, and then, again—nausea, pains; I went back to the Caucasus. Now the pains are gone again—I even drank a bottle of wine, just to see what would happen. . . ." The Commander interrupted himself: "If you'd like some wine, Alyoshka, there's some under the seat—I brought you a small case. Open a bottle!"

Popov sat leaning his head on the palm of his hand. He replied:

3. Formerly Smolny Institute for Daughters of the Nobility in Saint Petersburg; after the Revolution of 1917 the center of Communist leadership.—Eds.

"No, I don't drink in the morning. Go on."

"Well, so my health is in perfect order." The Commander paused. "Tell me, Alyoshka—why have I been summoned here—do you know?"

"No."

"An order came to leave directly from the Caucasus. I didn't even stop off to see my wife." The Commander paused. "Devil only knows what it can be. I can't think of anything—as far as the army goes, everything is in order; there are no conferences, nothing at all. . . . Have you ever been to the Caucasus? That is truly a wonderful country; our poets call it the southern clime; I could not understand it—why such an expression? I went there, and it's true, it is the southern clime! . . . Have a pomegranate, Alyosha—I can't eat them, I treat orderlies to them. How are things going?"

The Commander talked about the army and the war, and was doubtless unaware that when he talked about the army he ceased to be a weaver and became a leader of men, a Red General of the Red Army; the Commander talked about Orekhovo-Zuyevo and their life there, and was doubtless unaware that he then became a weaver—the same weaver who had fallen in love with a schoolteacher from the other side of the river, who had polished his boots for her sake and walked to her school barefoot to keep them from getting dusty, putting them on only when he reached a little wood near the school—the same weaver who had bought a fancy shirt with a bow tie and a hat à la devil-may-care. Yet somehow he never got any further with the teacher than talking about political pamphlets with her; nothing came of their friendship—the teacher turned him down. The Commander-weaver was a good, easygoing man who liked to joke and could see the funny side of things, and now he joked as he talked with his friend; only now and then would he suddenly return to the present and become restless: he remembered the mysterious summons, he shifted awkwardly, and then it was a healthy weaver talking about a sick Commander: "A bigwig, a field marshal, a senator—what a laugh! And I can't even eat buckwheat porridge. . . . Yes, my friend, the Central Committee plays strange tricks on a man[4]—you have to take it as it comes." He retreated into silence.

"Don't beat about the bush, Nikolasha; tell me, what do you suspect?" said Popov. "What was all that about a guard of honor?"

The Commander replied slowly, after a pause:

"In Rostov I met Potap" (he used the name by which a leading revolutionary, one of the "Glorious Band" of 1918, was known within the party)—"well, he told me. . . he tried to persuade me to have an operation, to have the ulcer removed or perhaps have it sewed up; there was something suspicious about the way he tried to persuade me!" The Commander fell silent. "I feel in good health; everything in me revolts against the operation; I don't want it—I'll get well without it. After all, there are no pains at all now, I've put on weight, and. . . , damn it all, I'm a grown man, an old man already, a bigwig, and I have to worry about my belly. I feel ashamed." The Commander paused, picked up the open book. "I'm reading old man Tolstoi—*Childhood* and *Boyhood;* the old man wrote well; he had a feeling for life, for the instincts in our blood. . . . I've seen enough blood, but. . . but I'm afraid of the operation like a kid. I don't want it; they'll kill me! . . . How well the old man understood what human blood means."

An orderly entered, came to attention, made his report: they had brought a dispatch from headquarters; an automobile from House Number One had arrived for the Commander; he was requested to go there; some new telegrams had arrived; so-and-so had sent someone to pick up a package from the south. The orderly placed a pile of newspapers on the table. The Commander dismissed the orderly. The Commander ordered his greatcoat to be got ready; he unfolded a paper. In the section in which appeared accounts of the most important events of the day the headline read: "Army Commander Gavrilov Arrives," and on the third page it was reported that "Commander Gavrilov arrives today; he has temporarily left his post in order to undergo an operation

4. A paraphrase of a line from a song: "Fate plays strange tricks on a man."—Eds.

for a stomach ulcer." In the same paragraph it was reported that "Comrade Gavrilov's health gives grounds for concern" but that "the professors are confident that the outcome of the operation will be positive."

Gavrilov—the old fighter of the Revolution, soldier, Army Commander, leader, who had sent thousands of men to die—the apex of a military machine which existed to kill, to die, to spill blood for victory—leaned back in his chair, wiped his forehead, looked intently at Popov, said:

"Listen to me, Alyoshka! There's something behind this! Y-y-yes. . . . But what can I do?" And he shouted, "Orderly, my greatcoat!"

The time was after ten in the morning when the greenish haze of the day crept over the city, when, actually, this greenish haze was invisible because over that patch of land where buildings were lined up the city machine had started running—huge, very complex, whirling and pulling everything into its vortex from drays, streetcars, and buses, from unmade beds in the houses to soldiers marching along the embankment, to the solemn quiet of the high-ceilinged bookkeeping halls and the offices of the People's Commissariats; it was a complex city machine that sent rivers of people to their places in factories, at tables, behind desks, in automobiles, on the streets—a machine that obscured the grayish sky, sleet, slush, the green haze of the day.

Two

At the intersection of two of the city's main streets, where automobiles, people, and drays flowed in an endless stream, a colonnaded house stood behind an iron fence. The house gave unmistakable signs of having stood behind its paling, supported by those columns, silent, held back by the paling for a century, in the calm of that century. There was no signboard of any kind outside the house. Two helmeted sentries stood at the gates, which were surmounted by griffins. Past the house flowed people, the sounds of automobile horns, crowds, human time—flowed the gray day, newspaper boys, men with briefcases, women in knee-length skirts and stockings that deceived the eye, making their legs seem bare; behind the griffins on the gates time took its ease and seemed to be coming to a standstill. And in a different part of the city was another house, also in the classical style, behind paling, colonnaded, flanked by outbuildings, and with some mythological nonsense of hideous, grimacing faces on bas-reliefs. This house stood on the edge of the city; in front of it spread a square, and above the square lay gray, in this part of the city spacious sky; nearby rose two factory chimneys, antennas, telegraph wires. In the yard, on flowerbeds near the house, instead of flowers and lilacs, grew birches, now, on this autumn day, bare, wet, drooping. Beyond the yard and the house a steep bank fell sharply, and a river flowed; above the meadows beyond the river again stretched a gray sky, factory chimneys, hamlets, a small church; the bank was overgrown with birches plundered by strong summer winds. There were two gateways to the house; fauns made faces from the gateposts; gatehouses stood on either side, and on benches near the gatehouses sat watchmen in aprons and felt boots, with brass badges on their aprons. A closed automobile, black with red crosses and bearing the word "Ambulance," stood near the gates.

That day the paper with the largest circulation carried an editorial "to mark the third anniversary of the return to the gold standard" which pointed out that a stable currency can exist "only when the entire economic life of the country is based on strict economic consideration, on solid economic foundations. State subsidies and the management of the national economy without regard for the budget will inevitably undermine a stable financial system." In headline type appeared: "China's Struggle Against the Imperialists." The foreign news section carried telegrams from England, France, Germany, Czechoslovakia, Latvia, America. Across the bottom section of one page was spread a long article entitled "The Revolutionary Movement and the Use of Force." There were also two pages of advertisements among which appeared in large type "Facts of Life—Syphilis" and "A New Book by S. Broide, *In the Madhouse*."

Incidentally, the same issue of the paper carried a goodly score of theater, variety, open-stage, and cinema programs. . . .

. . . If the day of work, fog, queues, reception rooms, solemn quiet of high-ceilinged bookkeeping halls, the chirping of the looms in cotton and wool mills, the thunder of hammers in factories and foundries, the whistles of trains, departing and in motion, the roar of buses and automobiles, the prattle of streetcar bells, telephone bells, doorbells, the whining of the radio—the day of the city machine, of people, men, women, children, old folk, mature people. . .

. . . if we look ahead and replace the day of labor and business with the evening, as time did, piling the day with twilight, spilling into the streets the light of streetlamps—which in the drizzle look like weeping eyes—destroying the sky. . .

. . . then in the evening tens of thousands of people made their way into cinemas, theaters, variety shows, open stages, taverns, and beer parlors. There in the places of entertainment all sorts of things were shown entangling time, space, and countries; they showed Greeks unlike any that have actually existed; Assyrians unlike any that have actually existed; unreal Jews, Americans, Englishmen, Germans; oppressed, unreal Chinese; Russian workers; Arakcheyev; Pugachev;

Nicholas the First; Stenka Razin;[5] furthermore, an ability to speak well or poorly was displayed, good or bad legs, arms, backs and chests were shown, and ability to dance and sing, well or poorly exhibited; furthermore, they showed all aspects of love and various amorous intrigues such as seldom if ever occur in everyday life. Dressed in their best, people sat in rows, looked, listened, applauded, and, streaming down the brightly lit stairs of the theaters into the wet streets, commented hurriedly, always trying to be clever. Then the streets emptied—to find rest in the night—and at night, past midnight—at the hour when in villages the first roosters crow—in houses, in beds husbands and wives, and lovers, mostly lonely couples, engaged in what animals, birds, and insects engage in at dawn and at sunset.

But the day moved along its usual order, counting off the hours on clocks in offices, banks, factories, and mills; on clocks in city squares; and on pocket watches. Many times rain began to fall, and many times it stopped. Once snow began sifting down to thicken the slush on the streets. The machine of the city worked, as any machine should.

At noon a closed Rolls drew up in front of House Number One—the house which made time slow down. A sentry opened the door of the limousine, and the Commander got out. In battle when people rush into attack they make more noise than when artillery is firing; the artillery roars louder than a regiment at an encampment; the regimental headquarters are noisier than division headquarters: in the army headquarters rigid silence must prevail; at meetings people shout louder than at the plenums of the soviets; at plenums there is more noise than in the presidium, and it is even quieter at the meetings of the presidium of the provincial executive committees.

5. Aleksei Andreyevich Arakcheyev (1769–1834); a reactionary court official in the reigns of Paul I and Alexander I; Yemelyan Ivanovich Pugachev (ca. 1742–75); a leader of a peasant and Cossack rebellion in Russia in the area of the Ural Mountains and the Volga; Nicholas I (1796–1855); tsar of Russia (1825–55); Stepan Timofeyevich Razin—Stenka (?–1671); a brigand, leader of a large peasant and Cossack rebellion.

In this house unbroken silence settled, telephone bells were muffled, abacuses were quiet, people walked about noiselessly, people were not agitated, people did not stoop; the walls, covered with posters that had replaced paintings, stood erect; red carpets lay on the floor; at the doors stood men with red stripes on their uniforms. In the study at the far end of the house the heavy curtains were half-drawn, and beyond the windows the street hurried by; a fire was burning in the grate; on the red felt of the desk stood three telephones as if to affirm, in company with the crackling logs in the fireplace, the quietness of the room; the three telephones brought three of the city's arteries into the study, so that from its silence commands could be issued and so that everything going on in the city's arteries could be known. On the desk stood a writing set, bronze and massive, and in the penholder were stuck a dozen red and blue pencils. To the wall behind the desk was attached a radio receiver with two pairs of earphones, and rows of electric buttons were lined up like a company of soldiers at attention—from one connecting with the reception room to one marked "War Alarm." Opposite the desk stood a leather armchair. Behind the desk the unbending man sat on a wooden chair. The heavy curtains were half-drawn, and on the desk an electric light burned under a green shade; the face of the unbending man was lost in the shadows.

The Commander walked across the carpet and sat down in the leather armchair.

Number One, the unbending man:

"It is not for us to talk about the grindstone of the Revolution, Gavrilov. The wheel of history, unfortunately, I suppose, is turned mainly by blood and death—particularly the wheel of revolution. It is not for you and me to talk of blood and death. You remember how the two of us led half-naked Red Army men against Yekaterinov. You had a rifle, and I had a rifle. Your horse was blown up under you by a shell, and you went ahead on foot. The Red Army men started to run, and you shot one of them down with your revolver to stop the rest. Commander, you would have shot me, too, if I had lost my nerve, and I suppose you would have been right."

Number Two, the Commander:

"Well, you have got a nice little setup here—quite the minister. Is smoking allowed? I don't see any cigarette butts."

Number One:

"Don't smoke—you shouldn't. Your health doesn't permit it. I don't smoke myself."

Number Two, curtly:

"Come to the point. What have you brought me here for? Don't play the diplomat with me. Let's hear it!"

Number One:

"I have asked you to come here because you need an operation. You are a man the Revolution cannot spare. I called in the professors, and they said you'll be on your feet in a month. The Revolution demands it. The professors are waiting for you—they'll examine you and find out what's wrong with you. I have already given the order. There's even a man from Germany."

Number Two:

"You do as you like, but I'll smoke anyway. My doctors told me there's no need for an operation and that everything will heal by itself. I feel perfectly well—there's no need at all for an operation. I don't want one."

Number One stuck his hand behind him, felt for a button on the wall, rang; a noiseless secretary entered: Number One asked, "Is there anyone waiting to see me?" The secretary replied in the affirmative. Number One made no reply, dismissed the secretary.

Number One:

"Comrade Commander, you remember how we debated whether or not to send four thousand men to certain death? You ordered them to be sent. You were right. In three weeks you'll be on your feet. You must forgive me, but I have already given the order."

A telephone rang—not the city telephone but the internal one, which had no more than thirty or forty lines. Number One picked up the receiver, listened, asked a question, said, "A note to the French?

An official one, of course, as we said yesterday. You understand—remember how we fished for trout—the French are a very slippery lot. What? Yes, yes. Get things moving. So long."

Number One:

"You must forgive me, but there is nothing further to discuss, Comrade Gavrilov."

The Commander finished his cigarette, stuck the butt in among the red and blue pencils, got up from the armchair.

The Commander:

"Good-bye."

Number One:

"So long."

The Commander walked over red carpets to the entrance; the Rolls carried him into the noise of the streets. The unbending man remained in the study. No one else came in to see him. Unbending he sat over his papers, a fat red pencil in his hand. He rang; the secretary came in; he said, "See that the cigarette butt is removed from here, from this stand!"—And again he was silent over his papers, red pencil in hand. One hour passed, and another, and still the man sat over his papers, working. Once a telephone rang; he listened and replied, "Two million rubles' worth of galoshes and textiles to Turkestan to plug up the hole in consumer goods? Yes, of course! Go to it! So long." An attendant came in noiselessly, put down a tray with a glass of tea and a piece of cold meat covered with a napkin on a small table by the window, went out. Then the unbending man rang for his secretary again, asked, "Is the confidential summary ready?" The secretary replied in the affirmative—"Bring it in." And once more the man was silent for a long time over a large sheet of paper—over columns headed: "People's Commissariat of Internal Affairs, Political and Economic Divisions of OGPU, People's Commissariat of Finance, People's Commissariat of Foreign Trade, People's Commissariat of Labor." Then into the study walked two men—the other two of the "troika" that ruled.

Over the city moved a yellow day steeped in foggy haze. Toward three o'clock alleys and the sky began turning blue and gray. The sky—like a huge factory—began trading in quilts, greasy to the point of a gray gloss.

At four o'clock, when the city began shedding tears from the wet glass of its streetlamps made up like the eyes of prostitutes, when there were more people on the streets than usual, when automobile horns roared, factory and train whistles blew, and streetcars clattered, several automobiles pulled up outside House Number Two on the outskirts of the city. The house hugged the darkness, as if darkness could warm the dampness that pervaded it. The windows that faced the open spaces beyond the river were burning with the reflection of the last slit of sunset, and there beyond the open spaces this slit oozed, poured forth clotted, purplish gore. At the gates of the house two militiamen took up positions next to the watchmen in aprons and felt boots. At the main entrance to the house two more militiamen took up positions. An officer with two orders of the Red Banner, supple as a willow rod, entered the front door with two Red Army men. In the house it was an hour of rest; quiet was descending; only somewhere in some remote room a nurse was singing a muted song: "Oh, she will go to the river bank, to look at the river, how fast it flows." The officer and the Red Army men were met in the entrance hall by a man in a white gown. "Yes, yes, yes, of course"; and then the nurse's song about the river broke off. The windows in the examination room faced the open spaces beyond the river. There were no curtains on the windows. The walls were painted white, and white electric light streamed from the ceiling. There were no telephones in the room. The room was vast and empty. Its center was taken up by a table covered with white oilcloth, around which stood oilcloth-covered, high-backed chairs—the standard variety found in railroad stations. Along the wall stood an oilcloth-covered couch with a sheet over it, and by the couch—a wooden stool. In a corner, on a glass shelf above a washbasin, were arranged medicine bottles with various labels, a huge bottle of mercury chloride, a jar of green soap; nearby hung yellowish, unbleached towels. The first automobiles to arrive brought professors, therapists, surgeons. People in frock coats and black jackets walked into the examination room; these people removed the coats and put on white gowns. Beyond the windows, the blood-tinged ooze of the sunset across the river had faded. People came in, exchanged greetings; they were met by the man in charge—tall, bearded, bald, with a good-natured face. In a vast majority of cases, men of science, and medicine in particular, are, for some reason, very ugly: their jaws are either too small or are overdeveloped so that they extend beyond their ears; their eyes are almost always behind glasses or near their temples or crawling into the very corners of their eyesockets; to some fate denied the blessing of hair, and on their necks grow sparse tufts of beard—with others, hair pushes up not only on jaws and chin but on nose and ears as well. Perhaps it is this circumstance that has created among scientists the tradition of eccentricity—every scientist must, without fail, be an eccentric; what is more, his eccentricity augments his erudition. At this time, though, there was probably no eccentric behavior in the examination room. The man who greeted the people as host, a surgeon, a professor, overgrown with hair to the extent that it grew on his nose, was quaint only on account of his abundant brown hair, into which was set a small pair of spectacles; there was also something quaint about the shine of his bald head. Coming forward to greet him was Professor Lozovsky—a man of about thirty-five, clean-shaven, wearing a frock coat and a pince-nez with a straight crosspiece, his eyes hiding in the inner corners of their sockets.

"Yes, yes, yes, of course."

The clean-shaven man handed the hairy one a wax-sealed envelope that had been torn open. The hairy man took out a sheet of paper, adjusted his spectacles, read it, again adjusted his spectacles, and with a puzzled expression passed it on to a third man.

The clean-shaven man, solemnly:

"A secret paper, as you can see—almost an order. It was sent to me this morning. You understand?"

First, second, third—snatches of conversation, whispered, hurried:

"How does the consultation come into this?"

"I came because of an urgent summons. There was a telegram addressed to the rector of the university."

"Army Commander Gavrilov, you know—the one who. . . ."

"Yes, yes, yes, of course—the Revolution, the man in command of the army—the usual formula—and then, if you please. . . ."

"A consultation."

"Have you seen him, gentlemen—Comrade Gavrilov? What sort of a man is he?"

"Yes, yes, yes, of course, my good man. . . ."

The electric light made sharp-cut shadows. The wound of the sunset carried with it into darkness the wide spaces beyond the river. Someone took hold of someone else by the button of the breast pocket of his white gown; someone took someone else's arm to stroll about the room. Then: loudly, slowly, calmly, first, second, third:

"Professor Oppel's report at the convention of surgeons on internal secretion. I opposed—the duodenum. . . ."

"Today in the House of Scientists. . . ."

"Thank you, my wife is well, the oldest boy has a touch of colitis. And how is Yekaterina Pavlovna?"

"Pavel Ivanovich, your article in the *Community Doctor*. . . ."

Then: from the doorway came the clang of rifles and the stamp of heels—the Red Army men froze to immobility; in the doorway appeared the tall, slender youth, supple as a whip, with the orders of the Red Banner on his chest, came to attention facing the door; the Commander walked quickly into the examination room, pushed his hair back with one hand, adjusted the collar of his tunic, said:

"Good day, comrades. Am I to undress?"

Then: without haste the professors sat down on the oilcloth-covered chairs around the table, put their elbows on the table, rubbed their hands, adjusted their spectacles and pince-nez, asked the patient to sit down. The man who had passed the envelope around, the one whose eyes had grown deep into their sockets behind his straight pince-nez, said to the hairy man:

"Pavel Ivanovich, I suppose that as primus inter pares you will have no objection to taking the chair."

"Am I to undress?" asked the Commander, and put his hand on his collar.

The chairman of the consultation, Pavel Ivanovich, gave no sign of having heard the Commander's question and said slowly, taking his place at the head of the table:

"I suppose we ought to ask the patient when he first became aware of the onset of the disease and what pathological indications made him realize he was ill. After that we'll examine the patient."

. . . A sheet of paper covered with illegible professorial script remains as evidence of this meeting of professors; the paper was yellow, unlined, rough-edged—made from wood pulp, the kind of paper that according to engineering specialists should disintegrate in seven years:

> The report of the consultation in which Professor So-and-So, Professor So-and-So, Professor So-and-So [and so on—seven times] took part.
>
> The patient, Citizen Nikolai Ivanovich Gavrilov, appeared before us complaining of pain in the epigastric region, vomiting, heartburn. He fell ill two years ago, without realizing that there was anything wrong at first. Was given outpatient treatment and visited health resorts. No improvement. At the request of the patient a consultation of the above-mentioned was called.
>
> *Status praesens:* Patient's general condition satisfactory. Lungs—N. Heart—slight enlargement and accelerated pulse observed. Mild neurasthenia. Other organs—apart from stomach—no pathological symptoms observed. It was agreed that in all probability the patient is suffering from an *ulcus ventriculi* and that an operation is necessary.
>
> Those taking part in the consultation suggest that Professor Anatoli Kozmich Lozovsky should operate. Professor Pavel Ivanovich Kokosov has agreed to assist.
>
> [City, date, signatures of the seven professors]

Subsequently, when the operation was over, it became clear from private conversations that not a single professor had in fact judged the operation to be in the least necessary, being of the opinion that the form which the disease had taken did not indicate an operation—but nothing was said of this during the consultation; only the taciturn German expressed the view that the operation was unnecessary, although he did not persist in face of his colleagues' objections; and it was also told that, as Professor Kokosov—the one whose eyes were overgrown with hair—was getting into his automobile to go to the House of Scientists, after the consultation, he said to Professor Lozovsky, "You know if a brother of mine had this disease I wouldn't operate," to which Professor Lozovsky replied, "Yes, of course, but. . . but it's a safe operation, after all. . . ." The engine came to life, and the automobile began to move. Lozovsky settled down comfortably, straightened out the skirt of his coat, leaned over toward Kokosov, and whispered so the driver would not hear:

"A frightening character, that Gavrilov—no emotion, no subtle shades about him. 'Am I to undress? I, you see, consider the operation inessential, but if you, comrades, think it is necessary, just indicate the time and the place where I must present myself for the operation!' Briefly and precisely."

"Yes, yes, yes, of course, my good man—a Bolshevik, you know, what can we do?" said Kokosov.

In the evening of that day, at the hour when thousands of people crowded cinemas, theaters, variety shows, taverns, and beer parlors, when crazy automobiles gobbled up street puddles with their headlights, carving up with those headlights crowds of people on the sidewalks that looked quaint in the lights, when in the theaters—entangling time, space, and countries, entangling nonexistent Greeks, Assyrians, Russian and Chinese workers, citizens of the American and Soviet republics—actors, by a variety of means, forced the spectators to remain silent or to applaud, at that hour above the city, above the puddles, above the houses rose the moon, for which the city had no use. Clouds moved swiftly, and it seemed that the moon was frightened, was in a hurry, ran, jumped to be on time, not to be late somewhere—white moon against blue clouds and black abysses in the sky.

At that hour the unbending man in House Number One was still sitting in his study. Drawn curtains completely covered the windows. Again a fire was burning in the grate. The house was steeped in silence, as if the silence had been hoarded for a century. The man was sitting on his wooden chair. This time thick books in German and English lay open before him; he was writing with pen and ink in his vertical script—in Russian on German linen paper. The books lying open in front of him concerned statecraft, law, and the use of power. Light fell from the ceiling of the study, and now the man's face could be seen: it was a very ordinary face, perhaps just a little hard, but there was great concentration and no sign of weariness in it; the man sat for a long time over his books and his writing pad. Then he rang, and a stenographer came in. He began to dictate. The landmarks of his speech were the USSR, America, Britain, the world and the USSR, British sterling and Russian poods of wheat, American heavy industry, Chinese manpower. The man spoke loudly and firmly, and every phrase was a formula.

The moon was moving over the city.

At that hour the Commander was sitting in Popov's room in a large hotel where only party members stayed—they had moved in in 1918 when in the smoke of rebellions Communists had to stay close together. The hotel room was large, luxuriously furnished, but like all rooms in all hotels it suggested something temporary, something of the road which, in its essence, is adverse to comfort. There were three of them—Gavrilov, Popov, and Popov's two-year-old daughter, Natashka. Popov lolled on the sofa. Gavrilov sat by the table, and Natashka fidgeted on his lap. Gavrilov was lighting matches one after another; Natashka looked at the flame with the wonder that only a child can feel before the mysteries of this world; then she stuck out her lips and blew at the flame. It took more than one puff to put out a match, but when it did go out, there was such amazement, such delight, and such awe in Natasha's blue eyes in the presence of this mystery that it was impossible not to light another match, impossible not to bow one's head before the mystery that was Natasha herself. Later Gavrilov put Natashka to bed, sat down by her crib, said, "You close your eyes and I'll sing you a song"—and he began to sing, not knowing how, not knowing a single song, making up a song on the spot:

> There came a goat and said:
> Sleep, sleep, sleep, sleep, sleep.

He smiled, looked slyly at Natasha and Popov, and sang the first thing that came into his head that was consonant with the words "sleep, sleep, sleep": he sang:

> There came a goat and said:
> Sleep, sleep, sleep, sleep, sleep. . .
> But don't pee, pee, pee, pee, pee. . . .

Natasha opened her eyes and smiled; and Gavrilov went on singing the last two lines in his unpracticed voice (he really couldn't sing) until Natasha fell asleep.

Then Gavrilov and Popov drank tea together. Carrying a red teapot on which was written in white enamel "To Comrade Popov from the workers of the Lysev factory on the Fifth Anniversary of October," carrying this teapot Popov went to the boiler in the kitchen to fetch some hot water. On a spread newspaper he set out glasses, plates of butter and cheese; sugar was in a bag, bread in another bag. Popov asked, "Shall I make you some gruel, Nikolka?"

They sat facing each other, talking slowly in low voices, taking their time; much tea was drunk; Gavrilov had unbuttoned the collar of his tunic and was drinking from his saucer. As they were drinking their second glass of tea, after talking about this and that, Popov pushed away his half-empty glass and said, after a pause:

"My Zina walked out on me, Nikolka, leaving the child on my hands; she ran off with some engineer she was in love with before—

devil knows who he is. I have no wish to judge her; I don't want to dirty myself by calling her names—but still, you have to admit, she ran off like a bitch, on the sly, without a word. It's hard to think that she never loved me but lived with me as a kept woman on account of my position, but still it turned out that she left me for the sake of silk stockings, perfume, face powder, and what have you. And I'm ashamed of myself; I pulled her out of a hole—it was at the front—took care of her, loved her, and like a fool took her to my heart—and she turned out to be a spoiled miss. I never really got to know the woman who lived with me for five years. . . ." And Popov went into all the trivial details of the separation, details which are always so painful because of their very triviality—the triviality that obscures the things that really matter. Then they began to talk about their children, and Gavrilov spoke of his family life, his three little ones, his wife, who was no longer young, but who would always be the only woman in the world for him. For a long time they talked about Natasha: how could Popov take care of her when he did not even know how to put her properly on a potty, or rock and hum her to sleep? Popov showed Gavrilov some books by Vodovozova, Montessori, Pinkevich;[6] he spread his arms in a gesture of helplessness. And all the time they drank cold tea.

The moon hurried over the city. At the hour when city streets were becoming empty—to rest in the night—and in villages the first roosters began crowing, when people digesting their suppers, the impressions and clever maxims of the day—husbands, wives, lovers—were crawling into their beds, Gavrilov was taking his leave of Popov.

"Give me something to read—but make it something simple, something about good people, about real love—something like *Childhood and Boyhood*," Gavrilov said.

Every corner of Popov's room was heaped with books, but a simple book about simple human love, simple relationships, simple life, a book

6. E. N. Vodovozova (1844–1923); educator, author of children's books and memoirs; Albert Petrovich Pinkevich (1884–1939); educator, author of books on methods of teaching; arrested in 1937; died in prison.—Eds.

about the sun, about human beings, and simple human joy—such a book was not to be found at Popov's.

"That's revolutionary literature for you," Gavrilov said jokingly. "All right then, I'll read Tolstoy again. I like that bit about the old gloves worn at the ball." And Gavrilov's face darkened; he paused, said quietly, "I didn't tell you, Alyoshka, so as not to waste time in useless talk—I saw the Chief today and I also went to the hospital to see the professors. That bunch put on a great show of learning. I don't want to be cut up—everything in me is against it. Tomorrow I have to go under the knife. Do come to the hospital; don't forget the old man. Don't write anything to my wife and my children. Good-bye!" And Gavrilov left the room without shaking Popov's hand.

A closed automobile was standing in front of the hotel. Gavrilov got in, said, "Home, to the station," and the automobile nosed into narrow streets. In the sidings the moon slithered over the rails; a dog ran past, yelped, and vanished where the rails stretched silently away into darkness. A sentry stood at the footboard of the car; he froze to attention as the Commander passed. The orderly suddenly materialized in the corridor; the attendant poked his head out; electric lights flashed on in the car, and a real provincial silence—deep, unbroken—descended. The Commander went through to his sleeping compartment, took off his boots, put on his slippers, unbuttoned the collar of his tunic, rang—"Tea." He went into the lounge, sat down by the table lamp; the attendant brought tea, but the Commander left it untouched; the Commander sat for a long time over *Childhood* and *Boyhood*, reading, thinking. Then he went into the sleeping compartment, returned with a large writing pad, rang, said to his orderly, "Ink, please," and began writing slowly, deliberating over each sentence. He wrote one letter, read it through, thought it over, sealed it in an envelope. He wrote a second letter, thought it over, sealed it. And he wrote a third letter—a very short one—wrote it hastily, sealed it unread. A numb silence filled the car. The sentry stood motionless by the footboard. Orderly and attendant were motionless in the corridor. It seemed that time itself was motionless. For a long time the letters in their white addressed envelopes lay in front of the Commander. Then the Commander took a large envelope, sealed all three letters in it, and on the envelope wrote "To be opened after my death." Casually he got up to go to bed. In the sleeping compartment he removed his tunic, then went out to wash before bedtime, got undressed, lay down, turned off the light. And for three or four hours the car remained in darkness and silence. This was the hour of the third roosters' crowing. If at the time the attendant had peeked into the Commander's compartment he would have seen, to his surprise, a red glow of a cigarette at the spot where the Commander's head was supposed to be—to his surprise, because usually the Commander did not smoke.

And then the bell from the Commander's compartment rang sharply, summoning the attendant.

The Commander spoke in the tones of an army leader:

"My clothes. Greatcoat. Call the garage—a racer, two-seater, open top; I'll drive myself. Get the House of Soviets, Popov's number."

The Commander said into the receiver, to Popov:

"Aleksei. I'm leaving to fetch you now. Come down to the entrance. This is Gavrilov speaking. Don't delay."

The two-seater hundred-horsepower racer jerked from the spot in second gear, swinging fanlike, casting shafts of white light—the chauffeur jumped out of the way, the Army Commander was at the wheel; the horn bellowed; the automobile began snipping splinters of puddles, alleys, shop and institution signs, tearing wind and space. Popov stood in sleepy bewilderment. The automobile must have given the rubber of its tires a good punishing, pulling up hard in front of the entrance to the House of Soviets; Popov got in silently. And the automobile began hurling back streets, alleys, the splash of puddles, the lights of street lamps. The air grew firmer and firmer, burst into the howling of the wind, whistled inside the automobile, became icy and biting. Streetlamps at crossings swung their lights, swooped down and retreated headlong—one militiaman then another blew his whistle. But the automobile had already torn itself free of the pile of houses and streets, was leaving the city limits, at first into the open spaces of vacant lots with the occasional streetcar-line gas burner, then into the black gloom of the fields. It was in top gear. Air and wind had gone crazy, slashing, stopping the breath. The highway beneath the automobile had long since merged into a smooth, white flatness, obscuring the hollows on the road and the piles of stone along the edges; only when the hollows were especially large, the automobile would take off and fly a few feet through the air, losing the noise of stones flying from under the tires. Once, twice, three times the automobile's lights struck walls of village huts, the huts scattered like sheep, and the village was left behind in a yelping of dogs. In a dip between two hills the automobile lights became entangled in the shaggy gray locks of an autumn mist, and it became clear that even a mist can fly, screech, rush, howl like a snowstorm and prick the face like a blizzard. Gavrilov sat bent over the wheel—all attention, precision and calculation—forcing the automobile forward, forward, forward, harder, harder, faster. Popov had long been down on all fours on the floor of the automobile, convulsively holding onto the floor with both hands and not looking out. In this way, in the space of less than an hour, the automobile broke through a distance of a hundred versts or so. There at the edge of some old forest the automobile lost speed, grew weak, fell silent, let wind and cold go their way—stood the rushing slant sleet upright, vertical; the automobile stopped. Popov sat down in his seat. Gavrilov said:

"Give me a cigarette, Alyoshka."

Popov answered:

"To the devil with you and all these tricks, my liver has gone down to my heels. There, have your smoke, damn you!"

Gavrilov lit up, leaned restfully against the back of the seat, said meditatively:

"When I'm overworked, when I'm at my wit's end, I take the automobile and race. This racing puts me and my thoughts in order. I remember every single one of these races. And I remember the smallest details of everything that happened during these races, all the conversations, all the phrases, down to the intonation of the voice, down to the way in which a cigarette stub glowed. I've got a bad memory, I forget everything—I don't even remember what happened in the crucial days of battles; they told me about it afterwards. But these races I remember perfectly. Just now I was driving like a madman, with a ninety-nine percent chance of having a smashup—but my every movement is precise, and it's not possible to have a smashup. I am intoxicated with the incomprehensible intoxication of precision. But if we did have a smashup, I'd only be glad! Let's talk."

Gavrilov threw away the cigarette stub with an energetic gesture, drew himself up straight, fell silent, no doubt listening to himself—fell silent solemnly, proudly.

"On the other hand, no need to say anything. We'll have a talk later. Sit still! We'll have another race. I feel good, because this racing, this rush forward is what a man should live for, is what makes life worth living—and for the sake of which we live. We've said everything to each other with our lives. Sit still! There are times when it's better not to say anything!" said Gavrilov proudly.

And the automobile began tearing up spaces on the return journey, stunning wind, time, mists, villages, forcing time and mists to dance a wild dance, to shout and run—all this to force Popov down on all fours again, to hook his hands to whatever turned up, whatever held firm, to shut his eyes tight in fear and send his liver down to his heels.

From the hill over the city the entire city was visible for several moments—down there in the mist, in the dim lights and reflections of lights, in the distant murmur and noise, the city seemed to be very miserable.

The automobile approached the city limits at the hour, at the gray dawn hour, when factory whistles sound over the city.

Three: Gavrilov's Death

The first snow, the snow that leads the earth out of autumn into winter, always falls during the night, so as to lay a boundary between the autumnal slush, mist, sleet, fallen leaves, and street rubbish that were there yesterday—and a white, brisk winter day, when all the cracklings and noises have vanished and when in the silence a man has to brace himself, to direct his thoughts inward and not to hurry anywhere.

The first snow fell on the day of Gavrilov's death. A white silence descended, blanching and lulling the city; blue tits that had flown in from the country with the snows were shaking snow from the twigs of trees outside the windows.

Professor Pavel Ivanovich Kokosov always woke up at seven o'clock, and it was at this hour that he awoke on the day of the operation. The professor stuck his head out from under the blanket, cleared his throat noisily, stretched out a hairy arm to the bedside table, felt for his spectacles with a habitual motion of the hand, and saddled his nose with them, setting the lenses into the thicket of hair on his face. On a birch outside the window a blue tit was scattering snow about. The professor put on a dressing gown, stuck his feet into his slippers, and went to the bathroom. The ceilings in Professor Kokosov's apartment were low, provincial; the professor must have lived twenty years or so in that apartment, because the leisure of at least a twenty-year span must have been spent on that thoroughly rubbed-in dust, on those yellowed curtains, on those faded pictures, on those leather-bound books, on wearing a hole in the couch, on polishing the felt cover on the desk to a silvery gloss, on the pointlessly neat disposal of every object in the house and on the desk, from the inscribed matchbox (a gift from his students), from the decaying pen covered with deerskin and made in the shape of a deer's leg (a memento of Switzerland), to the chamber pot under the bed, from which enamel was already chipping. It was quiet in the house at the hour when the professor awoke, but when he emerged, grunting, from the bathroom, his wife, Yekaterina Pavlovna, was already in the dining room stirring sugar into the professor's tea with a clink of spoon against glass; the samovar was hissing. The professor came out for his tea in dressing gown and slippers.

"Good morning, Pavel Ivanovich," said the wife.

"Good morning, Katerina Pavlovna," said the husband.

The professor kissed his wife's hand, sat down opposite her, settled his spectacles more comfortably into the hair on his face—and then behind the glass of his spectacles little eyes of a priestlike stamp became visible, eyes which were both amiable and cunning, simpleminded and intelligent. The professor took a swallow of tea in silence, preparing to make some customary remark. But the ritual of morning tea was interrupted by the telephone. A telephone call was unusual at this hour. The professor looked sternly at the door of the study where the telephone was ringing, looked suspiciously at his wife—a plump, aging woman wrapped in a Japanese kimono—got up, and went to the telephone, every step expressing suspicion. The professor's words, spoken fretfully in what was meant to sound like an old man's voice, were swallowed up by the receiver.

"All right, all right, I'm listening. Who's calling, and what's the matter?"

A voice at the other end of the line said that the call was from headquarters: they knew that the operation was scheduled for half-past eight, and they would like to know if the professor needed any assistance—should they send an automobile for him? And suddenly the professor lost his temper; he snuffled into the receiver, began speaking irritably.

". . . Let me tell you that I'm a servant of society and not of private individuals; yes, yes, yes, of course, my good man; I take a streetcar to the clinic, my good man. I do my duty according to my conscience, if you don't mind. And I see no reason not to take a streetcar today."

The professor banged down the receiver, cutting short the conversation, snorted, snuffled, returned to the table, to his wife and tea. He snorted once or twice, chewed his whiskers, and very soon calmed down. His eyes became visible again behind his spectacles; now they were wise and intent. The professor said quietly:

"Let's say Ivan the peasant from the village of Drakiny Luzhi gets sick—he'll lie on the stove ledge for three weeks, then he'll say a prayer, groan a bit, talk things over with his family, and go to the district hospital to see the doctor, Pyotr Ivanovich. Pyotr Ivanovich has known Ivan for fifteen years; during that time Ivan has brought a couple of dozen chickens to Pyotr Ivanovich as payment in kind, got to know all of Pyotr Ivanovich's children as they came along, and even pulled one of the boys' ears for raiding his pea patch. Ivan will come to see Pyotr Ivanovich, will present him with a hen. Pyotr Ivanovich will look him over, listen to what he has to say, and, if necessary, operate—quietly, calmly, competently—no worse than I would do it. And if the operation doesn't come off, Ivan will die, they'll put a cross over him, and that'll be the end of it. . . . Or even, let's say, some Anatoli Yuryevich Svintsitsky comes to see me. He'll talk about his symptoms till he's hoarse. I'll look him over thoroughly and look him over again half a dozen times, I'll find out all I can about him, and then I'll say, 'Go home, my good man, and live with your ulcer: be careful and you'll live another fifty years, but if you die, well, there's nothing that can be done about it: God has called you, my good man!'. . . If he says to me, 'Operate!' I'll do it, but if he doesn't want it—I would never think of doing it."

The professor was silent for a while.

"There's nothing worse than consultations, Katerina Pavlovna. I have no wish to insult Anatoli Kozmich. Anatoli Kozmich has no wish to insult me. We pay each other compliments and show off our learning, and the patient has nothing to do with it, just like all the fuss at Bolshevik trials—no one knows the patient properly, you see, neither Anatoli Kozmich, nor Herr Schieman. . . ."

The professor was silent for a while.

"Today I am assisting at an operation at the hospital; we are operating on a Bolshevik—Army Commander Gavrilov."

"The one who. . . ," said Yekaterina Pavlovna, "who. . . , well, according to the Bolshevik newspapers,. . . a terrible name! And why aren't you operating, Pavel Ivanovich?"

"Well, there's nothing particularly terrible about him, of course," the professor replied. "As for why they picked Lozovsky: such are the times we live in—youth is all the rage; young people have to make their reputations. And still, when you come down to it, nobody really knows the patient after all these consultations, even though all our big names have examined him thoroughly—prodded him all over, X-rayed him, purged him out. But they missed the main thing—the man himself. It's not a man they're dealing with, but a formula—some General X they write about every day in the papers to put the fear of God into people. But just you make one slip in the operation, and you'll end up in strange places—you won't even recognize your own father when they've finished with you."

Again the professor lost his temper, snuffled, snorted, hid his eyes in the thicket of his hair, got up from the table, shouted through the doorway leading to the kitchen, "Masha, my boots!" and went to his study to get dressed. He combed his eyebrows, his beard, his whiskers, his bald spot, put on his frock coat, thrusting a fresh handkerchief into the pocket of his coattail, pulled on his boots with vamps polished to the shine of a samovar and chestnut tops; he looked through the window: had the horse been brought up? The horse was already standing at the front porch; Ivan the coachman, who had lived in Professor Kokosov's kitchen for twenty years, was brushing snow from the seat.

Professor Anatoli Kozmich Lozovsky's room was not at all like Kokosov's apartment. If Kokosov's apartment had preserved the atmosphere of Russia at the turn of the century, Lozovsky's room had assumed its permanent shape between 1907 and 1916. There were heavy curtains, a wide sofa; naked bronze women served as candelabra on the oak writing table; the walls were covered with rugs, and over the rugs were hung second-rate paintings bought at exhibitions of the "World of Art." Lozovsky was asleep on the sofa, and not alone, but with a young and beautiful woman; his starched dickey lay on a rug on the floor. Lozovsky awoke, lightly kissed the woman's shoulder, got up energetically, and tugged sharply at the curtain rod. The heavy woolen curtain began creeping toward the corner, and the snowy day came into the room. Lozovsky looked out joyfully at the street, the snow, the sky, as people look who are in love with the life pulsing within them. Carefully, as bachelors do of a morning, he looked around the room, and, before going to wash, in pajamas and lacquered slippers, he began tidying up the room; he removed an unfinished bottle of red wine from the table and stood it behind the bookcase; he placed a dish of biscuits on the lower shelf of the bookcase; he arranged an ashtray, an inkwell, writing pads, books on the table. He plugged in the cord of an electric kettle, poured coffee into the kettle. The woman was asleep, and it was obvious that this woman was of the sort who love and give themselves up to love quietly and devotedly. Waking up, she said:

"Darling"; she opened her eyes happily, caught sight of the brisk winter day, the snow on the trees, lifted herself on the bed, clasped her hands as though in prayer, shouted happily: "Darling—the first snow, winter, darling! . . ."

The professor placed his large white hands on the woman's shoulders, rested her head against him, and said:

"Yes, yes, it's winter, my spring, my lily of the valley! . . ."

At that moment the telephone rang. The telephone in the professor's room hung on the wall near the rug over the sofa. The professor picked up the receiver: "Yes, yes, I'm listening." Headquarters was on the line: should they send an automobile for him?

The professor replied:

"Yes, yes, please do! There's no need to worry about the operation, I'm sure it will be a brilliant success. About the automobile—yes, please, especially as I have to make a stop on business before the operation. Yes, yes, please—about eight o'clock."

The professor hung up and said to the woman, joyfully and with pride:

"Get yourself dressed, my little lily of the valley; an automobile will be coming to pick me up; I'll give you a ride and I'll take you home. Hurry!"—and he embraced the woman, laying his head on her shoulder in the way that people do when they are very happy.

It was already a quarter to eight. The man and the woman got dressed, hurriedly, happily. As he dressed, the professor poured coffee into little Chinese cups. Smiling happily, the woman buttoned the studs of his starched dickey. Before leaving the house, the professor, with a solemn face and a sort of nervous respectfulness, made a telephone call; by means of all sorts of telephonic roundabout ways, the professor penetrated the network of about thirty or forty lines in all, calling the study of House Number One; he asked respectfully if there would be any new instructions; a firm voice in the receiver suggested that he come with a report immediately after the operation. The professor said: "Good-bye, it will be done," bowed to the receiver, and didn't hang up straightaway. An automobile was already roaring in front of the entrance.

In the morning on the day of the operation—before it took place—Popov came to see Gavrilov. It was not yet dawn, and the lights were still on; but there was no chance to talk, because a nurse came to take Gavrilov to the bathroom to administer a final enema. As he left the room, Gavrilov said:

"Alyosha, read that bit in Tolstoy's *Boyhood* about what is and what isn't comme il faut. What a feeling the old man had for the instincts in our blood!" Those were the last words that Popov heard from Gavrilov.

Popov went home in the rustlings of a frosty dawn quietness, went down a side street toward a steep bank facing the open spaces beyond the river; there on the horizon in a deep blue murk beyond the snows a blue moon was dying, and the east burned red, crimson, cold; Popov began to go down to the river to reach the city through the fields—behind him burned the east. At that moment Gavrilov was standing at the window gazing across the river—did he see Popov? Dressed in a hospital robe, in a bathroom by a window stood a man, a weaver from Orekhovo-Zuyevo whose name had become overgrown with legends of war, with the legends of thousands, tens of thousands and hundreds of thousands of men who had stood behind him—with the legends of thousands, tens and hundreds of thousands of deaths, agonies, mutilations, of hunger, cold, the ice-covered ground and the scorching heat of long marches, of the thunder of cannon, the whistle of bullets and night winds, of bonfires in the night, of marches, victories and routs, and again of thousands and of death. The man stood at the window in a bathroom, his hands clasped behind his back, looking into the sky, motionless; he lifted a hand and wrote on the misted window: "death. enema. not comme il faut," and began to undress.

Just before the operation people were hurrying back and forth along the corridor connecting the operating room with Gavrilov's room, whispering, bustling about noiselessly. The evening before the operation, a rubber tube had been inserted into Gavrilov's esophagus—a siphon to pump out gastric juice and to irrigate the stomach, the kind of rubber instrument that leaves a feeling of nausea and depresses the spirit as if it existed for the purpose of affronting human dignity. On the morning of the operation an enema was administered for the last time. Gavrilov came into the operating room wearing a hospital robe and shirt and pants of coarse linen (the shirt had laces instead of buttons), numbered hospital slippers on his bare feet (they had changed his clothes for the last time that morning—and given him sterilized things to wear); he entered the operating room pale, drawn, and tired. In the anteroom alcohol burners hummed, water boiled in long, nickel-plated boxes; there were silent people in white gowns. The operating room was very large and painted all over—floor, walls, ceiling—with white oil paint. The room was unusually light because one entire wall was a window, and that window looked out over the river. In the center of the room stood a long white table—the operating table. Here Gavrilov was met by Kokosov and Lozovsky. Both were wearing white gowns, and both put on white caps, like cooks; in addition, Kokosov covered his beard with a napkin, leaving only his thicketed eyes exposed. Along a wall stood a dozen people in white gowns. Gavrilov entered the room calmly, accompanied by a nurse; he bowed silently to the professors and walked to the table; he looked out of the window, at the far bank of the river, clasped his hands behind his back. A second nurse brought in a boiling sterilizer containing instruments—a long, nickel-plated box suspended from hooks.

Lozovsky asked Kokosov in a whisper:

"Shall we begin, Pavel Ivanovich?"

"Yes, yes, of course," replied Kokosov.

And the professors went to wash their hands over and over again, to pour mercury chloride solution over them, to swab them with iodine. The anesthetist checked the mask and fingered his bottle.

"Let's begin then, Comrade Gavrilov," said Lozovsky. "Would you kindly lie down on the table. Take your slippers off."

Gavrilov looked at the nurse and, slightly embarrassed, straightened his shirt; she gave Gavrilov a brief glance, as if he were a thing, and smiled as one smiles at a child. Gavrilov sat down on the table, kicked off one slipper, then the other, and quickly lay down, adjusting the roller cushion under his head—closed his eyes. Then quickly, deftly, with practiced skill the nurse buckled the straps around his legs, binding him fast to the table. The anesthetist laid a towel on the patient's eyes, smeared vaseline over his nose and mouth, put the mask over his face, took his hand to check the pulse, and poured chloroform onto the mask; the sweet, astringent smell drifted through the room. The anesthetist noted down the time when the operation began. The professors moved to the window in silence. Using forceps, the nurse began to take out and arrange on the sterilized gauze scalpels, sterilized towels, Peon's and Kocher's clamps, pincers, needles, and silk thread. The anesthetist continued to add chloroform. Silence settled upon the room. Then the patient began to jerk his head from side to side and groan.

"I can't breathe, take off the mask," Gavrilov said, and snapped his teeth.

"Please be patient a little," answered the anesthetist.

A few minutes later the patient began singing and talking:

"The ice is gone, the Volga flows to sea, my golden one, my precious one; a foolish girl am I, and love has come to me," sang the Commander, and then whispered, "Sleep, sleep, sleep." After a brief silence he said sternly, "And never give me cranberry *kissel*[7] again; I'm sick of it; it isn't comme il faut." He fell silent again, then shouted sternly, as he must have shouted in combat: "No retreat! Not a step! I'll shoot! Alyoshka, brother! Full speed ahead—the land is already out of sight. I remember everything. And so I know what the Revolution means, what a force it is. And I'm not afraid of death." And again he began to sing, "Beyond the Urals lives a carpenter, my golden one, my precious one. . . ."

"How do you feel? Aren't you sleepy?" the anesthetist asked Gavrilov softly.

And Gavrilov replied in his normal voice, also softly, like a conspirator:

"Not so good. I can't breathe."

"Be patient just a little longer," said the anesthetist, and poured on more chloroform.

Kokosov look anxiously at the clock and bent his head over the patient's case history, read it through once more. An organism can react peculiarly to certain drugs. For twenty-seven minutes they had been trying to put Gavrilov to sleep. Kokosov called over a junior assistant and thrust his head forward for him to adjust the spectacles on the professor's nose. The anesthetist whispered anxiously to Lozovsky:

"Perhaps we should give up chloroform and try ether?"

Lozovsky replied:

"Let's keep on with chloroform. Otherwise we'll have to postpone the operation. Awkward."

Kokosov looked around sternly and lowered his eyes, worried. The anesthetist poured on more chloroform. The professors remained silent. Gavrilov finally went to sleep in the forty-eighth minute. Then the professors rubbed their hands with alcohol for the last time. The nurse bared Gavrilov's stomach; the skinny ribs and flat belly were

7. A starchy jelly.—Eds.

exposed. With sweeping strokes Professor Kokosov rubbed alcohol, benzine, and iodine into the area of incision—the epigastric region. A nurse brought sheets to cover Gavrilov's legs and head. Another poured half a bottle of iodine over Professor Lozovsky's hands. Lozovsky picked up a scalpel and drew it over the skin. Blood spurted, and the skin spread apart, sliding off layers of fat, yellow like mutton fat, with interlayers of blood vessels. Lozovsky again cut into the human flesh, cutting through fascia—white and gleaming, interlayered with faintly lilac muscles. With a dexterity surprising in so bearish a man, Kokosov closed off blood vessels, using Peon's and Kocher's clamps. With another knife Lozovsky cut through the sac of the peritoneum. He put aside the knife and wiped away the blood with sterilized towels. Through the slit could be seen the intestines and the milky-blue sac of the stomach. Lozovsky put his hand in among the intestines, turned the stomach around, and kneaded it. . .

. . . on the gleaming wall of the stomach, on the spot where the ulcer should have been, was a scar—white as if molded from wax, resembling the larva of a dung beetle—a scar which showed that the ulcer had already healed and that the operation was pointless. . .

. . . but at that moment, the very moment when Gavrilov's stomach was in Lozovsky's hands. . .

"Pulse! Pulse!" shouted the anesthetist.

"Respiration!" Kokosov confirmed, automatically it seemed.

And then Kokosov's eyes, full of anger, of terrible anger, started out from behind his thicket of hair and spectacles, started out and swept around the room, while Lozovsky's eyes, close-set, pressing against the bridge of his nose, drew even closer together, sank deeper into their sockets, concentrated, merged into a single, frightfully piercing eye. The patient had no pulse, his heart was no longer beating, his breathing had stopped, and his legs were growing cold. It was a heart shock: the organism had been poisoned by the chloroform it had rejected. It was a certain indication that the man would never return to life, that death was inevitable and could only be postponed for an hour, ten hours, thirty hours, but no longer—by means of artificial respiration, oxygen, camphor, physiological salt solution; he would never regain consciousness; he was, in fact, dead. There was no doubt that Gavrilov was to die under the knife on the operating table. Professor Kokosov turned his face to the nurse, thrusting it forward so that she could adjust his spectacles. The professor shouted:

"Open the window! Camphor! Get physiological salt solution ready!"

An even greater silence fell upon the silent crowd of assistants. As if nothing had happened, Kokosov bent over the instruments on the table, inspected them in silence. Lozovsky bent over by Kokosov.

"Pavel Ivanovich," he whispered furiously.

"Well?" answered Kokosov in a loud voice.

"Pavel Ivanovich?" Lozovsky said in an even lower whisper, but now the fury had gone from his voice.

"Well?" replied Kokosov loudly, and said, "Carry on with the operation!"

The two professors straightened up, looked at each other—one with eyes fused together, the other with eyes starting out from behind a hairy thicket. Lozovsky swayed back from Kokosov as if from a blow, as if trying to focus his gaze; his single eye became two eyes wandering about the room; then they merged again, even more completely, even more piercingly. Lozovsky whispered:

"Pavel Ivanovich. . . "

And lowered his hands to the wound: he did not sew up the inner cavities but merely basted them together and began stitching the outer layers only. He gave an order:

"Release arms—artificial respiration!"

The enormous window of the operating room was opened, and the cold of the first snow came into the room. Camphor had already been injected. With the help of the anesthetist Kokosov was pulling Gavrilov's arms back and raising them, forcing him to breathe. Lozovsky was patching up the wound. He shouted:

"Physiological salt solution!"

And a woman assistant thrust two large needles, about the thickness of a cigarette, into the man's chest, to pour a thousand cubic centimeters of salt solution into the dead man's bloodstream to maintain blood pressure. The man's face was lifeless, blue; the lips had turned purple.

Then Gavrilov was untied from the table, transferred to a table on wheels, and taken back to his room. His heart was beating, and he was breathing, but consciousness did not return, and perhaps never returned, to the final moment when the heart, pumped full of camphor and salt, stopped beating, when—thirty-seven hours later—there were no more doctors and no more camphor, and he died, perhaps because up to the last minute no one was admitted to him, apart from the two professors and a nurse; but an hour before the death of Army Commander Gavrilov was officially announced, a patient who happened to be in the neighboring room heard strange sounds, as if a man was tapping out a message, as men do in prison. In that room lay a living corpse, saturated with camphor because the proprieties of the medical profession do not permit a man to die under the surgeon's knife. The professors guarded that room so carefully because the Army Commander was dying there—a hero of the Civil War, a hero of the great Russian Revolution, a man overgrown with legends, he who had had the will and the right to send men to kill other men and to die.

The operation had begun at eight thirty-nine, and Gavrilov was taken out of the operating room on a wheeled table at eleven minutes after eleven. At that time in the corridor, Professor Lozovsky was met by the porter, who told him that there had been two telephone calls for him from House Number One—and again the porter came and said that someone was on the telephone. Lozovsky went to the telephone. He was expecting a call from House Number One. In the receiver he heard: "Darling, I miss you so much," and for a moment Lozovsky bared his teeth and, perhaps, was about to say something vicious, but he said nothing, threw down the receiver. The professor went over to the window in the office where the telephone was, stood looking out at the first snow for a while, chewed his fingers, and then returned to the telephone; he penetrated the network that had thirty or forty lines, bowed to the receiver, and said that the operation had been successful, but the patient was very weak, and they, the doctors, had judged his condition to be grave; he begged to be excused from reporting in person immediately. Upstairs in the corridor between the operating room and the room of the patient, where people had been bustling and whispering that morning, there was now not a soul to be seen.

Gavrilov died—that is, Professor Lozovsky came out of his room with a sheet of white paper and, head bowed, announced sadly and solemnly that the sick Army Commander, Citizen Nikolai Ivanovich Gavrilov, had passed away at seventeen minutes after one in the morning, to everyone's great sorrow.

Three-quarters of an hour later, toward two o'clock in the morning, several companies of Red Army men entered the hospital yard, and sentries were placed at all passageways and stairways. Into the room where the Army Commander's corpse lay strode the same three general staff officers who had come to the station to meet him. Gavrilov—the helmsman in charge of the enormous machine known as the army—had been in charge of these men's lives, and now they had come to take charge of the Commander's corpse. At that hour the second roosters crow in the villages. At that hour clouds were creeping across the sky, and hurrying after them came a plump moon, already tiring of the chase. At that hour Professor Lozovsky was being taken in a closed Rolls to pay a special visit to House Number One: noiselessly the Rolls entered the gateway with the griffins, past the sentries, and drew up at the entrance. A sentry opened the automobile door. Lozovsky went through to the study where three telephones stood on the red felt of the desk and buttons were lined up on the wall behind the desk like a company at attention. It is not known what was said at that interview, but it lasted only three minutes; Lozovsky came out of the study—out of the main door—out of the yard—in a great hurry, holding his hat and coat in his hands like a character out of Hoffmann; the automobile had gone; Lozovsky walked unsteadily, like a drunken man. The streets were deserted at that still nocturnal hour, and the streets swayed together with Lozovsky.

The streets swayed beneath the moon with Lozovsky in the still wastes of night. Hoffmannlike, Lozovsky left the study of House Number One. The unbending man remained in the study. The man stood behind the desk, leaning over it on his fists. The man's head was bowed. He remained motionless for a long time. He had been torn from his papers and formulas. And then the man began to move; his movements were angular and precise as the formulas that he dictated to his stenographer every night. He began to move very quickly. He pressed a button behind him; he picked up a receiver. He said to the man on duty, "The open racer!" He spoke into the telephone to one of the ruling "troika" who must have been asleep at that hour; his voice was weak: "My dear Andrei, another one has gone—Kolya Gavrilov is dead, we have lost a comrade-in-arms. Would you mind calling Potap?"

To the chauffeur the unbending man said, "The hospital!" The streets were not swaying. In the clouds the moon was hurrying, bustling—and like a whip the automobile snaked through the streets. The hospital building, black in the gloom, blinked its restless windows. Sentries stood in black passageways. The building was numb, as a place of death must be numb. Through black corridors the unbending man made his way to Commander Gavrilov's room. He went in; there on the bed lay the body of the Army Commander; the smell of camphor was stifling. Everyone left the room, and only the unbending man and the body of a man—Gavrilov—remained. The man sat down on the bed by the feet of the corpse. Gavrilov's arms lay along his sides on top of the blanket. The man sat for a long time by the corpse, bending over it, quiescent. Silence filled the room. The man took Gavrilov's hand, pressed it, said:

"Farewell, comrade! Farewell, brother!" and he left the room, head bowed, not looking at anyone; he said: "Why doesn't somebody open a window; it's suffocating in there!" walked quickly down the black corridor and descended the staircase. At that hour in the villages the third roosters were crowing. Silently the man got into the automobile. The chauffeur turned his head to listen to the order. The man was silent. The man pulled himself together; the man said, "Out of town!—as fast as you can go!"

The automobile tore from the spot, in top gear, turning fanlike, casting shafts of light—began snipping splinters of alleys, street signs, streets. The air at once grew firm, began to blow as a wind, whistled inside the automobile. Streets, houses, streetlamps flew back—the streetlamps swung their lights, swooped down, and retreated headlong. At full speed the automobile tore out of town, striving to tear itself out of its very self. The gas burners of suburban streetcar lines had already disappeared; already the village huts were scattering like sheep in a yelping of dogs. The canvas of the highway was already invisible, and now and then, at those moments when the automobile flew through the air, the noise of the wheels was lost. Air, wind, time, and earth whistled, screamed, howled, leaped, rushed forward: and in this colossal rush, with everything rushing forward—only the moon behind the clouds, and the automobile, and this man sitting calmly in the automobile, moving in parallel motion, became motionless objects.

At the edge of the same forest where Gavrilov and Popov had been a few days before, the man gave the order: "Stop!" and the automobile broke speed, having rendered space, time, and wind superfluous, having stopped the earth and made the moon chase the clouds. The man did not know that a few nights before, Gavrilov had been near this forest. The man got out of the automobile and—silently and slowly—went into the forest. The forest stood still in the snow, and the moon hurried above it. There was no one for the man to talk to. It was some time before the man came back from the forest. On returning and getting into the automobile, he said:

"Let's go back. There's no hurry."

The automobile approached the city when dawn was already breaking. Red, crimson, cold, the sun was rising in the east. There, below, in violet and blue—in a radiant mist, in a haze—lay the city. The man took it in with a cold glance. Of the moon in the sky, all that remained at that hour was a barely perceptible, melting icy lump. In the snowy silence the rumble of the city could not be heard.

Last Chapter

The evening after Army Commander Gavrilov's funeral, when military brass bands had done blaring and banners were no longer lowered in mourning, after thousands of mourners had passed, and the body of the man was freezing in the earth and with the earth, Popov fell asleep in his room. He awoke at some strange hour, sitting at the table. The room was dark, and Natasha was crying softly. Popov bent over his daughter, took her in his arms, and walked around the room with her. A white moon, weary of hurrying through the sky, was pushing its way through the window. Popov went over to the window and looked out at the snow and the stillness of the night outside. Natasha slid down from his arms and stood on the windowsill. In Popov's pocket was a letter from Gavrilov, the last note that he had written the night before he entered the hospital. The note said:

"Aloyosha, brother! I knew that I was going to die. Forgive me, but you are not a young man anymore. I was rocking your little girl on my knee, and I was thinking. My wife is old too, and you have known her for twenty years. I have written to her. And you write to her too. Go and live together—marry if you like. Bring up the children. Farewell, Alyosha!"

Natasha was standing on the window sill and Popov saw: she was puffing out her cheeks, sticking out her lips, looking at the moon, taking aim at the moon, and blowing at it.

"What are you doing, Natasha?" her father asked.

"I want to blow out the moon," Natasha replied.

The moon, plump as a merchant's wife, swam behind clouds, wearying of the chase.

It was the hour when the city machine was beginning to come to life, when factory whistles were sounding. The whistles were long-drawn-out—one, two, three, many of them—merging into a gray howl over the city. It was quite clear that the whistles were the soul of the city—now frosted by the moon—howling.

Moscow
Povarskaya Street
January 9, 1926

Mother Earth

A peasant named Stepan Klimkov from the small village of Kadom went into the forest at Willow Spring to steal bark, climbed an oak, lost his footing, fell, and, caught by the bindings of his bast shoes, was left hanging head downward in the branches; both his eyes burst from the rush of blood to his head. That night the forest watchman Kandin took the thief to forestry headquarters and reported to Nekulyev that he had brought a "citizen forest thief." The forester Nekulyev ordered Stepan Klimkov's release. In the darkness Klimkov stood at attention, barefoot—his shoe bindings had been cut by Kandin when he was pulling him down from the oak, and his shoes had fallen off on the way. Klimkov said calmly:

"I could do with a guide, mister comrade; my eyes have run out down to the last drop."

Nekulyev leaned close to the peasant, saw a thicket of beard; what had been eyes were two dead slits, and blood trickled from the ears and nose.

Klimkov stayed at forestry headquarters for the night; they bedded down in Kuzya's hut. Kuzya, forest watchman and teller of tales, had been telling them the story about the three priests and the masses, the wily peasant Ilya Ivanych, his wife Annushka, and the drunkard Vanyusha. It was a moonlit June night. At the foot of the hill the Volga kept silence. Sometime during the night Ignat the wise man arrived—Minka the shepherd had run to fetch him from his cave. The wise man announced that there was no getting back Stepan Klimkov's eyes—neither by prayer nor by spell—and that they should apply ribwort leaves "so his brains won't run out."

* * *

The hero of this tale of forest and peasants (apart from the forester Anton Ivanovich Nekulyev, apart from the tanner Arina—Irina Sergeyevna Arsenyeva—apart from summer, ravines, and whistles in the night), the hero is a wolf pup, the little wolf pup Nikita, as he was named by Irina Sergeyevna Arsenyeva—that woman who was to die so senselessly and to whom the wolf pup—who was to die for his pelt—stood for so much. The wolf pup was bought for a few kopecks that spring in Tetyushi, in the Province of Kazan, on the Volga. A peasant boy was trying to sell it on the wharf, but nobody was buying; it was lying in a basket. And Irina Sergeyevna bought it.

It was barely able to open its eyes; its pelt was the color of black-leaf tobacco, and there was a reek of dog about it. She put it inside her coat and warmed it at her breast. She herself likened the color of its fur to that of tobacco—smaller than a kitten, it clouded her mind like tobacco with its enchanting remoteness. The boy who was selling the pup told her how it had been found in a forest clearing: some boys went into the forest after birds' eggs and stumbled upon a litter of wolf pups (they were still blind); five of the pup's little brothers died of hunger, and it alone survived. The pup was unable to lap milk. Irina Sergeyevna let the steamer go on without her and managed—by means of a special authorization—to obtain in Tetyushi a rubber nipple, the kind used to feed babies, and with this nipple she fed the pup. She whispered to the wolf pup as she fed it:

"Eat, my little silly; suck, Nikita, and you'll grow big and strong!"

She came to spend hours talking to the pup as a mother would to her child. The wolf pup was a wild creature; it never lost its fear of Irina Sergeyevna; it would creep into dark corners, curl its fluffy little tail under it, and from the darkness its black, watchful eyes would follow with a concentrated gleam every movement of Irina Sergeyevna's hands and eyes, and when their eyes met, the eyes of the wolf pup, unblinking, would become more hostile than ever, staring out of its triangular head like two intelligent, gleaming buttons; but the triangular head itself—the pointed muzzle, the black and likewise pointed ears—was silly, and not fierce at all. A terrible smell of dog came from the pup, and the rankness of it permeated everything.

* * *

There is a kind of dryness about the land along the quiet reaches of the Volga between Samara and Saratov. The Volga—the ancient waterway of Russia—flows among great plains, among solitudes and wildernesses. In July the grass on the hills is dried up, the smell of wormwood is everywhere, flint gleams in the moonlight; the traveler's feet become dusty and sore; the leaves of the oaks and maples are stiff, as if made of tin, and it takes more than a man's strength to split a pine; only the Tartar maple stands unperturbed; there are no flowers, and the bonfires on the hills—there is no mistaking them for lightning flares—are visible from the Volga for many scores of versts through the dust clouds rolling up from Astrakhan. And that is when you know that the dust is born of grasshoppers, of the grasshoppers' June chirping. To the right are wooded hills, and beyond the hills—the steppe; to the left are floodlands, and beyond the floodlands—the steppe. In the distance un-Russian church towers can be seen through the haze beyond the Volga: these are the German kolonkas.[1]

Many years ago, one of the tsars, most likely Paul, gave Prince Kakomsky a title deed in which was written in the imperial hand:

> . . . Your Excellency will come to the town of V. on the Volga; thirty versts thence lies the hill of Medyn. Your Excellency will mount this hill, and everything that the eye of Your Excellency will behold will be yours. . . .

1. German "colonies"—settlements established in the trans-Volga region in the latter half of the eighteenth century.—Eds.

Along the Volga, where it enters the steppe, the Medyn forests sprang up on hills and islands, extending seventy versts along its bank; pines for building timber, oaks, maples, elms, thickets, virgin forest, fir stands, saplings—covering an area of twenty-seven thousand dessiatines. In a hollow at the foot of Medyn Hill stood the Prince's house—stunned by the year 1917. In the forests there was nothing except watchmen's huts and guard posts; villages, big and small, moved away from the forests, making way for them and for the Prince. This is what the forester Nekulyev wrote to his friends on the Provincial Committee about how to get to him: ". . . you have to get to the village of Vyazovy by steamer; in Vyazovy you have to find either the forest watchman Tsipin—and he will jolt you for sixteen versts in his cart through woods, over hills, across gullies—or the fisherman Vasili Ivanov Starkov (you have to ask for Vasyatka the fisherman)—and he will pull you twelve versts up the Volga by the strength of his own back. It's a lie that only in China do people ride people: this is also the practice hereabouts—Starkov harnesses himself to the towline, his son takes the rudder, you get into the boat, and towing—just as people did three hundred years ago—by their own strength, taking turns, they'll pull you to forestry headquarters. If you ask this Starkov, 'How many Communists have you in Vyazovy?' he will answer, 'We don't have many Communists; what we have around here is mostly common folk; there's only two families of Communists.' And if you press him further about who exactly these common folk are, he will say, 'Common folk, like everyone knows, is common folk. Common folk is something like what you might call Bolsheviks.' "

The forests stood drooping, silent in the night. But if there had existed a giant ear able to catch every sound in the countryside thereabouts, it would have heard among the murmurs and rustlings of the forest at night many a crash of falling trees sawed through by forest thieves, ringing of saws, talk of moonshiners and deserters in hollows, on hills, in caves and lairs; it would have heard footsteps, shouted challenges, warning shots of watchmen and forest guards, whistled messages and exchanges, cries of owls and cries of men, groans of the beaten, the thud of horses' hooves. At night forest bonfires are visible from afar, and if these bonfires have been lighted in hollows, the smoke drifts far over the dewy ground; night bonfires are frightening, and frightening deeds are recounted at night around the bonfires of Russia. Wolves keep well clear of the bonfires. Days in the forest—in July—are always spacious; the smell of Tartar maple is everywhere. The men of the forest—foresters, watchmen, mounted guards, woodcutters—have the unshakable conviction that the whole of humanity is divided into two camps: themselves—foresters, watchmen, and woodcutters—and "citizen forest thieves."

* * *

It was a brisk, sunny day when the forester Anton Nekulyev, a brisk and cheerful man, succeeded in finding Tsipin the watchman in the village of Vyazovy, told him that he was the new forester and a Party member, that there had been a hell of a crush on board the steamer, that he had to get to the village soviet, that he had to be in Medyn that night, and that Lenin had a head on his shoulders, goddamn if he didn't! He made no mention of the sixteen trained men who were to follow him to protect the forests from plunder, or of the authority with which he and the sixteen had been invested to take strong measures—up to and including shooting. At the village soviet, in a drowsy, fly-buzzing silence, the chairman and secretary sat drinking samogon[2] and eating catfish; the chairman ordered the secretary to bring a third glass for Nekulyev. Tsipin listened and took careful note of things: that morning, as soon as Nekulyev arrived, he had sent an estafette to Medyn by way of the cordons, ordering Kuzya to come and fetch the new forester; the words *estafette* and *cordon*[3] were embedded in the vocabulary of the forest men and dated back to the time of the princes. Tsipin listened attentively to Nekulyev but, being a passionate hunter, responded with tales of grouse, foxes, and double-barrels. He did,

2. Home-distilled liquor usually made from grain or potatoes.—Eds.
3. As used here, estafette—relay message; cordon—guard post.—Eds.

however, tell how the peasants had killed the forester's predecessor: they killed him in the house, slit him open, pulled out his guts; with the guts they bound his hands and feet, tried hard to stuff him into the grand piano but couldn't do it, so they threw both him and the piano down the steep bank of the Volga—the piano hangs there to this day, stuck in the bush willows; and the hunting in these parts is fit for a king: if, say, a man should be greedy enough to lay traps in January when the fox is starving, he could pick up as many as a hundred skins in a single winter—but of course that's not the thing for a hunter with a gun to do: it would be a disgrace. Kuzya arrived in a carriage, the front wheels of which had been replaced by cart wheels, while those at the back still had rubber tires. He pulled himself to attention, arms stiffly at his sides, and began, army style, "I have the honor to report. . . ." Nekulyev gave him his hand, clapped him on the shoulder. Kuzya said:

"I have the honor to report. . . I mean, we'd better spend the night here or else—you never know—they're like to bash our heads in, them forest thieves. I have the honor. . . I mean, people are really swine these days; it's a disgrace, that's what."

Tsipin turned out to be of a different opinion about the situation. He reasoned:

"What? Touch Comrade Anton Ivanovich Nekulyev? Him, a Party member and a Bolshevik? The forests are ours now. And who would dare lay a finger on him? I'll come with you as far as Willow Spring; we'll take the steppe route, the roundabout way. Anton Ivanovich has a revolver, you have a rifle—I have a rifle—I'll tell my boy to go on ahead and give him a double-barrel. We'll shoot the lot of them, and no doubt about it! What, touch a Bolshevik? That's why he's come here—because the forests are ours. You can take as much as you like now without stealing, that's what the law says."

The steppe in July is stifling; the chirping of grasshoppers oppresses, and the air is filled with the smell of wormwood. Heat lightning winked incessantly. They descended a hill, crossed a ravine, passed some windmills, and suddenly the steppe was all around them, ancient as the ages. They took the roundabout route. Tsipin soon dozed off; Kuzya hummed to himself. It was very dark and quiet; only the grasshoppers kept up their rasping. They went down into another ravine and soon heard marmots squealing and whistling close by; Kuzya got down from the carriage and took the horse by the bridle: he said marmots had dug their burrows all over the track—the horse could likely break a leg. They came to the top of a hill and saw the sky—far away in the steppe, above the hills, over the Volga—torn with silent lightning: the thunder's roll did not reach them. "There's going to be a storm," said Tsipin sleepily. And again the sky flew open—silently—but this time to the left, above the steppe itself. The horse set off at a trot; the dry, black earth resounded to the thud of hooves and the rattle of wheels; the grasshoppers seemed to have quieted down, and one enormous half of sky was silently rent from east to west, opening up its infinities. By the side of the track sunflowers bent their heavy heads, and then the enormous distant thunder cart rolled over the steppe; the atmosphere became suffocating. Now lightning flares came thick and fast; the sky was ripped to tatters and became a bowling alley where the boisterous elements sent balls of thunder rolling. Tsipin woke up and said, "We'll have to go to the shepherds' dugout, Kuzya; we'll sit out the rain there; I don't fancy getting wet."

The storm, the open spaces, the thunder and lightning—all seemed a rare joy to Nekulyev, and all his days in the forests he remembered that night: how good it is sometimes when you are young to shout with the thunder, to outshout the storm! They did not reach the shepherds' dugout in time: the wind began tearing about the steppe; lightning darted and thunder roared on all sides; a torrent of rain came down on them when they were about a hundred paces from the dugout and instantly soaked them to the skin. The black earth of the path leading to the dugout turned to mud in a moment; water poured into the dugout in a stream. Someone shouted in alarm, "Who the hell is out there?" The horse stopped obediently by the wicket fence. In a brilliant flash of lightning Nekulyev saw his way to the dugout and—in the impenetrable rainy darkness—tumbled into a puddle. Through the

LEARN CHINESE - Headache
头(tóu)疼(tòng)
Lucky Numbers 36, 35, 31, 55, 23, 4

thunder he heard people talking close by, "That you, Potap? It's me, Tsipin." "Our matches are soaked. Did the Devil bring you out hunting?" "No, I'm taking a Barin somewhere—Party member, the new forester." Again the sky was rent by lightning; a little boy ran past into the dugout and said, as both he and the dugout were swallowed up by the darkness: "Dad, the wolves are here again, a pack of them. There's a strange horse standing out there, not ours, right where the pack is!" Kuzya had stayed behind with the horse, taking shelter under the carriage. They went out to the horse, Tsipin and Nekulyev carrying guns and the old shepherd a stick. They found the horse up the wicket fence, snorting, while Kuzya stood shaking off mud, sniveling and muttering curses: "I get under the carriage, and there's a big flash of lightning! And that gray nag takes a big jump up the fence! It's a wonder my neck wasn't broken." "It's wolves, you fool!" "N-o-o?" They pulled the horse down from the fence, replaced the broken bellyband with a rope. They decided to go on. They set off. The track had quickly turned to mud and running streams. They went down into a small ravine. Tsipin said, "Don't take the bridge away, Kuzya; the horse'll break a leg." "It was there at the bridge," he explained to Nekulyev, "that the peasants killed the Barin—the Prince." A stream whirled through the ravine. It had stopped raining; the storm was passing; lightning and thunder were less frequent. They began to climb out of the ravine; the horse slid about in the mud and went sprawling; the travelers climbed out. They began to push the carriage, got halfway up the hill, and started to slide down again, all together—horse, carriage, and men; the horse fell down and had to be unharnessed. Lightning blazed, and suddenly they saw a pack of wolves sitting side by side, above, on the edge of the ravine, no more than ten paces away. Tsipin said, "We'll have to pull the cart out; we can't spend the night here: the wolves won't leave us alone." They led the horse out first, then dragged out the carriage. Nekulyev was in high spirits all the time.

The rain had passed. They moved into the forest—into darkness, rustlings, fragrances, and water splashing down from leaves. Tsipin got down, dropped behind, and went to the hut of a watchman friend. Nekulyev wondered how Kuzya could find his way and not get lost in this damp and odorous darkness, where a man might just as well be blind. Kuzya was silent for a while.

"When the peasants took it into their heads to kill the Barin—the Prince—this Tsipin goes to Prince Kadomsky and says, 'Seeing as how things are, you'd better leave; they're going to loot the house—the peasants are after your blood.' The Prince says to his lackey, 'Have the troika ready!' And Tsipin says to him, 'There won't be any horses for you, Your Excellency, we won't allow that.' The Prince started hustling about, dressing himself up something like a tradesman—he took his coachman's boots, his cap too, and his red neckcloth. His wife put on a shawl. They left at night, as quiet as could be, and there by the bridge Tsipin comes up to them: 'Seeing as how things are, Your Excellency, how about a little tip from Your Grace for the warning?' The Prince gave him a coin—a silver ruble—but who killed the Prince nobody knows."

Kuzya fell silent. Nekulyev too was silent. They rode slowly in the pitch darkness. Here and there on the ground glowworms were burning.

"And, speaking of that, here's another thing. In a village there lived a peasant—a very cunning, thrifty man—his name was, let's say, Ilya Ivanych," Kuzya began in a leisurely singsong. "And he had a young wife—a beauty, and faithful, too—Annushka by name. The village was a big one—it had three churches, mark you, all consecrated to different saints. . . . And so one day Annushka goes to mass. And let me tell you that mass began at a different time in each church. So Annushka is walking along, and she meets a priest; he says to her, 'Good day to you, Annushka!' and then, under his breath, 'Annushka, how about us meeting some evening at sundown?' 'What are you saying, Father?' says Annushka, and runs straight to the second church as fast as her legs can carry her. And she meets a second priest, and he says, 'Good day to you, Annushka!' and, under his breath, like the other one, 'Annushka, how about spending a night with me?'"

"What on earth are you talking about?" Nekulyev asked in bewilderment.

"I'm telling a story, that's what; people like the way I tell stories."

⋆ ⋆ ⋆

And once again it was a brisk, sunny day—a day that emerged in benevolent sunshine from the wet darkness of a stormy night in the steppe, a day filled with the intoxicating smells of forest's and earth's abundance. The lungs swelled like a sponge in water—how good it smells when maples are baking in the sun! The stunned white house with its lizards and broken windows basked in the sun, and, at the slightest touch, ripe raindrops fell from the grapevines on the terrace. Below the steep bank the Volga was melting the sun; you couldn't look at it. All that had to be done was to put in windows, screw on doorknobs, fix vents and doors in the stoves, replace the stolen parquetry with new flooring—and the house would be in just as good shape as before—it wouldn't take much! And from the inner rooms to the one which bore the sign "Office" on its outside door, strode—the ceiling dully echoing his firm steps—a brisk man, handsome, curly-haired, youthful, wearing a dark-blue, high-collared blouse and hunting boots. The pince-nez on his nose sat neatly—in contrast with the rioting hair above. In the office, dull as all the bookkeeping in the world, plans and maps lay on one drawing table; the green baize of the other one was stained with the ink and candlewax of many nights and many scribblers; through the windows the sun brought in the vigor of the whole world. Holding his arms stiffly at his sides, Kuzya stepped forward to meet Nekulyev; he was barefoot and wearing the dark-blue woolen trousers of a gendarme's uniform and a shirt faded with age; he wore no belt, and his collar was unbuttoned; Kuzya had enormous—terrifying—brown whiskers that, far from making his good-natured, round face fearsome, merely gave it a rather foolish look. Kuzya said:

"I have the honor to report there are guards and peasants outside: the guards have brought in some forest thieves. And there's a woman asking to see you too. Do I let them in?"

"Let them all come in!"

"I have the honor to report, the old forester used to talk to everyone through this window—he ordered a hole to be made in the wall just for that."

"Let them all come in."

For a few minutes the office was the scene of an open meeting; the peasants came trooping in; there was no telling which of them had been caught stealing wood and which had come as petitioners. The guards lined up army style, rifles at their sides. The peasants all began talking at once; they were peacefully disposed but still on their guard: "The forests are ours now, we own them!" "Seeing as how you're a Communist, comrade—we want to cut wood in Wet Gully, seeing as how it belongs to Kadom!" "Those Germans across the river—if they set foot in the forests on our side, we'll break their legs for them!" "The same for Tartars and Mordvinians." "Look at it this way, Comrade Barin: we did the cutting, and we want to sell the wood at a good price in Saratov!" Nekulyev said gaily: "Its no use acting dumb, comrades, no use playing the fool. It's true I'm a Communist, but I'm not letting anyone plunder the forests. You know yourselves it's wrong; as for shouting, I can do that too—I've got a strong throat." A peasant, barefoot, wearing a coarse woolen coat and holding a fur cap in his hands, came up and stood by Nekulyev, who said, "Don't stand there cap in hand—aren't you ashamed?—put it on!" The peasant was abashed; he shot a glance at Nekulyev, hastily put the cap on, yanked it off again, and replied with a snarl: "This is a house, ain't it? There's icons hanging in the corner!" Two by two, unhurriedly, quietly, six men came into the room—Germans, all wearing vests but ragged like the Russians. "Können Sie Deutsch sprechen?" asked one of them. The peasants broke into shouting about the Germans: "Get out; the forests are ours!" Nekulyev sat down on a table, stretched out his legs, rocked back and forth a few times, and began in a businesslike way: "Comrades, why don't you sit down—oh, on the windowsills—and let's talk sense. Some of the men here are under arrest; I'll let them go and give them back their saws and axes—but that's not the issue. You can't cut down forests any old way; judge for yourselves"; and he began to speak about things that to him were as clear as day. Peasants and Germans went away in silence; many of them, though, had put on their caps toward the end of his talk. To those who left last Nekulyev said in a friendly manner, "I shall take what action is necessary, comrades—I shall do what has to be done, and you are on your own!" Nekulyev was a no-nonsense sort of man.

Kuzya pulled himself to attention and said:

"I have the honor to report. . . would you like a few eggs or some milk, perhaps? We haven't got any ourselves, but Maryasha can take a boat to the Germans across the river."

"I want to have a talk with your wife anyway—about her getting my meals. Let's eat together. Buy some eggs. . . ."

And so it was a sunny morning, and Nekulyev was cheerful and handsome in his youth and vigor, and Kuzya with his foolish face was standing barefoot at attention when Arina Arsenyeva, the tanner, came into the room. The green office baize was spotted with many waxes and many inks.

"I have to get a permit from you for bark. We'll strip it ourselves. Here's the order—I need the bark for the Shikhany tanneries." And in the top right-hand corner of the order were the words "Workers of the World Unite!" and on her documents, on her Party card were words beautiful to both of them: "Communist Party of Russia." "They killed the man who was here before you? They killed the Prince?" "The peasants hereabouts are fighting a war of their own against the forests." Their conversation was long, strange, and intense, with the intensity of the sun itself. For him—long ago and far away—a forestry institute in Germany, factories and factory settlements in Russia; being a revolutionary is a profession; dim lights are burning in the corridors of mill barracks, and sleep is so sweet at the hour when the man on night duty begins to bang on the doors of the cubicles ("Get up! Get up! It's your shift, the whistle's blown!"); and the world is beautiful; the world is full of sunlight because one's will is strong and one's faith in the goodness of the world is strong—and there's no nonsense about it: the will and the faith drawn from his childhood in the Urals (a mountain rises above valleys, and beyond the mountain is a wilderness where it seems that no man has ever set foot—where there are bears, and a hermit in a mud hut), from books in cardboard covers: the will and the faith which had sustained him through the forestry institute and the trenches of the Naroch front. All this was Nekulyev's, and all this had the precision of a game of chess—both out here in the Medyn forests and back there: in Moscow, Halle, Paris, London, and the mills of the Urals. And for her: the Volga, the Volga steppe and the land beyond, the fence at the edge of the village: on the other side of the fence—the outlaw steppe and rough trails; and on this side—vats with soaking skins and the corpse-like smell of skins and tanbark; and everything had this smell, even the house, even the Sunday pies—light as a feather—and the feather beds—light as Sunday pies; and her mother's incense (her mother died when she was thirteen, and she had to take her place in the house and learn the tanning business as well); and her father—himself like a tanned bull hide from the vat; and the cuckoo clock; and the house goblin behind the stove, and the devils; and at the age of thirteen she was in her third year at the gymnasium—her breasts already formed beneath the brown school uniform—and by the age of seventeen the young Volga beauty had grown to abundant womanhood; Saint Petersburg and her studies there unfolded in misty regularity, but the mists were low like the ceilings at home—and she had to rid her cubbyhole on Shestnadtsataya Liniya of bedbugs—yet later, when her father died, the ceilings at home seemed even lower—oppressive, smoke-blackened; the house goblin was no longer behind the stove, but the smell of skins brought back the mysteries of her childhood; she entered the house as the moon enters the night; the head clerk grumpily brought in greasy account books, and the police came, scuttling like rats, rummaging and rustling; there could never be any reconciliation with the house, the account keeping, and the rats; beauty gave the right to shout in protest, and the straight lines of prison corridors merged with the regularity of Petersburg, where there is no way of putting out the moon. All this was Arina Arsenyeva's—and all this, too, had the precision of a game of chess—and tanneries (the smell of them filled her childhood) are needed by the Red Army and must be put back into operation. With the years moonlight replaces sunlight in a woman's life: the abundance of seventeen is a heavy wine by the age of thirty when there has never been any time for wine. "I know the country round here through and through—the forests, the land along the Volga."

In the sunshine the green of the grapevine leaves makes the light greenish, and the air becomes liquid. Nekulyev noticed that in the green light the blood vessels in the whites of Arina's eyes turned blue, while the pupils deepened to an abyss—and suddenly it seemed to him that from her eyes came the smell of tanned hide. Three people came into the office: a man, a woman, and a boy. The man said uncertainly:

"I have the honor to report—I'm second watchman after Kuzya from the eleventh cordon. Yegor Nefedov. And this is my wife, Katya. And this is my son, Vasyatka."

The watchman was interrupted by his wife, who began in an injured tone: "You told Kuzya, Barin, that you want to eat with Maryasha. Do as you please—you're the master—but you could eat with us, too, and most likely no worse than at Maryasha's. We're building a new house; my husband's not strong; he got a rupture; we're from Kadom. Do as you please—you're the master. But Maryasha's got three kids, one smaller than the next, and there's only three of us." Katya pursed her lips, stuck her hands on her hips, and waited belligerently for an answer. Nekulyev said, "Go, God be with you—I'll decide later." And in the sunlight Arina Arsenyeva noticed: the bluish shaven skin of his cheekbones and chin was firm and tough. Arina said softly, with a touch of bitterness:

"Do you know, to this day when they have the 'crawling-in'—that's what they call moving into a new house—the peasants around here first let in a rooster and a cat, and only then do people go in—according to popular belief this has to be done by the light of a full moon. It's at night too that they drive the cattle over to the new place. And the same night, before dawn, the wife runs around the house three times—naked. All this is done to please the house goblin. . . ."

One: Nights and Days

Ask Maryasha, Katyasha, Kuzya, or Yegor about the forest—they will tell you:

In the depths of the forest and among the pines lives the wood devil—the Lyad. The forests stand dark, reaching from earth to sky, and there is no end to the things that Maryasha knows about them. The bluish woods rear an impenetrable wall. Man can hardly force a way through the close-growing pines; in the heart of the forest everything is slowly dying and becoming wilderness. Here by the side of new growth stand withered oaks and firs, eventually to crash to earth—smothering everything beneath them—and to be covered with a rich funereal brocade of mosses. Even in a July noon it is gloomy and damp here, and seldom does a bird cry out; if a wind blows in from the steppe, the ancient oaks rub against one another, groaning, shedding decaying limbs and showers of powdery rotten wood. Here Kuzya, Maryasha, Katyasha, and Yegor are overcome by feelings of terror, nothingness, loneliness, and impotence; their flesh creeps. The devil who is known as the Lyad has made his home in the pine woods from time immemorial, and Kuzya would even tell what he looks like: a wide belt of red cloth, caftan[4] buttoned up from left to right instead of right to left; bast shoes on the wrong feet, eyes glowing like coals, and himself all made up of mosses and fir cones. If you want to see the Lyad, you have to look over the right ear of a horse.

* * *

By day the white house in the hollow near Medyn Hill stood quietly amid greenery, cool as a pond. At night the house went mad: Nekulyev's straining eyes wandered over broken furniture, bindings of torn

4. As used here, an old-fashioned man's coat—long and gathered at the waist.—Eds.

books, all sorts of junk. In a rubbish heap on the terrace Nekulyev found an hourglass; it took five minutes for the sand to run from one glass sphere to the other; on moonlit nights the glass of the spheres had a faint greenish gleam; during the day Nekulyev never gave the hourglass a thought, but at night he spent many a five minutes with it. He was a no-nonsense sort of man; he was not aware that—independent of consciousness and will—every rustle in the house, every stupid mouse skitter across the floor, raised goose pimples on his back, and he fell into the habit of staying awake at night; he never lost his nerve, but all the time somebody else seemed to be there—some elusive, remote presence—and every night was the same. The moon was up, and hundreds of moons were shattered in the water at the foot of the hill; the house was numb; the trees surrounding it were of silver; a silence settled, broken only by owls. Moonlight furrowed the parquet floor in the ballroom. Nekulyev had carefully closed the windows, but there was no glass in them. He had barricaded the ballroom's three doors with broken furniture and wedged them with staves. A sofa stood by one of the doors, and on it lay Nekulyev. A revolver in an unbuttoned holster hung on a chair close by; a rifle was propped against the foot of the sofa. On the sofa lay a large, healthy, handsome body—the very same body that absurdly broke out in goose pimples at every rustle. Nekulyev was calm in the knowledge that two trained men, Kandin and Konkov, were guarding the forest at Willow Spring—they were tough men and wouldn't bungle the job. You couldn't cross the hills on foot, let alone in a cart, but if anyone got through to the house, then he'd go down to the cellar through a secret door which he had stumbled on by chance, and which dated back to the time of the Prince who used to own the estate; and from the cellar—through an underground passage—into the ravine; once there—just try to find him! . . . To distract attention, a small, battered lamp had been left burning in the right wing of the house, where the windows were carefully covered up. The moon peered through the windows into the wrecked interior of the house. Nekulyev got up from the sofa, picked up his revolver, removed the stake from the door, and made his way through the dark rooms—hesitantly, because he was still unused to the house; he took a drink of water from a bucket in the kitchen and went back; in the doorway he stood and listened to the sounds of the house—unaware of the goose pimples that covered his body; he wedged the stake against the door—and took it away again quickly: when he had picked up the bucket, he had laid his revolver on the windowsill and forgotten it; hurriedly he started back. In the dusty moonlight the hourglass lay on the windowsill in the ballroom; Nekulyev began running the sand from one sphere to the other, bending his curly head over the dull glass.

★ ★ ★

And then, all of a sudden, someone began knocking on the window in the room where the lamp was burning, and a voice called uncertainly: "Hey, whoever's there, come out. The militiaman wants you!" Lithe as a cat, Nekulyev picked up his rifle and looked out the broken window without making a sound: there in the moonlight by the house stood a boy with a boat hook, looking warily around in the silence. Nekulyev said calmly, "And who may you be?" The boy replied, relieved, "Come on, the militiaman wants you!" "What are you doing with that boat hook?" "It's to keep off dogs. Any dogs here? The militiaman's down below, in the boat!"

The boy, Kuzya, and Nekulyev (the last two carrying rifles) went down the steep bank to the Volga. Three flat-bottomed boats were moored by the bank. A militiaman, holding a revolver in one hand and a saber in the other, a rifle slung over one shoulder, was pacing the bank. The militiaman shouted:

"What the hell are you doing sleeping when timber's being stolen? I was out after moonshiners, got two flat-bottoms—been out three days, haven't slept. I was just going past Wet Hill, and what do I see: logs flying down from the top of the hill—timber thieves are at work and you're sleeping! I'd have taken the thieves myself, but all I've got is two witnesses: the rest are moonshiners caught redhanded. If I leave them, they'll run for it. Forty buckets of samogon I'm carrying—haven't slept in three days! . . . They come hurtling down right from the top, and two empty flat-bottoms waiting on the river! . . ."

The militiaman climbed into the boat, gave an order to the moonshiners, and the peasants harnessed themselves to the towline and started pulling the string of flat-bottoms in silence. The militiaman barked orders and moved his revolver threateningly. The moon shone down silently, and hundreds of moons splintered in the water. River and hills were numb. The boats disappeared beyond a spit of land. Kuzya brought up two horses, one of them saddled, the other with a sack of hay on its back. Without a word Kuzya and Nekulyev started at a gallop along forest paths and over hills in the direction of Wet Hill, rifles at the ready; they left the horses in Wet Ravine and came out to the Volga. River, hills, silence—a screech owl called, gravel loosened underfoot, the smell of wormwood drifted in from somewhere—silence—and on top of the hill a tree creaked, came crashing down, fell, rolling over the steep bank, dragging rocks after it. Kuzya and Nekulyev started to walk along the river below the sheer drop of the bank—two boats had been wedged among bush willows, one already piled high with logs; another log hurtled down from the hilltop, and close by—no more than ten paces away—a man whistled softly, another whistled on the hill, and a third,. . . and then the world played dead. Suddenly a solitary rifleshot burst on the hill. Kuzya crouched behind a rock; Nekulyev gave him a prod forward with his knee, flicked the bolt of his rifle, and strode resolutely toward the boats, pushed the empty boat out, and threw himself on the loaded one to get it moving. From above came a rifleshot; a bullet smacked the water. "Kuzma, come and push!" Above the drop came a red flash, a pop; a bullet smacked. Immediately Nekulyev fired in the direction of the flash, and somebody shouted from the hill: "Oi, what are you doing, you devil? Let the boats be!"

Nekulyev said:

"Kuzya, push off, push with the oar, take over the rudder, get it away from the shore or they'll hit us!"

* * *

The moon splashed from the oar. Shouts came from the bank: "Forgive us, Barin, for the love of Christ give us back our boats!"

Nekulyev said:

"Damn it, what if they steal the horses?"

Kuzya replied:

"How can they? We'll get them now. Nothing to be afraid of. The peasants have come to their senses—they've got the fear of God in them."

* * *

The boat touched shore at Wet Ravine; three men—peasants—one of them with a rifle—all from Vyazovy—came up tearfully and began to plead for their boat. Nekulyev said nothing, looked away. Kuzya, also without a word, went into the ravine, brought back the horses, and harnessed them to the towline; then he made a stern pronouncement: "Stealing wood, you swine! Get in the boat; you're under arrest! They'll get to the bottom of this, they'll show you how to steal wood!"

The peasants fell on their knees. Nekulyev whispered crossly:

"Why arrest them? What are we going to do with them?"

"That's all right—no harm in giving them a scare!"

Slowly the horses made their way along the shore over the rugged stones. Hills and the Volga were still, but the moon had already disappeared; in the vast spaces beyond the Volga the sky was ripening to red as day drew near; the dawn brought a chill, dew soaked their shirts.

"How about me telling you a story?" asked Kuzya.

They took the loaded boats around the spit of land below Medyn Hill and moored them securely. (The boats disappeared in the night two days later—somebody stole them.)

* * *

And again there came a hammering at the windows in the night. "Anton Ivanovich! Comrade forester! Nekulyev! Get up quick!" And the house was filled with the clumping of boots, with whispers and rustlings; candle and lighter flames rocked the ceilings. "Seeing as how you're a Communist, the peasants from Kadom—the whole lot of them and the priest, too—have gone to cut firewood near Red Ravine; estafettes have gone out to all cordons; the peasants have tied up Ilyukhin the watchman and dragged him off to the lockup!" Near the stable yard, opposite the servants' hut, stood lathery horses, and there was a strong smell of horse sweat (a smell sweet to Nekulyev from childhood); a bright star rested on the hilltop (what star was that?), and a glowworm burned under a tree nearby. Kuzya led out the horses, but they were one horse short, and he had to run.

"Yagor, you carry the rifle a bit—save me dragging it."

Into the saddle and off at a gallop to the hills, to the forest.

"Damn it! The trails are choked. One of these branches could take your eye out!"

The forest stood black, silent; on the hilltops the air was parched and dusty; there was a smell of dry grass. The hollows were damp and chill; fog crept along the ground; unknown birds cried out ("Oh, how beautiful the Volga nights!"). There is a strong smell of horse sweat; the horses knew the way.

"What swine these lousy peasants are! It isn't what they take—it's what they knock down and trample! These peasants have no sense of responsibility at all! They've tied up Ilyukhin like a bandit and taken him to the village—they've locked up his wife and kids in the watchman's hut and left someone to guard them; their boy Vanyatka crawled into the cellar, where the dog had dug a hole, got out through the hole into the yard, and ran to Konkov. Otherwise we wouldn't know anything about it. And it's every night you got to be on the lookout!"

Running at a trot, Kuzya caught up with the horsemen and said to Yegor:

"Yegorushka, you run awhile, and I'll ride and rest a bit."

Yegor dismounted and began running after the horsemen. Kuzya punched the bag that served as a saddle to make it more comfortable, settled down, got his breath back, and said cheerfully:

"Wouldn't it be good to strike up a song, like the robbers in the old days!" And his long-drawn-out robber's whistle pierced the blackness of the forest; nearby a large bird flapped its wings.

. . . Spread out among the trees at the edge of Red Ravine, a thin line of watchmen had been lying in wait since evening. A road led through the green wall of the forest among trails that cut the forest into squares, and disappeared into the hills. Nothing much was happening. The sun had sunk beyond the steppe; the moment had passed when—for a moment—trees and grass and earth and sky and birds fall silent; bars of deep blue fell across the earth; an owl flew out of the forest and winged by silently; no sooner had it passed than an unknown night bird cried out among the trees. And then, far away in the steppe, stirring up dust, a string of peasant carts came into view as they moved through a pass in the hills. But they were swallowed up by night, and it was only an hour later that the crude rattlings and creakings of native Russian wooden carts reached the edge of the wood. Then the dust cloud rolled up to the forest; creaking of wheels, rattling of wheel rims, snorts of horses, whispers of people, crying of a baby—converged, crowding against the forest. Two ancient oaks standing at the intersection of the road and a forest trail had been sawed almost through at the roots—the slightest push and they would topple and block the road.

And then out of the darkness—the stern voice of a mounted guard:

"Hey there! You Kadom people! You men! It's no good; turn back!"

And then from the line of carts all at once—shouting and laughter from a hundred throats; there is no making out the words or whether people are shouting or men and horses are trying to outneigh each other; and the carts creep forward. Then two bold trained men, Kandin and Konkov—agility, daring, a final effort—sent the trunks of the two oaks crashing down across the road; two shots explode convulsively into the sky. From the peasant camp—in the direction of the forest—comes a random hail of shots from revolvers, rifles, and shotguns. Half the carts jerk to a halt; horses rear onto the tailboards of carts in front. "Get off the trail!" "Go back!" "Shoot!" "Look out, you've run over a woman!" "The priest, hold the priest!" The forest is dark, incomprehensible; you can't get a horse off the trail; horses shy away from trees, from shots; shafts run into tree trunks, wheels crack against stumps. "The horse, leave the horse alone! You'll tear the collar, you swine!" Nobody knows who is shooting and why.

Nekulyev galloped up at dawn. A bonfire was burning near the edge of the forest. Watchmen were sitting around the fire, two of them singing a monotonous song. Rifles had been thrown in a heap by the fire. Horses stood dejectedly among carts in a little clearing. Men, women, children, and the priest stood under guard to one side. Dawn was catching fire above the forest. The crude encampment was a sorry sight. Kandin, who had come with Nekulyev to protect the forests, went to meet him, took him aside, and began in a distraught whisper:

"Things are a mess. We blocked the road, you see, knocked down two oaks, thinking we'd take, oh, maybe five carts; we cut them off. I fired a warning. We didn't use another bullet. It was the peasants themselves who did the shooting; they killed a boy and a horse, and another horse got trampled. When things got out of hand, I thought we'd make ourselves scarce while we could and let the peasants get out of the mess themselves, so we'd be out of it, but by that time there was no holding back our boys; they started chasing people, arresting, taking weapons away. . . ."

Nekulyev was holding a revolver; he said helplessly:

"Oh, hell, what a mess!"

A crowd of peasants rushed up to Nekulyev, fell on their knees, and began to plead with him:

"Beloved Barin and protector! For the love of Christ, let us go. We won't do it again, we've learned our lesson!"

Nekulyev roared—in bitter anger, no doubt:

"Get up this very minute! To hell with you, comrades! You've been told in plain language: I won't let you rob the forests, not for anything!" And in bewilderment, no doubt: "And look what you've done—you've killed a boy. A fine thing! Where is he? Every cart in the village is wrecked. A fine thing!"

"For the love of Christ, let us go! We'll never do it again! . . ."

"Do me a favor—get out of here. That won't bring the boy back. Get it into your heads, for Christ's sake, that I'm on your side!" And threateningly: "And if any one of you calls me 'Barin' once more, or pulls his hat off to me—I'll have him shot! Do me a favor—get out of here!"

Konkov, a Party member who had come with Nekulyev to protect the forests, turned on him angrily:

"What about the priest?"

"What about him?"

"We can't just let the priest go! That swindler ought to be sent to provincial Cheka."

Nekulyev said indifferently:

"All right then, send him!"

"I hope they shoot the swine!"

The sun rose above the trees—it was a glorious morning; the crude encampment was a sorry sight.

* * *

And once again it was night. The house was silent. Nekulyev went to the window, stood gazing out into the darkness. And then in the bushes nearby—Nekulyev saw it—there was a sudden flash of rifle fire; a shot echoed, and a bullet hit the ceiling with a sharp click; plaster showered down. They were shooting at Nekulyev.

* * *

And then came a brisk, sunny morning; it was Sunday; Nekulyev was in the office. Two moonshiners were brought in; Yegor was bent under the weight of a distilling vat. Tsipin arrived from Vyazovy with a message from the village soviet: "In view of the raising of the question concerning relegation of the forest, Comrade Nekulyev is to report immediately in person." Tsipin had been elected chairman of the village soviet. Nekulyev went; they rode through the steppe, listening to the ground squirrels; Tsipin told hunting tales and was calm, deliberate, matter-of-fact. Later, when Nekulyev recalled that day, he knew it had been the most terrifying day of his life and that only a stupid accident—human stupidity—had saved him from a most gruesome death—from being lynched, torn to pieces—arms, legs, and head torn from his body. In the steppe the squeaking of the ground squirrels seemed one with the suffocating heat. In the village young men and girls were milling in a square in front of the church and the building of the soviet, and a young fellow, barefoot but wearing spurs, was furiously dancing the squat dance; Nekulyev was struck by those spurs and got down from the cart to have a closer look: yes, that's what it was—spurs on bare heels, but the boy's face was not stupid. In the village soviet the peasants were waiting for Nekulyev. They were drunk. The room was stifling. When Nekulyev entered, silence descended upon the gathering—he could not hear so much as a fly's buzzing. Nekulyev and Tsipin went through to the table together, and Nekulyev suddenly noticed that Tsipin's expression, which throughout their ride had been relaxed and amiable, had become cunning and malicious. Tsipin began:

"All right, men! The meeting is open! Here he is—he's arrived! A Party member, too! Let him say what he has to say."

Nekulyev fingered the revolver in his pocket; the spurs came to his mind; the spurs confused his thoughts. He began:

"What's the matter, comrades? You demanded that I come here to make a report. . . ."

"The forests are ours now, we want to split them up, like the law says—to each man his share!"

Someone interrupted:

"To each household its share!"

There were shouts from all sides:

"No, to each man!"

"No, to each household!"

"No, I say, to each man!"

"What's the use of talking to him, men! Get the forester, let's get him!"

Nekulyev shouted:

"Comrades! You demanded that I come here to make a

report. . . . Our land is mostly steppe; forest is scarce. There's a civil war going on, comrades. Maybe you want the landowners back? If all the forests are cut down, you won't be able to make good the damage in forty years. Trees should be cut sensibly, according to a plan. There's a civil war going on, we're cut off from coal. These forests supply the whole of southeast Russia. You want the landowners back? I won't let anyone steal wood. . . ."

"Listen, men! Everything's ours now! Let him answer—how come the Kadom people can steal and we can't? Who is he to plague us?"

"We want to choose our own forester!"

"Get him, men—let's get our hands on him!"

All his life Nekulyev remembered those savage, drunken eyes closing in on him, full of hatred. He understood then that a mob smells blood, even though no blood has been shed. Nekulyev shouted with something like gaiety:

"Damn it, comrades, I won't let anyone touch me. You see this revolver? I'll stretch six of you out, and then I'll turn it on myself!"

Nekulyev pulled the table toward him and got into the corner behind it, gun in hand. The crowd pushed toward the table.

Tsipin bellowed:

"Minka, run get the rifle—we'll see who shoots who!"

"Shoot him, Tsipin; let's get him!"

Nekulyev shouted:

"Comrades, let me speak, damn you!"

The crowd assented:

"Let him speak!"

"Are you your own enemies, or what? Listen to me. Let's talk sense: suppose you kill me—what sense is there in that? You sit down, and I'll sit down, and we'll talk. . . ." That day Nekulyev talked about everything: forests, reforestation, what the Communists were doing, what was going on in Moscow and Brussels, about the locomotives that were being built, about Lenin. He talked about everything because while he was speaking the peasants quieted down, but the moment he stopped they began shouting, "What's the use of talking—let's get him!" And

Nekulyev would begin to feel dizzy from the smell of blood. Tsipin had been standing in the doorway with a rifle for some time. Day gave way to that time of dusk when swallows cut the air. Peasants came and went; the crowd got more and more drunk. Nekulyev knew that there was no escape, that they would kill him, and many times when his throat got dry it was only by a tremendous effort of will that he was able to conquer his pride—not to shout, not to send them all to hell, not to throw himself into the mob, but to keep on talking—talking about whatever came into his head.

Nekulyev was saved by chance. A group of young men, members of the Union of Front-Line Fighters, blind drunk, one of them with an accordion, staggered into the building; their leader—no doubt their chairman—climbed on the table in front of Nekulyev; he was barefoot, and wore spurs; he surveyed the crowd contemptuously and began with an air of authority:

"Listen, you graybeards! It's not up to you to judge Comrade Nekulyev, the forester! It's up to us, the front-line fighters. Look at Rybin there—shouting louder than anyone, but has he ever sat in the forester's cooler? No, he hasn't. Only them that's been caught stealing wood can judge him, and them that hasn't—get the hell out of here. And they think they can take the forest over—just like that! We're the ones that were caught and put in the cooler—so we've got first claim on the forests and we're the ones to judge him—and Tsipin along with him, seeing how he's his right-hand man and a devil himself!"

The swallow dusk had already given way to a grasshopper night. The young fellow was drunk, and around him stood his friends, also drunk. There was uproar: "Liar!" "That's right!" "Kill 'em!" "Get Tsipin, the old devil!" Then a shouting, gasping, knock-down fight broke out; beards, cheekbones, bruises went flying on all sides. Nekulyev was forgotten. Very slowly, apparently motionless, half step after half step, he reached the window and like a streaking cat threw himself out. Never before had he run with such headlong speed—so blindly; he regained memory and consciousness only at dawn, in the steppe, among the squeaking of ground squirrels—as oppressive as the heat itself.

(In the village soviet no one noticed Nekulyev's disappearance in the heat of the fighting, and that same evening Mother Grunya, the wife of Starkov the fisherman, said—and by morning many women were saying it—that with their own eyes—may the earth open up and swallow them if they were lying—they saw Nekulyev's skin darken; saw him strain every muscle, saw his eyes fill with blood, foam drip from his mouth, fangs sprout from his jaws, saw him turn as black as black earth—strain every muscle—and plunge into the earth, sorcerer that he was.)

* * *

And something else happened to Nekulyev. Again, as on a dozen previous occasions, a mounted guard galloped up and reported that the Germans from the other side of the Volga were on their way to Green Island in their flat-bottomed boats—to cut firewood. Nekulyev and his stalwarts set off in his flat-bottom to the rescue of the forests. Green Island was a sizable stretch of land; the forest men moored and went ashore unnoticed. It was a brisk day. They approached the Germans meaning to reason with them, but the Germans met the forest men with an attack organized on the best military lines. Nekulyev gave the order to fire; from the German side came the rat-tat-tat of a machine gun, and the Germans began to advance in a perfectly controlled line, attacking in accordance with all the rules of war. Nekulyev and his band soon ran out of ammunition and were faced with a dilemma: either to surrender or to try to escape in the flat-bottom; but the flat-bottom was a very good target for the machine gun, and the watchmen assured him that if a German gets really angry he will spare nothing. The Germans took them prisoner but later released all of them, except Nekulyev, whom they took back with them to the other side of the Volga, together with the wood and Nekulyev's flat-bottom. Nekulyev spent five days as a German prisoner. He was bailed out—for reasons incomprehensible to him—by the Vyazovy village soviet, headed by Tsipin (and it was Tsipin who crossed the Volga as negotiator). The passenger steamer that served the entire area stopped only at Vyazovy, and the Vyazovy peasants let the Germans know that if Nekulyev was not released they would not let them cross to their side and that any German caught would be killed; the Germans had to deliver butter, meat, and eggs to the ship; they let Nekulyev go.

Two: Nights, Letters, and Resolutions

In the evening Kandin came, bringing with him a forest thief; the thief had climbed a tree, was stripping bark, lost his footing, was caught in the branches by the bindings of his bast shoes; he was left hanging; his eyes ran out. Nekulyev ordered the thief's release. The peasant stood barefoot at attention in the darkness and said calmly,

"I could do with a guide, mister comrade—my eyes have run out." Nekulyev leaned close to the peasant, saw a thicket of beard; the empty sockets had already drawn together; the peasant stood cap in hand—and Nekulyev felt sick; he turned, went into the house. The house was alien, hostile; in this house they had killed the Prince; in this house they had killed his—Nekulyev's—predecessor: the house was hostile to these forests and this steppe—and Nekulyev had to live here. Again it was a moonlit night, and hundreds of moons splintered in the water at the foot of the hill. Nekulyev stood by the window, turning the hourglass over and over; abruptly he flung it away; it broke, spilling sand. . . . Sometimes when he was free, Nekulyev would climb alone to the bald rock at the top of Medyn Hill; there he would light a fire and sit by it, thinking; below was the broad sweep of the Volga and the land beyond, and there was a bitter smell of wormwood in the air. Nekulyev left the house and walked through the grounds; on the threshold of the servants' quarters sat Maryasha and Katyasha; Yegor and Kuzya sat on the ground nearby; a broad-shouldered giant of a peasant, dressed unseasonably in a caftan and bast shoes with white leggings, sat in a chair. Nekulyev did not come down from the hills until late.

Everything was peaceful near the servants' quarters. The moon glinted on the manure piled in front. Behind the hut a hill overgrown with hazel and maple reached up toward the forests. Maryasha kept listening for the sound of a bell among the hazels, lest the cow should stray too far. The door of the hut was open, and the groans of the blinded peasant came from within. Kuzya got up from the log he was sitting on, stretched himself out on the manure pile in front of the hut, and took up his tale.

". . . and so Annushka runs to the third church as fast as her legs can carry her, and she meets a third priest, who says, 'Good day to you, Annushka!' and then, under his breath, 'How would you like to spend some time with me, te-ta-te?' And so Annushka didn't get to mass at all; she came home and cried for shame, let me tell you. She told her husband everything without fail, mark you. And her husband, Ilya Ivanych—a cunning one—says, 'Go to church, wait until the priest comes from mass, and then tell him to come at half-past nine. And tell the second priest to come about ten, and the third priest—and so on. And keep your mouth shut.' Annushka sets off and sees one of the priests coming from church. 'Well, Annushka, how about sundown?' 'Come about half-past nine, Father; my husband will be visiting his cousin, and he'll get dead drunk, for sure.' And she meets the second priest. 'Well, Annushka, how about spending the night?' Well, she said what her husband had told her to say, and so it went on. . . . Evening came, and let me tell you, the winter was bitter cold, it was the time of the Epiphany frosts. The priest arrives, smooths his beard, crosses himself in front of the icon in the corner, and takes out from under his coat, mark you, a bottle of vodka, the very best. 'Well,' he says, 'hurry up with the samovar and the herring, and then—to bed.' And she says to him, 'What's the hurry, Father? The night is long; we can sleep all we want—enjoy your tea.' Well, let me tell you, the way things are, two's company and three's a crowd. No sooner has the priest warmed up, sat close to her, slipped his hand inside her blouse, when—'knock-knock' on the window. Well, Annushka gets all aflutter. 'Oh-oh! My husband!' The priest tries to hide under a bench, can't squeeze himself in, starts groaning—he's real scared. And Annushka says, as her husband ordered, 'I just don't know where to hide you! Maybe in the storeroom; my husband's build a new bin—get in there.' The first priest hides himself, and the second one takes his place; he's brought vodka too—the very best. And no sooner has he slipped his hand inside her blouse, when—'knock-knock' on the window. And so the second priest finds himself in the bin, lying on top of the first, and there they are, whispering, pinching, and cursing each other. And as soon as the third priest begins to snuggle up, there's a knock at the gate, and the husband shouts, playing drunk, 'Open up, woman!' And so the three priests find themselves piled one on top of the other. The husband, Ilya Ivanych—mark you—walks in and asks his wife in a whisper, 'In the bin?' Annushka replies, 'In the bin!' And now the husband, Ilya Ivanych, starts to throw his weight around like a drunk. 'Woman,' he says, 'I wish to put the new bin out in the cold, in the barn, and fill it with oats!' He starts climbing up to the storeroom. What Ilya Ivanych had in mind to do, mark you, was to put the priests out in the cold, lock them up in the barn, and let them freeze there for a day or so; in the end the cold would get them, they'd break out of the barn, run like crazy, and be the laughingstock of the whole village. But things turned out quite different, and there was nothing to laugh about: he started to drag the bin down from the storeroom; the priests were fat—each of them weighed nine poods—too heavy for Ilya Ivanych, and the bin went flying down the stairs. And the way it landed, the priests all cracked their heads open and gave up the ghost on the spot! . . . Yes. . . ." Kuzya took out his tobacco pouch, squatted down, and began to roll himself a dogleg[5]—carefully sealing the piece of newspaper with his tongue—about to go on with his story.

The moon rested on top of the hill. The cowbell tinkled peacefully close by; the cow was chewing her cud. Nekulyev went by, walking uphill toward the steep bank. They fell silent, followed him with their eyes until he was lost in the darkness. Yegorushka said in a whisper:

"Look, there goes Anton! He's off again; he's on his way. To light bonfires. . . Grunya from Vyazovy—she's a sharp one—says he's a sorcerer for sure. I went up there and had a look: he breaks up dry branches, builds a fire, lies down beside it, props his head up with his hands—and looks and looks into the fire; his eyes are terrible to see, and those glasses on his nose glow like coals—and all the time he's

5. A paper funnel filled with tobacco and bent in the middle.—Eds.

chewing a blade of grass. . . . It's real frightening! Sometimes he stands with his back to the fire, right at the edge of the rock, hands behind his back—and there he stands and stands looking across the Volga; it's a wonder he don't fall off. Oo-oo, I got scared, and kept crawling and crawling until I got to the trail—and home at a run. Then I see him walking home just like nothing's happened."

"And he goes to see his woman," said Kuzya. "He gets there, and right away they go walking in the steppe, holding hands. And they start making a fire there too, mark you. . . . One time they went into a wood; I hid myself, and they sat down—oh, no more than two paces from me, no farther than that; I couldn't move, and the gnats were eating me up. They began talking about communes and kissed once—genteel-like—they put up with the gnats, but I couldn't—and I couldn't move neither, and so I said, 'Excuse me, Anton Ivanych—the gnats are eating me alive!' She jumped up, and turned on him. 'What does this mean?'—angry-like. He didn't say nothing to me, like nothing'd happened. . . ."

"I've got to go read the Hours; I'll be off—good-bye to you," said the old peasant in the caftan.

"Go, and may God be with you; time for bed," responded Maryasha, and yawned.

Kuzya struck a spark, kindled a piece of tinder, and lit a rolled cigarette; his cat whiskers showed in the glow. "And so, the way things are, there's no help for the man's eyes?" he asked sternly. "Neither by prayer nor by spell?"

"There's no help for him at all—the wood-devil's gouged out his eyes. You have to lay on ribwort leaves so his brains won't run out," said the old man. "I take my leave of you!" He got up and started to walk unhurriedly down toward the Volga, stick in hand; his white leggings and bast shoes showed pale below his caftan.

Katyasha called after him, "Father Ignat, come by sometime, don't forget—see if you can heal my walleyed bull calf!"

Kuzya began in a singsong voice, "yes. . . . And so that's how it turned out, let me tell you—Ilya Ivanych wanted to play a joke on the priests, but things turned out quite different. . . ."

"I brought you some eggs, Maryash," said Katyasha, interrupting him. "For the Barin. What do you charge him?"

"Forty-five."

"I gave the Germans twenty. We'll settle later."

"How are you off for flour, Yegorushka?" asked Kuzya.

"We don't have any—we've spent everything on the house. The peasants don't buy wood anymore—they steal it themselves. As for flour—things couldn't be worse. Now my brother had a lucky break in town, you might say he really struck it lucky. A brother-in-law of his comes to him from the depot and says, 'Here's forty poods of flour, sell it for me in the market and I'll make it worth your while—I just don't have time to do the selling.' So my brother agreed, sold the flour, hid the money in a barrel, and buried it—there were only three poods of flour left. And then the militia got him, my brother—it turns out the flour's been stolen from the depot. So they take him off to the cooler. 'Where's the rest of the flour?' 'I don't know.' 'Where did you get the flour?' 'At the market from somebody—don't remember who.' He stuck to it like a bull in a gate, didn't give his brother-in-law away; three weeks they kept him in jail—questioned him all the time—then, of course, they had to let him go. The brother-in-law lost no time in coming around, but my brother jumped on him: 'You no-good bum, selling stolen goods! You should thank me on your knees for not giving you away!' 'What about the money?' 'They took everything, brother; thank God I got off with a whole skin. . . . ' And so the brother-in-law went away empty-handed; he even thanked my brother and stood him a drink of samogon. . . . The money started my brother off, he opened up a shop, he wears galoshes now—there's luck for you straight out of the blue.

Yegor was silent for a while. "The eggs are in my cap—eight of them. Take them, Maryash."

"The forester, let me tell you, ever since he arrived he's lived on butter and eggs; he puts bread away and thinks nothing of it—brought flour with him. And he notices everything, doesn't miss a thing, mark you, he's got a real sharp eye," said Kuzya.

"He eats and eats, nothing but sour cream, and butter, and eggs—he's living like the masters!" began Maryasha with animation. "He brought some buckwheat—in all my born days I've never seen it; we don't sow it around here; I cooked it and took some for myself—the kids ate it licking their chops like it was sugar. And his underwear he tells me to wash with soap; he wears it a week and takes it off—it's as clean as can be, and still with soap! . . . I was washing dishes and he says, 'Wash them with soap!' and I say to him, 'In these parts we hold soap to be unclean! . . .'"

Suddenly inside the hut a bucket fell with a clatter, a crushed chick squeaked, a hen started clucking, and a peasant appeared in the doorway—the one who had been blinded; his white shirt was blood-soaked, his arms were stretched out in front of him, his bearded head was thrown back, the dead sockets could not be seen; his hands groped the air. Suddenly he shrieked in unbearable pain and rage:

"Give me back my eyes, my eyes, my sharp eyes! . . ." He stumbled on the threshold and fell forward into the manure.

"That'll learn you to steal bark," Kuzya said comfortingly. "You saw we called Father Ignat, and he said nothing can be done."

Kuzya and the women began dragging the man back into the hut. Yegorushka walked a few paces away from the hut toward the barn and the riverbank to relieve himself; he returned and said thoughtfully, "The fire's out, that means he's coming back. Time for bed." He yawned and made the sign of the cross over his mouth. "So give us the eggs, we'll settle later." Yegor and Katyasha went home to the watchman's hut at the other end of the grounds. In the servants' quarters Kuzya lit a homemade candle and took off his cap—cockroaches skittered over the table. The peasant lay groaning on a bunk. The children were sleeping on the stove ledge. A cradle hung in the middle of the room. From the oven Kuzya took an iron pot. The potatoes were cold; he poured a little mound of salt on the table (a cockroach came running up, took a sniff, and went away slowly); he began eating a potato, skin and all. Then he lay down, as he was, on the floor in front of the stove. Maryasha also ate some potatoes, took off her dress, but kept on a shift made of sacking; she let down her hair, gave the cradle a gentle push, threw Kuzya's sheepskin coat on the floor beside him, blew out the candle, and, scratching herself and sighing, lay down by Kuzya's side. Before long the baby in the cradle began crying; taking up an incredible posture, one leg in the air, Maryasha began to rock the cradle with her foot and, rocking it—slept. In the passageway a cock crowed peacefully.

* * *

In the morning both Kuzya and Yegorushka had things to do. Maryasha got up at dawn, milked the cow; her swollen-bellied children, who had not been washed for a year, ran about the yard after her; the oldest, six-year-old Zhenka—the only one who could talk—tugged at the hem of her mother's skirt, crying, "A-rya-rya-rya, tyap-tya, tyap-tya,"—asking for milk. The cow was drying up and gave little milk; what there was Maryasha took down to the cellar, and the children got none. Later Maryasha sat out on the veranda of the manor house, waiting—bored—for the forester to wake up, chasing the children away lest their noise should disturb Nekulyev. The forester, in a cheerful mood, came out into the sun and went down to the Volga to bathe. He greeted Maryasha—she snickered, dropped her head, stuck her hand inside her blouse, and, murder in her face—"Get away, you little devils!"—ran straight into the hut, dragged the samovar out onto the veranda, then brought the milk pot up from the cellar and the eight eggs—cradled in her skirt. Katyasha passed by, carrying water buckets, and said with venom and envy in her voice:

"Trying hard? He'll take you to bed with him soon!" Maryasha snapped back: "What of it—it'll be me and not you!" Maryasha was no more than twenty-three, but she looked like a woman of forty—tall and skinny as a rake. Katyasha, on the other hand, was short, bigboned, and covered with wrinkles like a dried-up puffball, as befitted her thirty-five years.

That morning Kuzya went into the forest; he hung the rifle from his shoulder by a string, barrel down, and stuck his hands in his pockets; he walked unhurriedly, looking solemnly from side to side—not along the track but taking hidden paths known to him alone. He went down into a ravine, climbed a hill, and came to a wild and overgrown part where oaks and maples grew thickly together, with hazel pushing up from below. He began to descend a steep bank, grabbing hold of bushes, sending stones down in a cloud of dust. Among some dry leaves he found a slough—a castoff snakeskin—picked it up, smoothed it out, put it inside the lining of his cap, and stuck the cap on his head at a rakish angle. He walked another quarter verst along the slope and came to a cave. Kuzya called out: "Anybody there? Andrei? Vasyatka?" A young man came out, said, "Father's gone down to the Volga; he'll be back right away." Kuzya sat down on the ground near the cave, lit a cigarette; the young man went back inside and said, "Want a glass of the new stuff?" "No," said Kuzya. They fell silent; the stifling smell of raw samogon came from the cave. Ten minutes or so later a peasant with a beard an arshin[6] long came up the hill. Kuzya said: "Stilling as usual? I'm out of flour and grain. Get me, let's say, two poods. And Yegor'll be having his crawling-in feast, so he'll need samogon, the best you've got. Bring everything over. In the afternoon the forester'll go to the bark stripping, and later he'll stop by at his woman's place. That's the time to aim for—leave everything with Maryasha." They talked about their affairs, how high prices were, the quality of samogon, then said good-bye. The young man came out of the cave, said, "Kuzya, let me have a bang!" Kuzya handed him the rifle, replied, "Shoot!" The young man fired; his father shook his head dejectedly, said, "You know, Vasili's a deserter. . . ."

On his way back Kuzya stopped at Ignat's bee garden in Linden Valley; they sat and smoked together. Ignat, nicknamed "the Renter," sat on a stump and discoursed on the vagaries of life. "For example, once I was sitting on this very stump, and a siskin says to me from a

6. A measure of length, approximately twenty-eight inches.—Eds.

tree, 'You'll be drinking vodka today!' And I say to him, 'What's this foolishness you're talking, where should I get vodka?' But it turned out as he said: a cousin of mine came in the evening and brought some samogon! . . . Birds are the wisdom of God. Or take your new Barin, for example: I stopped at his place, we got talking; I ask what does he think—during the marriage rite should you walk around the lectern with the sun or against the sun? And he says, 'If you have to take the sun into account in such a matter, you'll have to stand still and have them carry the lectern around you, because the sun stands still in the sky and it's the earth that goes around.' Yes, he shot right back at me! And I say to him, 'If that's so, then Joshua stopped the earth and not the sun?" And it was Koopernik[7] who started it all. They burned this Koopernik at the stake; too good for him—I'd have cut him up with my own hands, piece by piece, bone by bone. . . . As for tobacco, it's true that it's the Devil's own weed. I planted some here for smoking and had to throw away two hives of honey. . . ."

When he was quite close to home, near the grounds of the estate, Kuzya came across a clearing overgrown with sorrel. He lay down on the ground, crawled all over the clearing on his belly, eating sorrel. At home Maryasha gave him a dish of kvass[8] with bread and onions in it. He ate and went out to groom the horse; he curried it, washed it down, and began harnessing it to the droshky. Nekulyev came out of the house, and they set off for the forest.

* * *

Katyasha and Yegorushka had been building a new house in the village. The house was finished, and it only remained to have it blessed and to celebrate the crawling-in. Some time before, Yegorushka had made an icon case from one of the Prince's mahogany cabinets, and since early morning, after milking the cow, Katyasha had been busy

7. Nicolaus Copernicus (1473–1543), the founder of modern astronomy.—Eds.
8. A thin, sour beer made by pouring warm water on rye or barley and letting the mixture ferment.—Eds.

with its adornment. Somehow she had managed to get hold of some brewery labels—"Volga Hawk Beer"—with a golden hawk in the middle; she was pasting them all over the mahogany of the icon case, some upside down, for she could not read. For Yegorushka and Katyasha the crawling-in was a holiday; Nekulyev had given Yegor a week's leave. That same morning Yegorushka and Katyasha visited Father Ignat in his bee garden to have their fortunes told. Ignat did his best to fill them with terror. He was sitting on a coffer in his hut and did not even glance at Yegorushka and Katyasha but simply waved his hand for them to sit down. Between his feet Ignat had placed an earthenware cook pot; he began peering into it and saying—heaven knows what. He spat to the right, to the left, and on Katyasha, who wiped herself submissively; then a spasm began to twist his face. Presently he got up, came from behind the table, went into the storeroom, beckoned silently to Yegor and Katyasha to follow him; inside it was dark and stuffy, and there was a stifling smell of honey and dry grass. Ignat picked up two church candles from a shelf; he took Yegor's hands and turned him around three times with the sun, ending up with Yegor behind him; he bent forward and began to twist the candles together in an intricate fashion; he gave one candle to Yegor and the other to Katyasha, mumbling something rapidly to himself; then he took the candles back, pressed them together, and, holding them at both ends, sank his teeth in at midpoint, his face contorted in a snarl, while Yegorushka and Katyasha stood in awestruck silence. Ignat began hissing, roaring, and gritting his teeth; his eyes filled with blood, so it seemed to Yegorushka and Katyasha in the darkness. He shouted, "May he be racked with convulsions, head over heels, feet in the air! May he be broken into seven hundred and seventy-seven pieces; may the sinew of his gut be stretched thirty-three *sazhens!*"[9] A measure of length. One *sazhen* is equal to seven feet.—Eds. When this was all over, Ignat explained with perfect calm that they would live well in their new house, eat their fill, and reach a ripe old age; they would have a black-haired

9. A measure of length. One *sazhen* is equal to seven feet.—Eds.

daughter-in-law, and only one misfortune would befall them: "After a dark number of days, nights, and months have passed"—the bull calf would go blind and would have to be slaughtered. Katyasha and Yegorushka walked home happy, in renewed harmony, a little subdued by all these wonders; Ignat had given them the candles with instructions about what was to be done with them: in the new house they were to go to the gatepost, light their candles, and singe the post; then they were to go into the house with the lighted candles and stick them to the doorjamb—this to be repeated three nights running; they were to see to it that on the last night the candles burned right down and went out together, but the first two nights they were to put out the candles with the thumb and fourth finger of the left hand, without fail, and not to get it wrong, or else their fingers would drop off. Nekulyev had already left when Katyasha and Yegor got back; a vedro[10] of samogon had been delivered. Yegor began harnessing the horse; Katyasha lingered, caught up in preparations, sticking labels on the icon case: "Volga Hawk Beer," "Volga Hawk Beer." To while away the time, Yegorushka went into the manor house, wandered into the room that Nekulyev occupied, felt the bed, lay down, trying it out for size; on the table were some leftover sour cream and some granulated sugar in a box that had once contained hard candies—several times he wet a finger and stuck it first in the sour cream, then in the sugar, then licked the finger; on the window sill lay some toothpowder, a toothbrush, and a razor; Yegorushka lingered here for some time—he tasted the powder, chewed it, and spat it out, shaking his head in bewilderment; he picked up a mirror and brushed his beard and whiskers with the toothbrush; near the mirror lay a safety razor, and several blades were scattered about. Yegorushka examined them all, counted them, picked out one of the worst, and stuck it in his pocket. In the office he sat down at Nekulyev's writing table, put on a stern face, rested his hands on the arms of the chair, spreading out his legs and elbows, and said: "All right, them as are forest thieves! Come forward!" In the domestic life

10. A liquid measure equal to 3.25 U.S. gallons.—Eds.

of Yegorushka and Katyasha, it was Katyasha who had the upper hand. Soon a loaded cart was standing in front of the house; in the cart were the icon case covered with "Volga Hawks," a broken-down armchair with a gilt back, two baskets—one with a black rooster (obtained from Maryasha and paid for in kind) and the other with a black tomcat (kept specially since spring; both rooster and tomcat were needed for the crawling-in)—and a trunk containing the possessions which Katyasha had brought with her as a bride. On the very top of the load sat Katyasha herself; she had already been at the samogon; she was waving a red kerchief, bouncing up and down, and singing "Saratov" and "*Sharaban,* my *sharaban*"[11]—at the top of her voice. Maryasha with the children stood near the cart, looking on entranced and envious; Katyasha stopped singing, crossed herself; Yegor and Maryasha and the children crossed themselves too; Katyasha said: "Let's go! God be with us!" She called out to Maryasha: "Look after the animals; when Ignat comes, show him! . . ." They started; Yegor went on foot, holding the reins; again Katyasha began shrieking, "My *sharaban,* my two-wheeled carriage, and me, I'm just a no-good baggage! . . ."

* * *

It was during Nekulyev's time as forester that the only meeting of the Workers' Committee took place. It was called by those good fellows Kandin and Konkov, trained workers and Party members. Many of those attending arrived the day before the meeting was scheduled—some had to travel as many as forty versts. In the evening they built a bonfire on the croquet court in the park and cooked potatoes and fish. The shrewdest among them, and the Party members, gathered at Nekulyev's to get things settled before the committee got down to business. Konkov was sullen and determined; Kandin did his best to be patient; they talked about the Revolution, about the forests, and about thieving—the absolutely unheard-of amount of thieving that was going on in the forests; they talked quietly, sitting in the ballroom in a

11. Charabanc.—Eds.

close circle by the light of a single candle; Nekulyev lay on the sofa. Konkov said unhappily: "Shoot them—that's what we ought to do, comrades—and our own forest men first of all to show we mean business. The way things are, what have we got? We fight the peasants, and the more cunning among them go to a forest watchman they know, talk him round, slip him a pood of grain, and the watchman lets them take whatever they want. What we've got, comrades, is nothing but hypocrisy and plain disgrace. Forgive me, comrades, but I'll confess: a peasant from Shikhany kept after me to let him have some wood for a house—two whole days he won't leave me alone—and there I am starving, and he keeps pushing samogon and white flour at me; I couldn't stand it any longer, and gave him such a beating they had to take him to the hospital!" Kandin replied, "I'll give it to you straight; I've given more than one beating, not that it does much good. But you have to take this into account: a forest watchman gets a wage; if you convert it to the cost of bread—it's one and a half rubles; he can't live on that, and so he's forced to steal; just look how they live—the gentry's pigs used to live more decently. You can't manage forests without statistics: we have to set a limit on what they can steal, and pretend not to notice, because they're stealing from need. And if they steal over the limit, that means they're stealing out of deviltry, and in that case shooting might be a good idea. We're none of us saints—but we have our job to do!" They talked about the Workers' Committee. The committee had to be formed to bind everyone together in collective responsibility. Nekulyev was silent, listening; the candle cast its light no further than the sofa. Neither Konkov nor Kandin knew how they were to conduct the meeting of the Workers' Committee in the morning in such a way as not to set the rest of the forest men against them. In the park a song rose and faded; Nekulyev went out in the park to join the others. People sat by the bonfire, a ragged crowd, no two of them dressed alike, all with rifles. Kuzya lay by the fire, resting his head on the palms of his hands; he was staring into the fire and telling a story. Alarmed by the blaze, crows were screaming in the trees. Nekulyev sat down by the fire and listened.

Kuzya was saying:

". . . And so, like I was saying, Ilya Ivanych wanted to play a joke on the priests, but it turned out different. Ilya Ivanych opens the bin, and there are the three priests lying one on top of the other, all dead and stiffening in the cold already. Ilya Ivanych gets scared, carries the priests into the barn, and lays them out side by side; he goes back to the house, sits down at the table, puts on his thinking cap, and, mark you, he's in a cold sweat. . . . But Ilya Ivanych was a clever one; he sat there for an hour or so racking his brains—and all of a sudden he slapped himself on the forehead! He went into the barn—the priests were stiff by now—took hold of one of them, stood him up by the shed, and poured water over him—icicles were soon hanging from him. Then Ilya Ivanych went to the tavern and, mark you, took a bottle along with him—the one the priest hadn't finished. At the tavern an accordion is playing, people are sitting around, and it so happens that Vanyusha the drunkard is sitting by the counter waiting for someone to treat him to a drink. Ilya Ivanych goes straight up to Vanyusha: 'Have a drink!'—gives him the bottle. Vanyusha tosses it back and gets drunk straight away. And Ilya Ivanych says to him: 'I'd give you some more, but there's no time. I've got to go—a drowned man has come into my yard; I'll have to carry him to the Volga and drop him through a hole in the ice.' Well, Vanyusha grabs at the chance: 'I'll carry him, if you'll treat me!' And this is just what Ilya Ivanych is waiting for; he says, unwilling-like, 'Well, all right—if it's for friendship's sake—you take him away, come back to the house, and I'll treat you!' Vanyusha can't get there fast enough. 'Where's the drowned man?' 'Over there!' Vanyusha grabs hold of the priest, throws him over his shoulder, and makes straight for the gate. And Ilya Ivanych says to him, 'Wait a bit, you'd better put him in a sack, or you'll scare people.' So they put him in a sack, mark you; Vanyusha sets off with his load, and in the meantime Ilya Ivanych brings the second priest out of the barn, stands him up, pours water over him, and waits. Vanyusha comes running, straight to the house: 'Where's the drink?' But Ilya Ivanych says to him, 'Just a minute, brother; you did a poor job of carrying him away; you didn't say the right word—he's come back again.' 'Who has?' 'The drowned man.' 'Where is he?' They go out into the yard. The priest is standing by the shed. Vanyusha's eyes pop out of his head, and he gets angry: 'Oh, you so-and-so, you want to make trouble!' He grabs hold of the second priest and runs toward the hole in the ice. And Ilya Ivanych shouts after him, 'When you're shoving him in, say "May his soul rest in peace," and then he'll go in easy!' This was so that the priest had some kind of prayer said for him. No sooner is Vanyusha gone than Ilya Ivanych brings out the third priest and stands him up by the shed. Vanyusha comes running, and Ilya Ivanych tells him off: 'You're a fine one, Vanyusha! Can't even carry away a drowned man—look, he's come back again. Seems like I'll have to go with you myself to make sure things are done good and proper. You carry him, and I'll walk behind and see how you handle things.' So they carried off the third priest; Ilya Ivanych watched and saw that Vanyusha had been launching the priests like he ought to, so he stopped worrying and said, 'Well, all right, Vanyusha, you've worked hard enough, come on—I'll treat you!' And he got Vanyusha so drunk that he couldn't remember a thing and forgot how he hauled away the drowned men. And they never found out about the priests—what the Devil has done with them. And so ends my story, and mine be the glory," said Kuzya.

Nekulyev walked away from the bonfire into the darkness, skirting the grounds; he went up the hill toward the riverbank, to be alone with his thoughts for a while. The tale seemed to him a bad omen.

In the morning, on the same croquet court where many had bedded down for the night by the fire, about seventy men—woodcutters and forest watchmen—gathered. A table was set up under a linden tree; benches were brought—but many of the men lay on the grass around the court. The fire was kept going. Rifles were stacked army-style. A presidium was elected.

The following minutes of this meeting survive:

Reports	*Resolutions*
1. Comrade Konkov made a report on the international situation.[1]	1. Duly noted.
2. Comrade Kandin made a report on the plan of activities of the Workerks' Committee. a. Cultural-educational work. b. Income and expenditure of the Workers' Committee.	2. In view of the wide dispersion of forest workers throughout the forests, no cultural commission to be elected; a collective subscription to a newspaper for each watchman's hut to be made;[2] expenses; a. Office supplies. b. Transportation to town. c. Daily allowances.
3. Comrade Konkov proposed that a contribution should be deducted from wages toward the fund for the building of a monument of the Revolution in Moscow.	3. One day's pay to be deducted.
4. Chairman of the Kadom village soviet Nefedov charged that there were fictitious names on the payroll of the twenty-seventh cordon, for which mounted guard Sarychev collected. Sarychev produced the above-mentioned payroll and pointed out that its correctness was certified by the stamp and signature of Chairman Nefedov, who had made the above-mentioned charge.	4. In view of the absurdity of making a charge against oneself, an inquiry should be initiated by sending a copy of the charge to the Department of Criminal Investigation.

1. In his report Konkov made a mistake in indicating that Europe and Russia are geographically situated in different continents.

2. It was discovered that half of the forestry workers were illiterate; as he voted, Kuzya whispered to Yegorushka, "It's all right, we'll use them for smokes!"

Reports	*Resolutions*
5. The case of the pedigreed bull eaten by mounted guards and woodcutters of the seventh cordon: the bull was hired from a breeding farm on a collective guarantee—it was killed and eaten and a report sent to the breeding farm to the effect that the bull had died of anthrax.	5. In view of the illegal act concerning the bull, three days' pay to be withheld monthly from woodcutters Stulov, Sinitsin, and Shavelkin and from mounted guard Usachev, and sent to the cashier's office of the breeding farm.
6. Comrade Soshkin expressed a wish that no general meetings should be held on Sundays.[3]	6. Carried.
7. Mounted guard Sarychev proposed that all present immediately join the Russian Communist Party.	7. No action to be taken at present.[4]

Here is part of the first letter that Nekulyev wrote from the Hills of Medyn—he never finished it:

". . . in the middle of nowhere—there is no post office for sixteen versts, and no railway for a hundred—in an accursed house on the Volga, a house which has passed the curse of the landowners on to me;

3. A barefoot young fellow in a coat of coarse cloth got up from the grass and said in some agitation: "This is what I think, comrades; it seems like we shouldn't have meetings of the Workers' Committee on Sunday, as citizen forest thieves are all out in the fields on weekdays—you can't catch them there—but on Sunday they sit at home, and that's the place to go after them with the militia."

4. Comrade Kandin said at this point that the question of joining the Russian Communist Party should be left to each man's conscience. Sarychev took offense at Kandin's remarks, and said: ". . . and if you think that Vaska Nefedov from Kadom, chairman and informer, was telling the truth about me, let me tell you he's the biggest crook himself; as for the names that were signed, those people were from other parts; by now they'll have gone home to Vetluga."

the heat and the goings-on here are truly devilish! I live like Robinson Crusoe; I sleep without sheets, eat raw eggs and milk—nothing cooked—and go about half-naked. All around me there is savagery, shame, abomination. The nearest village is sixteen versts from us, but the 'Great Waterway' flows at the foot of the steep bank, and I often talk with the men who haul boats on the Volga; there are a great many—a good score of flat-bottoms pass by every day, and the men often stop for a rest and cook their fish stew near our place. About five days ago a peasant was pulling his wife tied up in a flat-bottom; he informed me that she was possessed by three devils, one under the heart, another in the backbone, and a third in the armpit, and that there was a wonderful soothsayer some hundred versts from us who could cast out devils—and so he was taking his wife to him; yesterday he was on his way back, and this time it was his wife who was in harness, while he took it easy in the boat; he told me that the devils had been cast out. The people I am living with are two watchmen and their wives and children. One of them has built himself a house out of stolen wood—the wood which it is his duty to guard—and filled it with broken furniture from the manor house; but that's not the main thing; the main thing is that before moving into the house he let in a black cat and a rooster, put a hunk of bread and salt under the stove for the house goblin, and his wife ran around the house naked 'to ward off the evil eye.' His bull calf got sick—its eyes started running; there's a veterinarian not far away—in Vyazovy—but he called in a local soothsayer (this soothsayer, a peasant who rents an apiary, came around once or twice to talk to me; I had no idea he was a sorcerer—he seemed just like any other peasant, only a bit sharper; he can read, and talks some nonsense about Copernicus), and so this soothsayer examined the bull calf, whispered something over it, removed (!) some kind of film (!) from its eyes, sprinkled salt in them—and the calf went blind! Then Katyasha, Yegor's wife, got hold of a snake slough, dried it, ground it to power—and this snake slough is what she uses to treat the calf, sprinkling the powder in its already blind eyes. The other watchman's wife is called Maryasha. At first I called her Masha, but she said to me, 'What's that you're calling me? Everybody calls me Maryasha!' She has three children and is about twenty-three years old; my 'way of life' makes her drool: 'Eee, and everything with butter, and milk to your heart's content!' She gives no milk to her children—she sells it to me; this disgusts me, but I know—if I don't buy from her I'll starve to death, as I'm not used to constant starvation the way they are, and she would only use it to make butter and cottage cheese and sell it all the same. Maryasha has never been to town—her own district town, thirty versts away; she has three children living, who run about naked, and had two that died; she is twenty-three and already has some kind of female ailment about which her husband Kuzya readily talks to all and sundry; none of her children was delivered. . . not even by the local wise woman: she gave birth alone, cut the umbilical cord herself, and herself cleaned up the blood afterward, sending her husband out into the forest for the occasion. What savagery, what horror, God damn it all! This is their attitude toward me: yesterday a German from across the Volga came and offered to sell me butter. I asked, 'How much?' 'The same price you paid before—twenty-five.' And Maryasha, Kuzya, and Katyasha had been charging me sixty. My patience gave way, and I called Maryasha and Katyasha and told them they ought to be ashamed of themselves, and that I knew very well they were cheating and robbing me right and left—after all hadn't I treated them as friends and been fair with them? From now on I should be forced to consider them thieves and no longer respect them—such a lyrical homily I delivered to them! They didn't bat an eye: 'We did it special, on purpose like! . . . '

"And that very day at dinner time they suddenly bring me a sterlet:[12] 'This is a present to you from us!' I told them to go to hell with their sterlets. For them I'm just the Barin and nothing else: I don't plow, I wash my clothes with soap, do things incomprehensible to them; I read, live in the manor house, and so—I'm the Barin; if I were to order them to crawl on all fours—they'd do it; if I ordered them to lick the floor clean—they'd do it; and they'd do it 50 percent out of servile fear

12. Small sturgeon.—Eds.

and 50 percent because—who knows?—maybe the Barin really needs it done, because much of what I am doing—what we are doing—seems as absurd to them as licking floors; they will do anything you like, still I have got into the habit of making sure there is no one behind me, as I never know if Katyasha or Kuzya may not find it unavoidable at a given moment to stick a knife in my back: perhaps this is a superfluous precaution, because they look upon me as their milch cow, and I have heard Katyasha say enviously that I was 'a godsend' to Maryasha, because Maryasha, in getting the samovar for me and cleaning my room and office, has every right and every opportunity to rob me systematically—with Katyasha's approval! Yes, that's how it is—and I am an honest Party member. I don't understand our peasants' conception of honor—after all, they must have honor. They live understanding nothing, nothing at all—and here is Yegor building a new house according to all the soothsayers' rules at a time when the world revolution is taking place! . . . All the people I see every day are like that, and in addition to them there are the unseen ones—the hundreds, perhaps even thousands, who all around me are carrying off the forests, and with whom I am engaged in a fight to the death. I have a feeling that all those who surround me are thieves, one worse than the next, and I don't understand how it is they don't steal each other—but I was forgetting that I was stolen myself by the Germans and kept prisoner in a dark storeroom! . . . Maryasha's children run about naked because they have nothing to put on, and they're covered with terrible itching sores; at first I used to eat at Kuzya's table, but I was nauseated by the filth and felt ashamed to eat in front of the children because they were hungry; they don't even get enough bread and potatoes—as for meat or butter, say, or eggs—they never see them. . . . And then take Mishka the shepherd—who talks to cows in cow language that hardly resembles human speech, and is almost unable to talk like a human being—he found a tumbledown hut in a ravine in a remote part of the forest; the hut had sunk into the hill, and inside was a crumbling Psalter—no doubt some pious man had sought salvation there; it would be interesting to know if he considered soap holy or unholy. . . . And a siskin foretells when the soothsayer—the one they call the Renter—is going to drink samogon. As for Minka the shepherd himself—he is famous because last year, before I came, a cow in his herd gave birth to a calf with a human head; the women killed the calf, and rumor has it that Minka was the father. Of course that couldn't have happened, but if Minka, who talks to cows more easily than to human beings, had lusted after cows—let that be on his own conscience. . . ."

Nekulyev did not finish the letter. He sat down to write it in the evening, after coming back from the hill, where he had lit a fire, and remained at the table late into the night. He was writing in the office; two candles burned on the table, dripping wax which spilled onto the green baize, adding to the marks of other candlewax nights passed in the house, this house bitter as honey gathered from tobacco flowers. And suddenly Nekulyev felt his flesh creep—for the first time he became aware of the goose pimples which had so often made his skin tingle—quickly he felt for his revolver, jumped up from behind the table, grabbed the revolver, ready to shoot—at that moment Konkov walked into the office, revolver in hand, covered with dust, his face the color of earth. Konkov said:

"Comrade Anton! Ilya Kandin has been killed—by peasants he caught stealing wood. Reconnaissance detachments have arrived in Kadom, Vyazovy, and Belokon—we can't find out if they're Whites or Reds. The peasants are rioting!"

Three:
About Mother Earth and the Beauty of Love

If you ask a peasant about Mother Earth, and if you are weary as you listen, there will rise before you terrors, devils, and that mighty force concealed in the earth with which the legendary hero Mikula, had he found it, would have turned the world around. Peasants—old men and women—will tell you that ravines were dug out and hills piled up with their horns by huge devils, such as no longer exist at the very time when the archangels were driving them out of Paradise. Mother Earth, like love and sex, is a mystery: for her own secret purposes she divided mankind into men and women; she lures men irresistibly; the peasants kiss the earth like sons, carry her in small bags suspended from their necks, talk softly to her, cast spells in her name to charm love and hatred, sun and day. The peasants swear by Mother Earth as they do by love and death. Spells are woven over her, and in the night a naked widow who has known all things is harnessed to a plow, and the plow is guided by two naked virgins who have the earth and the world before them. It is for a woman to take the part of Mother Earth. But Mother Earth herself is fields, forests, swamps, coppices, hills, distances, years, nights, days, blizzards, storms, calm. . . . You can either curse Mother Earth or love her. . . .

* * *

Nekulyev's task was a hard one. The Don and Ural armies were cutting off the southeast; the Czechs were marching from Penza toward Kazan. The Volga was caught, pressed from all sides. The Volga was saved by places like Medyn. At various Wet Ravines, Hamlets, Islands, Old Fields—at dozens of places—barges were being loaded with firewood, timber, eight-inchers, twelve-inchers, boards. By day and by night steamers arrived, at their last gasp; in the darkness they sent up showers of sparks and took on firewood—their life's sustenance—in order to slap the daybreak waters with their wheel paddles, frightening the empty distances. From Saratov, from Samara, from provincial districts, from steppe towns came bands of people with saws, people with the will to achieve victory and not to die—factory workers, professors, students, women teachers, mothers, doctors—old and young, men and women; they went to the forest; they sawed wood, bruising hands and knees, raising blood blisters, fighting for life with blunt saws. At night they made bonfires, sang hungry songs, slept on the forest grass, wept and cursed the night and the world—and still the steamers came, coughing up wood smoke; professors worked as stokers; their jackets became oil-stained like work shirts. Nekulyev was here, there—dashing from one place to another astride the Prince's bay, while Kuzya limped behind on a lame gelding; everything they did had to be done—at all costs—and Kuzya waved his revolver often enough.

★ ★ ★

It was night. Nekulyev had not finished his letter; the candles were recording a new wax chronicle on the green office baize. It was then that Konkov walked into the room, revolver in hand, covered with dust, his face the color of earth, and said in a whisper, like a conspirator: "Comrade Anton! Ilya Kandin has been killed—by peasants he caught stealing wood. Reconnaissance detachments have arrived in Kadom, Vyazovy, and Belokon—we can't find out if they're Whites or Reds. The peasants are rioting!" Nekulyev met Konkov in gooseflesh fear, both hands grasping a revolver; he lowered it and sat down helplessly on the table to mark his friend's death by a moment of silence. Suddenly both of them tightened their grips on the handles of their revolvers as they drew closer together: from outside the window came the rustle of a dozen stealthy footsteps; rifle locks flicked, and the next moment the black holes of rifle barrels appeared in doorways and windows; a sailor walked into the room, calm and businesslike, his revolver still in its holster.

"Don't move, comrades. Hands up, comrades. Your papers!" "Are you a Communist, comrade?" "You're under arrest. You will go with us to the ship." The earth was moving into autumn, the night was black, and the broad reaches of the Volga breathed a damp hostility. Near the boat the women were wailing in the darkness, and Yegorushka and Kuzya were taking leave of them like recruits leaving home. Steamers were snorting in the dark, but none of them had lights on board. They got into the boat and cast off. Kuzya eased down next to Nekulyev: "What's happening—are they taking us to be shot?" He was silent for a moment. "I figure at least I'm barefoot—I'll jump in and swim for it." A sailor shouted, "No whispering!" "All right then, where are you taking us?" Kuzya snapped back. "You'll find out when you get there." The boat nudged the side of a steamer. "Grab the line." "Make fast!" The steamer was humming with voices. Nekulyev was the first to climb on deck. "Take me to the deckhouse!" The deckhouse was crowded with armed men; some had belts hung with hand grenades the way Indians' belts are hung with feathers; others wore machine-gun cartridge belts slung around their hips; the smell of makhorka[13] was enough to knock you over.

And this is what happened:

The Seventh Revolutionary Peasant Regiment had lost its chief of staff, and he had been the only one on board who could read German—a map torn from a German atlas served as a field map; it was spread out on the table in the deckhouse, upside down. The Seventh Peasant Regiment was on its way to fight the Cossacks and break through to Astrakhan, but the farther they went following the map, the more confused they became. Nekulyev turned the map around; they argued, not trusting him. In the end Nekulyev sat all night with the staff men—sailors—teaching them how to read Russian words in Roman script; the sailors were quick to understand and hung on the wall a sheet of paper with the Russian equivalents of the Roman letters. Dawn came pale and glassy. Nekulyev was released; Konkov said he would remain on board; Yegorushka and Kuzya were asleep by the funnel; Nekulyev shook them awake.

13. A coarse tobacco.—Eds.

And when they had already pushed away from the steamer, a cannon shot exploded beyond the hill, and with a roar the water near the boat leaped wildly skyward. It was the Cossacks firing, those who were advancing to meet the Seventh (also the First and Twentieth) Revolutionary Peasant Regiment, named in honor of the sailor Chaplygin.

⋆ ⋆ ⋆

Men like Nekulyev are shy in love: they are chaste and truthful in all things. Sometimes, for the sake of politics and for the sake of life, they tell lies—but this is not lying and hypocrisy but rather a blithe cunning; within themselves they are chaste and innocent, straightforward and exacting. That first day in Medyn the sun burst into the office, and everything was full of life; and then a few days later, that same moonlit week, in the moonlit and dewy darkness, Nekulyev said, "I love you, I love you," swearing by the sun itself and by all that is finest in man, so that this love would be all sun and humanity. There was an intoxicating smell of linden, the moon was red, and they were coming into the fields from the wood where Arina and her workmen stripped bark—living bark from living trees—to tan dead hide. Arina Arsenyeva's childhood had been filled with the smell of rich pies, but she had wanted to reshape it to the regularity of Petersburg; she grew abundantly, like Mother Earth, like the steppe, tulip-covered for a brief two weeks in the spring—Arina Arsenyeva the leather tanner, a woman. The house was as it had always been, but her days were different—very spacious; there were neither clerks nor bookkeepers nor father nor mother. Work had to be done at all costs. Everything had to be cut to a new pattern. The house was the same, but the pies had vanished, and where the dining room (a place to eat those pies) had been stood workmen's bunks, and Arina was left with an attic, a suitcase, a basket of books, a bed, a table, a rifle, samples of leather; and in the corner lived the wolf pup. But beyond the house and the fences—the house stood at the edge of the village—was the steppe, as always dried up, lonely, with its long, low hills and ravines, the moonlit steppe so well remembered from her childhood. And every woman is a mother. She had to rush to the forest in her tarantass[14] to supervise bark stripping; she had to rush to the Council of National Economy in town and have things out with them; she had to throw herself into all sorts of battles at village meetings and at town conferences; she had to talk about rawhide, flesh side, derma, liming, tanning, scraping, drying, about *shaksha* (meaning bird droppings); and sometimes she had to curse workmen out—necessity is a stern master—using language that made even the leather dressers respect her; inside the fence were low barracks; vats for washing and liming stood in rows; at the back a small slaughter yard had been added; the barracks were being built to house the soap-and-glue works; there was a shed where horse bones were ground up: everything had to be rebuilt, done over again in an entirely new way. She had to wear a man's jacket, to carry a revolver on a strap, but boots—for those small feet—had to be made to order. And in the evenings she shouldn't—she really shouldn't—have bent over the wolf pup, looking into its eyes, saying tender words to it, breathing in its bitter forest smell. And one brisk, sunny day the urgings of Mother Earth rose within her, choking her, and she fell in love—in love! And in that same moonlit week, in the moonlit and dewy dark when Nekulyev said, "I love you, I love you," there were only the moon and Mother Earth; she gave herself to him—a woman of thirty and a virgin—yielding up everything she had garnered in those thirty springs. He would come to see her in the evenings and go up to the attic; sometimes she was not at home, and then, as he waited, he would rummage through books, strange to him, about the tanning industry and try to play with the wolf pup; but the pup was hostile; it would cower in its corner, and two eyes—alien, unblinking, utterly watchful—would stare out, following every movement, not missing a thing; and the wolf pup would bare its little teeth in a helpless snarl; there was a vile smell of dog about it, something rancid, repellent to man. . . . Arina would come in, and every time it seemed to Nekulyev that the sun was coming into the room, and he was blinded with happiness. Nekulyev

14. A four-wheeled cart.—Eds.

accepted unthinkingly the good things she always gave him to eat: ham, pork, and very often there were either pies as light as a feather or rich puffs which Arina baked herself—somehow she found the time! He gave no thought to the strange, indefinable smell which permeated everything in the house, even the pies—could it be leather? Later Nekulyev and Arina would go out into the steppe and descend into the ravine—at the top sunflowers bowed their suns, and at the bottom marmots whistled to each other and froze like sentries; then they would climb up the other bank and find themselves in places where man had never set foot, where not even the Tartar hordes had passed. Arina gave herself to Nekulyev with all the abandon of Mother Earth; it seemed to Nekulyev that he held the sun in his arms. They had no need of a crawling-in with black rooster and black cat (although the moon was full)—because they were happy and in love.

And this happiness was smashed to pieces as earthenware is smashed to pieces at peasant weddings in the villages. Nekulyev suddenly understood the smell that surrounded Arina and could not overcome his revulsion.

One day he arrived in the afternoon. The attic was deserted, except for the wolf pup. At the gate of the tannery sat a watchman, an old man, who said, "The army sent us some mangy nags, no good and half dead—Arina Sergeyevna went over." Nekulyev started to walk through the tannery, passed huge, stinking vats; he was too squeamish to enter the barracks and went through the gate into the other yard—and there he saw. . . . In the yard stood forty or so horses, complete wrecks—hairless, blind, "legless" (when horses become "legless," their legs are bent like bows); the horses looked like hideous old beggar women; crazy with fear, they bunched together, heads to the center; they had no tails, only gray, scaly stumps which trembled convulsively. And it was here, behind a low fence, that the horses were slaughtered one after another, each one dragged away forcibly from the herd. The small gate leading to the slaughter yard opened, and four men began to shove a struggling horse through, one of them twisting its tail stump, forcing the horse on to the slaughter—Arina came out through the gate and struck the horse on the neck with a club; it staggered and lurched forward. Arina was wearing a blood-soaked apron and leather pants. Nekulyev started running toward the gate. When he ran into the slaughter yard, the horse was already lying on the ground; the legs jerked convulsively; the dead lips sagged away from teeth that clenched a tongue covered with yellow saliva, and a pair of workmen were busy with the horse, cutting open the still-living skin; the broken tail stump stuck up in the air. Nekulyev shouted, "Arina, what are you doing?" Arina began to speak in a matter-of-fact way, but hurriedly—so it seemed to Nekulyev. "The skin is used for leather; the fats are used in soapmaking; we feed the proteins to the pigs. The bones and sinews go to the glue works. Then the bones are ground to make fertilizer. We waste nothing here." Arina's hands were covered with blood; the ground was running with blood; workmen were skinning the horse; other carcasses lay about already skinned; using a pulley, they hung the horse by its legs from a gallows. And then Nekulyev understood: the smell here was the same as Arina's smell, and he suddenly felt his throat contract in a spasm of nausea. He pressed his hand to his mouth, as if to hold back his vomit, turned around, and without a word walked out of the yard into the steppe. Nekulyev was chaste in love. He had always been a cheerful and no-nonsense kind of man—and now he was walking through the steppe like a fool; he was without his cap—he had left it in the wolf pup's attic. Nekulyev never saw Arina again.

⋆ ⋆ ⋆

The forests lay in wait, silently—the wood devil (according to Kuzya) lived in the depths of the forest, and among the pines; at night bonfires burned, ill-omened fires. If there had existed a giant ear, it would have heard watchmen shouting to each other, trees falling—millions of logs (to fuel the Volga and the Revolution)—it would have heard whistles that conveyed all kinds of messages, warning shouts, yells. Beneath the forests lay Mother Earth. It was dawn when shells came flying over the forest—shells that were to establish truth. Nekulyev went into the house, calling to Kuzma and Yegor to follow him; standing behind the table, he said:

"Comrades. We have to decide what to do. There's fighting on all sides. Are we going to stay, or are we going to leave? . . ."

Kuzya did not answer at once; he asked Yegor, "What do you think, Yegorushka?" Yegor replied: "I can't go—I've built a new house, I can't go noways, they'll carry off every last thing; I'd better hide in the village." Standing at attention Kuzya answered for both of them:

"I have the honor to report we're staying with the forests!"

Nekulyev sat down at the table and said: "Go now; I'm staying too. We'll shoot it out. If I get killed, divide up whatever things there are between you. Kuzma, come back in an hour's time, and I'll give you some letters; you can deliver them." Kuzma and Yegor went out. A shell burst over the house.

Nekulyev began to write, slowly:

"To Irina Sergeyevna Arsenyeva. Arina, forgive me. I have been honest, both with you and with myself. Good-bye, good-bye forever; you have taught me to be a revolutionary. . . ."

⋆ ⋆ ⋆

But he never finished the letter, because suddenly goose pimples rose all over his body; the smell of rotting skins and tobacco honey came flooding in; his hands began to tremble; the hair on his head stirred; there came fear, horror. Night was giving way to gray murk; far away the east was turning lilac; far away shells burst; around him all was quiet. Nekulyev crouched down behind the table, straining his ears; his eyes were the eyes of a madman; he ran on tiptoe to the door: it was quiet outside; he put out the candle on the table, held his breath, shouted, "Go away!" Then he sprang to the window, flung it open, vaulted out; he ran headlong like one possessed toward the hills. Goose pimples covered his skin ever more thickly; his curly hair must have been turning gray as it stirred on his head. . . .

⋆ ⋆ ⋆

In the morning Kuzya found the letter on the table—just the three lines—and set off to deliver it.

About the Wolf Pup

It was a moonless night. A fine rain was falling. Irina was returning from the steppe; she passed through the village, listened to the dogs howling; the village seemed dead in the silence and darkness. She entered the yard, passed by the vats, meeting no one, and went up to her attic. She listened intently to the silence—the wolf pup was breathing somewhere close by in the room. She lit a candle, bent over the pup, whispered, "My darling, my little animal, don't be shy, come to me! . . ." The wolf pup crouched in the corner, its fluffy tail curled under it, its black eyes following every movement of Irina's hands and eyes. And when their eyes met, the pup's unblinking eyes became more than ever remote and eternally hostile. When Irina found the pup, it was still blind; she fed it with a rubber nipple; she nursed it as if it were a baby; she sat with it for hours at a time, whispering to it again and again all the tender words she had learned from her mother; the wolf pup thrived in her care, learned to lap from a saucer and to eat unaided, but it sensed that it was and always would be Irina's enemy. There was no taming it; the bigger the wolf pup grew, the more hostile and remote it became; it shied away from Irina's hands and stopped eating in her presence; for hours they sat facing each other, its dish between them; she knew it was hungry; she coaxed it with the tenderest words: "Eat, eat, my darling, don't be silly, eat—because I won't go away!" The wolf pup followed her eyes and hands with its little, glinting eyes, not moving, refusing to look at the dish—until she left, and then it gulped the food down; it would growl and bare its teeth when she stretched her hand out to it; it was and always would be her enemy; there was no taming it. Irina had often noticed that when it was alone the pup led a very contented life, absorbed in its own concerns: it ran about the room, examining and sniffing things, basked in the sun, chased flies, lay about at its ease, rolled on its back, legs up—but the moment she walked in, it would retreat into its corner, and two black and utterly vigilant eyes would stare out. . . . Irina put the candle on the floor, squatted down in front of the wolf, and began talking: "My darling, my little animal, my little Nikita, don't be shy, come to me; you haven't got a mamma—I'll take you in my arms and stroke you!" The candle was smoking, winking; the world—the world of Irina and the wolf pup—was confined by the back of the bedstead, a wall, a stove; even the ceiling was out of sight, because the candle was smoking and because both pairs of eyes were looking into each other. Irina stretched out a hand to stroke the pup—and the pup threw itself on the hand with boundless hatred, in a fight to the death; it sank its teeth into the fingers and fell over in its rage, jaws still clenched; Irina snatched her hand back, but the wolf pup hung on by its teeth; then it dropped, tearing the flesh from her fingers, hitting against the bed—and immediately retreated to its usual place in the corner: a pair of unblinking, utterly vigilant eyes looked out as if nothing had happened. And Irina wept bitterly: it was not the pain, not the blood flowing from her hand; she wept from loneliness, hurt, and helplessness; love a wolf pup as you may, it still looks to the forest; Irina was powerless before instinct—before the little, stinking, fluffy bundle of forest and animal instincts now entrenched behind the bed, powerless before those instincts that were alive within her and ruled her, and that had driven her out into the rain, into the steppe, to weep on the hill where she had given herself to Nekulyev; and in her helplessness, hurt, and loneliness (the more she loved the wolf pup, the more savage it was toward her) she hit the pup hard about the head and eyes, and fell in tears on the bed in her loneliness and misery. The candle remained on the floor near the wolf. . . .

At that moment a stone hit the window, glass scattered, and someone outside called in a stifled voice:

"Comrade Arsenyeva! Run for it! What are you waiting for?—everyone's gone. The Cossacks are in the village! Quick! To the woods!"

And from outside came the rapid beat of a horse's hooves. . . away from the village, toward the steppe, toward the forests. . . .

* * *

In fall the steppe fades all at once, enveloped suddenly in a vast, gray sadness. Morning came in rain and sleet, unwashed, dreary. A detachment of Cossacks rode past the shattered gate of the tannery, singing lustily. Three Cossacks rode out of the gate and mingled with the rest; no one heard them talking about the beautiful woman Communist they had been lucky enough to have for the night. . . . And when the singing died away, the shattered gate of the tannery again stood in silence. Vats reeking of dead skins and tanbark stood in the tannery yard; a stake had been driven into the central vat, and Irina—Arina Sergeyevna Arsenyeva—was impaled on the stake. She was naked. The stake was driven between her legs; her feet were tied to the stake. Her face—the face of a beautiful woman—was hideous with horror, the eyes popping out of their sockets. She was alive. She died toward evening. The whole of that day no one went into the tannery yard.

* * *

Kuzya was late in delivering Nekulyev's letter to Arina. He came at night. Home and yard were unlocked; there was no one about. He made his way to the attic, lit a match; everything was in wild disorder. In the corner behind the bed a holder with a candle stub was standing on the floor; two wolf eyes stared out from behind it. Kuzya lit the candle, examined the room carefully, picking at the bloodstains on the floor with his fingernail, and said to himself aloud: "Killed her, have they? Or just wounded her maybe—and they've smashed up things here too, the devils!" Then he fixed his attention on the wolf pup, looked at it closely, chuckled, and said: "And they said it was a wolf pup—they're not all there! It's a fox!" Kuzya heaped together all the things in the room, wrapped them in a blanket, and tied a rope around; he took the sheet from the bed, calmly picked up the fox cub by the scruff, wrapped it up, threw the bundles over his shoulder, put out the candle, stuck the candle holder in his pocket, and went out of the room.

Soon Kuzya was walking through the forest. The forest was silent, black, still. Nekulyev would have wondered how Kuzya could move in the dark without having his eyes poked out by branches. He took the shortest route, following narrow paths over hills; he gave no thought to the wood devil, but he did not whistle either. The bundles were heavy.

The affair of the wolf pup must have made a great impression on Kuzya, because Yegor, Maryasha, and Katyasha each heard the story many times over: "And they said it was a wolf pup—they're not all there!—it was a fox all the time! A wolf's tail is like a cudgel, but this one has a black tuft on the end, and the ears are black, mark you. Of course, how should the gentry know about that?—not every hunter can tell the difference—but I know!"

By the time the snows came that fall there was no longer any doubt that the wolf pup had turned out to be a fox. Kuzya killed the fox, skinned it, and from the pelt made himself a cap with earflaps.

Moscow
November 20, 1924
On Povarskaya Street

The Nizhni Novgorod Otkos[1]

A Story

One day in February, at the sunset hour, the high school student Dmitri Klestov, who had stayed behind at school for a rehearsal in preparation for the Shrovetide ball and play, returned home and chanced to go into the drawing room. His mother stood by the window. The room was deep in twilight; beyond the window lay a deep blue, only the odd cloud gleamed golden in the sky. The room was filled with the silence of the heated stoves and the peaceful house. His mother Natalya Dmitrievna's face, her expression, could not be made out, only her silhouette could. She was looking out the window; her head was lowered, her hands were lowered, her shoulders drooped in their heavy shawl. It was very quiet in the room. If a third person had been in the room, he would have said that the woman was standing at the window in very great sadness, grief it must have been—a grief of which she herself perhaps was unaware. Dmitri ran over to his mother, laid his head on her shoulder, pressed against his mother, and said:

"Mama, Mama, what a terrible thing life is! Forgive me, but I have been watching you. It is given to a man to live, yes, every day, every hour. After that comes death. You get me up in the morning, see Papa and me off, and you have such long days, one the same as the other. I can't put it into words. . . . All of us, all of us will die—and each peaceful minute you pass is a step on the way to death. I understand why you began studying music with me at the age of twenty-eight, why it is you

1. *Otkos* means "steep bank." In Nizhni Novgorod (now Gorki) the Otkos is a wide boulevard that runs through the town above the Volga.—Eds.

are learning English—and you're ashamed to speak it, not knowing how to pronounce the words in English—it's to fill empty time. It's simply frightful—empty time! That's why you read books, that's why you go visiting and to the theater and skating—all that doesn't interest you; you're just killing time. I can't find the right words—it's frightful. And sometimes I feel such pain for you, such misery, that I could put my head in a noose. . . . If only I could die for you, Mama, if only I could! . . ."

. . . That evening the mother went to the Otkos. The Otkos exists in the town of Nizhni Novgorod to purify and sadden human beings and to plunge people into the unconscious and incomprehensible. The town of Nizhni Novgorod is situated on a hill above the Oka and above the Volga, a medieval principality town and now provincial capital, overgrown with kremlin, stone mansions, with splendid generations of Russian ways, traditions, legends—and the town with all its traditions and ways breaks off at the Otkos, and particularly sharply at the place where the kremlin too breaks off. From there the widest reaches of the Oka and the Volga are visible, the water meadows beyond the Volga, the pastures, the Melnikov-Pechersky[2] forests. These forests are primeval to this very day; the gaze is lost in them. In the town of Nizhni Novgorod, months, fairs, traditions pass, and there beyond the Volga, where man's gaze is lost in the blue of the forests, snowstorms pass, wild beasts have their being; during the summer steamers and sailing boats pass on the Volga, disappearing into the silver of the Volga's reaches, their whistles reverberating through empty spaces. These spaces sadden and purify.

Natalya Dmitrievna had a tradition—to go to the Otkos, to stand for hours on the Otkos, to gaze into space, to be silent, to think, to be sad—these reaches of the Volga and beyond plunge a human being into that unreality that troubles a man and calms him with a great peace.

2. Pavel Ivanovich Melnikov-Pechersky (1818–83), a novelist whose best-known books, *In the Forests* and *On the Hills*, describe the life of the Old Believers along the upper Volga.—Eds.

That evening the mother wandered for a long time through the frosts of the Otkos, in moonlit silence. At home that evening there was tranquility of quiet and warmth, and the house rested in the darkness of unlighted lamps like a cat on a stove ledge. The son was sitting in his room at his lessons and then took up a book. That evening Natalya Dmitrievna was searching the town for her husband by telephone, found him, and said into the telephone wire:

"I feel very bad today, Kirill. Will you be home soon?"

Kirill Pavlovich answered cheerfully:

"I'm playing whist, Natasha. Come over here; have the horse harnessed. They've brought some tasty stuff from Moscow, from Yliseyev's. Will you come?"

"Yes, I'll come," answered Natalya Dmitrievna, and that entire evening she sat in the dark drawing room on a sofa, not turning on the light, wrapping her shawl tightly about her. The son didn't leave his room, falling asleep over his book. The husband arrived after midnight.

On sunny days on the Otkos, in February, the sun already hints of March. At midday then the Semyonov forests are visible for vast dozens of versts, and the light and the snow are so sharp that they stab your eyes. On the Otkos the frost makes it hard to breathe at that time, that's when the hoar frost comes, hoar frost that settles on the eyelashes, and the string of sledges that is visible thirty versts away on the Volga ice carries away with it the human will. And on the Otkos at noon, in the fierce February frost, Dmitri attentively examining the land beyond the Volga, those snowy expanses that stab the eyes, said to his friend and classmate Sergei Beryozin:

"You know, Seryozha, I'll probably shoot myself soon."

* * *

The Nizhni Novgorod Otkos!—It exists to shatter the common run of everyday human existence: it can happen that the ultimate human happiness is an abomination, that an abomination is happiness—and each man, like the epochs, drains his cup of life in his own way, as it is given to him.

The town of Nizhni Novgorod is a medieval principality town, a forest town. The upper reaches of the Volga are fettered in winter by heavy ice. At that time there is skating in Osharskaya Square, and behind the monastery settlement, in Devichya Grove, near Pechery, above the Oka and above the Volga there is deft skiing. The Klestovs, mother and son, skied and skated together. Houses in Nizhni Novgorod were built broad-hipped, warm, roomy, for such were needed in an existence of long evenings, slow tea drinking, a book in the study, and a grand piano in the twilight of the drawing room.

This was a family of the Russian intelligentsia, the kind that had become extinct in the decade of the October Revolution. The father was a railroad engineer, and every morning at half past nine he would take his seat in the sledge with a bearskin rug, greeting the sedate Ivan, who has been grunting into his frost-whitened beard going into the second decade of his coachman's service. The horse, which had been broken in as a foal, would carry him to Kunavino, to the railroad board, scooping up the broad expanses and the silvery snow of the Oka so that later it and Ivan would wait for the engineer in the board's stable. He was an engineer who worked in the offices of the board in order, about four o'clock, frosted by the Oka and the slanting beams of the red sun, to remove the overcoat of his uniform, lined with kangaroo fur, in his warm vestibule, tossing it into the arms of a maidservant in a cap; there would be warm water on the washstand; in the dining room at that time the lid would already have been taken off the soup tureen in clouds of cheerful steam; the engineer, freshly washed, besprinkled only the moment before with eau de cologne, would go into the dining room; he kissed his wife's hand; his wife kissed him on the forehead; the son kissed his father's hand; the father kissed his son on the forehead. Then there was his study in the semigloom of the ministerial bell glass on the lamp and with the latest numbers of *Russian Thought*, the *European Herald* and the *Herald of the Ministry of Transportation*—until nine o'clock, when he would meet his friends for grand slam and for arguments about the State Duma and about the victories near Naroch. He was forty, and he was a calm, neat, clean engineer, a family man, and a loyal subject of his country. And that's all there is to be said about Kirill Pavlovich Klestov.

She, the wife and mother, was in her thirty-sixth year. Every living being knows maternal love, because everyone has had a mother, and every living man, every living woman has to love children, for it is given to mankind to preserve itself in the face of eternity through birth. It must be true that every mother who devotes herself to her son, loves herself in her son, her own body, her own pain, her own blood, her own immortality, which she passed on to her son. If a woman has one child and cannot have more children, all her love is given to that one and only child, who came into being in portents of daydreams about him, in the first movement there, beneath her heart, in the pain of birth, in the shame of birth, that shame of which mothers in the pangs of giving birth are not aware—to that one and only child who came into being from her blood and sucked the milk of her breast, all the wonder of whose life has gone by in her arms. Natalya Dmitrievna was slow-moving and beautiful. The whole of her preceding Nizhni Novgorod life she had thought herself happy—in her house, her husband, her child, in her days and deeds and cares. She had an only son, born in the first year of her marriage; having once given birth, she could bear no more children. She had a great deal of leisure, and there always remained in her the slowness of movement and speech of an eighteen-year-old blue-eyed Russian girl, the kind of slowness that makes one suppose the blood of such girls to be not red but blue, like their eyes, like the little blue veins around their eyes, on their temples, on their hands—that slowness of movement was the legacy of a difficult birth. She lived, in fact, a good, slow, pure life, devoted to her family, her husband, her son. Her son! Dmitri!—she had given her life to her son—his first movement, his first tears, his first word—all this she would remember forever, as she remembered her son even before his birth. With her son she repeated the multiplication tables when he was preparing for school. From his first school years she would get up at the same time as her son, so as to see the boy off, and, with her own hands, make him lunch to take to school, with some unexpected sweet.

With her son she began to study music (and she was always a lesson ahead because she had a great deal of leisure for canons and scales). For her son's sake she began to study English. Every day she sensed the hour when her son was to arrive—her son arrived back from school about three, and the hour that preceded four o'clock was the sweetest one for her; they would be in her son's room, she would stand by the stove, her son—a girlish youth—would walk about the room in his father's manner, and they would talk about teachers and classes, about Blok, and Maeterlinck, about Kant's *Critique of Pure Reason*, about Mechnikov's *Forty Years's Search for a Rational World View*, and about the latest show at the town theater. At half past five every day, mother and son would go skating; the son would skate with his friends, his mother with ladies and students of her acquaintance—to watch over her son, her only son. Her son! Dmitri! Time extends and contracts like an accordion: that's really him, a student in the eleventh grade, and only yesterday he sucked the milk from her breast and clung to her knees with his weak little hands, it was he whom she had taught prayers to the Virgin, and he had brought her his first A, and he was the one who had asked her what it was that people lived for, and he too had asked her what death was.

Her son, Dmitri, was sixteen. The son of a strong, big father and a fragile mother who at thirty-five looked like a girl; the son was born with health like his mother's and a character like his father's. The young Blok, Dmitri's favorite poet, must have been like Dmitri. Dmitri was calm, collected, practical, judicious beyond his years, and slow in his actions like his father. He was of delicate health, fragile and beautiful like his mother, and he resembled a girl, with a dimple in his chin, with a girlish blush on his cheeks, as bashful as a girl. His mother knew that people build their mental world in different ways and define their place in the world differently: there are those who feel a certain guilt before life into old age; others are never conscious of their right to life, feeling guilty for being alive; from early childhood Dmitri knew unconsciously where his right to life began and where it ended; he had the right to live, simply because he was alive. He was a little reserved—

he was liked, but he didn't have many friends. As with his mother, the entire life of this adolescent and then youth was very simple and transparent in that childish wisdom which preserves its purity. Life did not present him with upheavals; he was pure in thought and deed. His friend Sergei knew better than his mother, and his mother knew better than his father, that the awakening of human instincts, so tormenting in young men—the instinct of death, the instinct of the right to life, the sex instinct—passed barely discernibly in his case, absolutely painlessly. The most frightening for his mother was the sex instinct—she was inclined to think that this instinct had not yet awakened in him by his sixteenth year, and she worried about her son with her maternal sex instinct (his friend Sergei knew that one day Dmitri had gone voluntarily and willingly to a brothel on Millionnaya Street with his classmates and sat through the evening in the drawing room listening to the grand piano and waiting for his friends, and when they were leaving the brothel, when his friends felt themselves to be thieves who had stolen something beautiful from their very selves, Dmitri said cheerfully, glancing at the gleaming lindens: "Rubbish, filth, not interesting").

The town of Nizhni Novgorod, which with its Otkos plunges into the human unknown, was living out its life according to set rules and traditions, in its solid kremlin streets, in its solid families. It was taken for granted that every new issue of a magazine had to be discussed by the whole family, at Christmas there had to be a trip to Moscow to see the productions of the Art Theater—and to see all the productions of their own town theater, where his father and mother sat in the third row of the stalls, always in the same seats, and their son in the amphitheater with his friends. The father had a day of grand slam, and the mother had her hour of afternoon tea—and on Saturdays friends of both sexes gathered at the son's in a study group to read Buckle, Marx and Büchner, on the instructions of the father, and to discuss them fiercely, under the mother's guidance.

Her son! Dmitri!—he whose warmth, from the day of his birth, whose physical warmth had been her warmth—he told his mother what a terrible thing life was. At the twilight hour on that day his mother stood long at the window of the dark drawing room—and long did she wander along the Otkos. Her husband arrived after midnight. She sat on the sofa in the dark drawing room, wrapping her shawl tightly about her. She had stolen into her son's room, where the moon disturbed the room's darkness; the mother had sat down on her son's bed and kissed the sleeping boy as she had kissed him when he slept in his cradle; her son was already a man, and his mother had whispered to him:

"My son, my little darling, you're grown up now, my defender, my darling. . . ."

The father arrived after midnight. He was a little fatigued with mulled wine and whist. And then, when father and mother were alone together, he said:

"You don't notice anything strange about our son? He has stopped getting his study group together. I asked him why—he answered that he considered it pointless. I insisted and tried to show that collective work with friends develops social know-how—but apparently he's read his fill of Schopenhauer and had nothing to say. He refused a part in the Shrovetide school play; the principal told me about it today over whist—stupid!" The father lit a cigarette. "Forgive the vulgarity, Natasha. Pay attention to what I say and don't misinterpret me. I've been wanting to talk this over with you for some time. Life is life, and in life there is a great deal that is revolting. My mother dealt with me in exactly the same way when I was sixteen. I explain our son's behavior—how shall I put it?—biologically. . . . We'll have to get rid of Dasha and hire a new maid. . . . Do you understand me? It's easier for you to do that, so that he doesn't notice."

But Natalya Dmitrievna didn't let her husband finish. Not with anger, but with the most acute pain, with outrage, revulsion, she began to speak, stretching out her hands and begging for mercy.

"What are you saying, what are you saying, Kirill?! You should be ashamed! That I should. . . . Aren't you afraid?—how can you insult me in this way?"

"I'm speaking as a naturalist," said Kirill Pavlovich.

"How can you insult me like this?" whispered Natalya Dmitrievna. Her head and shoulders dropped. She fell silent. Her husband clicked his cigarette case in irritation.

The ministerial lamp burned surrounded by midnight, quiet, peacefulness, and twenty degrees of frost outside. The hoarfrost covered the windows with plants that predated the Ice Age.

* * *

Friendship!

Dmitri had a friend, his classmate Sergei Beryozin. The boys understood friendship as brotherhood, as a vow, as a heroic deed, when the friends have no secrets from each other, when there is nothing which is not in common and when one must be ready to do all and give all for the other. Their friendship went back to their first school year, a school friendship such as occurs once in a lifetime. Dmitri was an orderly young gentleman, a fragile youth with hair parted straight, with a collar under his gray school blouse, as fresh as his thoughts, with the slow habit of gazing at his girlish palms. Sergei was awkward, nihilistic, impetuous, always without a belt and with hair like Mark Volokhov's.

The friendship had many events in its memory. One day Sergei had rushed into Dmitri's room and hidden something under Dmitri's bed—with bristling seventeen-year-old side-whiskers he demanded from the maid, for the whole house to hear, a tricolored bit of ribbon from the pastry they had eaten at tea three days before and, having obtained the ribbon, grunting with embarrassment and shaking his nihilistic curls, asked Natalya Dmitrievna to leave the room; Natalya Dmitrievna went out, Sergei closed the door and triumphantly dragged out from under the bed a horse's leg, a hoof with a piece of bone, with flesh the dogs had not finished eating, all covered with hoarfrost; moving the photographs of Blok and Dmitri's mother to one side, Sergei spread on Dmitri's desk the paper from the pastry shop which he had brought with him and carefully wrapping the leg in the paper—to

Dmitri's great surprise—tied it with the ribbon; Sergei then explained that today was the name day of the classics teacher Sega and that he, Sergei, intended to take the leg to Sega as a gift, together with a visiting card of the principal, which has been filched from the principal's study. (Dmitri tried to dissuade Sergei from the enterprise, which carried with it the threat of expulsion, scornfully shrugged his shoulders, and argued that there was nothing in the least clever about this; but friendship is above reason, and the boys emerged onto Osharskaya Street with the leg in the pastry-shop wrapping; the leg was to play a tragic role in the history of Nizhni Novgorod cinemas; cunningly, Dmitri told Sergei that Lelya Knabe would be at the movies today and that she had insisted that Sergei come too; Sergei's courage weakened at that point, and the boys entered the cinema, resolved to deliver the leg afterwards; in the cinema the leg thawed out and began to ooze blood-tinged liquid. Lelya insisted that Sergei accompany her home, and the leg was left in the cinema, in the foyer, behind the drapery, to the amazement of the janitor; the story of the leg surfaced behind school desks, and ever since then every student, from sniveling sixth-grader to senior, considered it his duty to dump some piece of filth when he went to the cinema.) Week after week Sergei, carried away with Nietzsche, would discourse on true human freedom, which is connected in mankind with rudimentary instincts of conscience, and sought ways of getting rid of conscience, constructing his own moral system by reason alone; saddened by the existence within himself of a conscience and seeking for some means of destroying it, Sergei then came to the conclusion that it was essential to steal something or to rob or kill someone; but stealing was somewhat repellent, unaesthetic—and one day Sergei came running in in great spirits, announcing that he had discovered someone whom it would be possible to rob and inviting Dmitri to the robbery. Dmitri agreed, for he too had read Nietzsche, and he thought long and hard about Nietzsche and Sergei's suggestion; Dmitri took his father's revolver; several times the friends went to Devichya Grove to learn to shoot; then one dark evening they went out to commit a robbery; Dmitri found himself the leader; he was not in the least nervous; Sergei on the other hand was frightened; they went into Pushkin Garden, which had just been laid out and was completely empty; it was dark and cold; Sergei had discovered that every evening a man in a fur coat went walking there, with his hands behind his back, a cane held between his shoulder blades; it was decided to take his fur coat, watch, and money. The man appeared in the darkness; Sergei bared his dagger; Dmitri cocked the revolver; Dmitri was to shout "Hands up!"; toward them walked a man, straight as a rod, his hands behind him; Dmitri went up to him; the man looked closely at Dmitri, and just as Dmitri was about to shout, "Hands up!" the stranger said with the greatest calm; "Hello, Mityusha, what are you doing here?" Dmitri answered politely; "Hello, Aleksandr Pavlinovich!" and lifted his cap; it was the chief forester, a friend of his father's, whose wife had recently run off with a student probationer; the chief forester walked on past; the boys stood in perplexity; it was unaesthetic to rob an acquaintance; Dmitri gave Sergei a scolding; Sergei scratched the back of his head, and they went home, arguing that what was essential was not the fact but the awareness of the fact, all the more in that there is a great deal which is ridiculous as fact (the boys made no further attempts at robbery and murder, and in two weeks or so the chief forester, Aleksandr Pavlinovich, shot himself). These were the secrets of friendship. There is no point in explaining that every day Sergei fell in love with another girl, sometimes even with several at the same time, and all his tempestuous secrets he would carry to Dmitri and to Natalya Dmitrievna in the same tempestuous way that he reacted to the books he read and to the injustices of school life. Dmitri's secrets were simple, ordinary, and brief. When his mother was not in the room, Dmitri would take his mother's place at the stove, warm his hands, and calmly, always as if it were the most ordinary thing in the world, would confide to Sergei the idea that Tatyana Larina[3] was wrong not to return to Onegin (Beryozin's father was a steamship owner from across the Volga, an Old Believer with a beard as thick as a forest, wearing a red

3. Heroine of Aleksandr S. Pushkin's novel in verse, *Eugene Onegin*.—Eds.

shirt with blue polka dots under his velvet vest; on holidays Dmitri would travel to the forest beyond the Volga to stay with Sergei; Sergei's mother would then bake enormous pies, regular pies, cheese tarts; the Beryozins lived in the forest in a house built of logs; benches lined the walls; the icon corner was loaded with icons and the rooms smelled of incense; on a holiday morning, coming from their attic room to the kitchen, where the dining table stood, the boys ate meat dumplings, drank tea with honey, and talked about Liza Kalitina;[4] in the corner beneath the icons sat the father, bearded like a forest, in a vest and felt boots; he listened to the boys mistrustfully and said, stressing his *o*'s in the Nizhni Novgorod manner, spreading his beard sedately:

"You talkin' about them girls, huh? Forget it! Their little thing is so tiny, but at the fair one of them took care of seven of my steamships, and two barges to boot.")

At school Sergei would get up lankily from his desk in class and say to the physics teacher Nadezhdin: "Yevgeni Ivanovich, you gave me a C in physics in the quarterly report. I request that you give me a D, because I know myself that I only know enough physics to deserve a D!" And in the wake of Sergei, Dmitri would get up modestly with the request that his B should be changed to a C. Nadezhdin, the physics teacher, would correct their marks, but the class preceptor, the classicist Sega, would always be annoyed: "Vat it this? I know vat mark I vant to give a pupil, if I vant I'll give you a B; if I vant I'll give you an F!"

According to Sergei's code, friendship was a knightly quality, inspired by the devotion of Ostap Bulba, the son of Taras.[5] On that day, on the Otkos at noon, in the fierce February frost, Dmitri, attentively examining the land beyond the Volga, those snowy expanses that stab the eyes, said to his friend:

"You know, Seryozha, I'll probably shoot myself soon."

This was during the free hour after the lunch break. Sergei became excited; he began to pester Dmitri: "What's the matter, Mitri? What

4. Heroine of Ivan S. Turgenev's novel *A Nest of Gentlefolk*.—Eds.

5. Characters in Nikolai V. Gogol's story "Taras Bulba."—Eds.

has brought you to such a decision? Explain." Dmitri didn't say another word, failing for the first time to confide in his friend. Sergei was indignant. The boys had to go to class.

⋆ ⋆ ⋆

The laws of friendship were sacred to Sergei. Sergei knew his friend's reticence. In the drawing class Dmitri with a slow eye measured a head of Zeus to draw it on paper. He was calm, and he kept silence. Sergei skipped the fifth class, and while Dmitri was drawing the head of Zeus, Sergei paid a visit to Natalya Dmitrievna. He arrived very upset and feeling like a thief—he didn't know whether or not he was betraying friendship. Sergei came straight out with:

"You know, Natalya Dmitrievna, I was out with Mitya on the Otkos, and he said to me: 'You know, Seryozha, I'll probably shoot myself soon.' I tried to question him, but he didn't say anything."

Frost and light streamed into the room through the horsetails predating the Ice Age; the room was filled with a white, very sharp light; the heavy shawl weighed down Natalya Dmitrievna's shoulders. The frost on the windowpanes was cold and blank. All the little wrinkles around Natalya Dmitrievna's eyes and temples stood out sharply; the lines around the eyes had become as empty as the eyes themselves; the shawl had become weightless.

"Seryozha, Seryozha, find out immediately, find out at all costs, find out, find out!"

. . . There are in the fates of men and women—in human fates in general—matters which every being must live through, think through, and decide only for himself, because only himself alone, this particular individual, do these matters concern; he must come to a particular decision about his love, his honor, his time; with these matters a human being defines his place in relation to men and to the world, not only in the face of mankind but also in the face of the indifference of that terrible, or merely indifferent, personage the name of whom is death, the names of whom are birth, time, death. And then, in the solving of these matters, in the face of their solution, a man's sufferings, his tomorrows, his petty concerns and possessions and the people who surround him become a matter of complete indifference to him.

Dmitri arrived after classes that day, calm, a little preoccupied, and slow as always. His mother saw him through the window taking leave of his friends, shaking hands, and then touching the peak of his cap and bowing. The mother met her son in the hallway.

"Hello, Mama," said the son, slowly removing his coat.

He went to his room. His mother followed. His mother closed the door behind her. The shawl fell from the mother's shoulders. She held out her hands to her son; she put her hands on her son's shoulders; she lowered her head on her son's chest. She was powerless and resolute. The son embraced his mother convulsively. The son began convulsively to seek his mother's lips with his own. The son murmured:

"Mama, Mama, darling, darling. . . ."

And convulsively the son pushed his mother away, with deathly anguish throwing his hands behind his neck, pressing his neck with his hands; like a whipped dog he went over to the bed, fell face down in the pillow, said softly and firmly:

"Go away, Mama—Mama, go away from me, I beg you, Mama."

The mother didn't go away. The mother—like any mother—covered her son's head, protecting him from whatever there was; she shielded her son with her breast, spoke words from which there was no retreat:

"What do you want, Mitya my son, my own dear boy, what do you want? I'll do anything for you. Tell me, just tell me what's the matter with you and I'll do anything you want. . . ."

Her son said nothing. Her son lifted and freed his head. Her son said:

"Only never tell Father anything. Swear to it."

"I swear," said his mother.

"Mama, I can't tell you anything. I can't; you must understand me. Leave me now. Papa will come soon. I won't do anything against your will, I promise you. Go away from me, Mama."

The mother left her son's room. The mother stood for a long time on the threshold of her son's room. There was no shawl on the mother's shoulders.

The husband's ringing of the doorbell broke the twilight silence.

The husband came into the dining room, rubbing his cold hands.

The son kissed his father's hand; the father kissed the mother's hand.

. . . Friendship—for Sergei—was not only happiness but a heroic feat. Sergei left the Klestovs that day as the September wind blows, without purpose and in confusion. In his attic, over his father's supply shop, books went flying into corners so that he, the friend, should have more space to think; now he sat at his desk, resting his head on his palms; now he lay down on the bed in his boots; now he rushed about the room, energetically spitting, and kicking rubbish around the corners with the toe of his boot; now he sat down to write his diary. His hair was no longer nihilistic but stood up like porcupine quills. In the evening Natalya Dmitrievna came to visit him for the first time in all these years; she stood at the door of the untidy room with a submissiveness not characteristic of that threshold. The mother asked Sergei, as adult and conspirator, to find out all he could from Dmitri. Friendship meant more to Sergei than a mother's entreaties.

Late that evening Sergei went to Dmitri to demand the rights of friendship and to put to him categorically the questions of the honor of friendship. And it was a difficult evening for the two boys. Dmitri stood by the stove; Sergei rushed about the room, storming Dmitri. The parents were not at home; in the house, Nizhni Novgorod–style, silence settled, in warmth, in the occasional crackling of frost in the street and in the slow song of the cook from the kitchen, singing while the masters were away. A candle burned on the desk; Sergei's shadow fled the candlelight around the walls and across the ceiling, the image of the devil.

And Dmitri submitted to the laws of friendship with desperate grief.

"Yes, I want to shoot myself," said Dmitri, "because a terrible thing has happened to me, which I cannot define and which I'm powerless to cope with. I love my mother. No, wait a moment. You love Lelya, and you live with your maid, and you've been to a brothel. I never loved any Lelyas, I never slept with a woman, and I never will, because I find that disgusting and utterly unnecessary. And in the way that you love Lelya and your maid and a girl from a brothel, in that way I love my mother, but much more strongly. I love her more than life, more than anything in the world, and much more than I love myself. I'm ashamed; I'm disgusted with myself. I worship my mother as I worship God; she is all that is most beautiful in the world, but at night I stand at the door of my mother and father's bedroom and I listen to all the sounds coming from there—and I'm ready to kill my father from jealousy. Twice, as if by accident, I went into the bathroom when my mother was bathing—and she wasn't embarrassed—but I don't do that any more, because I'm afraid that her beauty will make my heart burst."

Dmitri stood motionless by the stove while he was saying this. He was gazing upward with a transfixed gaze, and large, slow tears ran down his cheeks. Sergei ran about the room and also wept, rubbing his eyes with his fist so that tears didn't get in the way, but not ashamed of his tears. For a long time the boys wept in silence.

Now and then Sergei would put his arms around Dmitri and smear his forehead with Dmitri's tears—now and then he would run into the kitchen to drink water and would sit for a long time in a chair, spreading his legs, resting his elbows on his knees, and drooping his curls, crushed with sorrow.

"Stop, wait a minute; let's discuss this sensibly. Well, there's you and there's me," said Sergei, but couldn't find words and ran about the room, chasing his shadow and shaking his head, as if he wished to shake off his thoughts. "Well, you then,. . . you must fall out of love. But that's nonsense. Well, as for me. . . ."

"I'll have to shoot myself," said Dmitri, "because I can't think of anything else. I can't try to possess my mother, and I can't kill my father, whom she loves and who is my father. But perhaps I can do both those things, because I dream about Mama and about how I'll kill my father. I've thought about it—I don't understand anything. All my life the closest person to me, apart from you, has been Mama, and now I can't tell her anything because I don't dare to insult her—and I insult her because I kiss her not as a mother but as a woman."

Sergei brushed his thoughts from his curls and said:

"Stop, wait a moment; let's discuss this sensibly. It needs to be discussed. It goes against nature—to love your own mother. I can't understand it. Forgive me, but it's an abomination, against nature, incest. . . ."

"I'll have to shoot myself," said Dmitri, and wept.

It was at that moment that Kirill Pavlovich rang the door bell with an accustomed hand. Sergei ran out through the kitchen. In taking leave, he kissed Dmitri, smeared his tears, and said:

"Stop, wait a moment—give me your word you won't shoot yourself for a week. Give it a week. It needs to be discussed."

Sergei ran off. Kirill Pavlovich went into his son's room.

"You're not asleep."

"No, I'm not."

"Someone was here."

"Sergei."

"What a way is that to answer questions? Why the tears?"

"It's the way I find necessary, the way I find necessary, do you hear! The way I find necessary, necessary, necessary. . . ."

The son was hysterical.

Sergei walked in moonlight and frost, devastated by his friend's problems. He was going to the Otkos. The moon shone with beyond-the-Volga expansiveness, the frost scattered diamonds in the snow, and the frost rustled with Sergei's footsteps. Sergei's shadow leaped after him like an abandoned wolf cub—as lost and abandoned as Sergei's thoughts, as his heart and his ideas of friendship and duty disturbed by Dmitri's problems. "He that is able to receive it, let him receive it"[6]—Sergei was unable to receive it. He did not want his friend to die, for he loved his friend; he had a physical sensation of the fear of death, a fear of death as odious as their nocturnal conversation. With his healthy

6. Matt. 19:12.—Eds.

body, with the roots of his curls, with the tingling of his spine he felt the perversity and abomination—so he defined it—of his friend's love. The silence of Dmitri's room and the candle on the table—here on the Otkos in the blue moonlight—seemed to him as frightful as Dante's Inferno. He kissed his friend, and with his healthy body he felt it repugnant to kiss this handsome boy, in whom an abomination had taken root.

"He's got to shoot himself—no—he's got to shoot himself—no." Sergei fell asleep in his attic without undressing and woke up in the morning much too late for school; he woke up with a headache of oppression, of horror, of uncleanness, when the world is nauseating, and it is better not to wake up. He woke up in the awareness that—well, let Dmitri shoot himself, but in his subconsciousness it came to him that night that their friendship was over, that he felt terrified to see Dmitri, terrified to speak to him, to touch him. "He that is able to receive it"—Sergei couldn't receive it, and he simply desired, physically desired, to wash himself, to wash his hands and his mind. Sergei awoke because he was roused. On the threshold—for the second and last time—stood Natalya Dmitrievna. And Sergei spoke, he said what he had no wish to say, he spoke and was horrified at what he was saying, choking over the words as if they were hangman's nooses.

"I know what's the matter with him. I'm betraying a friend; I won't be able to see him any more; I gave my word of honor that everything would be kept secret, but he's got to shoot himself. This concerns you directly. I don't accept responsibility for his death. I can't bear it. He loves you as a man loves a woman; he spied on you in the bath; he's jealous of Kirill Pavlovich. You too should shoot yourself. Good-bye. He's got to shoot himself. Good-bye!" Sergei stood in the middle of the room while he was saying this, and he ran out of the room into the dark of the attic passage, sniffling and in tears. "Let him shoot himself!"

Natalya Dmitrievna remained in the middle of the room—a chess queen. She didn't see, didn't notice Sergei running off. She said into emptiness:

"Yes—yes. Don't ever tell anyone, don't ever tell anyone about this, Seryozha, anyone, ever. Yes—yes."

Natalya Dmitrievna's head sank; her shoulders drooped. For several moments she was motionless. Then she smiled as people in their sleep, her brows relaxed at first in powerlessness and helplessness and then drew together in severity and resolution. Deep sorrow replaced the smile—and again the smile gleamed. She glanced around the garret with an awakening gaze. As though in her sleep, she strode to the table, leaned on the table, raised herself on tiptoe, threw back her head, arched her spine, and once more whispered:

"Not to anyone, ever. Yes—yes. My son, my own darling boy."

* * *

And indeed from that time Sergei never spoke with Dmitri, just as Dmitri had no words for Sergei.

* * *

At that time the last snowstorm before March descended on Nizhni Novgorod, dumping snow, howling with winds, covering roads, houses, streets. At that time Kirill Pavlovich traveled the railroad line to oversee snowdrift clearance. The chimney and eaves of the house on Osharskaya Street howled in the stormy night. By nightfall the house was well heated. The house was in darkness. Along the roofs, along the walls, above the roofs, behind the walls, thousands of winds raced, wept, shouted. Nobody saw how in the middle of the night, in the howling of the snowstorm, and in the deathly hush of the house the mother prayed before the icons and then walked through the rooms in a dressing gown, with a candle in her hand, walked with great heaviness, halting at every doorjamb for a long time, leaning her head against it, with a trembling candle in one hand, the other at her throat, clutching the collar of her dressing gown. Above the town the Otkos was vanishing, because everything was becoming Otkos: the greatest human happiness can sometimes be abomination, as abomination can be happiness—and every human being, like the epochs, drains the cup of life in his own way, in the way that it is given to mankind and to the epoch. On the twenty-seventh of February in that year, in those three days of snowstorms, the Russian Empire fell: the greatest human joy is for some the greatest horror—that March in Russia arose a revolution, horror to some, happiness, great happiness, to others, Russia went into horror and happiness, into holiness and abomination. At that time Blok, Dmitri's favorite poet, wrote his poem "The Twelve"; poets and writers, in Blok's wake, made obeisance to the snowstorm.

On that February night, when the snowstorm was howling, the student Sergei Beryozin sat on his bed in the attic. His head was lowered, and in his hands was a revolver. The lamp had burned out and was smoking. The snowstorm howled. Sergei was asleep. He had gone to sleep with the revolver in his hands, having hypnotized himself with the thought of death, because by shooting he wanted to rid himself of the abomination there is in life.

Moscow, Yamskoye pole
December 29, 1927

A Dog's Life

The Vicissitudes of Destiny

Our hero was simply of canine origin, for he was quite without a pedigree. He did not even know his father and mother. And he did not even have a proper name, for each new owner gave him a new name, totally disregarding his personality: at one time or another he was Malysh or Sharik or Volchok or Stek; he was also frequently called Zhuchka, for it is an old, established fact that all street dogs are Zhuchkas.

Soon after his birth he was sentenced to death. He was born on the back stair of a large family house; not knowing any better, he was constantly underfoot, and the yardman decided to take him to the river and drown him. But since in those days they were still selling alcoholic beverages, the yardman stopped at a tavern, had a drink, a bite to eat, and completely forgot about the pup.

The frightened pup crawled under a bench and sat there until everybody had left the tavern. After the people had gone, rats arrived. An old she-rat, the leader of them all, who was almost as big as our pup, immediately noticed our hero, in spite of the darkness in the tavern, and approached him with an air of importance.

"Who are you? Where are you from, and what is your origin?" the rat asked.

"To tell the truth, I don't know," the pup replied. "Our yardman wanted to drown me, but he didn't get me to the river, and I don't know whether this is good or bad."

"What is your origin?" the rat interrupted him. "Are you in any way related to the breed of cats?"

"I am not related to any breed," the pup replied. "I am a dog."

"Aha! That is all for the best," said the rat, reassured. "Allow me to teach you a few rules: first—have fear of cats. Had you been of the cat breed, we would have eaten you. Second—be afraid of death, for death is very unpleasant; in particular, death by drowning means that you are forced to drink water and breathe water until blood starts pouring out of your ears even though this is completely against your wishes. Third—always be as one with your brothers and sisters; help them and they will help you. Fourth. . . fourth—although you can live tolerably well in the society of human beings, always depend on your own resources. . . . But conversation is not nourishment," the rat interrupted herself; "you must have a bite to eat."

And the rats gave him some suet and sausage skins and then put him to bed on towels under the counter, where it was very warm.

In the morning the old rat awakened him and, bidding him good-bye, said:

"Perhaps we'll never meet again. I want to teach you one more rule—never put on airs, and remember your friends. In time you will grow big, and if we should meet, please don't eat me. Our life is full of troubles, so why complicate it further?"

"Rest assured," the pup replied, "gratitude is the only thing that I shall retain in my memory."

The rats left. The sun rose. The owner of the tavern came, and a gramophone began playing on the counter. The music had a depressing effect on the pup; at first he felt melancholy and began considering the rules taught him by the rat (when melancholy, we always ponder our situation) and then simply began to howl:

"Oo-aoo, oo-aoo, oo-aoo. . . ."

"Strange," said the tavern owner, and crawled under the counter. "Well, what do you know, a puppy, a little one. . . ."

The tavern owner picked up the pup, looked him over, and put him in his pocket; he took him to his son Mitka and said:

"Here is a little one for you. Beat him coming and going."

Soon, very soon, Malysh, the little one, learned to judge people on first sniff, and one thing was certain: whoever Malysh approached willingly was a good person.

At Mitka's house Malysh settled down in the corridor in a box next to the brick heating stove. The stove was, in Malysh's estimation, a good person, because one could hide from Mitka in it and keep warm near it; the stove's only defect was that it bred fleas.

Mitka, on the other hand, was a bad person, although he spent all of his spare time with Malysh. Mitka greatly enjoyed fastening a piece of paper to Malysh's tail, which made Malysh lose his mental equilibrium and whirl around like a top, much to Mitka's amusement and his own misery. Mitka also blew tobacco smoke into Malysh's nose when he secretly smoked cigarettes stolen from his father.

The tavern owner was also a bad person, because coming home from the tavern he would bring friends with him and turn on the gramophone; and when Malysh would begin howling, he would stick his nose into the horn.

The cook, Mavra, who fed Malysh, and the tomcat, Semyon Matveyevich, on the other hand, turned out to be good people.

When Malysh first met Semyon Matveyevich—remembering the lessons taught him by the estimable rat—he growled and put his tail between his legs; but Semyon Matveyevich, on the contrary, raised his tail and shook it reproachfully.

"You are behaving badly, young man, badly," said the tomact. You and I are not even acquainted, and you are already hostile to me."

"Pardon me; I was so instructed by a respected rat," Malysh replied.

"You are behaving badly, badly," Semyon Matveyevich continued. "It is an age-old prejudice. Considering the present level of culture and condition of the minds—there cannot be and should not be any caste enmity. All together, as brothers, we must strive for unity and mutual help. In my social circles I have long been preaching reconciliation with rats. It's high time. . . ."

The tomcat nodded his tail in parting and said:

"So long for now. Remember, I am your best friend. Come to me for any explanations you may need."

At that time a great change took place in the house of the tavern owner and in Mitka's life: the tavern owner put on a mouse-colored suit and kept coming and going; the tavern was closed, and the customers would come to the house and drink on the sly behind the heating stove—"half-a-jar" and "twenty-five-rubles-worth." As for Mitka, he completely lost his wits: he would put on a jacket, get a bow, and with the bow shoot at Malysh, shouting:

"Beat the Germanth. Do you know what a high-explothive shell ith?"

Malysh knew no rest and no respite and went to Semyon Matveyevich for explanations.

"Pardon me, Semyon Matveyevich," said Malysh. "Mitka has completely worn me down, and the impression remains that I have become a German."

The tomcat sighed deeply.

"The people have completely taken leave of their senses," said the tomcat. "They kill each other, when everybody knows that pain and death are the worst things there are. What is more, people do everything they can to derive profit from it and sell alcohol, encouraging vice. It is very hard for me, young man. Mitka gives me no rest either, in spite of my age; and although I am convinced that it is immaterial who you are, a German or a Russian, as long as you are a good person, I am still giving some thought to the idea of leaving this house, where we live as spongers, and going to find a new shelter."

"If you do, don't forget me, Semyon Matveyevich."

"Yes, yes, I will certainly let you know beforehand, young man."

Semyon Matveyevich and Malysh Travel

Early one morning Malysh and Semyon Matveyevich left the house. Semyon Matveyevich traveled mainly over fences; Malysh, on the other hand, used gateways, for our travelers had decided not to use streets so as to shorten the journey.

"The most valuable thing in life is freedom," said Semyon Matveyevich, jumping from a fence to a gate.

The sun was strolling leisurely in the sky; on earth it was an autumn day. Beyond the fences, along the street, soldiers were marching and singing: "Nightingale, nightingale—little brown bird. . . ."

Malysh and Semyon Matveyevich walked all day and toward evening reached a large, dark barn smelling of flour and rats.

"This is my birthplace," said Semyon Matveyevich. "I was born here, and here, in freedom, I shall spend the rest of my days. The most precious thing of all is freedom."

"Yes," replied Malysh, "that is true; however, I am very hungry. . . .

"To tell the truth, I too am hungry," the tomcat sighed, "but. . . we'll face that tomorrow, for, as they say, the morning is wiser than the evening."

They crawled into the barn, snuggled into a dark corner, and went to sleep.

In the morning, having barely awakened, Malysh announced that hunger not only had not left him but, quite the contrary, had become worse.

"Yes, yes, let us hasten to obtain provisions," said the tomcat.

And they went in search of food. Not far from the barn they came upon a street market. Our travelers saw meat and milk being sold there and licked their chops in bitterness. Malysh summoned all his courage and, approaching a woman stallkeeper, said in his dog language:

"Madam, I'd be obliged if you would give me something to eat."

The stallkeeper apparently understood Malysh, because she threw him a small piece of tripe, with which Malysh completely satisfied his hunger. Having eaten, he went back to join Semyon Matveyevich.

But Semyon Matveyevich was not where he had left him. Malysh basked in the sun for a while and then went home to the barn. Semyon Matveyevich returned toward evening.

"Where have you been? Did you get something to eat?" Malysh asked.

"No," the tomcat replied sullenly.

"And I had a meal and took a walk," said Malysh. "Freedom is a wonderful thing."

"I suppose so," Semyon Matveyevich replied sullenly.

The friends went to sleep. Malysh quickly dozed off, but was soon awakened by the sound of crying: Semyon Matveyevich sat on his haunches and wept most bitterly, his tears flowing in streams.

"Semyon Matveyevich, my friend, what is the matter?" Malysh cried out.

"Something awful has happened. . . ," Semyon Matveyevich cried out, his tears flowing in streams. "I abandoned my principles. Freedom is a wonderful thing, but when freedom is idleness—it brings crime in its wake. Hunger drove me to eat a rat. I abandoned my principles."

The tomcat cried for a very long time, his tears flowing in streams, and then calmed down.

"No, without compromises one can't survive," said Malysh, who, half-awake, had begun to feel hungry again. "We have to seek new pathways. What are we going to do?"

The tomcat sighed and said:

"I think we should return to our former owner. . . ."

"But," Malysh replied, "there every day Mitka twisted my tail and stuck my nose into the gramophone horn. . . ."

"Let that be the payment for a piece of bread," the tomcat said sadly.

"Oh, no!" Malysh cried out, "that would be sinecure. I am going to find more honorable work."

"Do as you wish," the tomcat sighed. "In that case I'll go alone. If you succeed in living an honest life, remember me."

"I surely will!" Malysh cried out.

Semyon Matveyevich and Malysh shook paws, hugged and kissed, and parted for the time being. Limping slightly, the tomcat climbed the fence and trudged off home, and Malysh set off for the street market to get a bite to eat before looking for work.

Not Malysh, but Sharik, and Then Stek

By the time Malysh and Semyon Matveyevich parted, Malysh, properly speaking, was no longer Malysh, the Little One, and although he was not of any kind of breed, he had grown to be a dog of respectable size, in his appearance somewhat resembling a fox, but with jet-black pelt, legs more sinewy than a fox's and a tail less long and fluffy.

That day, arriving at the street market, Malysh met the house painter, Sergei Terentyevich. Sergei Terentyevich put his pail on the sidewalk and shouted:

"Sharik, Sharik!"

Malysh was somewhat surprised and even offended that he was not called by his name and was treated so casually, but, remembering the saying "Beggars can't be choosers," he obediently approached Sergei Terentyevich.

"A-aa, doggie, a-a," said Sergei Terentyevich, and patted him on the neck.

Then they went to Sergei Terentyevich's house; the painter lived in a small, three-window cottage; buckets of paint stood every-where, and paintbrushes lay about. The paints smelled delicious.

They lived alone, just the two of them. Sergei Terentyevich would come home in the evening, climb on the stove, and begin a soliloquy:

"Yes, brother Sharik, there is a war going on. Not a war, actually, but a robbery. Drying oil, for example, used to cost sixty-five kopecks, and now it is two rubles eighty. And whitewash. . . . And red lead. . . . Red lead is bad enough; potatoes, even they are running crazy. . . . So help me God, they are running crazy. And in addition to everything else, I have to feed you. Yes!"

Sharik would stand there with a doleful look in his eyes.

"Come on now, don't feel hurt. You are guarding the place, and keep on guarding it."

Nevertheless, Sharik's stay at Sergei Terentyevich's came to an end in an absolutely unbelievable way. Sharik was already used to being

Sharik, rather than Malysh; he was used to barking at people, carrying out his duty, even though he was not cross with visitors. . . . But, little by little, Sergei Terentyevich fell out of the habit of feeding Sharik and once, for about three days, did not give him a single potato. The paints always smelled appetizing, and when Sergei Terentyevich left, Sharik went over to the bucket of whitewash and ate the whole contents; he also ate the red lead. He ate them and nearly died of heartburn; he felt as though all his insides had been scalded with boiling water, scratched up, and had pieces of paper tied to them, the way Mitka used to tie them to his tail; a thousand gramophones roared in his ears. But the misfortune did not end there; Sergei Terentyevich, a man of gentle disposition, arriving home, roared like a camel, grabbed a firelog with one hand and Sharik by his tail with the other and began beating these two objects against each other.

Sharik could not endure such ingratitude and ran away from Sergei Terentyevich.

The search for new employment was lengthy. One night he spent at the barracks, enticed there by the soldiers. But at the barracks they talked about war all the time, and Sharik, remembering the principles of tomcat Semyon Matveyevich, and thinking that war had something in common with whitewash and red lead, made haste to depart. One day he was chased with a noose so as to be taken to the pound and hanged there. Once a peasant woman threw slops over him. Not once but many times, boys threw stones at him. Finally, one beautiful day, Sharik arrived at the boulevard. On a bench there sat an old lady surrounded by five dogs of different breeds: pugs, spitzes, and fox terriers. Sharik approached the pug and said:

"Good day, comrade."

"A goose is no comrade to a pig," the pug quipped, and burst out laughing; and having had his joke, he turned and added: "Well, what do you want?"

"You see, I am looking for employment. Won't you help me?"

"And what is your breed?"

Sharik turned over the matter in his mind and resorted to cunning:

"I am, you see, an ex-mutt."

"An ex?" the pug asked. "That is not a bad breed. There is a resemblance to a pug, that is, to me. You see, we are in the service of Countess Matilda Karlovna Krinkis-Tazens."

"And what do you do?"

"We adorn the countess's old age."

"Aha, I'd say that is not hard work. Do engage me."

The pug smiled condescendingly and said:

"Oh, all right. We'll engage you. And what is your name?"

"Formerly I was called Malysh, and now I am Sharik."

"No, that name does not suit the countess's society. Henceforth you will be Stek. And now, my friend, run down to the river, wash up, and come back here—we'll wait for you. At home the bath day is not until Saturday."

A New Life, an Unexpected Encounter, Thoughts, the End

It was quite by chance that Sharik had described his breed as exmutt, but the description was very apt, because the service involved flunky's duties, and "ex" and "pug" have something in common with "If you please, Madam," and "Yes, Madam?" Countess Krinkis-Tazens, besides being a titled person, was also the widow of a general and in addition to the six dogs had two lackeys. The dogs tended the general's widow, and the lackeys tended the dogs.

Besides various other rooms in the house, there were a bedroom with a number of beds—one belonging to the general's widow and the rest to the dogs—and a dining room where there was a separate table for each dog.

The general's widow awoke before the dogs did and rang for the lackeys. The lackeys came, and the morning toilet began: the dogs were washed, perfumed with various colognes, brushed, and adorned with bows and trinkets. After having their faces washed, the dogs jumped onto their mistress's bed to lick her good morning on her nose. The lackeys left on tiptoe. The general's widow relaxed a bit with the dogs; then she dressed, and afterward everybody went to the dining room to have breakfast and drink coffee.

The lackeys served the various dishes, saying:

"If you please, Mr. Pug, sir."

"We beg you to eat, Madam Nelly."

The dogs were fed till they were stuffed, and after breakfast they and the general's widow went to the boulevard or rode in the carriage to the country or to visit friends.

Every Saturday the dogs were bathed, and afterward Viktor Savvich, the veterinarian, came, took their temperatures, and examined their stomachs.

In the presence of the general's widow, the lackeys called the dogs various affectionate names, but when her back was turned, they beat the dogs savagely, saying:

"You pigs' bastards! Scum's spawn!"

As for the general's widow, they called her Dog Mommy or Dog Pot, the latter on the basis of her name, Krinkis-Tazens.[1] In the presence of the general's widow the dogs were supposed to be affectionate and to look fawningly into her eyes, like the lackeys. But when the general's widow was absent and the lackeys were not beating them, the dogs also abused the general's widow. The job gave one plenty to eat, but it was worthless and mean; remembering the principles of the friends of his youth, Malysh often felt sad, could not sleep at night because of his overstuffed belly, and wandered about the empty rooms yielding to pessimism.

And once, in the corridor on his way to the kitchen, he met his old acquaintance—the estimable rat.

1. The name Krinkis-Tazens suggests the Russian words *krinka*, or *krynka*, "pot"; and *taz*, "basin."—Eds.

"What brings you here?" the ex-mutt cried out.

"You see," said the rat, "the tavern was closed, and I moved from one cellar to another."

"What a pleasant encounter!" the ex cried out again. "I remember your principles very well; you were wrong in only one respect: I shall introduce you to tomcat Semyon Matveyevich, who preaches brotherhood between cats and rats. What is new?"

The rat sighed.

"I live in the underground. Revolutionaries work down there together with us. They have now formed a union—a universal brotherhood in conjunction with the class struggle. Never take that point of view—it means the end of culture. We must walk hand in hand. Your friend Semyon Matveyevich is right. It is too bad that not everyone is as sensible as he is. . . . You ask, what is new? Well, taking advantage of the war, the revolutionaries in the underground have decided to stir up a revolution. . . ."

Malysh and the rat parted friends and promised to meet again.

But then the revolution came, and the worst possible turmoil began. Class struggle won. The general's widow was put in her own carriage and taken to jail. The lackeys ran away to parade with red banners. And the dogs were given complete freedom.

"The devil only knows what this is all about!" Pug exclaimed.

"Well, I don't know," Malysh replied. "Of course, they should not have taken the general's widow to jail, for it is not her fault that God made her what she is. On the other hand, oppression must be curbed. Take us: we lived as parasites and for that reason derived no satisfaction from life."

"So what are we going to do now?" Nelly growled.

"Work," replied Malysh. "Class struggle has triumphed, and if you are not going to work, you will be judged a bourgeois, like the general's widow, and sent to jail. And personally. . . "

But Malysh did not finish because some people burst into the house and began looting the place.

The dogs ran in all directions. . . .

New Life and the End of the Story

By the time the revolution came, Malysh (also Sharik and Stek) was full grown—a sturdy dog of an average dog size. He found the estimable rat, and together they went to see Semyon Matveyevich. They found Semyon Matveyevich on the fence, because the house where the tavern owner and Mitka had lived was also being divided in the name of the class struggle.

"Semyon Matveyevich, we have come to see you!" Malysh shouted.

"What horrors I have lived through!" the tomcat said. "One of the citizens tried to hang me on the fence by my tail, and it was my luck that they began dividing the fence also."

"Comrades," said Malysh, "I have lived in this world long enough and have pondered fate long enough. I have lived with people and was not satisfied because my will was taken from me; instead of serving I had to be servile. I have lived a free life too and was not satisfied because I was idle, out of touch with society, and hungry. I have eaten my fill, and I have been hungry, and when I had enough to eat, I felt even worse than when I was hungry because my conscience bothered me. . . ."

"So what is your idea?" asked the tomcat.

"My idea is to begin a new, brotherly, community life, completely free but based on work. We'll earn our daily bread working in the sweat of our brows for the good of our neighbors."

"Makes sense," said Semyon Matveyevich.

"I agree," said the rat. "In our society there will be neither rats nor cats nor dogs but only brothers. Let's go."

"Let's go!" cried out the tomcat. "This is exactly according to my principles."

"Let's go," said Malysh.

And they left the people where class struggle was uppermost and went into a field and toward the woods. In the woods they built a little house. The rat was the cook. The tomcat and Malysh toiled in the sweat of their brows getting provisions. Soon they were joined by other dogs, rats, chickens, and one duck. They all were free, and they all toiled from morning till night.

And in the evening they sat around a common table, drank tea, ate the bread procured by brotherly hands, and talked about principles.

[1919]

A Year of Their Life

I

To the south and the north, to the east and the west—in all directions for hundreds of versts—forests and swamps lay wrapped in moss and laced with moss. Grayish-brown cedars and pines stood in the chill. Below them grew impassable thickets of firs, alders, bird cherries, junipers, undersized birches. And in small meadows, amid shrubbery, in layers of peat framed by red whortleberries and cranberries, covered with moss, lay "wells"—frightening, full of reddish water, bottomless.

In September frosts came and went. Snow lay hard and blue. Light arose for three hours only; the rest of the time it was night. The sky seemed heavy and pressed close to the earth. It was quiet; only in September elk bellowed as they mated; in December wolves howled; the rest of the time a silence prevailed such as can exist only in a desert.

On a hill by the river stood a village.

A slope—bare, of grayish-brown granite and white shale, furrowed by water and wind—led to the river. On the shore lay clumsy grayish-brown boats. The river was big, gloomy, cold, bristling with murky bluish-black waves. The huts had turned grayish brown with age; their roofs—steep, projecting, made of planks—were covered with greenish moss. The windows gazed blindly. Nets were drying nearby. Trappers lived here. In winter, for long stretches of time they went into taiga and killed wild beasts there.

II

In spring the rivers overflowed broadly, freely, in powerful upsurge.

Heavy waves were set in motion, rippling the body of the rivers, giving forth a damp, subdued noise, disquieting and uneasy. The snows melted. Resinous, strong-smelling candles appeared on the pines. The sky rose higher and turned a rich blue, and twilight was tremulous green, with an enticing sadness. In taiga, after winter death, the first animal business was under way—the business of birth. And all the forest dwellers—bears, wolves, elk, foxes, polar foxes, owls, eagle owls—retreated into the vernal joy of birth. On the river, loons, swans, geese made a great noise. At twilight, when the sky became green and tremulous, changing to a satiny, star-studded blue at night, when the loons and swans quieted down and went to sleep, and only mole crickets and land rails rasped in the soft, warm air, girls gathered above the river steep to sing of Lada[1] and dance round dances. The village lads returned from taiga, from their winter huts, and also gathered here.

The cliff fell sheer to the river. Below, the river rustled. And the sky spread above. Everything was quieting down, but at the same time one could sense life's stir and hurry. At the top of the cliff, where stunted moss and wayside grasses grew on granite and shale, the girls sat in a tight cluster. All of them were sturdy and glowing with health; they wore bright dresses and sang sad, widespanned, ancient songs; they gazed somewhere into the darkening greenish haze. The girls sang their eternal broad-spanned songs for the lads. And the lads stood around the girls—dark, tousled silhouettes—with abrupt bursts of laughter and rowdiness, just like male animals in the forest mating grounds.

These gatherings had their own law.

The lads came and selected wives for themselves, contending for the girls and confronting one another as foes; it was all the same to the girls, and they subjugated themselves to the men in all things. The lads

1. Some folklorists claim that Lada was a Slavic goddess.—Eds.

argued, roared with laughter, fought, kicked up a row; and the lad who won—he was the first to choose himself a wife.

And then they—man and woman—departed these gatherings.

III

Marina was twenty years old, and she went to the top of the cliff.

Her tall, somewhat heavy body was strikingly formed—strong muscled and with mat-white skin. Breast, stomach, back, hips, and legs were in bold relief—firm, resilient, elastic. High was the rise of her broad, rounded breast. Her heavy braids, her eyebrows and lashes were jet black. Black and moist were her eyes, with their deep pupils. Her cheeks were ruddy with a warm bluish undertone. And her lips seemed soft, animal, thick and very red. She always walked with slow movements of her long, strong legs, barely swaying her firm hips.

She would join the girls on the top of the cliff.

The girls sang their age-old, smoldering songs of allurement.

Marina would squeeze into the cluster of girls, throw herself on her back, close her misty eyes, and join in the singing. The song went its course, spreading in broad and luminous circles, a song in which everything was absorbed. Her eyes would close languorously. The eternal body ached with a sweet pain. The heart contracted with a tremor, as if benumbed, and from the heart this numbness passed through the blood to arms and shanks; it enfeebled them, and it clouded her brain. And Marina would stretch her limbs passionately, numbness spreading throughout her body, would retreat into song, would sing; only at the excited, raucous voices of the lads would a shudder run through her body.

And then at home, in her stuffy cubicle, Marina would lie down on her bed; she would throw her arms behind her head, at which her breast rose high; would stretch her legs; would open wide her dark, misty eyes; would press her lips together and, once more, overcome with vernal languor, would lie there motionless for a long time.

Marina was twenty years old, and from the day of her birth she had grown like thistle on the cliff, in freedom and solitude, surrounded by trappers, taiga, cliff, and river.

IV

Demid lived on an isolated plot of land.

Like the village, the plot was above the river. Only the hill was higher and steeper. Taiga moved in close; dark-green cedars and pines with grayish-brown trunks reached out paws of forest right to the house. A broad view opened from here: restless, dark river, floodlands beyond, taiga, jagged and deep blue on the horizon, and the sky—low and heavy.

The house, built of huge pine logs, with timbered walls, white unpainted ceilings and floors, was piled with hides of bears, elk, wolves, polar foxes, ermine. Hides hung on the walls and lay on the floor. Gunpowder, smallshot, buckshot lay on tables. The corners were piled with snares, nooses, traps. Guns hung about. There was a sharp, strong smell about the place, as if all the smells of taiga were gathered there. There were two rooms and a kitchen.

In the middle of one of the rooms stood a table, sturdy and homemade, and near it a low trestle covered with a bearskin. In this room lived Demid; in the other room lived Makar the bear.

At home Demid would lie on his bed of bearskin—motionless for long at a time—hearkening to his great body, to the life coursing within it, to the strong blood moving through his veins. Makar the bear would approach, lay his heavy paws on Demid's chest and sniff his body amicably. Demid would scratch the bear behind the ear, and there was a feeling that they, man and beast, understood each other. Taiga looked in through the windows.

Demid was burly and broad-shouldered; his black eyes were large, calm, and kind. There was a smell of taiga about him—healthy and strong. He dressed—as all the trappers did—in furs and coarse homespun cloth, white, veined with red thread. His feet were shod in high, heavy boots made of deer hide, and his hands—red and broad—were covered with a hard crust of calluses.

Makar was young and, like all young animals, oafish and stupid. He waddled about and often got into mischief: he gnawed on nets and hides, broke snares, licked up gunpowder. Then Demid would punish Makar—give him a thrashing. And Makar would roll over on his back, his eyes all innocence, and emit plaintive squeals.

V

Demid went to the top of the cliff, where the girls were, and led Marina away to his plot of land, and Marina became Demid's wife.

VI

In the summer, turbulent grasses grew—deep green and of an urgent succulence. By day the sun shone from a blue and seemingly humid sky. Nights were white, and then it seemed that there was no sky at all: it had dissolved in the pale haze. The nights were short and white; sunset merged with sunrise to shed a perpetual scarlet glow; tremulous mists crept over the earth. Life moved hard and fast, sensing that its days were short.

At Demid's place Marina took over Makar's room.

Makar was moved in with Demid.

Makar met Marina with hostility. When he first set eyes on her, he bared his teeth, growled, and struck her with his paw. Demid gave him a whipping for this, and the bear quieted down. Then he and Marina became friendly.

During the day Demid went to taiga. Marina stayed home alone.

She decorated her room in her own way, with rough elegance. She hung hides and rags embroidered—in bright red and blue—with roosters and deer, in a balanced way; in the corner she hung an icon of the Virgin; she washed the floors clean; and her room, gaily colored and still smelling of taiga, took on the air of a forest chapel where the people of the forest pray to their little gods.

In pale-greenish twilight when a skyless night was on its way and only eagle owls cried out in taiga and mole crickets creaked by the river, Demid would go to Marina. Thinking was not Marina's way—her thoughts turned over like huge, heavy cobblestones, slowly and clumsily. Sensing things was her way; she gave all of herself to Demid, her husband; and on pale, skyless nights, her body in odorous heat, writhing on her bearskin, she took Demid to herself and gave herself to him, submitting her whole being, wanting to dissolve herself in him, in his strength and passion, while draining her own passion.

White, tremulous, misty were the nights. The nocturnal silence of taiga prevailed. Mists floated past. Eagle owls and hulking wood demons hooted. And at daybreak the sunrise burned like a crimson conflagration, a huge sun lifting herself into the sky's deep-blue humidity. Grasses shot up with an urgent succulence.

Summer was passing, day followed day.

VII

Snow came in September.

As early as August the days had begun to shrink and gray perceptibly, and the huge black nights grew longer. All at once taiga grew quiet and dumb and vacant. Cold came and shackled the river with ice. The twilights were very long, and in these twilights the snow and ice on the river seemed deep blue. In the nights mating elk bellowed. Their bellowing was so loud and so strange that it was frightening, and the walls quivered.

That fall Marina became pregnant.

One night, Marina awoke just before dawn. The room was stuffy from the overheated stoves, and there was a smell of bear. It was just beginning to grow light, and the windows glimmered faintly as patches of deep blue on the dark walls. Somewhere near the plot an old elk was bellowing: you could tell he was an elder by the sibilant notes of his rough voice.

Marina sat up in her bed. Her head was going round and round; she felt nauseated. The bear lay nearby. He was already awake and was watching Marina. His eyes glowed with soft greenish sparks, as though a twilight spring sky—peaceful and tremulously quiet—were visible through crannies.

Once more the nausea mounted to her gullet; she felt dizzy—and those sparks in Makar's eyes, subconsciously, in the very depths of her being, were transfigured into an enormous, unbearable joy from which her body began to tremble painfully—she was pregnant. Her heart was beating like a quail caught in a snare, and she was overcome with dizziness, tremulous and misty as summer mornings.

Marina got up from her bed—from the bearskin—and quickly, with awkwardly uncertain steps, naked, went to Demid. Demid was asleep—she encircled his head with her hot arms, pressing him to her ample breast.

Night was slowly graying, and a deep-blue light came in through the windows. The elk stopped bellowing. In the room gray shadows began to swarm. Makar approached, heaved a deep sigh, and laid his paws on the bed. Demid took him by the scruff of the neck with his free hand and, roughing the fur affectionately, said:

"That's the way things are, Makar Ivanych—get the idea?"

Then he added, turning to Marina:

"D'you think he gets the idea? Marinka! Marinka! Marinka!"

Makar licked Demid's hand and wisely, understandingly, lowered his head onto his paws. Night was graying; lilac shadows soon began to pass over the snow, slipping into the house. The sun rose, red, round, remote. Below the cliff lay the deep-blue ice of the river, beyond that rose the ribs of taiga.

That day, and many days that followed, Demid did not go into taiga.

VIII

Winter came, stayed, went its way.

Snow lay in thick layers; by day and by night it was deep blue—and lilac in the brief sunsets and sunrises. The sun, pale and weak, hardly lifted itself above the horizon, rose for three hours, seemed remote and alien. The remaining time was night. Nights were irradiated by the tremulous darts of the northern lights. Frost had set in as a milky-white mist, painting everything with rime. It was the silence of the desert, a silence that spoke of death.

Marina's eyes changed. Before, they had been mistily dark and filled with intoxication; now they had become amazingly clear, filled with a joyous calm, direct, and gentle—a chaste modesty had come into them. Her hips broadened, and her belly swelled, and this gave her a new kind of grace, sluggishly soft and heavy, and again—a kind of chastity.

Marina didn't move much, sitting in her room, which was like a forest chapel where people pray to their little gods. By day she went about her simple domestic chores: heated the stove, cooked meat and fish, skinned the wild beasts killed by Demid, cleared her plot of land. In the evening—evenings were long—Marina twisted the warp on her spindle and wove linen on her loom; she did sewing for the baby. And as she sewed, thought of the baby, singing and smiling softly.

Marina thought of the baby—and a rare, potent, all-embracing joy took her body in thrall. Her heart was beating, and an even deeper joy came over her. But she gave no thought to the fact that she, Marina, was to give birth, to suffer.

In the lilac dawns, when a round moon stood in the southwest, Demid would ski to taiga with a rifle and a Finnish dagger. Pines and cedars stood outlined in hard, heavy patterns of snow; beneath them clustered spiny firs, juniper, alder thickets. A snow-crushed silence prevailed. In the dead, noiseless snow Demid went from trap to trap, from snare to snare, stunning the captive beasts. He would fire a shot, and the echo would dance long in the stillness. Tracking elk and packs of wolves, he would descend to the river, keeping a lookout for beavers; he would catch benumbed fish in unfrozen patches of water in the midst of the ice and would set up creels. All around was what he had always known. The red sun slowly dimmed, and tremulous shafts of the northern lights began to glimmer.

In the evening, standing on his plot of land, he cut up fish and flesh, hung the pieces up to freeze, threw chunks to the bear, ate some of the meat himself, washed in icy water, and sat close to Marina. A strapping, thickset fellow, he spread his strong legs and, ponderously resting his hands on his knees, made the room seem too small. He smiled calmly and good-naturedly.

The lamp was burning. Beyond the walls were the snows, the silence, and the frost. Makar came up and scratched around on the floor. A sense of comfort and joyous calm settled within the room with the look of a chapel. The walls crackled in the frost; murk gazed in through the frozen windows. Towels hung on the walls, embroidered with deer and roosters in red and in blue. Then Demid would get up from his bench, take Marina strongly and tenderly in his arms, and carry her to the bed. The lamp went out, and Makar's eyes glimmered softly in the gloom.

In the course of the winter Makar had reached maturity and had become a full-grown bear like any other: gloomily earnest, heavy and clumsily adroit. He had a very broad muzzle, with a protuberant brow and gloomily good-natured eyes.

IX

From the last days of December, from the snowy holiday when the wolves were howling, Marina began to feel the child moving beneath her heart. It was moving there within her, moving so tenderly and gently as though her body was stroked with eiderdown.

Marina was overcome with joy—she was aware only of the little one within her, who had taken a strong hold on her from within, and the words she uttered to Demid were shameless and incoherent.

At dawn the child would stir within her. Marina would press her hands—with amazing tenderness—to her belly, stroking it solicitously, and sing cradle songs about how her son would become a hunter who in his day would kill three hundred and a thousand deer, three hundred and a thousand bears, three hundred and yet another three hundred ermine, who would take the village beauty to wife. And the child moved within her, scarcely to be felt and with the greatest tenderness.

At this time, beyond the house, beyond the plot of land, there were: a misty frost, night, and a silence which spoke of death. And only sometimes wolves would begin to howl; they approached the plot, sat on their haunches, and howled to the sky long and monotonously.

X

In the spring Marina gave birth.

In the spring the rivers came to life and overflowed far and wide, rippling with gloomy, gristling, leaden waves; the banks were hidden beneath white flocks—swans, geese, loons. Life came to taiga. Animals there were giving birth; the woods buzzed vigilantly with noises of bears, elk, wolves, polar foxes, eagle owls, wood grouse. All sorts of grasses, dark green in color, burgeoned and bloomed turbulently. Nights shrank, and days grew bigger. Dawns and dusks were lilac and broad. Twilights were pale green and tremulous, and in the twilights above the river in the village girls would sing of Lada. At break of day a huge sun would lift itself upon the moist blue sky to travel its celestial course for many a springtime hour. The spring festival had arrived when, according to legend, the sun smiles and folk exchange red eggs, symbols of the sun.

On that day Marina gave birth.

Delivery began during the day. A big, joyous spring sun came through the window, settling in abundant sheaves on the walls and on the skin-covered floor.

All that Marina remembered was the savage pain tearing at her body and making it writhe. She was lying on her bearskin bed; the sun was shining through the windows—that she remembered, remembered that its rays had fallen on the wall and on the floor at an angle that indicated midday, then moved away to the left—half an hour, an hour. From then on everything was swallowed in pain, in the writhing convulsions of her belly.

When Marina came to, it was already twilight, green and quiet. At her feet, all covered with blood, lay a red, bawling infant. The bear stood close by and in a special way—understandingly and sternly—looked on with his good-naturedly gloomy eyes.

This was the time when Demid arrived—he broke the umbilical cord, washed the baby, made Marina comfortable. He gave her the child—the look in her eyes was astonishing. In Marina's arms lay a little red human being, who was crying for no apparent reason. There was no pain any more.

XI

That night the bear left Demid, left for taiga to find himself a mate.

The bear left late at night, breaking the door open. It was night. A barely perceptible streak of dawn lay on the horizon. Somewhere in the distance the girls were singing of Lada. Above the cliff of granite and white shale the girls sat singing in a tight cluster, and close by—dark, tousled silhouettes—stood the lads who had returned from their winter huts in taiga.

Kolomna
1916

Selected Works of

Boris Pilnyak

"Arina." *Byl'e*. Revel: Izdatel'stvo "Bibliofil," 1922, pp. 51–64.
"Afrikantsy." *Krasnaia Niva* 3 (1924): 58–63.
"Bol'shoe Serdtse." *Zvezda* 4 (1927): 40–61.
"Bol'shoi Shlem." *Novyi Mir* 11 (1934): 5–18.
"Che-Che-O." *Novyi Mir* (1928): 249–58.
"Chelovecheskii Veter." *Novyi Mir* 10 (1925): 59–65.
"Dva Rasskaza." *Russkii Sovremennik* 1 (1924): 132–50.
"Ded Perependen'." *Krasnyi Zhurnal Dlia Vsekh* 1–2 (1923): 3–6.
"Emel'ka Svistunov." *Mirskoe Delo* 1–2 (1919): 12–13.
"Fel'dshera i Akademiki." *Literaturnaia Gazeta*, April 22, 1929, p. 2.
"God ikh Zhizni." *Spolokhi* 11 (1917): 139–48.
"Grego-trimuntan." *Novyi Mir* 1 (1926): 104–12.
"Ivan-da-Mar'ia." Petersburg-Berlin: Izdatel'stvo Z.I. Grzhebina, 1922.
"Ivan Moskva." *Krasnaia Nov'* 6 (1927): 42–83.
"Kamen', Nebo." *Novyi Mir* 12 (1934): 34–45.
Kamni i Korni. Moscow: Sovetskaia Literatura, 1934.
"Kolomna." *Mirskoe Delo* 13–16 (1919): 54–55.
"Ledokhod." *Russkii Sovremennik* 3 (1924): 76–99.
"Lesnaia Dacha." *Krasnaia Niva* 2 (1923): 11, 14–15, 18, 20.
Mashiny i Volki. Leningrad: Gosudarstvennoe Izdatel'stvo, 1923.
"Mastera." *Literaturnyi Sovremennik* 2 (1937): 113–28.
"Nizhegorodskii Otkos" ["The Nizhni Novgorod Otkos"]. *Zvezda* 2 (1928): 38–52.

"Noch'iu v Stepi." *Spolokhi* 9 (1916): 95–108.
"O-kei, Amerikanskii Roman." *Novyi Mir* 3–6 (1932).
"O Nizhnem Novgorode." *Zori* 1 (1923): 6–7.
"Pozemka." *Mirskoe Delo* 14–15 (1918): 15–19.
"Prostye Rasskazy." *Krasnaia Nov'* 4 (1921): 21–33.
"Rasplesnutoe Vremia." *Novaia Rossia* 3 (1926), cols. 53–58.
"Rozhdenie Cheloveka." *Novyi Mir* 1 (1935): 111–26.
"Snega." *Put'* 4 (1919): 10–23.
"Speranza." *Krasnaia Nov'* 6 (1923): 33–47.
"Tatarskie Ser'gi." *Spolokhi* 7 (1922): 3–8.
"Tri Brata." *Kul'tura i Zhizn'* 1 (1922): 16–21.
Volga Vpadaet v Kaspiiskoe More [The Volga Flows into the Caspian Sea]. Moscow: Izdatel'stvo "Nedra," 1930.
"Volki." *Krasnaia Nov'* 3 (1923): 125–42.
"Zemlia na Rukakh." *Krasnaia Nov'* 8 (1928): 98–101.
"Znakhari." *Krasnaia Niva* 13 (1924): 298–300.

Index

Aden: 33
Alexander I: 160, 178
Alexander II: 120n.
Alexander III: 120n.
Allilueva, Svetlana: 7& n.
Arakcheyev, Aleksei Andreyevich: 177, 178n.
Astrakhan: 213, 262

Bab el Mandeb (strait): 34
Bastille, taking of: 49
Batavia: 96, 97
Belokon: 259, 261
Bely, Andrei (Boris Nikolayevich Bugayev): 3
Berlin: 9
Blok, Aleksandr Aleksandrovich: 278, 281, 292
Bogorodsk: 91, 160, 172
Boucher, François: 138
Brindisi: 172
Bruges: 114, 123, 126, 144, 157, 159
Brussels: 235
Büchner, Ludwig: 279
Buckle, Henry Thomas: 279
Bunin, Ivan Alekseyevich: 2, 64n.; "The Gentleman from San Francisco," 64
Byzantium: 63

Canton (Kwangchow): 32, 39, 43, 66, 73, 74
Catherine II: 113, 119, 121, 128, 144, 156, 157
Caucasus: 170
Chekhov, Anton Pavlovich: 2
Chicago: 172
Christ, Jesus: 151, 152, 229, 232, 233
Christiana (Oslo): 160
Cleopatra: 65, 71
Constantinople: 33
Copernicus, Nicolaus: 247n., 256
Cosway, Richard: 138
Czechoslovakia: 177

Dairen (Talien): 23, 40

Elizabeth, Empress: 112, 113, 156
England: 177
Esenin, Sergei Aleksandrovich: 34& n.

Fedin, Konstantin Aleksandrovich: 10
France: 177
Frunze, Mikhail Vasilyevich: 7, 8, 9, 13, 165
Furmanov, Dmitri Andreyevich: 85 & n.

Germany: 128, 177, 180, 222
Gogol, Nikolai Vasilyevich: *The Inspector General*, 96n.; "Taras Bulba," 284n.
Gorky, Maksim (Aleksei Maksimovich Peshkov): 8, 12, 124

Halle: 223
Hamsun, Knut: 100

Hang-chow: 84
Hankow: 23, 25, 27, 28, 29, 31
Honan (province): 25, 57, 74, 93
Hong Kong: 34
Honolulu: 64
Huang-p'u (river): 18, 61, 80, 87
Hwang Ho (Yellow River): 26, 27

Indian Ocean: 33, 34
Ivanov, Vsevolod Vyacheslavovich: 10

Japan: 5, 42, 43
Java: 96

Kadom: 211, 221, 224, 230, 231, 235, 254, 255, 259, 261
K'ai-feng: 94
Kalgan (Wanchuan): 36, 102
Kamakura: 114, 123, 157, 159
Kant, Immanuel: 98, 278
Kastalsky, Aleksandr Dmitriyevich: 122& n.
Kazan: 212, 260
Kiangsi (province): 102
Kiev: 172
Klyazma (river): 171
Kolomna: 31, 41, 63, 317
Koreisha, Ivan Yakovlevich: 109 & n., 110, 111
Kunavino: 276
Kwangchow (Canton): 32, 39, 43, 66, 74

Latvia: 177
Leipzig: 171n.
Lenin, Vladimir Ilyich (Vladimir Ilyich Ulyanov): 120 & n., 131, 171n., 215, 235;
Leninists, 150
Leningrad: 9, 10, 156
Lomonosov, Mikhail Vasilyevich: 75 & n.
London: 7n., 223

Maeterlinck, Maurice: 278
Manila: 96, 97
Marx, Karl: 279
Mayakovsky, Vladimir Vladimirovich: 12
Mechnikov, Ilya Ilyich: 278
Medyn: 213, 214, 215, 223, 225, 229, 239, 255, 260, 263
Melnikov-Pechersky, Pavel Ivanovich: 274 & n.
Mirbeau, Octave: 70
Mongolia: 36, 60, 63
Montessori, Maria: 189
Moscow: 1 & n., 3n., 4 & n., 5 & n., 7, 10, 31n., 33, 35, 37, 38, 41, 53, 59, 60, 63 &n., 84, 85, 90, 91, 92, 95, 96, 101, 108, 109 & n., 110, 111, 112, 113, 114, 124, 141, 142, 153, 156, 165, 172, 210, 223, 235, 254, 271, 275, 279, 292
Mozhaisk: 1, 91
Mukden (Shen'-yang): 23

Nanking: 31, 38, 77
Naroch (Narosz, lake): 223, 276
New York: 39
Nicholas I: 113, 115, 120n., 178 & n.
Norway: 100
Novikov, Vasili Vasilyevich: 4, 6
Novyi Mir: 7, 12

Oka (river): 274, 276
Orekhovo-Zuyevo: 171, 173, 199
Ostrovsky, Aleksandr Nikolayevich: 124

Pacific Ocean: 31, 36, 39, 40, 65
Panama: 97
Paris: 99, 112, 172, 223
Paul, Emperor: 113, 117, 156, 178n., 213
Pei-ho (Pai, river): 23
Peking (Beijing): 22, 24, 25, 26, 27, 28, 31, 32, 36, 47, 58, 65, 70, 71, 72, 74, 81, 83, 159
Peter I (Peter the Great): 2, 62 & n., 112
Piccadilly: 31
Pinkevich, Albert Petrovich: 189 & n.
Port Said: 33, 36, 40
Pugachev, Yemelyan Ivanovich: 177, 178n.

Pushkin, Aleksandr Sergeyevich: 87, 94, 114, 152; *Eugene Onegin*, 283n.
Putung: 20

Radek, Karl: 8
Razin, Stepan Timofeyevich (Stenka Razin): 178 & n.
Red Sea: 34
Reid, Mayne: 100
Rostov: 174
Rostov-Veliki: 114
Rumania: 172
Russo-Japanese War: 74
Rykov, Aleksei Ivanovich: 120 & n., 172

Saint Petersburg: 112, 159, 160, 172, & n., 223
Salonika: 172
Saltykov-Shchedrin, Mikhail Evgrafovich: 63n.
Samara: 213, 261
San Francisco: 18, 62, 64
Saratov: 23, 63, 213, 221, 250, 261
Saxony: 160
Schopenhauer, Arthur: 280
Seifullina, Lidia Nikolayevna: 10
Sevastopol: 120
Shanghai: 5, 6, 31, 32, 42n., 64n., 66
Shantung: 90
Siam: 33, 34
Siberia: 159
Siccawei (Zi-ka-wei, Ziccawei): 64 & n., 68
Singapore: 33, 34, 35, 84, 98
Sino-Russian Society for Cultural Relations ("Sino-Russ"): 43, 59, 60, 95, 97, 103, 105
Smolensk: 110
Sorrento: 8
Sparrow Hills (Lenin Hills), Moscow: 41
Stalin (Iosif Visarionovich Dzhugashvili): 7, 8, 9, 120n.
Su-chou: 84
Suez: 34
Sun Yat-sen: 26, 32

Tetyushi: 212
Tientsin: 23, 24, 59, 66
Tobolsk: 159
Tolstoi, Aleksei Nikolayevich: 10
Tolstoi, Lev Nikolayevich: *Childhood, Boyhood*, 174
Trotskyites: 150, 154, 155
Tsarskoye Selo (Pushkin): 159
Tula: 172
Turgenev, Ivan Sergeyevich, *A Nest of Gentlefolk:* 79n., 284n.
Turkestan: 181
Tver (Kalinin): 114

Udmurt Autonomous Soviet Socialist Republic: 63n.
Uglich: 114
Urals: 202, 223

Vetluga: 255
Vienna: 112, 172
Vladivostok: 40, 55, 61, 93
Vodovozova, E. N.: 189 & n.
Volga: 1, 7, 17, 23, 27, 28, 30, 42, 63, 114, 116, 125, 126, 130, 151, 158, 178n., 201, 211, 212, 213 & n., 214, 216, 217, 220, 223, 224, 227, 228, 229, 230, 237, 238, 239, 242, 245, 246, 248, 249, 250, 252, 255, 256, 257, 260, 262, 266, 273n., 274 & n., 275, 276, 283, 284, 289
Voltaire, François-Marie Arouet de: 134
Voronsky, Aleksandr Konstantinovich: 8, 164
Vyazovy: 214, 215, 229, 233, 238, 241, 256, 259, 261

Wright brothers (Orville, Wilbur): 131

Yangtze-Kiang: 18, 27
Yaransk: 159, 160
Yaroslavl: 114, 124
Yekaterinov: 179

Zamyatin, Evgeni Ivanovich: 10
Zhukovsky, Vasili Andreyevich: 55 & n.

AVAILABLE FROM ARDIS

PUBLISHERS OF RUSSIAN LITERATURE, HISTORY, CRITICISM, & CULTURE

THE DOUBLE
Fyodor Dostoevsky
Translated by Evelyn Harden
978-0-88233-757-9 • PB • $16.95

THE PETTY DEMON
Fyodor Sologub
Translated by S.D. Cioran
978-0-88233-808-8 • PB • $17.95

CONTACT SALES@OVERLOOKNY.COM FOR OUR MOST RECENT ARDIS CATALOG

THE OVERLOOK PRESS
New York, NY
www.overlookpress.com
www.ardisbooks.com

AVAILABLE FROM ARDIS 

PUBLISHERS OF RUSSIAN LITERATURE, HISTORY, CRITICISM, & CULTURE

New in paperback
NOTES ON THE CUFF
Mikhail Bulgakov
Translated by Alison Rice • 978-1-59020-506-8 • PB • $17.95

CONTACT SALES@OVERLOOKNY.COM FOR OUR MOST RECENT ARDIS CATALOG

THE OVERLOOK PRESS
New York, NY
www.overlookpress.com
www.ardisbooks.com

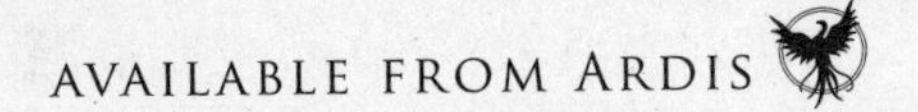

PUBLISHERS OF RUSSIAN LITERATURE, HISTORY, CRITICISM, & CULTURE

New in paperback
PUSHKIN THREEFOLD
Alexander Pushkin
Translated by Walter Arndt • 978-1-59020-507-5 • PB • $29.95

CONTACT SALES@OVERLOOKNY.COM FOR OUR MOST RECENT ARDIS CATALOG

THE OVERLOOK PRESS
New York, NY
www.overlookpress.com
www.ardisbooks.com

AVAILABLE FROM ARDIS 

PUBLISHERS OF RUSSIAN LITERATURE, HISTORY, CRITICISM, & CULTURE

COLLECTED NARRATIVE
AND LYRICAL POETRY
Alexander Pushkin
Translated by Walter Arndt
978-0-88233-826-2 • PB • $18.95

A HERO OF OUR TIME
Mikhail Lermontov
Translated by Vladimir Nabokov
978-0-87501-049-6 • PB • $14.95

CONTACT SALES@OVERLOOKNY.COM FOR OUR MOST RECENT ARDIS CATALOG

THE OVERLOOK PRESS
New York, NY
www.overlookpress.com
www.ardisbooks.com

AVAILABLE FROM ARDIS

PUBLISHERS OF RUSSIAN LITERATURE, HISTORY, CRITICISM, & CULTURE

SELECTED POEMS
Anna Akhmatova
Translated by Walter Arndt
978-0-88233-180-5 • PB • $17.95

ENVY
Yury Olesha
Translated by T. S. Berczynski
978-0-88233-091-4 • PB • $13.95

CONTACT SALES@OVERLOOKNY.COM FOR OUR MOST RECENT ARDIS CATALOG

THE OVERLOOK PRESS
New York, NY
www.overlookpress.com
www.ardisbooks.com